OBSIDIAN OATH

FIREBIRD UNCAGED BOOK 3

ERIN EMBLY

I WAS TRYING to decide between gummy cola and regular cola when I heard the shotgun rack.

My left eye twitched, and I snatched the gummies off the shelf. Crinkling the plastic loudly, I opened the bag and popped one in my mouth as I made my way up to the register of the rundown gas station, where Carina was staring down the shaking barrel of a weapon far too big for the boy holding it behind the counter.

I crinkled the bag again, chewing casually until the boy's eyes shifted over to me. Then I smiled. Never sneak up on an amateur holding a gun unless you mean to take him down.

"You . . . have to pay for those," he stammered, snapping his eyes back to Carina when she sighed dramatically. His fingers were turning white around the metal of the weapon.

"Happy to," I said. "Should I come around there to ring myself up, or are you going to put that thing down?"

"I . . ." He glanced wildly between me and my little terror of a niece before his eyes narrowed on her again. "She's not human."

"And you're not very smart," Carina said, a wisp of smoke

sneaking out from her nose. My eye twitched again as I realized it wasn't just the boy behind the counter who needed to calm the fuck down.

"She looks pretty human to me," I lied. "Just a harmless little girl." Not taking any chances, I slid myself in between the two of them, putting the gummies on the counter and trying to ignore the weapon that was wavering right in front of my chest. "Well?"

"Get out of the way, ma'am. The police will be here soon." The boy's voice was surprisingly steady now, which was good. A steady voice meant a steady trigger finger less likely to accidentally shoot me.

"Did she try to steal something?" I asked, getting out my wallet.

"She turned it to *stone*." The way he said it told me he expected it to mean something to me, so I twisted my head around to raise my eyebrows at Carina.

She shrugged, then pulled her hand out of her coat pocket. A single obsidian bunny sat in her palm, resting its shiny black head on her fingers. "You mean this?"

The boy clutched his weapon tighter when the bunny's ears twitched. "Why is it still moving?"

"Because I didn't kill it, dummy," Carina said. "It was always made of stone. It's a magic rabbit and it doesn't like you."

I breathed out a huff and made a mental note to teach my hot-headed niece about the merits of de-escalation. But when I turned back to the boy, he had miraculously lowered his weapon.

"So . . . it's not like what happened last week?" he said, his jaw going slack.

"What happened last week?" I asked.

He shifted his eyes at me, a moment of confusion passing before he said, "You're not from around here, are you?"

"Just passing through."

The boy's shoulders drooped, his whole body relaxing as he set the shotgun down behind the counter. "Sorry, it's just . . . We don't get a lot of magic types here, and last week . . ." He swallowed.

"What happened last week?" I repeated.

"My girlfriend's parents," he said. "I took her out on a date, and when we came back . . . they were just rocks."

"Dumb as rocks, to let their daughter date someone like you," Carina piped up from behind me.

The boy's face hardened again, but he didn't get a chance to say anything before I turned on my heel and wrapped my fingers tight around Carina's upper arm.

"Hey!" she protested, but I dragged her over to the door and shoved her out of the store.

"Wait in the car," I snapped before slamming the door shut, the chimes at the top jangling to make my words sound less threatening than I'd hoped. But then, nothing was going as I'd hoped it would lately. Every day, this road trip felt less like an escape and more like something both the angry little dragon and I wanted to escape *from*.

A beep at the register reminded me to turn around with a smile, only to see the boy frowning at me. "Three seventy-nine, please," he said flatly.

"What did you mean about them being rocks?" I asked as I dug into my wallet for cash.

"Exactly what I said. Rocks. Stone. Statues. Like they were killed by Medusa or something." He blinked, giving his head a small shake before softly saying, "They looked terrified."

I had to stop myself from correcting him with "petrified." That wouldn't be helpful. Not to mention it was exactly the kind of thing Adrian would say. "Damn," I said instead, shaking my own head to banish the thought of the man I'd left in DC. "Any idea what happened?"

"No. There were DSC agents in town the next day, but they didn't do shit. Just asked a bunch of questions and then left."

"No wonder you're still jumpy," I said as I placed a few bills on the counter. I wanted to tell this kid I'd look into it for him, that I knew some DSC agents and I'd call them. But that was one road I didn't want to go down right now. I was supposed to be taking a break from all that.

"Not just me," he said, a grim half-smile on his face. "I'd keep that rabbit out of sight around here. It's a small town and people talk."

"Noted." Good thing he'd only seen the one. There was a whole horde of those obsidian bunnies along for the ride with me and Carina, and I wouldn't know how to keep them all out of sight if I tried.

Red and blue lights flashed down the road as I walked out to my bunny-infested car, not looking forward to telling the tired little girl inside that we'd need to drive a few more hours before stopping for the night. The boy wasn't kidding when he'd said the cops were on their way. Jumpy indeed.

Popping another cola gummy in my mouth, I frowned at the flavor that was not quite the same as I remembered it from when I was a kid. Sweet but disappointingly flat—just like my piss-poor attempt at this vacation.

Not that this was ever going to be a real vacation.

I picked up my pace and slid into the driver's seat just in time to hit the gas before the cops pulled into the parking lot. Couldn't risk having to answer their questions when the little girl quietly fuming in the passenger's seat was technically a fugitive.

"I should have eaten him," she said. It didn't come across as intimidating as it might have had she not been scratching a content bunny between the ears while she said it.

Still, it was worrying, and I said nothing as I pressed my foot down harder on the gas pedal. I honestly didn't know what to say. I was supposed to be driving this girl out of the country, helping her flee back to her god—our god—in Mexico after she'd been forced to murder a handful of innocent people a couple weeks ago in DC.

It hadn't been her fault, not in the least. But at the end of the day, she was still a child with blood on her hands. Blood that hadn't been there before. And now, she was joking about eating random humans when I was pretty sure she'd never actually eaten anything bigger than a baby goat.

"Did you see how skinny he was?" I eventually joked back, forcing myself to bury my worries. "Eat these instead."

I tossed the open bag of gummies at her, and a couple fell into her lap when she caught them. A few more bunnies popped their shiny black heads up from beneath the edges of her seat, scurrying over her legs to snatch up the stray candy.

They might be spies for the ancient volcano god I was kind of running away from right now, but at least they kept my car clean.

"Am I wasting my time here?" I asked once Carina was chewing on a gummy. She swallowed and looked at me, and I tried to keep my eyes on the road as the dusk slowly overtook the clear sky above.

"What do you mean?"

"I mean, if you *want* to get caught and go to jail, it'd be way easier for me to just drop you off at the nearest police station. You don't have to keep picking fights with everyone we meet."

"I wasn't—he started it!"

"This time, maybe. But we've gotten kicked out of nearly every place we've stopped." I wasn't even exaggerating, and if I weren't so annoyed I might actually be impressed.

Carina huffed, another puff of smoke blowing out from her nostrils. Something I'd never seen her do before we set out on this trip.

"Look," I said with a sigh. "We would be out of the country

already if we were doing what your dad wanted us to do. And at this point, if you can't control whatever *this* is . . ." I took my right hand off the wheel and waved it around at her. "I'm starting to think we should just head south. I can visit my family without you."

"No!" Carina sat up straight, the bunnies scurrying off her lap at the surprising boom in her voice.

"Why not?" I asked calmly.

She deflated a bit, tucking her chin down and squeezing the bag of gummies tight in her fist. "I want to meet them," she said eventually. "You said I could."

"You *can*, sure, but only if you'll let me get you there in one piece." I decided not to press her on why she wanted to meet them so much. Not when we'd been so careful to avoid the subject this whole time. With Popo's bunnies along for the ride, our godly benefactor had constant eyes and ears on us. It didn't bother me that he knew where we were going, but I didn't think it'd be a great idea for him to know what we were planning on doing when we got there.

I still wasn't sure what my niece would decide, but I was going to ask my aunts and uncles to help me redo the tattoo—the mage mark—Carina had ripped off my ankle months ago. For most of my life, that tattoo had blocked Popo from influencing me, made me an independent magic user—a mage rather than a witch. And independent was how I preferred to live my life.

Was it duplicitous of me to try to get it back? Maybe. I had willingly accepted the god's help in exchange for my witchy servitude, after all. But that had been in an emergency. I did a lot of crazy things when faced with emergencies, and I wasn't above regretting the ones that made my life hell after the fact.

The road ahead was empty and Carina unusually quiet, so I turned my head to look at her. She was leaning against the window now, one of the bunnies pressed against her chin as her eyes focused on nothing. Deep in thought.

I turned back to the road and was met with blinding light.

"Ahh!" I squeezed my eyes shut and slammed on the brakes, tightening my grip on the wheel as the car started to spin out of control.

Carina was screaming something now, but I couldn't understand it. The words melted into nonsense as they assaulted my ears, part of a humming cacophony that faded slowly into silence as the blinding light dimmed.

The car halted, and I opened my eyes.

Fire.

Something in front of us was on fire. A car wreck? But then why had it been so bright, so sudden—and why was it so quiet now?

The something in front of us moved. Flames burned in strange directions, not just upwards but sideways and down, almost like ... feathers.

Great wings unfurled and tapped against the pavement before lifting into the air, scattering wisps of fire into the darkness on either side of the narrow road. The bird's head lifted from the ground and turned to me, its dark eyes sucking me in like black holes as it opened its beak and shrieked.

And just as Carina's words had turned into nonsense when they'd met my ears before, this shriek turned into something else.

"Darcy." A voice inside my head, resonating disapproval strong enough it threatened to stop my heart.

I shut my eyes again, wanting to cover my ears even though I knew it wouldn't help. The cacophony returned, humming and shrieking at once before exploding into silence.

"Darcy!" Carina's little angry voice washed over me along with an immense feeling of relief.

I breathed out slowly, releasing the tension in my face and my arms as I opened my eyes and let go of the steering wheel.

The road was empty and dark again, the fiery bird gone. When I turned to Carina, licking my dry lips, she met me with wide eyes and a twisted mouth.

"What was that you were saying about getting me to California in one piece?"

2

"Bats." I shook my head, emitting a low groan. "Birds, actually."

The former curse had always been my way of blaming all my problems on vampires. Not that vampires actually turned into bats—but centuries of incorrect lore had forever fused the two, and that made it a hard connection to shake.

Now, I was beginning to think birds would take their place as the bane of my existence. Starting with the spirit of the phoenix that lived inside me.

Was that what I had just seen? Was the damn bird trying to kill me? Because that was what would happen if it decided to blind me again while I was driving.

"Are you seeing things, Darcy?" Carina piped up. "You should tell me if you are . . . That's how it started with me." Her voice became low and soft as she finished.

I swallowed. It was good that she was mentioning what had happened to her with the chaneques, right? Maybe seeing me go off the deep end would make her feel less ashamed of having gone off it herself.

"You didn't see anything in the road?" I asked.

She shook her head.

"It must be the bird," I said. "It doesn't like that I'm so far away from your dad." That was my best guess, anyway. The phoenix needed both its hosts to thrive, and I'd left my brother—its other half—in DC.

"Oh." Carina turned her head away from me, and I frowned.

Shaking the tension out of my hands, I pressed on the gas and got back on the road. It wasn't long before the bright lights of a motel beckoned me to pull over again. Maybe we were still too close for comfort to the town where people had been turning to stone, but we both desperately needed some rest and some space.

Carina was out as soon as her head hit the threadbare pillow. Or at least she wanted me to think she was out. She shut down like this every time I brought up her dad. Complicated kid feelings, apparently.

But then, Ray had decided to send her back to Mexico alone rather than go with her. And it was hard for me to not feel guilty about that, since I was the reason he "needed" to stay in DC.

Yet here I was, the one accompanying his daughter in his stead, even though it was only temporary.

Nowhere near tired enough to sleep, I crept back out of the quiet room and slid into the back seat of my car with my glowing phone.

Was it too late to call Etty? I could really use some sane adult conversation right about now, but Carina and I were already in Arizona and two hours behind DC time. Etty liked to go to bed early, so she would be asleep unless she was working.

I tapped my fingernails on the screen impatiently after sending her a text, a heaviness taking root in my chest as I realized us being in Arizona meant we would make it to California tomorrow. I'd see my adoptive family for the first time in almost ten years.

My phone buzzed, keeping me from contemplating my imminent family reunion. I turned on the screen to see a picture of

Etty's legs, dark and slim and shiny, ending in a pair of ruby-red heels pressed together.

Click-clack, bitch, it said underneath.

"There's no place like home," I whispered. Something Becca had always said when she'd worn her sparkly red shoes. I wondered if Etty was really wearing those things tonight, or if she'd taken that picture just to have on hand to send to me.

It didn't matter—message received. She was working, and if I wanted to talk to her then maybe I should come the fuck home.

Without thinking, I swiped over to my list of recent calls and messages, my glazed-over eyes focusing automatically on Adrian's number, which was still only a few numbers down despite the fact that I wouldn't be using it again anytime soon—or ever. He'd made it very clear last time we'd spoken that he wanted nothing more to do with me, and I honestly couldn't blame him.

Still, though . . . I couldn't bring myself to erase him from my phone. My thumb hovered over his name for a moment, remembering the intoxicating warmth of his lips on mine before I squeezed my eyes shut and locked the screen, stuffing the tiny evil device in my pocket.

My face hot, I flopped over so I could bury it in the seat cushions. I'd expected the leather to be sticky and cold, but it felt velvety and warm on my cheek. Opening my eyes, I squinted at the mess of black bunnies staring at me with glowing red eyes from beneath the driver's seat. They'd been warming the cushions for me with their little volcanic asses.

"Thanks," I said, then sank into the cozy haze of sleepiness that promised to numb the pain in my chest.

SEARING heat enveloped me as I blinked my way into the dream I'd dreamed every night for the past two weeks. Only this time, I recognized the flames surrounding me as the phoenix's wings.

After seeing the massive bird in front of me on the road, the pattern in its fiery feathers was unmistakable.

Still, I couldn't spare it much thought. Not with my hands wrapped around Simeon's neck in front of me. Every night since I'd let him slip between my fingers in real life, I'd throttled this man in my dreams. Every night, I held the moon in my mind's eye as I attempted to channel the magic wind I'd used to shred the other vampire to bits.

The phoenix's wind.

Was that why it never worked on Simeon in my dreams? Why the bird was shrieking at me now? Was my focus on the moon a trick that had only been necessary before I'd accepted Popo's help and connected myself fully to the phoenix's magic? Probably.

For the first time in this dream, I sighed and gave in. The moon disappeared in my mind and the bird's invisible talons gripped my arms. Magic sliced through me, from my shoulders to my wrists to my fingers—but then it stopped.

It didn't pour through my fingers into Simeon's soft, vulnerable neck. It didn't explode through his cold veins and turn him into ribbons of gore. The comforting splatter of his brains didn't spill out onto my arms and rain softly down onto my face.

Instead, he stared at me with mischief in his eyes.

My fingers went cold and numb, black crystals forming on the tips of my nails and then climbing up along my arms, paralyzing me as my flesh transformed into something with a dark sheen—obsidian.

I thought at first he must be freezing me, harnessing the icy magic of his new god, but instead he was using the power of my own new god against me. Turning me to stone, not ice.

Turning me to stone.

Why did that sound so familiar?

Tiny sharp claws bit into my cheek, and I woke to the solid warmth of a rabbit on my face. Its little red eyes stared into mine, assuring me as I involuntarily stretched my fingers that it was the only obsidian on me. The rest of me was still flesh and blood.

The sound of glass rattling above my head made me jerk, and the bunny on my face hopped off. I sat up, squinting my bleary eyes at the withered face of a police officer peering down at me through the car window.

Groaning, I hit the unlock button on my keys and rolled down the glass. "Hi," I said, not wanting to wish him a good morning in case it wasn't actually morning.

"Morning," he said, answering that unspoken question. "Of all the places I've seen folk sleeping in cars . . . a motel parking lot?"

I clenched my jaw, wondering what I could say to make him go away.

"Couldn't make it into your room last night?" he asked. I licked my lips, about to answer when he cut me off. "Hey . . . wasn't it you I saw speeding off yesterday after Matthew called me to the gas station down the road?"

"I wasn't speeding," I said, immediately regretting it. I knew better than to start arguments with cops. I wasn't exactly my best self right now, though.

"Alright, alright." He took a sip of his coffee, and I counted myself lucky that he hadn't caught me here before he'd had his fix. "But you're loitering now, and this lot is only for paying customers, and . . ." He tilted his head to peer in further. "Did I just see some kinda carved animal in there?"

"Sorry, Officer," I said, my manners finally waking up with the rest of me. "I am a paying customer." I dug in my pocket and brought out my room key to hold up. "Just fell asleep here by accident." I ignored his other question about the rabbit, knowing I was likely to get sucked into a small-town magical murder investigation if I answered it.

Out of the corner of my eye, I saw Carina's dark head of hair poke out from behind the white curtains in our motel room. I sucked in my breath.

"Hmm." The old man took another sip of coffee, forehead creased with what I assumed was the difficult decision of what to do with me.

Before he could decide to make my morning worse than it already was, a scratchy voice came through his radio, which was strapped to his left side. I couldn't make out much through the jumble of static, but his forehead creased further when he heard it.

He moved to switch his coffee cup to his right hand, but it fell swiftly to the ground. The paper rim hit the pavement beside my car with a wet thwack, and I cringed as I pictured the delicious-smelling beverage splattering all over my tires.

A wisp of red dust blew in my face as the only answer for why he had dropped it.

It turned out he had dropped his whole right hand along with it—after it had turned into red stone.

"What the hell?" he muttered, squinting at the stump of crumbling rock sitting where his wrist used to be. Sleepy confusion quickly turned to panic, his left hand grasping his radio and bringing it to his lips just in time for them to harden in an eerie oval that quickly cracked over in the same red rock. It had swept up his arm and neck as quick as flames, and it went on to consume the top of his head before I could blink.

He stood there looking like solid fire, all orange and red and crackling, and a hollow feeling sank into my gut as I stared at him.

Could I still be dreaming? Was this a new mind game the phoenix was playing with me?

I blinked again, and the stone man was still standing in front of me when I opened my eyes.

No. Not a dream, not a mind game—this was the universe

trying it's damnedest to suck me into that small-town magical murder investigation I'd been avoiding.

He'd turned into stone, just like the boy at the gas station had said happened to his girlfriend's parents. Like I was fucking Medusa or something.

I knew I couldn't look amazing after sleeping all night in my car, but still. It wasn't like I had snakes growing out of my head.

"Damn it," I muttered, pushing down the ache in my chest that was trying to remind me I'd probably just watched an innocent old man die. Any whiff of death made my training take over, and I didn't have time to be sad for him right now.

I fumbled around the seat for my phone, then snapped a quick picture of the stony statue of a corpse before getting out of the car on the other side. I didn't want to touch him. Didn't want to risk knocking him over and smashing him to pieces. Somehow that would make him seem even more dead than he already was.

I slid into the motel room, quick and quiet, and grabbed the bag I hadn't gotten a chance to unpack last night.

Carina gaped at me, a glint of excitement in her eyes. "Did you just—"

"Let's go. Now," I hissed, cutting her off, and she miraculously seemed to understand I meant business.

She buried herself under her unpacked pile of dirty clothes from the night before and trotted out to the car, her eyes lingering on the red statue of the man beside it that had been living and breathing just moments prior.

I avoided her questioning stare as I hurried my ass into the driver's seat, only pausing long enough to text the picture I'd taken of the statue to Dirk, my Guardian contact who was now also Etty's boyfriend.

Dirk was an asshole, but he would tell me if he knew anything about what I'd just witnessed. And if not, he could help me make a report to someone in a better position than me to do something about it.

Because I was not in a good position for that, regardless of how much the universe was trying to tempt me right now.

It didn't take long for the dusty, ragged buildings of the small town to disappear in my rear-view window, gigantic rock formations taking their place on the horizon.

Gigantic *red* rock formations. The same fiery-colored sandstone I'd just seen consume the police officer.

The wavy striations in the rock danced like flames in my peripheral vision as I did my best to keep my eyes on the road.

"Darcy."

Was it the phoenix again, casting its fiery glare over everything in my path?

"Darcy?"

I blinked, then shifted my eyes over to Carina. "Yeah?"

"Your family in California . . . Can they teach me how to do that?"

"Do what?" I asked, hoping she didn't mean what I thought she meant.

"*That.* What you just did to that guy."

"That wasn't me," I said, my words as icy as the chills running down my spine.

"Oh," Carina said.

I swallowed and pressed harder on the gas, hoping it wasn't a twinge of disappointment I heard in her voice.

3

"IF YOU DIDN'T KILL him, why are we running away?"

Carina's question hung in the stale air of the car. Cold coffee and leftover candy had been our only breakfast, and my niece was squirming in the passenger seat in a way that begged for a bathroom break. But I wanted to get as far away as possible from that town before stopping.

"You know why," I said. Did she want me to spell it out for her? To remind her, in so many words, that *she* had killed people back in DC? That if she showed her face anywhere near these new mysterious deaths, the police would not only arrest her but also try to pin *more* charges against her?

"But shouldn't we try to help?" she asked. When I looked over, she was squirming with her whole body now and not just her legs.

I sighed, a tingling relief flooding through me at the humanity in her question. It was the kind of question she should be asking.

"Maybe," I answered. "If we knew how to help. But I don't."

It wasn't like there'd been a course in my Guardian training on how to save people from being turned into stone. If something that looked like Medusa reared its ugly head, I'd be the first one to squeeze my eyes shut and hack it to pieces. But there didn't seem to be a clear culprit here, and I was no expert on spontaneous petrification—my unfortunate experience with spontaneous combustion notwithstanding.

My phone buzzed against the empty cup holder. I took a hand off the wheel to answer.

"You're on speaker," I said quickly.

"Well hello to whoever's listening." As usual, Dirk sounded far too amused for the circumstances. "So . . ." he started.

"So," I answered.

"You turned someone into a statue and took a picture for evidence?"

"It wasn't me," I said. "I don't know why that happened to him, but it wasn't a solitary incident. Spoke to someone yesterday saying it happened to at least two others last week."

"Serial killer, then . . . Medusa running loose over there?"

I let out a light chuckle. "That's what I said. But I haven't seen anything to suggest that."

"You wouldn't have, though," he said firmly.

"What do you mean?"

"If you'd seen her, you'd be dead too. Don't need to be a genius of mythology to remember that's how that works."

"True . . ." I paused, tapping my fingernails on the steering wheel. "But the officer this morning was looking right at me when it happened. No one else was around."

"Well how long's it been since you washed your hair? It gets pretty wild when you go too long, could look like snakes in the right—"

"Ha ha," I said while staring daggers at Carina, who was actually giggling under her breath. "Very funny. You have anything useful to say?"

"Not really," he said. "What did Crane say?"

"What do you mean?" I asked, my heart jumping just a little when I heard him say Adrian's last name.

"About the people turning to stone," Dirk clarified. "What did he say?"

"I haven't asked him. You're the only one I've told." I paused again, trying not to squirm in my seat like my niece had been doing a moment ago. "I thought that's what I was supposed to do —that you wanted me to come to you first if I notice anything weird. Right?" I was careful not to mention why that was in front of Carina, who didn't know that I was still working for the Guardians and that Dirk was my main point of contact.

No one knew, and that was the whole point. With my ruined reputation as a bodyguard, I was useless to the Guardians for anything other than covert work. And right now, I was in between assignments. That wouldn't last long, but while it did I was just tasked with reporting anything I happened upon that might be of interest.

"Well, sure," Dirk said, "but you tell that boy everything. Hell, that's who I'd ask first about something like this. Our people will take time to dig up any theories, but Crane's got a whole mess of useless information just knockin' around in his head."

"Right." I should have seen that coming, of course. Dirk and Adrian were police partners, so they tended to work together on anything not directly related to Dirk's covert assignments. And so far, these stone deaths weren't tied to anything Guardian related. "Well, you should tell him then."

"Me? Nah," Dirk said. "He's been outta the office this week, and I'm busy picking up his slack. You're the one who saw it happen and it ain't technically my problem—you call him."

I swallowed, wondering if there was a diplomatic way to tell Dirk his partner wouldn't answer the phone if I called.

"Let me know what he says and I'll call it in to our people," Dirk continued. "And Darcy?"

"Yeah?"

"Remember to wash your hair."

He hung up before I could think of something sufficiently rude to answer him with, so I just narrowed my eyes and tried to resist the urge to push away the stray curl that had fallen out of my messy bun in front of my eyes.

Was it a bit greasy? Sure. But if I washed it too often, my shiny curls would become a poofy hot mess. Becca had taught me that before she'd died—embarrassingly late in my life. None of the mages who'd raised me had hair like mine, and none of them cared much about appearances anyway.

Neither had I, until recently. Grumbling under my breath, I picked my phone up out of the cup holder and clicked through to my abandoned text conversation with Adrian. My heart pounded faster in my chest, left hand sweating on the steering wheel as my right sent him the picture of the statue corpse along with a message telling him to call Dirk.

It wasn't the dangers of texting while driving that had my nerves spiking. I swallowed down my unease, aware that Carina was watching. *Set a good example, Darcy—break some driving laws while you break a boundary the man clearly set.* I let out a grunt that wanted to be a laugh.

This should be fine, right? Adrian had only said he never wanted to *work* with me again, not that I should never contact him. And I was clearly just referring him to Dirk.

Sucking in my cheeks, I refocused on the road ahead of me. Steep hillsides had replaced the flat desert we'd been driving through for hours. They were covered in dry brown grass, the same color as the drab tunics I'd worn as a teenager at the clinic. We were in California now, uncomfortably close to home.

Carina had stopped squirming. I narrowed my eyes. "You still have to pee?"

"Nope," she said brightly.

I grimaced. "Do I want to know why?"

"Nope," she repeated, but then she held up my large gas-station paper coffee cup from yesterday and grinned a devilish grin.

"Gross," I said, my grimace deepening. "You spill any of that, you're dead."

Carina shrugged and popped another piece of candy in her mouth.

I turned the radio on, looking for something to take my mind away from the unwanted thoughts spinning around in there with nowhere to go.

When the staticky annoying beat of a horrible pop song blared through the speakers, Carina nearly jumped out of her seat. I cringed as the coffee cup in her hands jumped with her.

"Put that down!" I said at the same time as she said, "Turn it up!"

"It's Oya oh my god it's Oya!" she yelled, bouncing up and down as far as the seatbelt would let her.

I frowned and took a hand off the wheel to pluck the disgusting coffee cup out of her grasp myself. I shoved it firmly into a cupholder while Carina took it upon herself to turn up the volume.

"Yeah, yeah, yeah . . ." she sang, wiggling her butt in the seat. "We shake our tail feathers!"

Holy birds. We hadn't even gotten to our first destination yet, and I already wanted to kill her.

Carina blocked me from touching any of the buttons on the radio until the song ended, at which point she turned it off and hooked her phone up to the speakers instead. "I just want to listen to more Oya," she said exuberantly. "He's the *coolest*—Don't you love him?"

I blinked. "Isn't that the failed vigilante vampire who goes everywhere in purple tights?" How did I even know that? I wasn't sure, but I hated myself a little bit for it.

"He's not a failure, Darcy. He just can't be a hero himself anymore because he's too famous. But he helps other people become heroes every day and—oh my god!"

I cringed, knowing I would regret it when I asked, "What?"

"He just posted a casting call!" Carina shrieked.

"A—"

"Do you have a special ability?" she read, words mashing together as her voice sped up in excitement. "Even the strangest talents can be useful in the right circumstances, and my super-power now is matching the right people with the right circum-stances." She looked up from her phone, wild energy practically spilling out of her. "Do you think he would have a use for me? It's supposed to be anonymous, so maybe . . ."

I frowned as Carina looked back down at her phone. "You want to be a *superhero*?" I asked.

"Who doesn't?" she answered quickly. Then she looked up at me. "Isn't that what you were, before you let that creepy old vampire witch get away?"

"I was a Guardian," I corrected her. But she wasn't entirely wrong. Take away the gaudy outfits and the corny masked identi-ties, and most people who signed up to be superheroes probably wanted the same things I had when I'd signed up to be a Guardian so many years ago. "And I'm not letting the creepy old vampire witch get away. That's why we're passing through Cali-fornia on our way to Mexico, *remember*?"

"Whatever," Carina said as she put on another Oya song and adjusted the volume.

I sighed. Simeon obviously wasn't the *whole* reason we were passing through California, but he was a big one. After my twice-decapitated vampire ex-boyfriend had apparently been reunited with his head again and run off with his crazy new ice god, I had no idea where to even start looking for him. But the assassin who'd taken off his head the first time had found him even when I'd been the one hiding him—so I figured she should be able to help me find him again now. According to the pictures on her wife's phone, she was currently in Los Angeles, which was only a stone's throw from my family's coven where Carina and I were headed.

Carina belted out the final words to the song as it ended, and she didn't even pause to catch her breath before turning to ask me, "Are we there yet?"

I took a deep breath to calm the pounding in my temple. I'd been dreading our arrival for the past few hours. Now, as far as I was concerned, we couldn't get there soon enough.

THE SMELL of Aunt Sassie's medicinal tea filled my nostrils as I walked up the stone steps to the front door of the main house. It was a perfectly normal-looking house, one story, painted in a pale orangey hue that matched the hills surrounding it on either side.

I breathed in deep, relishing the sting of the ginger in the air. I'd always hated that tea, but I'd missed it all the same. Funny the way something can creep under your skin and become an inextricable piece of your identity just for being part of a place you once called home.

But this hadn't been my home for a long time.

"Smells tasty," Carina said from behind me, and I half expected to see a forked tongue snake out from between her lips when I turned around.

"It isn't," I said, busting out my fakest smile as the door opened in front of me.

It took Sassie a moment to match my expression, her cheeks going slack in shock before they lifted in a loud welcome. "Darcy . . ." She shook her head, graying dark hair sifting loose from the low bun she kept it in when she was at home. "I almost didn't recognize you!"

She reached out with a slender arm and gently tugged on one of my curls before letting it bounce back into place. Her eyes moved up and down, taking in my tight jeans and camisole, the jacket with all my weapons in it tied around my waist on this sunny day. It was a far cry from how I'd looked growing up, my hair always pulled back tight and my clothes always loose.

Comfortable, maybe.

But that look had had nothing to do with comfort and everything to do with hiding. I was meant to be one of the coven, a healer, a servant to the sick and dying rather than my own person, and I'd needed to look the part. We all had.

Sassie still did. Her brown robe wrinkled along with the corners of her eyes as she bent over to level her face with Carina's. "And who is this little one?"

I pressed my lips together, hoping Carina wouldn't breathe fire in her face. But when I looked at my niece, she was smiling just as wide as the two of us—only her smile was genuine.

"Carina," she said, holding out her hand.

Sassie shook the dragon's hand firmly, and my heart beat faster for a moment as I watched her take in Carina's baggy sweater. It was bright yellow and way too warm for this weather, and I silently begged my aunt to refrain from commenting on it. Carina's torso was still covered in burns, and although they were mostly healed, I knew she was dressing to hide them. But Sassie just stood up and motioned for us to come in.

"Well Carina," she said, "would you like some tea?"

"Yes, please!" The girl ran through the doorway, practically skipping, and left me standing on the doorstep wondering where my sulky murderous niece had gone. Had I left her in the last town and brought some impostor here instead?

I shrugged. The befuddled part of my brain could take a back seat if it meant I could relax for a moment. No one would be calling the cops on us here, and if Carina was behaving well then that was icing on the cake.

My head spun with a strange familiarity as I walked into the house. It was like walking into a dream, everything warped, the colors just slightly off from my memories and the space just slightly too small. But then, I'd been slightly smaller when I'd lived here. A child, like Carina was now.

A buzz from my pocket snapped me out of my memories, and I grabbed my phone out just a little too quickly. My heart sank before I even realized what I'd been hoping to see on the screen. It wasn't anything from Adrian—just a text from Etty complaining about some drama with Baz.

Had the old genie found out I'd left his precious club with her and skipped town? Thankfully, there was only so much he could meddle in his own business affairs from prison. I hoped I'd be back to help my roommate before he could do too much damage.

"Do you like ginger?" Sassie's voice called as I rounded the corner into her sunny, cluttered kitchen. She wasn't talking to me.

"I love anything spicy," Carina answered as she followed my aunt, a fresh bounce in her step.

Sassie picked up the kettle with a worn hand towel and poured two cups of tea. She handed one to Carina and left the other on the counter in front of an empty stool that had always been mine to occupy when I'd lived here.

"You made it," Sassie said, focusing her attention on me as Carina flopped down in one of the other stools and sipped her tea.

"I did," I said stiffly, a lump in my throat keeping me from getting any more words out.

Sassie stared at me silently for just a little too long before saying, "I wasn't sure it was really you when you called."

"Who else would it be?" I asked.

"One of your enemies trying to sneak their way in so they can kill your family and everyone you ever cared about," Carina said, peering at us over her steaming mug. "It's supervillain 101."

"I'm not a superhero," I reminded her. "I don't have supervillain enemies."

Carina scoffed at me and rolled her eyes. Okay, I kind of did have supervillain enemies. Or at least one. But he would know better than to come to Sassie if he were looking for someone to use as leverage or kill for vengeance.

"That's reassuring," Sassie said in her darkly monotone voice.

I stepped up to the counter and grabbed my cup of tea, downing half of it in a few gulps without sitting down. I grimaced at the spicy, earthy flavor that filled my mouth. Yeah, still hated it. But I needed to distract myself from how horribly awkward this was.

Just stepping into this room had brought back the memories of Sassie and I screaming at each other over this same counter the day I had left for Guardian training almost ten years ago. She'd hated the idea of me doing anything other than following in her footsteps as a healer, and I'd hated that she couldn't see how miserable I would have been in her shoes. How had we even found so many words to scream at each other over such a simple and obvious issue?

It didn't matter now. I wanted to just rip off the bandage—ask my aunt about the mage marks so I could get mine back and slap a new one on Carina and then get us both back on the road to track down the assassin I was eager to find.

But I couldn't slap a mage mark on Carina until and unless she decided she wanted one. And that wasn't a decision that should be rushed.

"How long are you planning to stay?" Sassie asked calmly

when I set down my empty mug on the counter with a loud clack.

Good fucking question. "I don't know," I said tentatively, looking up at her. "Is that okay?"

"You know your room will always be here." My aunt spread out her hands in front of her and then reached for the kettle to pour me more tea.

My heart beat faster in my chest. My room? Had she really kept my room as . . . mine? After all these years? Had she not believed me when I'd said I was never coming back?

"And I'm not planning on hosting any other visitors anytime soon," she continued, either oblivious to my discomfort or ignoring it. "Except your friend, of course."

"My friend?" I asked, eyebrow quirked. I didn't think she was referring to Carina.

"The redhead who showed up earlier today," Sassie replied as I heard someone open the sliding-glass door to the garden from the other room. "That should be her coming in now. She went out back to take a phone call."

My chest tightened as a cheerful voice with a familiar English accent called out from the other room, "Is Darcy here yet?"

"Minnie?" I muttered to myself, blinking as she walked into the room until I was certain her red hair and sly smile were really there. Not another dream or vision or phantom phoenix spirit there to taunt me. No, this was the actual woman whose wife had decapitated Simeon and blown up my life a year ago—the woman whose wife I'd come to California to find.

I squelched the urge to ask her what the fuck she was doing here. My face was probably doing a good enough job of that all on its own.

"Took you long enough," Minnie said, her smile fading only slightly when she turned to me. "I'm shocked you didn't fly here, what with the hurry you're always in."

"I'm not always in—" I stopped, clenching my teeth as I took a deep breath. I probably *had* always been in a hurry from her point of view; Minnie only showed up in my life when crazy shit was going down. Which didn't make her appearance now, in a place she shouldn't even know about, bode well. "What are you doing here?" Fuck it, the question was warranted.

"You invited me. Don't you remember?" Before I could answer with a definite no, she added, "So I can surprise my wife for our anniversary—we got married just nearby, of course. It was so thoughtful of you."

"Hmm," Sassie said as she poured another cup of tea. "Very thoughtful. I wish you'd thought to warn me, though, Darcy."

"Must have slipped my mind," I said, wondering if it actually had. Minnie had a history of stealing my memories, after all. But as far as I knew, she'd been delirious and half dead of blood loss the last time I'd seen her, in Soma's crypt. I'd honestly expected the ancient vampire to kill her after that, even though I'd asked him not to.

But clearly, he hadn't. It would appear he hadn't even had the decency to cloud her memory of our last encounter, or she would have had no reason to follow me across the country like this. Maybe he had tried, and her abilities had stopped him? I still didn't completely understand what she could do, but I knew it had something to do with memories—both past and future. Whatever that meant.

"Your aunt makes delicious tea," Minnie said brightly. "I can taste the vitality in the ginger; those roots must be well established and well cared for." She took a sip and looked at Sassie. "You grow your own, I assume?"

"I do." Sassie gave her a wry smile. "But don't expect me to be impressed that you knew that; I'm sure you caught a glimpse of my garden on the way in."

I scowled at the both of them, almost wishing Carina would

put on another annoying song to distract me from the over-whelming anxiety I felt from seeing my past and present clashing here like this.

Aunt Sassie was where I had learned my skepticism. In a world full of magic and mystery, she only ever believed in what she could perceive with her own senses. She had always cautioned me against the idea that magic could make anything possible. Magic wasn't the stuff of wishes and dreams; it was real and dangerous and it had rules. So if a self-proclaimed "diviner" walked into her kitchen and promised to tell her fortune, she would either politely decline or make the woman prove herself. It seemed she was leaning towards the latter.

"Do you want a tour?" I asked Minnie quickly. "Of the garden," I added. "I can show you the ginger." I wanted to get out of that kitchen, and I wanted to nip this relationship in the bud. Minnie was the real deal, and once Sassie discovered that, there was no telling what use for her she might find.

"That sounds lovely," Minnie said as she put down her tea.

"You two can help me with the weeds while you're out there." Sassie handed me a small key, which I guessed would open the garden shed. Ever the delegator of chores. "I'll show the little one something more exciting."

Sassie's voice went up an octave as she addressed this last part to Carina, who already looked like she never wanted to leave.

"Yep," I said. "You two try not to burn anything."

At Sassie's perplexed expression, I did the same thing I'd always done as a teenager and just fake-smiled, the corners of my lips only lifting halfway as I turned on my heel and walked outside.

I only knew Minnie had followed me when I heard the safety of her weapon click off.

4

I FROZE.

Normally, if someone got it in their head to try and shoot me, I did one of two things: de-escalate or disarm. Try to talk them out of it or attack them before they could get a shot off. And normally, it wasn't hard to determine which was the best course of action. Normally, I could tell just by looking at someone just how determined and just how dangerous they were.

Minnie, however, was still a fucking mystery to me.

If I had to guess, I'd say her intent was to heroically murder me before I could get to her wife—she probably thought I was still out for revenge after what the blonde had done to Simeon.

If I could convince her I wasn't—that I wanted Simeon dead twice over—she would stand down.

Probably.

But since she knew exactly who she was dealing with in me— an opponent who could kill her easily if given a window . . . would she give me a window?

I turned around slowly.

Minnie's hands were shaking, and it wasn't from the weight of the small firearm she had pointed straight at me. Bad sign.

This was the woman who hadn't batted an eyelash when I'd used her bread mixer to tear off the head of a vampire who'd chased me into her kitchen. She'd simply dusted off her apron, chopped him up, and baked him to a crisp in her ovens. I hadn't thought it would be possible to shake her, but here we were.

I ducked, knees scraping against the stones of the garden path before I pitched myself forward and rolled towards Minnie's feet.

The sudden movement had her wide eyed as she pulled the trigger, setting off a booming shot that went over my head. Minnie wouldn't kill me today, but Sassie might. I hoped the stray bullet had found its way into a pile of compost and not into someone I knew.

The weapon flew out of her hands when I tackled her from below, her knees buckling against the force from my shoulder. She let out a short yelp as she fell, and her arms flailed out at me, panic in her eyes.

Her fingers reached my face as her ass hit the ground, and my world darkened at her touch.

My face went numb, followed by the rest of me. Minnie's wrath filled me, clawing at my insides like a trapped beast desperate to get out.

I gasped, choking against her suffocating touch, even though her hands were nowhere near my neck.

How dare she . . .

How dare she what?

How dare she murder my love . . .

Simeon's laughing eyes stared at me from my dreams, his thick eyebrows raised as he lifted a glass to his lips, minutes before his neck painted the wall behind him red. His head rolled towards me, leaving a trail of dark wetness on the dusky blue carpet of the hotel room. His eyes still laughing as my insides clawed at me with even more desperation.

It wasn't Minnie's wrath I was feeling . . . it was my own. The memories she had taken from me, of the night Simeon had been decapitated. This was what I had felt as I'd hovered over her as she was hovering over me now. Even though he wasn't actually dead then. Even though Minnie hadn't been the one to kill him— nor had the blonde assassin when she'd cut off his head.

Somehow, I had remembered the gist of what had happened without remembering the details. Minnie had said that was her fault, her being the one who'd fucked with my head, albeit accidentally. And now it seemed she was accidentally correcting her mistake.

She was giving me back my memory of the fearful, panicked rage I'd felt when I'd realized someone had come after the person I'd loved. It must be similar to what she was feeling now, as she imagined me going after her wife in retaliation.

Hell, if I hadn't forgotten so much of that night . . . I might have gotten that retaliation.

But it was too late now. I didn't want it. All I wanted was Simeon dead. Again. For real.

I let my anger at him slice through the shock of the memories Minnie had thrown me in. Would it find its way to her?

Her hand burned on my forehead, and she let out a strangled yell as she fell back. Her eyes were almost as red as her hair as she scrambled to find the weapon she'd dropped.

I found it first.

If my assailant had been anyone else, I'd have moved to restrain her before going for her weapon. But Minnie apparently had the upper hand when it came to close contact, since all it took for her to mess with my brain was a simple touch.

I aimed her weapon at her chest, following her as she climbed to her feet. My grip was much steadier than hers had been, but my finger was light on the trigger.

She reached up as if to fix her hair, but her hand landed on her left earring instead. The same black feathers she always wore.

The redness drained from her eyes as soon as she touched it, and I could tell by the movements of her chest that her breathing had slowed.

"I don't want—"

"You don't want to hurt her," Minnie said, her words taking mine over.

"No," I said. "Turns out she was doing me a favor when she took the head off the lying bloodsucker I was dating."

I had promised Soma I wouldn't go around telling people the vampires' secret, that they could survive decapitation—but Minnie had probably seen it all when she'd touched me. There was no keeping secrets from her.

She threw her head back, laughter rushing out of her as fast and hard as the bullet she'd just sent after me. When she finally came up for air, she said, "That's a bloody relief!"

I let out a slow breath, trying to nudge my nervous system out of fight mode. My fists opened and my neck stretched to the side as my stance echoed her jarring shift in mood.

"Why did you sneak off without me then, love? And stealing my phone at that. You didn't think I'd want to introduce you to my wife?" Minnie paused, tilting her head with a sly look in her eyes. "Unless you're trying to steal her away . . ."

I almost laughed at the implication, but the mirth could only bubble up so far underneath the weight of the fight still knotting my insides.

"She is very beautiful," Minnie said pointedly.

"Sure," I said, finally calming my heart enough to smile. "But unless she has a dick or a twin brother, I'm not interested."

"Suit yourself." Minnie picked herself up from the ground and dusted off her pants as she shook her head at me. "Shall we see about these weeds?"

There she was again, the ever-cheerful woman she'd been before I'd seen her half-drained in Soma's crypt.

"Did he say anything to you?" I asked the back of her head as we walked further into the garden. In a way, it was calming to be around someone else who could snap back to normalcy so soon after a fight.

"Who?" She paused just long enough to turn her head at me with an arched eyebrow. "I'm not a mind reader, you know. I can only see your memories, not your thoughts—and only when we touch."

"Soma," I said.

She didn't turn back to look at me this time, but her stance shifted just slightly as she walked, her steps more rigid than before. "No." It wasn't until she halted before the locked shed, waiting for me to rustle up Sassie's key, that she continued, "He expected I'd forget it all, I'm sure."

"Why didn't you?"

Minnie blinked. "You can wash blood out of clothes, but you can't wash out memories."

"Is that a riddle?" I turned the key in the shed door, then creaked it open and peered into the dusty darkness inside.

"No." Minnie sighed. "It's confusing, I know. Hard to imagine the concept of memories existing outside of the sentient mind, but they do. Or maybe it would be more accurate to say I can see beyond the limitations of time. Be it a person or a plant or a shoe, I don't always just see it in the present, like you do. Past and future like to pop up and toy with me. So when a vampire erases the memories in my brain, it's only a matter of time before the shirt I was wearing tells me the whole story."

I chewed on my tongue as I handed her a pair of garden gloves. "Does that mean you just know . . . everything? Everything that's happened in the past and everything that will happen in the future?"

"Of course not. I can't touch everything in the world, firstly. And even if I could, it's not easy to control what I see. Things slip by me all the time. And sometimes I can't tell the difference between future and past."

"So you don't know how you're going to die?" I wasn't sure why my mind went there. Maybe it was what I would want to know if I had her ability.

Minnie's eyes went vacant for a moment. Her cheerful expression stayed put, but something within her had changed. "Not exactly, no."

Sore subject, then. I broke the awkward silence in two when I tossed Minnie a rusty hoe. Her eyes popped open wide, life returning to them as she fumbled to catch the tool. "Well it's not death by hoe, apparently," I said in an attempt to lighten the mood.

Minnie took a breath and adjusted her grip to put the glove between the handle and her skin. "Not a garden hoe, at least," she said with a mischievous grin.

I rolled my eyes. I'd spent enough time with Dirk at this point that I should have seen that one coming. "While we're on the subject of deadly women . . ."

"Yes, of course I'll introduce you," Minnie said as she made her way to a weedy patch of earth beneath the ginger plants. Their leaves looked like long blades, shooting out from the central stalks as pointy warnings to keep people away.

I knelt down beside her. "Great. Does tomorrow work?" I had been planning on doing a bit of investigative work . . . okay, stalking . . . to find Minnie's wife, so her help was more than welcome now that she'd stopped trying to kill me.

"The thing is . . ." Minnie said slowly, not looking up from the earth she was turning. "I don't exactly know where she is."

I raised my eyebrows, pinching my lips together.

"She's on a job, is all." Minnie dug her hoe into the ground a little too forcefully. "She sort of disappears when she's on a job."

"Sort of?"

"Yes, well, there's one place I know she'll always be, but—"

"But what?"

"I can't go there."

I narrowed my eyes, beginning to lose what little patience I had left with this woman after the attempt she'd just made on my life.

"Ever heard of Celestial?"

I let out a harsh breath, closing my eyes. "Of fucking course." Opening my eyes again, I fixed them on Minnie. "Is she really one of those nuts?"

On its surface, Celestial was a club. Everyone knew it—the glowing windows at the top of the tallest building in downtown LA broadcast its presence every night, like a halo. An angelic skyscraper, doing its best to lord over the city like any angelic presence would. Only the creatures inside weren't angels.

"They're not nuts," Minnie protested. "Just very old. You know what that does to a person, certainly."

I did know. Sighing, I punched into the earth with my gloved fingers and grasped an especially tenacious weed by its roots, then yanked it up. At this point, I'd spent far too many of my relatively few years on this earth dealing with nutjobs who had been living for far too long.

"What is she?" Celestial didn't allow vampires to be members, and their minimum age requirement was something more like twenty-one *hundred* rather than twenty-one. So if Minnie's wife was a member, she must be something much more sinister than I'd imagined. "Besides a cradle robber," I added.

"Don't start." Minnie huffed. "After everything you got up to with that stodgy bloodsucker . . ."

She had me there. I didn't bother arguing that there was a difference between a few hundred years old and a few thousand, because it didn't matter. At the end of the day, she was the happily married one while I was on a mission to kill my ex and make sure he stayed dead this time.

"And I don't know," Minnie continued.

"You're married to her, and you don't know what she is?"

"She won't say."

I narrowed my eyes at Minnie, suddenly wondering whether they'd included the "till death do us part" bit in their wedding vows and whether Minnie understood that really just meant until *her* death. Commitment for life wasn't exactly the same thing when it was between a mortal and . . . whatever this woman was.

"Hmm," I said. "She won't tell you where she is, and she won't tell you what she is . . . If she were a man, I'd say those are classic 'He has a second family' type of red flags."

"She *does* have a second family—Celestial. It's one of their rules. They're not supposed to say what they are."

"I see," I said, but I really didn't. My knowledge of Celestial didn't go beyond the fact that it was full of ancient nuts who acted like they owned the city.

"It's not so much a club as a support group," she went on, looking at me now with eagerly wide eyes. "They help each other navigate the human world and stay in the present. When you get to be that old . . . it gets harder and harder to leave the past behind."

"And we have to go there to find her, you said?"

"Yes, well . . ." Minnie shoved her hoe in the earth and left it there while she wiped the sweat off her forehead. Flecks of earth stuck to her damp skin, adding to the freckles that already dotted her complexion. "*You* have to go there. I can't."

I frowned. "I'd accuse you of using me to stalk your wife— very healthy, by the way—but I don't see why you think I can get into Celestial when you can't."

Minnie raised her eyebrows at me. "Don't be dense, Darcy. It's not becoming."

"I mean, I know the stress of the past year or so has given me a couple white hairs, but I'm not even thirty yet. Need to add a few zeros to that before they'll even consider letting me in."

"But you're not just you, are you?" Minnie asked, rubbing something at the back of her head.

"I'm not . . ." I paused, realization dawning on me as some of Minnie's fiery red hair fell out of her braid onto her shoulders. Hot embers charred the edges of my memories from the road. "Oh, right."

The phoenix. That fucker was probably ancient.

"It's settled, then," Minnie said brightly. "You'll go the night after next." She pursed her lips, tilting her head as her eyes darted around the garden. "I'm going to see if your aunt has any dill growing—so I can make a loaf of her favorite bread."

"You're sending me to Celestial to deliver her a care package?"

"You're the one that wants to ask her a favor. The least you could do is help me feed her; she eats terribly when she works."

Minnie was off, ambling through the plants, before I could even think of how to respond. My head was spinning from how many turns the day had taken already, and I'd been here less than an hour. This place hadn't been nearly as chaotic when I'd called it home, but I was a fool if I'd thought the new chaos in my life wouldn't follow me here.

I'd been prepared to hunt down an assassin—but an assassin member of Celestial was a whole different ball game. We wouldn't be on anything like equal footing. How could I ask a favor of this kind of killer when I had nothing to offer in return?

I grimaced, taking a step to follow Minnie towards the herbs. Hopefully, her bread was delicious enough to do the trick.

A shrill yelp cut through the okra stalks in front of me, and Minnie's head of red hair jerked to the side before falling out of my view.

I grumbled, picking up my pace and wondering if Sassie had

been hiding gnomes in the garden again. Supposedly good for the plants, but very easy to trip over their pointy little hats.

I pushed the stalks aside to emerge in the little clearing before the herb garden, where the wildflowers in the ground covering were allowed their small space to shine. This spot had always made me want to take my shoes off and sink my toes into the soft leaves and vines and rugged blooms.

Today, though, my feet would have been bloody if not for my boots. A person-sized pile of sharp crystals lay beside Minnie in the clearing, its greenish-yellow hue almost blending with the soft plants beneath it.

Drips of Minnie's blood shone crimson on the jagged edges at the top, where her bare legs must have scraped against it when she'd fallen.

Not another . . .

I ran forward, hoping a closer look would reveal that the person-sized crystal was not also shaped like a person—was not in fact another person who'd just been turned into some kind of stone.

But it was. Tiny droplets of Minnie's blood coated even tinier crystal eyelashes, a red-spattered comb of glittering stone framing two crystal eyes above a scrunched nose and an open mouth. I could see the terror in the petrified face, the tension in the body positioning even though it must have fallen over from standing.

One of the arms had broken off and lay at a grotesque angle, but at least it hadn't all shattered or crumbled like I'd worried the police officer from this morning would do.

Not that it would have mattered. An intact crystal person was no more alive than a shattered one would be. There was no life in those prisms, even as they glimmered in the sunlight and bathed in blood.

Minnie's blood. I shook my head, finally registering the fact that Minnie wasn't moving. When I knelt down beside her, I saw why—her hand was resting on the crystal person's shoulder. It looked relaxed, accidental, just a casual touch as if to reassure a friend that everything would be alright.

Except Minnie's touches were never casual, were they?

Her eyes stared up at the sky, unmoving, unfocused. Her mouth hung open loosely, and I had to hold my wrist above it to confirm that she was breathing.

I moved my hand to hers, pushing it off the crystals as I rolled her to her side. The edges of my world began to darken again at the touch of my fingers on hers, and my throat tightened.

I let go like she was on fire.

Flexing my fingers to try to shake off the lingering feeling of her touch, I frowned. I'd been planning to heal her—grasp her wrists in my hands and close my eyes and let the magic all around us flow through me, into her and back again, while I assessed and repaired whatever damage she might have incurred from her fall.

But I couldn't do that if I couldn't touch her. And I couldn't touch her if her psychic memory bullshit was trying to strangle me, even though I had no idea why it would.

I was pulling out my phone to call Sassie when Minnie's eyelids fluttered open. Her eyes locked on mine, and in an almost robotic voice she croaked, "The moon."

Minnie's forehead creased as she squirmed to get away from the crystalline corpse.

"The moon brought this death," she whispered before her eyes closed again, and then she was still.

5

PUFFS OF FLOUR clouded the air in front of the wall-hanging in Sassie's kitchen, making the crescent-moon mirror appear to be shrouded in fog.

I coughed. I hated baking.

Clumps of gluey dough were already crusting around my fingernails as I rubbed my hands together over the sink. I sucked in my cheek, biting it against the urge to rub the skin clean off my bones.

Minnie's blood had been easier to wash away than this night-mare. But at least she was still breathing, even though she was too unconscious to do the baking herself.

The water gushing from the faucet had started to steam, so I thrust my hands under it and stretched out my fingers. Warmth filled me, tension leaving my muscles even as I winced from the sting on my skin.

When my hands were as clean as they were going to get, I turned off the water and picked up the limp, grayish-brown hand towel that was hanging on the cabinet. Not even the fixtures in this house were allowed to wear anything colorful.

"What are you doing here?" Sassie asked from behind me.

I let out a breath, hanging the damp towel back in its place as I eyed the ticking timer above the oven. Was it time for us to get real with each other, now that we were alone? "Making bread," I said. *Or trying to.*

"I meant here in my house."

"Is there another house I would have been more welcome in?" I knew that wasn't what she'd meant, but the hitch in her breath told me I'd touched a nerve anyway.

I turned around to look at her, to see the damage I'd done unwittingly.

"Where's Fred?" I asked before I could stop myself. Sassie sucked in a long breath, and I tried not to feel satisfied for having hit the nail on the head so precisely.

"Just a few doors down."

"Not living here anymore?" *Not with you* were the words that went unsaid.

"No. Not since you left."

My gut clenched, guilt punching at my insides before I could remember to harden them. I wasn't responsible for her failed marriage, even if she had driven us both away in tandem.

My mouth opened, so many words trying to escape and none managing to make it out. Surprise that Fred would leave Sassie without leaving the coven entirely—I'd always thought she was the only thing that kept him here. Apparently not. Hurt that he would leave her and not tell me. Not find me. Not visit me. Not anything.

"It wasn't because of you," Sassie said.

That was hard to believe. Before I'd left, the fights Fred had picked with her had always been about me. "Why then?"

"He wanted more children. I didn't."

I nodded. My head felt light as I processed her words. *More* children. But they hadn't had any children to start with—only me. And it had never really felt like I counted. I'd always called them aunt and uncle, not mom and dad.

"You haven't answered my question," Sassie said. I didn't know if she was changing the subject more for her benefit or for mine. "Why are you here?"

I leaned towards her, spreading my hands out on the counter as I looked her straight in the eyes. "My mark is gone."

"Your . . ." Sassie's eyes bulged as they followed mine down to my left ankle, where I pulled up the cuff of my jeans to show her the bare skin. The tattoo of the moon that had been there for as long as I could remember was gone, as if it had never existed. "How did you—"

I held up a hand to stop her, shaking my head. "That's not important. I want to know why you lied to me about it."

She looked away from me. Her jaw shifted from side to side as her knuckles rapped on the granite countertop, displacing the light dusting of flour I'd left there. "How much do you know?"

It was a reasonable question, so I answered it. The tattoo was actually a mage mark, meant to block me from the influence of the god who had taught me to channel magic. Without it, I was his servant, by definition a witch. And then there was my long-lost brother, and the phoenix spirit we carried between us. I hadn't known whether Sassie had known about that part all along, but her unchanged expression told me that she had.

"And Carina . . .?"

"Is my niece," I said. "Also one of Popo's servants."

"Is that why you brought her here?"

I frowned. The answer was yes, of course. I wanted to give Carina the same opportunity Sassie had given me when I'd been brought to her as a child. The chance for independence. But it wasn't safe to say that when we were probably being watched.

"We're on the way to bring her back home," I said instead. "I brought her here because she wants to learn . . . about healing."

The timer dinged.

I snapped my eyes to the oven, then spun around and stuffed the oven mitts over my hands. Steam blasted me in the face when I opened the door, along with the enticing savory scents of toasted wheat and fresh dill. My mouth watered. But when I squinted into the dark pan and slid it out into the light, my heart sank. The loaf looked more like a pancake. Completely flat.

"You didn't develop the gluten enough," Sassie said, tapping her fingernail on the golden-brown crust. "It doesn't matter how much you let it rise if you don't give it the strength to hold itself up."

My stomach growled at the bread.

I reached across the counter to Sassie's knife block and pulled out the long serrated blade from the back. It felt strange in my hand; the balance was off, the blade too long and unwieldy. It would be terrible in combat. *But no one needs killing right here, right now, so that's fine.*

The crust cracked and crumbled as I sliced into the bread, cutting myself a heavy wedge that looked gummy on the inside. I took a bite and chewed.

"Stubborn as always," Sassie remarked.

"The flavor is good," I said once I'd swallowed.

She chuckled, her shoulder brushing mine as she moved past me to reach the kettle on the stove. Two steaming mugs of tea later, she plopped down on a stool beside me and said, "Cut me a slice."

We ate in silence, me checking my phone for messages and her with her eyes closed, just like the good old days that I'd never thought of as very good at all. I still didn't remember them fondly, but everything that had come after certainly made them seem . . . less bad.

"Why did you lie about the mark?" I asked, not sure when

we'd become such experts at avoiding each other's uncomfortable questions.

Sassie sighed, opening her eyes as she brought her tea to her lips. After a careful sip, she looked at me and said, "I couldn't think of anything good that would come of you knowing the truth."

My head rushed, all the possibilities flitting around as I tried to think of what I could have done differently, had I known about my witchy origins from the start. About the phoenix that had burned Becca. I couldn't have saved her from death, but I could have saved her from burning and then coming back as a zombie. That would have at least been one good thing. I almost opened my mouth to tell Sassie that, but for some reason, I didn't want to.

"Is everyone here a witch hiding from some god?" I asked instead. "Or was it just me?"

"Not everyone, but some others. You were the only one that didn't know. The only one that came to us as a child young enough to forget. The others agreed that letting you forget was the kindest thing to do."

My phone buzzed. There had been no messages when I'd checked a few minutes ago, but something had just come in from Etty—a text clarifying that Baz was sick in prison and freaking out about it. Sick? Could that even happen to an immortal djinn like him? I didn't think too hard about it because she followed it up with picture of Noah standing in the middle of my bed, hugging my pillow with an exaggerated pout on his little pudgy face.

Ugh. So fucking cute. I clenched my jaw, to keep from smiling or crying, I didn't know which. It was annoying how much I wanted to be there with him, to chase him around the apartment until he relinquished my pillow in a fit of shrieking giggles, to "help" him with one of his puzzles and have him chew me out for putting in the middle pieces before finishing the edges, to play our version of magical mood catch, where I infuse his apple juice with good vibes and he gives them back to me in different versions of happy emotions, always pushing me to generate more nuance.

My chest ached. Was this what it was like to be homesick? *What am I doing here anyway?*

Putting my phone down, I stared at the half-eaten pancake loaf of gummy bread, which was meant to be my peace offering to the ancient assassin I hoped would help me find and kill my psychotic vampire ex-boyfriend.

Oh, right.

"How is Minnie doing?" I asked Sassie, who had opened her eyes to pour herself more tea.

"Still unconscious, but stable. All her wounds were superficial, but we healed them anyway. Kia was working on her, last I checked."

"She's in good hands then." Kia was one of the specialists at the clinic who dealt in magical maladies. She could sense curses like I could sense souls. "Not making any bread anytime soon, though."

"No," Sassie agreed. "Are you going to try again?"

"No," I said. "I have something else in mind."

I FOUND Carina sitting on the floor in my old bedroom, buried under a pile of my old anatomy books.

"How old are you?" I asked quickly as I knocked on the open door.

"Eight." She looked up, her eyes wild. "Why?"

"Just thought you might be, like, a thousand and lying about your age," I said, still not entirely convinced. "Don't worry about it. I need you to come help me with something in the city."

"No thanks; I'll stay here." Carina shrugged off my presence and peered down at the open book in front of her, her fingertip squeaking slightly as it ran over the page to follow her gaze.

I narrowed my eyes and cleared my throat, and she looked up at me again.

"Your aunt said if I read these books, she'll let me cut open a dead body."

If I narrowed my eyes any further, I wouldn't be able to see her.

"Is this how you learned to heal people?" she asked without waiting for my response. "Or how you're so good at knowing where to stab?"

I would kill Sassie. Or better, stab her in the gut to cause her the most pain possible without killing her. "Only partly," I answered to both questions. "You also need practical experience to learn those things. Which is why you should come with me now."

Carina's eyes widened. "Will you be healing someone?"

"No." I pursed my lips.

"Stabbing, then?"

"Maybe. I'll be infiltrating a secretive group of ancient magical beings, at least one of whom works as an assassin. You'll be my backup."

"Yawwwwwn," Carina said, rolling her whole head with her eyes. "I'm more interested in the healing."

A jolt of frustration ran through me before I realized that was actually a good thing. I didn't like the idea of leaving her here without me—but if the prospect of stabbing ancient magical assassins hadn't swayed her, maybe I didn't need to be so worried.

Or maybe she was just trying to get under my skin.

"Fine," I said, then glanced around the room, subconsciously checking for anything that might explode if it came in contact with Carina.

Nothing gave me pause, and that in itself made me feel uneasy considering I'd grown up in this room. Sassie hadn't changed the steely blue decor, and everything in here had once belonged to me.

It didn't feel as familiar as I would have expected. I had erased it all from my mind because, when I'd left, I hadn't intended on ever seeing it again. Now, after so much had happened, it was hard to remember exactly why that was.

"Don't burn anything," I added, stopping myself before saying "or anyone."

THE CAR FELT empty without Carina. Candy wrappers and soda bottles decorated her spot on the passenger side, where only my jacket was sitting, and even the warmth of the fire bunnies under the seats seemed weaker than usual in the cool desert night.

I shifted my legs without lifting my foot from the gas. In the distance, the tall buildings of downtown LA sparkled against the cloudy black sky, Celestial's halo of windows shining brighter than all the rest.

My phone buzzed. A text. Probably another picture from Etty. I reached across to fish it out of my jacket, but my eyes had to stay on the road, so it slipped out of my grasp and fell onto the floor.

"Birds," I mumbled. I would have to pull over and unbuckle to get it now. But it was hooked up to the car's system, so theoretically I could . . .

I pushed some buttons on the dashboard, hoping for a robotic voice to read me whatever message I'd just received. Instead, I got a ringtone.

It only rang twice before it stopped with a click and a man's low voice said, "Hey."

I froze, my muscles trying to jerk into a sprint and then stopping when they realized there was nowhere to go. "Hey," I said back, then swallowed against the tightness in my throat. "Sorry—I didn't mean to call." I cringed as soon as I said it; it might be the truth, but it sounded like the lamest of all lame excuses.

"Yeah, it's fine," Adrian said.

Is it? My heart jumped with the horrible excitement that he might have actually meant it.

"It'll be easier over the phone," he continued. "I need you to tell me what you saw."

Of course. As much as he wanted to avoid me, Adrian couldn't resist finding out about the crazy-ass bullshit I encountered on the regular. That would always be his downfall.

"Didn't Dirk tell you?" I asked.

"He told me you *didn't* see Medusa, and then he told me to call you. Apparently he's busy."

"Apparently." Apparently Adrian had left him with all their work. I wanted to ask where he was and what he was doing, but that was the kind of question I shouldn't be asking during this conversation we shouldn't be having.

"So, can you tell me what happened?" It felt like he might have added "in your own words" to the end of that, like I was a run-of-the-mill witness on one of his cases.

"Honestly, I can't tell you much that isn't self-explanatory. You saw the picture I sent?"

"I did."

"Well, that guy was living and breathing and talking to me and then all of a sudden, he started turning into *that* . . ."

"Started turning into . . ." Adrian mumbled. "So it wasn't immediate?" And then, before I could answer: "Where did it start?"

"His hand," I said. "He was holding a coffee and then the whole hand just crumbled off—"

"How fast did it spread?"

I sighed. I could hear the excitement in his voice. The rush of joy he always took in trying to understand things that didn't want to be understood. My stomach clenched. Why hadn't he tried harder to understand *me*?

"Darcy?"

"Fast," I answered. "It was done before either of us really realized it was happening."

"What happened to the body?"

"I don't know."

"What do you mean you don't know?"

"I mean I didn't stick around to find out. He was a cop." *She says to the detective,* I thought, groaning internally.

"Good to know what you'd do in the event of my death." There was a twinge of laughter in his voice, and I felt anger bubbling up around the edges of my good sense.

"I wouldn't be there if you died, Adrian," I snapped. His name felt wrong on my tongue. "Or did you forget?"

"I didn't forget," he said, the laughter gone.

"You're calling me to talk about work, so it seems like you might have forgotten."

"You're the one who called me."

"Fine," I said through gritted teeth. "You texted."

"In response to the cryptic picture of a dead body you sent me this morning."

I clutched the steering wheel, my newly polished nails digging into the leather.

"Fine," I said again. "Look, we don't have to do this. You aren't the only person I know who likes researching weird shit—I don't need your help."

"Is that what you think is happening?" he asked. "Darcy, I

have . . ." He paused. "Close to two dozen reports of similar deaths across the country, and that's just in the last week. Not to mention the few I've stumbled on already from overseas."

I gaped at the road in front of me. Not just because of the horrifying idea that I'd stumbled upon something so massive, but also because I hadn't expected Adrian to know anything about it. Had he left the office just to do more work that he was hiding from his partner? *Didn't Dirk do the exact same thing just weeks ago?* Did any of us even know how to take an actual vacation?

"This isn't me trying to help you through a rough spot on your road trip," Adrian went on. "This is me interrogating a witness in a desperate attempt to make sense of something that, if it continues at its current rate, could lead to the deaths of millions of people."

Well, fuck. "Oh," I said. "Then you should know about the others."

"You've seen others?"

"I didn't see them *happen*, but . . ." I took a sharp breath, then told him about the boy in the gas station whose girlfriend's parents were turned to stone, and then about the crystallized mage Minnie and I had found in Sassie's garden. "Minnie said something about the moon when she touched it. And . . ." I pressed my lips together, not sure if or how I should say what I wanted to say.

"And what? Please don't keep anything from me now, Darcy."

"That's—" I shook my head, frustrated. "That's exactly what I was going to say. That I'm trying not to." He was silent for a moment, and I resisted the urge to repeat myself. *I'm really trying.* It was on the tip of my tongue as tears welled in the corners of my eyes. What was wrong with me?

"Thank you," he finally said. "Call me if there's anything else."

"Okay," I said, but he had already hung up.

Gods.

I growled at the car in front of me, swerving into the left lane to speed up.

Why was I so bad with men?

Why did I even care so much about this particular man? He wasn't my usual type. Not dangerous. Not mysterious. Not someone who made me put up with bullshit and expected to put up with mine. Not someone I could ever see myself hunting down to murder.

Not Simeon.

I breathed in at the reminder of what I was doing here, where I was going. It was another reminder of something I'd fucked up, yes—but this was something I could fix.

Invigorated, I stepped harder on the gas, letting the glittering lights of downtown be my beacon.

6

"JUST A SECOND," I yelled over my shoulder to the valet who was holding my door open and waiting for me to get out of the car.

Twisting my body, I peered underneath the passenger seat and held my hand out, palm up.

"Come on," I said in as sweet a voice as I could manage. "I only need one of you."

A single pair of glowing red eyes met mine.

I made a clucking noise with my tongue. I didn't think rabbits clucked, but it seemed the thing to do.

The pair of eyes grew closer until a glossy pair of floppy obsidian ears emerged from the shadows, twitching as the rabbit inspected the piece of gummy candy sitting in my hand. It darted forward, its mouth engulfing the candy like a little vacuum. No chewing, no swallowing—the gummy was simply gone, and the little black bunny sat in my hand, looking up at me as though pleading for more.

"Stay cool and you can have all the candy you want." I lifted the creature to my shoulder and sat up straight. It burrowed quickly in my voluminous tangle of curls, which I was wearing loose tonight, and I hoped it would be able to find its way out again.

I gave my keys a brief squeeze before tossing them to the valet. I wasn't possessive about my car, but it made me feel naked to part with the keys. The car was a thing to get me from point A to point B—the keys were certainty and control.

No one stopped me from walking into the building, which seemed to extend into the sun from this angle. The doors looked exactly like the mirror-plated windows covering every inch of the building's surface, until they slid open to reveal a market of shops that felt too quiet.

My footsteps echoed through the space, highlighting the fact that no one else in here was moving. Shop attendants stared at me from behind counters, all wearing smiles that failed to reach their eyes. One of them waved and another bowed, robotic motions that made me wonder if these people were human—or if they were even really alive.

I made it all the way to the elevator doors before I felt it. A tingle of magic that started at my wrists and quickly floated up to my throat. A clear threat.

"Excuse me, Miss," called a melodic voice. "Are you a member?"

"Not yet," I said, turning around. My throat was getting tighter by the second. "I'd like to join, though."

The tall man who had stopped me seemed to come to life at my words, eyes sharpening as the corner of his mouth twitched up and his fingers tensed. I knew that look—I'd just given him permission to hurt me.

"Unfortunately, that isn't how it works," he said. "You aren't eligible. And even if you were, there's a formal process to follow."

Something hit the back of my neck with a clink. I stumbled forward a step, scrunching my forehead in confusion. What could have made that sound? Warmth spread over my skin, from

OBSIDIAN OATH | 55

the back of my skull to my chin, and I reached up to find my entire neck plated in something hard.

When I saw the anger in the narrowed eyes of the tall man, it hit me—the bunny in my hair had turned itself into armor to protect my neck.

From what?

Something above me glinted in the light. A long, thin spike attached to . . . the tail of a giant scorpion?

I blinked.

The tail of a giant scorpion *man*.

He had reached out and tried to sting me while we were talking, and I hadn't even noticed.

"Cute," he said, and my mind spun in circles as my eyes tried to work out what was real in front of me. He was a man and a scorpion both, at the same time, like two images layered on top of one another—neither of which I could see clearly.

I sprang into action, trying not to think too hard about how dead I would be already if I hadn't had the bunny in my hair. I didn't have any weapons on me, so I did the only thing I could do.

I jumped.

My hands reached up above me and grasped onto the glistening, segmented brown tail still wavering threateningly over my head.

The man hissed. His tail thrashed wildly as I swung my legs up and wrapped them around it. I hung on tightly.

I had no idea how I was going to get out of this fight alive, but gluing myself to the thing that would kill me was at least an effective way of postponing my death.

"Get off of me," the scorpi-man ground out through his teeth, "you vexatious worm."

Vexatious worm, huh? I can do that.

Like I'd seen Etty do countless times on the pole, I pushed my butt up and scooted my way down the monster's tail, away from the deadly stinger and towards its ugly scorpion ass.

When I got there, I hugged the base of the tail tightly with my legs and one arm. With my other arm, I reached into my hair and plucked out the rock-hard bunny that was clinging to my curls. It chittered at me as I set it down on the thrashing scorpion's abdomen and gave it a nod.

Can you turn molten please and burn a hole in this ugly thing? I asked in my thoughts, hoping it was an obvious request.

It wasn't.

The bunny chittered at me even louder and then clambered its way right back into my hair.

The scorpion laughed. It was a grating sound, making my bones vibrate and my teeth sting in my gums.

"Do you think I am afraid of the little witch pet?" it said, seething at me from over its shoulder. "I had seen ages come and go when your god was but a screaming infant human."

That rang of too much truth for my tastes. I needed to find a way out of this.

Muttering a curse at the bunny, I reached inside myself and felt the phoenix's magic buzzing in my veins, overflowing from my scrye. Ready and waiting for me to come play. I'd come here intending to use the bird, hadn't I?

I took a deep breath and let go of the scorpion's tail, pushing the phoenix's magic into the muscles on my back as soon as my feet hit the floor.

Scorpions couldn't fly, as far as I knew, and I would just have to hope that unhinged, ancient scorpion men were similarly grounded.

I started running away from the giant bug, expecting my wings to lift me up at any moment.

Instead, the shiny tile floor came rushing swiftly up to meet my face.

The world went black for a moment, and then I was watching through bleary eyes as the bug-man dragged me across the floor, its pincers gripped tightly around my ankles. Soft, ghostly brown feathers brushed my cheek as they slipped beneath me on the tile.

I'd managed to get my wings out, but I hadn't been fast enough to escape.

Pain was blooming at my low spine, creeping out across my back and into my limbs.

I groaned.

No . . . I didn't groan.

I tried to groan. Nothing happened.

My heart raced. The pain diminished as it spread over my body, and within seconds I was numb all over. My arms should have been stretched out—I'd just moved them towards my ankles —but they weren't. I hadn't moved.

I *couldn't* move.

I felt nothing.

My mind spun in circles, trying to work out what I could have done to prevent this from happening. To guard against this attack.

But there was nothing obvious—I was just seriously outclassed. My only mistake had been coming here at all.

Well, fuck. At least I wasn't dead quite yet.

The man dragged me further, his legs looking human in one instant and monstrous the next. Somehow stepping and scuttling, both and neither with each stride.

I tried to breathe, but my lungs were paralyzed now too. There it was—the thing that would kill me.

I reached for the phoenix's magic, hoping it wasn't too mad at me for getting my wings dirty.

Where are you, bird? I asked in my mind.

Flames licked the edges of my consciousness.

Warmth surrounded me, bringing feeling and pain back to the

surface of my skin. The scorpion in front of me disappeared, hidden behind a billowing veil of glowing, sparking feathers that engulfed me. The world was on fire, bright orange and blue, but none of it touched me. A thin layer of wind rushed over every inch of my skin, my own personal atmosphere whispering promises of freedom and flight in my ears.

I gasped. Crisp air filled my lungs as tingling energy crept back through my body. And then it was all gone.

The scorpion stopped scuttling, its human parts staring at me in something that looked like disappointment. Its pincers released my ankles, which dropped to the floor with a feeling of stinging relief.

"I'm sorry, miss." He said it as though he had spilled coffee on me, not almost killed me. "You're welcome to—"

His neck exploded.

I scrunched up my face as brown goo splattered into my eyes and mouth.

"Blech . . ." I spat. That was unnecessary, and exactly what I'd been afraid of in calling on the phoenix for help.

The bird was a loose cannon, completely unpredictable, and now there would be consequences for killing one of Celestial's own. Even though I didn't know how I had done it.

His head rolled to the ground, but his torso and scorpion body stayed upright—having eight legs to hold itself up and all.

Behind him, a blonde woman stood dressed in a white sundress, every inch of it pristine. No goo.

She smiled at me and licked her lips.

"You're Minnie's friend, right? Darcy?"

A flicker of rage came to life and died in my chest at the sight of her. Minnie's wife. Simeon's supposed killer. For over a year, this woman had been a vague shadow in my memories of his death. A symbol of my failure, of my loss. And she didn't even acknowledge who I was to her—not her victim's bereaved, just some rando her wife had befriended. But that didn't matter, not anymore.

"Did *you* just kill that thing?" I squinted at her through the scorpion goo in my eyelashes, both hoping her answer was yes and irritated with her for interfering if it was. "Do you know how to do *anything* but take people's heads off?"

She gave an exaggerated shrug, the kind you might expect from a bad actress playing a giggly teenager. Flipping her hair even though it was tied back tightly. "Girt isn't a person," she said, "and he's six thousand years old—it would take more than that to kill him."

My shoulders fell in relief. It wasn't the phoenix who had beheaded the scorpion man, and I wouldn't be blamed for his death. Maybe.

This woman did have a history of leaving me to clean up her intentionally created messes.

I looked down at the head of the scorpion man and tried to see Simeon in his eyes, but I couldn't. I couldn't see Simeon clearly in my memories anymore, not since I'd discovered that everything I'd known about him was a lie. He was only ever clear in my murderous dreams, his face fading back into obscurity as soon as I woke.

"I'm Tula," said the woman who had cut off Simeon's head the first time. She stepped closer to me and pulled a white cloth out of the pocket of her white blazer. Handing it to me, she looked me over thoroughly and asked, "Did you bring me bread?"

"No." I wiped the cloth over my face. "Minnie was going to make some, but then she tripped over a dead body and passed out."

Tula crossed her arms, staring down her nose at me as if I were a child out of line. "She's not allowed around dead bodies without me. Didn't she tell you?"

"It was a surprise body," I said bitterly. "I'm sure she didn't mean to be naughty."

Tula chuckled. "I see why she likes you."

By this point, two of the expressionless shop attendants had made their way over to us with mops. Leaving the scorpion man's head and body carefully untouched, they began cleaning up the brown goo from the pearlescent tile floor.

The elevator dinged.

"Well," Tula said, "Let's get you cleaned up, and you can tell me why you're here."

MY SKIN SIZZLED underneath the spray of water from the shower in Tula's apartment. Every member of Celestial had a place in the building, apparently, although they mostly went unused. I would have expected Tula's to be as pristine as the assassin ice queen she appeared to be, but it wasn't. A couple stray shoes had been tossed into the corner of the bathroom, and rumpled towels hung over just one too many surfaces.

Either she was good at her job because she was too damn powerful not to be, or she was good at knowing when it was okay to turn off the perfectionism anyone halfway normal would need in her shoes.

I rinsed the last remnants of scorpion slime out of my hair and squeezed the water out of it. The droplets spattered heavily at my feet as I shut off the shower. Naked, I stepped out and resisted the urge to wrap a towel around myself as quickly as possible.

I needed to get comfortable with this feeling of vulnerability —get used to the fact that I was playing with power I could never expect to control.

For years, I'd managed to convince myself that my Guardian training and skill with a blade would be enough to get me through anything that came at me. Now, after all that had happened, I had to face the fact that it simply wouldn't. How many times in the last few months would I have been dead if not for the phoenix inside me?

I didn't know exactly, but whatever the number, I could add one to it after what had just happened in the lobby. I wasn't above using the bird's power when I needed it, but I couldn't rely on it.

I had to start working smarter, and that meant letting go of the instinct to tackle potential threats head on. I wouldn't win any fight I started here.

There was strength in knowledge, even if it was the knowledge of my weakness.

I dried myself off and slipped on the robe Tula had left for me before stepping out to join her in the sitting room.

"You're lucky I was here today, or Girt would have eaten you," she said as I made my way over to my purse, which was slung over the corner of a white leather sofa. I normally didn't wear one, but I was carrying more than just my weapons, phone, and wallet today. "Do you know scorpions liquify their prey before ingesting it?"

I picked up my purse without meeting her eyes. "He was going to let me in."

"Ah yes, maybe. Or maybe he would have changed his mind again once he realized *you* aren't that flamboyant firebird." She paused. "Are you really going to apply for membership?"

"Maybe," I lied.

"I don't recommend it."

"Why not?"

"Our age restrictions are there for a reason," she said in a sing-song voice. "You would have nothing to gain by joining, and that phoenix in you is too feral for us to do it any good."

"What did *you* have to gain?" I asked, finally looking up at her.

It was one step away from asking for her age, and the dip of her chin told me she knew exactly what I was getting at.

"It's not easy, you know—living this long. Things change, and anyone who doesn't change with them will get left behind. Or go mad." Her eyes glinted, and I turned away from her again to walk towards the kitchen.

"So this place . . . keeps you sane?" I said, looking around as I went.

"Oh no," she called after me. "I wasn't sane even back when I was your age."

I opened a few cabinets in the kitchen until I found the glass-ware. No shot glasses, so the tumblers would have to do. I plucked out four of them.

Tula leaned forward as I walked back towards her and lowered her voice. "This place keeps me from showing my hand. Or getting too much worse." She took in a short breath through her nose and wiggled a little as she let it out, spreading her hands out beside her and tipping her head up to the space around us. "It's a progression—a learning module for those who need help assimilating in today's world. You'd be surprised how many *things* survive on the outskirts of civilization for centuries, only to step out of their lairs to find the world unrecognizable." She pointed down. "The lower floors are for basics—public spaces, blending in—with more complex and intimate experiences as you go up."

"And the very top?" I asked, thinking of that famous halo of windows.

"That's where we let loose," she said. "No diet works without a regular cheat day."

"Don't go up to the very top then," I said, setting the tumblers down on the coffee table. "Heard."

She chuckled, twirling her hair around a finger. "So you see, I don't think you came here to join unless there's something about you I'm missing. Why *did* you come?"

I gave her a short nod, then sat down adjacent to her on the sofa. "Do you remember Senator Simeon Drake? About a year and a half ago. You took off his head in front of me in a hotel room in London. I'm told your wife was there too."

"Of course I remember. Are you finally going to enact your revenge?" She cocked her head at me. "You haven't tried to kill me yet."

"That's because you didn't actually kill him, and I'd like your help to finish the job."

Tula looked at me for a long moment, slightly sucking in her cheek in a way that seemed to hold in a smile. "And what would I get out of this arrangement?" she finally said.

I opened my purse and pulled out two of Sassie's small tonic bottles I'd filled with something better. I split them each between two glasses and set one of each before her, the first a golden amber color and the second a dull green. My fingers lingered on the second glass until it frosted at the edges, the magic around me pulling heat into my skin to chill the drink.

I picked up the glass with the amber liquid in front of me and raised it up between us. "What's in it for you? Me, as a friend and ally."

"Hmm," she said, but she lifted her glass and clinked it against mine, then followed my lead when I knocked it back in one gulp. Notes of butterscotch and oak burned the back of my throat as I swallowed.

"Chase it with this," I said, bringing the second glass to my lips. The cold green liquid hit my tongue with a salty, herbaceous zing—perfectly refreshing after the hot shower I'd needed to scour away the scorpion goo.

Pleasure and confusion crossed Tula's face at the same time. An unlikely combination, given how old she was. She looked at me in question.

"I'm a shit baker," I said, "but Minnie said you liked dill, so here we are. Pickleback."

"Pickleback?"

"Pickleback," I repeated. "Whiskey and pickle juice."

"Hmm," she said again, then tilted her head to the side and peered at the empty glass in her hand. "I like it. But if you want my help, it will come at a higher price than that."

That was a better response than I'd expected. "What do you have in mind?"

Tula looked at me with narrowed eyes, evaluating, calculating. Then she put down her glass. "Vampires like you, don't they?"

"At least one vampire has, obviously." *More than one*, I realized, thinking of the weird truce I'd landed on with Soma.

"And somehow, you know their secret."

"The fun fact about their heads being re-attachable? I wish I'd known it sooner."

"There aren't many people who do," Tula said as she sat up straighter, all business now.

"How did you learn it?"

She shrugged. "I was around before it became a secret. But that's not important. The important thing is that knowing it puts me at a unique advantage among hired killers working for vampires. So—"

"Wait," I said, shaking my head. "You knew about this *before* you cut off Simeon's head?"

"Of course," she said slowly. "Vampires are nothing if not precise. It's not enough to put a hit out on someone you want dead when the method of their death is critically important. Soma would have faced too much opposition from the senator's followers if he'd had him killed permanently, and even the most professional killers can't be trusted to do anything but get the job done unless they understand the importance of the request.

Soma picked me because I understood *why* the senator needed to be decapitated specifically."

"That makes sense," I mumbled, not looking at her. It did make sense, but it was just one more blow to the lie I'd spent so long building up in my mind. How many blows would it take to dismantle it completely? It was already too many.

"So," she continued, "now that you know too—and no one is paying me to kill you to keep you quiet—you would also be at a unique advantage in my line of work."

I breathed in, not sure whether I should be glad I wasn't on her hit list or disconcerted about the possibility. "Are you offering me a job?"

"No," she said. "I don't do that. What I'm offering is my help killing your vampire in exchange for your help killing mine."

"I'd ask who your vampire is," I replied, "but I'm not an assassin."

"Oh?" She raised her eyebrows, genuinely looking surprised.

"I have nothing against killing, but I won't do it for a paycheck and I won't do it for a favor. I'll only do it to keep innocent people safe."

"Ever the Guardian, I see." Tula licked the rim of her empty glass as she eyed me. "That won't be a problem in this case."

"Why not?"

She set down the glass in front of her, then picked up my little bottle of pickle juice and poured out the last drops, humming a familiar tune as she did. "Because the vampire I need to kill is Oya Vane."

"Oya Vane," I repeated, realizing what Tula was humming. "The superhero pop star my niece is obsessed with? He's not a danger to anyone, unless you count his flagrant abuse of all our eardrums."

"I assure you, he is a danger," Tula said. "And a nasty one at that." She stretched her long body across the sofa to pick up a tablet off the side table, then turned it on and slid it in front of me.

A gallery of exsanguinated bodies displayed on the screen. Some with the telltale double-puncture wounds at the neck— others torn limb from limb, displaying bloodless flesh and hollow veins.

"I don't get it," I said. "Are these supposed to be his victims? How do you know they're his?"

"They're not his. Not directly. He didn't kill any of these people," Tula said.

"Then . . ."

"He sold them to the vampires that did."

I narrowed my eyes, looking more closely at the pictures. "How . . .?"

"They've all been identified as people who auditioned for Oya's program."

I blinked. "So his superhero recruitment agency is really just a . . ."

"A blood farm. Very clever. His victims self-select as vintages with unique flavor—all with some kind of magic making them tastier than the average human." Tula made a slurping sound with her mouth, laughing, and then pouted when she saw the disgusted expression on my face. "Too soon?" She took the tablet back from me. "I thought this would be good motivation, but maybe you're more squeamish than I imagined."

"I'm not squeamish," I said. "I just don't find this funny."

"I'll keep it boring then," Tula said, her smile disappearing unnervingly fast. "I've been offered a handsome sum to take out Oya, but he knows me. His people know me. He's employed me before, to erase one of his buyers who was disappointed with a shipment and threatened to expose him." Tula rolled her neck and leaned a little closer to me. "None of this makes it impossible for me to do the job, but it's taking me longer than I'd like to find a way in. It would be easier for you."

I leaned away from her slightly. "Hmm."

"Just like you know killing the senator permanently would be easier for me."

"I only need your help finding him," I protested. "The killing part, I can do."

She gave me the universal look I knew well as *"Oh, honey."*

"What?" I snapped. "I can. I already would have if I hadn't lost him before I could figure out *how* to kill him." My throat tightened at her relentless glare of sympathy as I resisted the urge to continue with *"I even have a flamethrower."* I was starting to sound like Carina, and I didn't like it. "Fine then. Same. I'm sure it would be easier for you. Which one do we do first?"

Tula smiled crookedly and gave her shoulders an enthusiastic shake. "Both, of course—we'll split up. You go after Oya and I'll find your man."

I frowned. That wasn't what I'd had in mind, but I couldn't deny I would prefer to not literally work *with* this woman if I didn't have to. "One condition."

"Yes?"

"Bring me his head," I said, feeling like some queen in a fairytale—*fantasy story.* "I need to see it burn with my own eyes."

"Fair. Let's make it fun and you do the same. We'll meet here when it's done and trade."

I grimaced, not sure I agreed with what Tula considered "fun." But I nodded and held out my hand all the same, ready to shake on it.

Instead of taking my hand, Tula held up a finger and then rose from the sofa. She disappeared into another room, leaving me staring out at the wide window behind her and abnormally clear view of Los Angeles it offered.

That had to be magic. Those hills in the distance were never visible except just after rainfall, and the air outside was dusty and dry.

Before I could lower my still outstretched hand, Tula glided back into my view and dropped something heavy in my palm.

I closed my fingers around it on reflex, then brought it closer to my face to inspect.

A black feather pendant, crystalline and lifelike as the rabbit in my hair, stared back at me from the end of its silver chain. It reminded me of Minnie's earrings.

"What is this?" I asked.

"A gift to celebrate our partnership. Put it on."

When I looked up at her, ready to tell her I didn't accept expensive jewelry from anyone I wasn't sleeping with, I held my tongue. All the mirth had left her expression. What had replaced it was hard, cold and—if I'd had enough sense to be afraid —frightening.

I put on the necklace.

"If you fail to hold up your end of the deal," she said, "I'll know. And then, I don't know, things might get worse for you somehow."

"Of all the vague threats I've ever heard, that's got to be the worst." And yet, my chest itched where her crystal feather lay against my skin.

"Sorry." She yawned. "I promise, I mean it. I just haven't figured out the best way to destroy you yet, should I need to." She shook herself until a gleam returned to her eyes. "Once we spend some more time together, I'm sure it will come."

"Right," I grumbled. "Just give me what you have on Oya and I'll get out of your hair."

She smiled, then started humming Oya's song again as she plucked my phone from my purse and tapped something in it. "Ah," she said, her phone ringing softly at her side as she handed mine back to me. "My wife—is she still out from that dead body she touched?"

"I'm not sure," I said. "She was unconscious when I last saw her, but she's at a mage clinic and they may have been able to help her."

"Oh, they shouldn't bother," Tula said. "She'll come to on her own. But when she does . . . Make sure you aren't there."

"Why?" Was this a jealousy thing? Why did both of these women seem paranoid I was going to make a play for the other?

"Because it will be dangerous." Tula shrugged, as if her reasoning were obvious. "She's most powerful when she wakes. I wouldn't want my little mouse to kill you before you can get to Oya."

7

No one answered the phone at Sassie's house, not the first time I called and not the fifth. She had no answering machine either, and I couldn't remember the number for the clinic, so I drove for the better part of an hour listening to nothing but a monotonous ringtone and the occasional chitter of the bunnies in the passenger seat. They weren't happy about the necklace I'd tossed at them as soon as I'd gotten in the car. I didn't care how intimidating Tula actually was—I'd cart around her creepy jewelry for now, but I wouldn't wear it.

Finally, after I'd almost forgotten why my ears were ringing, the tone stopped with a click and a sleepy voice said "Hello" at me. Carina had probably fallen asleep after the novelty of the medical books had worn off. They were only interesting until you realized they were all filled with slightly different versions of the same thing.

"Where's Sassie?" I asked her.

"Not here," Carina mumbled.

"Obviously," I said. "She would have picked up the phone sooner. Where is she?"

"I don't—Oh." Carina paused. "At the clinic. She left a note by the phone."

"Does it have a number on it?"

"Yep," Carina said, then stopped. As I was opening my mouth to ask her what it was, she started reading it out.

"Thanks," I growled, then picked up my phone—which was safely in my lap this time—and dialed it in.

A voice I didn't recognize greeted me brightly on the other line, asking if this was an emergency call.

"Kind of," I said before asking for Sassie. It didn't get me anywhere until I mentioned my name.

"Darcy?" The voice brightened again. "Sassie's daughter? Oh, that's wonderful—she talks about you all the time. I'll go get her."

The pit in my insides hollowed further, and I swallowed against a dry throat. I wasn't Sassie's daughter. But even now, she was still acting like I was. Like I had intended on returning when I'd left. And the joke was on me, clearly, because I *had* returned.

"Darcy?" Sassie's voice rang out not two minutes later. "Is everything okay?"

It was the same thing she might have asked me fifteen years ago if I'd called her in the middle of the night from a sleepover at a friend's house after having a bad dream. I didn't answer the question. I didn't know the answer. "Minnie might be dangerous," I said instead. "Don't let anyone get too close, and . . ." I took a breath. "Has her condition changed at all?"

"Not that I know of, but I'll go check. What is this about?"

"Honestly, I'm not sure." I shook my head, even though she couldn't see me. "I don't understand the first thing about her abilities. Just make sure no one goes in her room until she's awake and lucid."

"Ok, I'm here with her now," Sassie said, true to form failing to take me seriously. "She's still unconscious and . . . Oh."

"Oh?"

"I'll call you back." *Click.*

That was not reassuring.

"Damn it," I muttered, glaring daggers at a bunny that had perched itself in the passenger seat to stare at me. It quickly scurried into the back.

My phone buzzed. An image text from an unknown number. I squinted at it, unable to get a good look with one hand on the wheel and one eye on the road. Grumbling, I pressed on the brakes and pulled over.

Bright lights zipped by me on the dark road, swallowing my mirrors and threatening to make me dizzy as the car subtly swayed from side to side. I zoomed in on the picture and saw Minnie lying in a cot at the clinic, still unconscious. What was I supposed to be looking at—*Oh.*

Her fingers.

Where there should be a human hand resting at her side, yellow-green crystals glinted in the fluorescent light. It was the hand that had touched the dead body, and it had crystallized, starting with the tips of her fingers and moving up her wrist.

My heart beat faster. If Minnie died, Tula would probably kill me and throw our tenuous agreement into the wind.

But if Sassie'd had time to take a picture, Minnie couldn't be crystallizing as fast as the police officer had turned to stone the other day.

I'm assuming she's contagious until we rule it out. Quarantining everyone here who's been near her.

I breathed out as I read the follow-up text, which must be from Sassie's mobile phone and implicitly confirmed that Minnie was still mostly flesh and blood. Without thinking, I forwarded the texts to Adrian. The tension in my body seemed to spill out through my fingers as I pressed **Send**. He would figure out what was happening. He always did. And it didn't matter what he thought of me in the meantime.

I looked up and frowned at the road. I'd already been headed to the clinic, but if I went there now I'd probably just end up quarantined with Sassie.

Should I be quarantined with Sassie? I didn't know. So far, there was no evidence this turning-to-stone stuff was contagious except in exactly one case—Minnie's. And Minnie's case was different from the others. *Minnie* was different from the others. Probably.

I rubbed my eyes. If I couldn't go to the clinic, I also couldn't go back to Sassie's house.

Change of plans, then. Taking a leaf out of Carina's book, I opened one of the many unused social media apps on my phone and bumbled my way through it until I found Oya's feed.

If I had to pick somewhere else to go, at least I wouldn't let it be a waste of time.

I needed coffee. I needed to think. And in a weird twist of fate that almost seemed too good to be true, Oya was already headed to the perfect place.

I looked over my shoulder, stepped on the gas, and swung the steering wheel sharply to the left to make a U-turn.

THE PANTRY HAD ALWAYS BEEN one of my favorite places in LA. I'd been a typical teenager in some ways, and one of those ways was that I'd had a propensity for sneaking out of the house at night when I was supposed to be sleeping. But hey, what had Sassie and Fred expected after giving a girl the moon as her magical focus and then telling her bedtime was at 9 o'clock sharp?

The din of clanking dishes and sizzling flat-tops and giggly chatter and yelled orders embraced me like an old friend, making me feel at home in a way I never had at Sassie's house. A server rushed by in a blur, managing to refill my mug with steaming coffee on the way. This was where I'd first learned to love coffee —and, I realized only now, it was also one of the reasons I'd felt so at home in the strip club. The late-night crowd had always been my crowd, an eclectic group of moths that were drawn to the few lights that always remained on in the darkness no matter what. The Pantry was the quintessential moth flame, a diner open 24 hours a day, and it had been open pretty much every night for over a hundred years—since before the Opening, when so many other places had begun bolting their doors at night for fear of vampires.

I brought the thick ceramic lip of the coffee mug up to rest against my chin before taking a sip. Jolts of euphoric energy ran through me, the piping hot bitterness bringing back memories of all the hope and wonder I'd had when I was younger. I hadn't always wanted to be a Guardian.

There was a time when I'd been exactly like Carina with those medical books. The idea of so much knowledge felt like power at my fingertips, and the idea of helping people by healing felt so perfect, so noble—I couldn't find any fault in it, until I'd actually started doing it.

The healing itself was fine, and if it had been just that, I might have gone to medical school like Sassie wanted and then stayed at her clinic forever. But it wasn't just healing. I'd had a special knack for coaxing souls to stay in ruined bodies long enough to help the healers make a difference, which I probably had the phoenix to thank for. And I was sure it looked wondrous from the outside as I helped save patients there should have been no way to save.

But stealing a soul from death's door was agonizing for the soul in question, and to me it had always felt like I was holding someone down for a maniac to torture them. I couldn't live like that, and somewhere along the line I'd realized that the only way to escape that fate while still saving lives would be to prevent people from getting hurt in the first place.

I closed my eyes, willing the warmth of the coffee on my lips to bring me back to a time when I'd thought that was possible. I'd never believed outright that I could save everyone—but it was what I'd wanted, deep down, in a place I'd always kept buried because of how utterly foolish it was.

I looked up when someone across the room said, "That's disgusting."

His voice would have stood out even if he hadn't said something so hopelessly out of place here—nothing in this glorious, greasy godsend of a place was ever disgusting. It was a voice I'd been subjected to over long hours of driving with Carina, and it was the owner of that voice I'd come here tonight to find.

Oya Vane had told all his followers online just hours ago that he'd be here tonight, and here he was. I'd only had to wait for three cups of coffee, and I'd have been happy to wait for three more.

I put down my mug and stuffed a piece of thick, buttery, toasted sourdough in my mouth, staring at Oya as my teeth crunched through the crust.

He was a slender man with tanned skin, contoured and shimmery in all the right places by a professional makeup team he probably kept in his pocket. Or by vampire magic. He didn't look much like a vampire to me in person, but what did I know?

"No eggs," he said to the huge man sitting across from him, who looked like he probably ate a dozen eggs for breakfast every morning.

The man shrugged, then turned to the other two people at their table and repeated, "No eggs."

I swallowed my piece of toast, hoping it would hide the grimace on my face. Who came to The Pantry—or any diner, for that manner—and refused to even watch someone else eat eggs?

If Oya was a vegan, I was pretty sure the only thing he could eat here would be the coleslaw.

I shook my head as I watched him order a patty melt, medium rare. Of course he wasn't a vegan. He was a vampire. A vampire who hated eggs, apparently.

A slice of cheesecake slid across the table in front of me, the server another blur who was already gone by the time I looked down. I breathed in, something inside me melting at the nostalgic anticipation. Simple but delicious, coffee and cheesecake had been my favorite order as a teenager.

I broke off a chunk with my spoon and let the sweet, cheesy goodness coat my tongue as I watched Oya sip his water and stare into his phone. Why was he even here? It was common for celebrities to come here—vampires, not so much. They could ingest non-blood substances, but not frequently, and most didn't enjoy it.

Swallowing the bite of cheesecake, I lifted my coffee mug again and was tempted to close my eyes when the palate-cleansing bitterness filled my mouth. Gods, this was good.

My phone buzzed, and I looked down at the screen. Sassie's house. Could be an update on Minnie, even though Sassie had just been at the clinic. I answered.

"Darcy, oh my god, are you at The Pantry right now because Oya just posted a video and it looks like you're at The Pantry right now and is that really—"

I held the phone away from my ear, grimacing as Carina's shrill voice assaulted the air beside my face. When she seemed to have stopped, I brought the phone back and said, "You're breaking up. Get to the point."

"Please please please can you get him to sign something for me?"

I sighed. How had Oya even managed to post a video while I was watching without me noticing? He must have hidden cameras coming out of his ears. But Carina could actually be a convenient excuse if I wanted to approach him. "I can ask," I said, "after I finish my cheesecake."

"Please please please Darcy please you don't even—"

I hung up, then rubbed my face. There was a better way to deal with Carina when she was being this annoying, but right now I couldn't find it in myself to figure out what that was. *Rarely* could I find it in myself, if I was honest.

A new respect for my brother bubbled up around the edges of my frustration, and in the same instant I found myself opening the last picture Etty had sent me of Noah. Would I be this bad with him once he got a little older and developed his own ways to push my buttons?

I didn't want that to happen. So maybe I needed to try harder to recalibrate my buttons.

I tapped my spoon on my plate and breathed in the steam from my coffee as I watched Oya. I should go over there. I wouldn't get a more natural opportunity to approach than the one I'd just been handed.

Just as I planted my feet on the floor to stand up, someone shrieked beside me.

"Help!" a middle-aged woman was yelling. "Help! She can't breathe!"

The young woman across the table from her had her hands to her neck, eyes wide and panicked as she tried fruitlessly to gasp in air. Textbook choking signs.

I hopped over the table between us and had my arms around her midsection before anyone else could get to her, ready to administer abdominal thrusts. But her companion slapped me away.

"She's not choking—she's allergic to tomatoes. They must have put them in her sandwich."

I shook my head, ready to proceed anyway because that

couldn't be right; an allergy wouldn't look like such a straightforward airway obstruction. There would be other symptoms, even if they were subtle. But the woman with the allergy in question squirmed out of my grasp, a little too deftly for someone who supposedly couldn't breathe.

"I'll help you!" a clear voice called from a few tables over. A teenage girl sped over, pushing past me to take the panicked woman by the shoulders. My mouth contorted into a lopsided frown as I watched the girl's pale skin crust over like the bark of a tree. Tiny branches leapt out of her forearms, green tips gluing themselves to the distressed woman's neck like veins.

The woman's round eyes stopped jerking around as she focused on the treeish girl in front of her. Her hands moved away from her throat, fingers glancing appreciatively over the green branches attached to her skin. She didn't sigh—she didn't breathe. But she didn't need to. It looked like those branches were breathing for her.

I stepped back as yet more branches grew from the girl's arms and back, these blooming with emerald-green leaves and wrapping around the allergic woman to cocoon her in a nest of life-giving foliage.

"Someone should call an ambulance," the girl said softly to the room, which was now more silent than The Pantry had probably ever been since it had first opened its doors. "I can't stay like this for too long."

Or find her non-existent epinephrine injector, I thought bitterly. That woman wasn't allergic to shit, and she certainly hadn't been in any real danger at any point tonight. I'd seen and heard and felt and saved enough people in life-threatening situations by now to know when someone was faking it. The question was *why*?

I slinked my way back over to my cheesecake, not wanting to get involved if I wasn't needed. Enough other people had their phones out that I didn't bother with that, either. My coffee was cold, but I sipped it anyway as I watched the room. What had just happened here? An attack against whoever owned The Pantry? No—this place wouldn't take much of a hit even if they did have a customer die from an allergic reaction. It was too iconic, too established. Maybe a distraction?

My eyes found Oya, then narrowed as I realized he was watching the room as intently as I was. Maybe more so. Or not watching . . . waiting.

I didn't take my eyes off him again until the emergency responders arrived, and he didn't take his eyes off the tree girl during those long few minutes. Once the tomato-stricken woman had been safely detached from her branches and carted off in an ambulance, Oya turned on.

It was like a switch had been flipped on his back; he held his phone out in front of him and infused his face with life. Mouth open in awe, he was by the tree girl's side in only a few long strides.

"Did you just see that? It was fannntastic!" He gaped at the tree girl and looked her up and down, tilting his phone at her to match his gaze. Running a hand over her arm, which still looked like bark, he asked, "What is this? What *are* you?"

The girl wasn't even an iota as annoyed as I would have expected her to be. She smiled sheepishly at Oya's phone. "I'm . . . nothing special. My grandmother was a forest sprite."

"Looks like you inherited her sprite spirit!" Oya's words almost bounced out of him as he bounced up and down next to her, putting his face close to hers as if they were posing for a picture together.

I dug in my jacket for some cash. The longer I stayed in here watching this shitshow, the more likely it was I would vomit up my cheesecake or kill Oya right here.

Killing him was the job, but I probably shouldn't do it in

public. That, and if I didn't want to hate myself later then I really needed to verify Tula's intel beforehand. The only thing I had real evidence of now was that he was a disgustingly fake, manipulative showman who hated eggs.

"What would you say if I told you I could help you save lives like this every day?" Oya was saying now, not even trying to hide the rehearsed nature of his schtick. He'd set this whole thing up, and he'd probably recruited tree girl weeks ago.

"That would be everything I've ever wanted!" she responded with a squeal as bright purple flowers bloomed from the tips of her branches. All I could see were the puncture marks that would soon appear on her neck if Tula was right about the game Oya was running.

I shook my head. If she was right, he couldn't sell *all* his recruits for their blood. At least, not right away. Someone would notice that many people going missing and you know, not becoming superheroes—wouldn't they?

Not if the sensation he's selling the most of is the dreams-coming-true hype of the recruiting process. That would make for a tidy little revolving door of hopefuls picked up and then promptly forgotten about, their lives changed forever but not in the way they'd expected.

I paid my bill and stepped outside into the cool night, my body instantly relaxing out of earshot of the farce inside. That wasn't the most pleasant late-night coffee and cheesecake I'd ever had, but at least it hadn't been a total wash. I had a better idea of how I would approach Oya now. And it would make Carina happy, I thought as I pulled out my phone to enlist her help.

My breath caught in my throat when I saw the message from Adrian at the top of my notifications.

I'll be at LAX in 8 hours. Send clinic address.

I coughed, then scowled at the phone. He'd sent it two hours ago, at around nine pm. That would be around midnight his time, which meant he'd gotten on a red-eye right after I'd sent him the news about Minnie. And it meant he would be here in the morning.

No, not here—at the clinic, which was a stone's throw away from my childhood home. With my aunt and the other people who had raised me.

I sent him the address, then put my phone away and started walking towards my car. Quarantine be damned—I wasn't going to let him come into my world like that without being there to do some damage control.

8

I SLEPT BETTER than I could have expected that night.

I'd never been a morning person. My magic perception was so much stronger in the dark, with the moon glowing in the sky, that the rise of the sun tended to make my nerves frayed and my brain foggy and my energy lacking.

So whenever I needed to set an early alarm, I tossed and turned more than usual, unable to relax fully with the dread of needing to function amidst the destruction of the quiet calm of the dark.

Now, I sipped my coffee peacefully while I watched that destruction, reclining in a lawn chair in Sassie's garden. I had slept like a baby next to Carina in my childhood bed, the little dragon giving off faint puffs of smoke as she snored, and I'd woken just in time to turn off my alarm before it could disturb her.

The sky was coming alive above me, deep purple making way for soft pink and orange and blue, all dappled and smeared like watercolors between the thin, wispy clouds. Sunrises were softer than sunsets, gentler almost, despite the fact that they usually felt more violent to me. I didn't know why I was enjoying this one so much, but I could put aside my suspicions until I'd finished my coffee, at least.

My second alarm chimed just as I slurped the last lukewarm sip from the bottom of the mug. Seven o'clock. If Adrian had rented a car and driven straight here from LAX, he would be arriving at the clinic around now.

I hopped up and slid the squeaking glass door to go inside, rinsed out my coffee mug and then splashed some water from the kitchen sink onto my face. I'd showered and washed my grimy hair quickly last night before slipping into bed, so my curls were wilder than usual and stuffed into a loose scrunchie. Waking up this early, some sacrifices had to be made.

Carina was still snoring when I grabbed my sunglasses and popped out the door, my steps falling lightly along the winding stone path that led through the other houses of the coven to the clinic. I wasn't alone in my distaste for mornings here, with all the other mages of the moon. So nothing was stirring except the insects and the birds in the garden. With every step I took away from my coffee and towards the clinic that had at one point been my personal hell, it felt more and more like the calm before a storm.

By the time I arrived to see the parking lot full of DSC guards in their ridiculous crimson uniforms, the bright sun had finally begun to put a scowl on my face as it dulled my senses and dampened the skin on the back of my neck.

"Excuse me, ma'am," said one of the guards as I approached. "This is a restricted area. You'll need to turn around."

My eye twitched. Had the DSC seriously closed down the entire clinic? How had they even found out about what was going on—Oh, of course. Adrian must have told them. Or Miriam. He had said this was connected to a massive case with widespread implications, so I shouldn't have expected he'd come alone. But the DSC? Really?

These robots weren't likely to provide any real help other than keeping my aunt and the rest of the mages in the coven from taking in new patients needing care. If I were screaming and crying and bleeding out, would it still be a "restricted area"?

"I have an appointment," I lied, eyes quickly scanning over the guards and their equipment. Those skin-tight uniforms were woven with powerful armor, and they were all armed with weapons and gadgets I didn't even recognize. If I was going to force my way in, it would have to be by sneaking.

"Let her in," a gruff voice called from across the parking lot, and I saw Adrian walking over from the building entrance. "She's with me."

I barely recognized him at first. The usual boyish glint in his eye and dimple in his cheek were nowhere to be seen, and his large frame looked almost brutish in the crimson and gray suit worn by DSC officers. He looked tired, the red in his clothes bringing out the red in his eyes—but more than that, he looked hard. Like someone who might fight me if I crossed him. And I'd never thought that of him before.

When he came closer, though, I saw the warmth return slightly to his cheeks and the life to his eyes. He didn't smile, but it was lurking there behind whatever mask he was wearing today.

"Yes, sir," said the guard who had stopped me, and she stepped aside to let me pass.

I raised my eyebrows. "Sir?" I said, looking right at Adrian.

He gave me a slight nod and hardened his jaw further. "Come in and I'll brief you." Then he spun around and headed for the entrance to the clinic.

Rude, I thought as I picked up my pace to catch up with him.

The waiting room was empty of patients when we entered, all DSC in red except for a mage I didn't recognize sitting at the front desk. Must be someone who'd joined the coven after I'd left. She gave me a questioning stare as Adrian led me down the hall to the right into a spare room I'd used for mid-shift naps once upon a time.

"My provisional office." He waved his hand around at the jumble of mismatched furniture that had been moved around to accommodate his things. "Sorry for the mess."

It took everything in me not to laugh. And even then, I only lasted a minute before I let out a chuckle. I opened my mouth to ask him if this was a joke, only to close it a moment later when his stern eyes told me it most certainly wasn't. "I don't know where to start with the questions," I said honestly. Wow, I was doing great with this whole honesty thing.

He sighed and dipped his head down, his thumb and forefinger rubbing into his eyebrows. "It's bad," he eventually said.

I took a deep breath. Right. Of course it was bad. Here I was, off on my murder vacation and not thinking about anything except getting revenge on my ex and keeping my fugitive niece out of trouble—not thinking about anything except myself. Meanwhile, Adrian had been out there in save-the-world mode. Apparently the world needed saving.

"Tell me," I said, and he looked up.

Our eyes met. My stomach dropped.

There's a certain energy that exists between two people alone together, when they've fucked or come close to fucking. I wasn't sure Adrian and I had really come close, but this feeling I had said otherwise . . . an inviting, comfortable warmth, drawing me to press myself against his chest even though his arms were currently crossed stiffly in front of it.

I missed him. I missed the man he'd been the last time I'd seen him. He was different now, and it had only been a few weeks.

He swallowed, then reached for a file on his makeshift desk. "It started with Miriam—well, that's how I first noticed it." He handed me the file.

"Is she . . ." I trailed off as I opened the file and saw a chalky white version of Miriam lying on a bed, still as stone.

"That's not her," Adrian said quickly. "She was still alive, last I checked. That's a distant relative of hers, in Bulgaria."

I squinted down at the image. "Looks exactly like her. Except, you know, for the rock thing."

"Salt," Adrian corrected me. "This woman was turned to salt. And amoeboids reproduce asexually. All of Miriam's relatives look exactly like her. Well, most of them—there are occasionally mutations in the—" He shook his head. "That's not important."

I couldn't suppress the small smile that crept into my cheeks. There it was, just a glimmer of the Adrian I knew. That, and I was glad Miriam wasn't dead—yet. "Ok, so Miriam's distant-cousin evil-twin gets turned to salt. She piss off that god that did that in the, uh . . ."

"The Bible? No, not that I'm aware of. The common thread here is—" Adrian stopped and rubbed his eyebrows again. "I'm getting ahead of myself. Miriam's distant-cousin evil-twin was the first case I found after her mother hired me to check up on their family tree."

I scrunched my face up. "Her mother?"

"Miriam's mother is the head of the DSC."

"Ah . . ." I breathed out and nodded slowly. "That explains the . . ." I gestured at his uniform. "Nepotism?"

He raised his eyebrows.

"Didn't you say you'd applied to work at the DSC and they wouldn't take you?" If I remembered correctly, he and Dirk had implied it was because he was human with no extraordinary abilities. Although in my experience, he had plenty of extraordinary abilities—just not magical.

"Yes," he said in a clipped tone. "But that was years ago, when all they'd seen of me was on paper."

"And now suddenly you're leading a team that calls you 'sir'?"

I shook my head. "All in such a short period of time that your partner with the local police just thinks you're temporarily out of the office?"

"You've been talking about me with Dirk?" Adrian asked.

I pursed my lips. "You're dodging my questions."

He rolled his neck like it was stiff and then grabbed a half-full water bottle off his desk. "You're asking the wrong questions," he said before putting the bottle to his mouth.

"Fine." I waved my hands at him. "Why did Miriam's relative turn into salt, and what's happening to Minnie, and what can I do to help you keep the horrible things from happening to more people?"

"I don't know yet," he answered. "At first I thought it had something to do with Miriam's species, because it happened to a handful of her relatives. But all the dead Miriams turned into different minerals, which was odd. Then I started combing through recent reports of odd deaths and found the same thing happening to humans all over the world. Some shifters, too."

I sat on the edge of a cot as he spoke, gripping the edges to keep from fidgeting.

"Then . . ." he continued, turning to face the world map he had pinned to the wall. "I noticed that the minerals they turned into weren't random; they tended to be tied to locations." He glanced back at me as his hands swept over the map in quick, deft motions I didn't understand. "Not always, and not precisely, but if there were two deaths in the same town, the victims usually knew each other and usually turned into the same thing."

The mix of emotions in me was disorienting, the cold dread forming because of the words he was saying and the nervous desire building up because of the way he was saying them. Half of me was paralyzed, wishing he would take his hands off the map and put them on me—and the other half was toying with an idea I really didn't like.

"Sandstone," I said, thinking of the police officer. "Did everyone who died in that small town in Arizona turn into sandstone?"

He nodded.

"It's what all the landmarks in the area are made of . . ." I said.

"It's also the favored building material of the god they all worshipped," he said.

The dread inside me took shape, a heavy ball of ice in my gut. "So you're saying—"

"They were witches."

I nodded, breathing in as my brain tried to escape the walls that were quickly closing in around it. "Just the people in Arizona?"

"Those I've confirmed. But my theory is that they were all witches. Everyone this has happened to so far. Except Minnie."

"That's why you're here," I said, closing my eyes in resignation.

"That's why I'm here."

I took a deep breath. That explained why he'd flown across the country so quickly and set up an office in my coven's clinic. What it didn't explain was why Minnie was the one unconscious and turning to crystal and not me—Darcy the witch. "Minnie is the first outlier you've identified?"

"In more than one way. I'm fairly certain she's not a witch, and—"

"How?" I asked. "What makes you fairly certain?"

"She told me about her abilities when I was debriefing her after the incident with the raging ifrit outside her coffee shop. The things she can do and the way she does them—she isn't using any magic but her own. I'm not sure exactly what she is, but it's something different."

Since when did you become such an expert on witches? I wondered, but of course he was an expert on far too many things most people never thought about twice. If he was confident about Minnie not being a witch, he was probably right.

"But also," he continued, "she's the only case I've come across of someone being only partially petrified. No one else this has happened to has survived. We've only ever found the remnants of their bodies."

I swallowed and stretched out my right hand, fingers tingling. "Any indication it's contagious?"

"It's spreading somehow," he said. "But I don't know what the method of transmission could be. If you'd asked me yesterday, I wouldn't have thought it had anything to do with physical proximity or touch, but that's clearly how it infected Minnie—and she's clearly infected. The crystals forming on her fingers are citrine, the same crystals as the body she touched. That body belonged to the newest member of your coven who wore a citrine amulet around her neck before she died, a relic of worship to the sun god she hadn't yet severed ties with."

"Has anyone else here been affected?"

"Not yet. We have a handful of people in quarantine—most were already sequestered before we got here—and we'll monitor them closely."

"Are you going to ask me to join them?" I asked cautiously.

"Do I need to?" He stared right into my eyes as he asked it, the simple question a challenge that neither one of us wanted to name.

"I'm a witch," I said, and he only continued to stare at me. Apologies and excuses danced on my tongue, ready to spill out if only I could remember how to open my mouth and speak. I should have told him sooner—I would have if he hadn't bailed on me so soon after it happened—or would I have been too ashamed to tell him, even if he hadn't?

None of that mattered now. I was a witch, and it was one more thing I'd failed to tell him. I was a witch, and that now meant I was in danger of turning into a Darcy statue at any moment. I was a witch after Sassie had done so much to ensure I would never need to be one—I was a witch, and the thought of it made me more and more nauseous the longer I lived with it.

"I'm sorry," Adrian said, suddenly standing only a foot away from me. When did he get so close?

"What are you sorry for?" I asked, confused.

"For expecting too much from you."

The words hit me like a punch to the gut, even though I wasn't sure exactly what he meant by them.

"No, that's not it," he continued, his words coming out a little faster. "It's not that I expected you to be better. It's that I was going through my own thing and took it out on you because you weren't *perfect*. I . . ." He took a step closer. "I look at you and see something that's so close to perfect I sometimes forget you're human. Or . . . mostly human."

A million thoughts raced through my mind. Me, anywhere near perfect? Maybe Adrian wasn't as smart as I'd thought. But I didn't want to push through the door to that conversation now that he'd cracked it open. Not when he'd been acting so hot and cold. There was more to it, and his warped perception of me wasn't what needed addressing. "What was the thing?" I asked instead. At his questioning stare, I continued, "You said you were going through your own thing. What was it?"

He took in a sharp breath and blinked his eyes. He didn't step away from me, but he stood up straighter, and he was so much taller than me that it had the same effect. "That's not something I want to get into," he said. "Not with all this . . ." He gestured at the map behind him and the files on his desk.

I narrowed my eyes. "But you and I—we're good?"

"On my end, yes." He must have seen the skepticism in my expression, because he continued softly, "I appreciate that you've been trying."

I needed to get out of here. A fire was burning in my chest, getting hotter and brighter and harder to contain by the minute. Only I wasn't entirely sure what was fueling it. Fury that he could be so calm and civil and businesslike about this—check. Fear that he had hurt me so much that *I* couldn't be calm and civil about it —double check. "Where's Minnie?" I asked.

He frowned. "Are you sure you want to—"

"I can see her through the glass, right?" I interrupted. "Or are you keeping her in a windowless cell?"

Adrian tilted his head at me. "You never answered my question," he eventually said. "Do I need to quarantine you?"

"No." The truth was, I didn't know. But I wouldn't be able to help anyone if I was locked up in the clinic waiting to turn to . . . *Obsidian*, I realized. I would turn into obsidian, like the rabbits but cold and dead. "Not enough risk to justify taking me off the board. There must be something I can do to help you."

"There is," Adrian said, and his eyes told me I wasn't going to like it. "Talk to your god."

"Excuse me?"

"You're a witch. That means there's a god you follow, whose power you draw from—but it also means you can communicate with them somehow, right?"

I tapped my fingers on my thigh. "I suppose it does."

"The way I see it, if something is wiping out witches all over the world, those witches' gods are the ones with the most to lose. And so many have been affected recently that I'd think any god would be concerned, if not at least interested in getting to the bottom of it."

I frowned. He was right. Witches drew their power from the gods they followed, but it was a symbiotic relationship. Our belief and reliance on those gods was what kept them alive. It had always been that way—that was the incentive for the gods to have created witches in the first place.

Only I still didn't remember ever having met mine. If what my brother had said was true, it had happened when I was still a child, before my mother had stolen me away and taken me to Sassie. I was supposed to be on my way to his volcano with Carina right now, but I'd been stalling . . . Okay, I'd just signed up to assassinate a pop-star vampire, so stalling was a gross understatement.

I'd been dreading my reunion with Popo, dreading the inevitable oath I still officially needed to swear to him. In denial about the loss of my short-lived independence. I sighed.

"Okay," I said. "I'll talk to him."

"If you—" Adrian started, but someone knocked on the open door before he could continue.

A short man in DSC uniform poked his head in. "Sir? We have the new figures you requested."

I ducked out while Adrian was busy answering him, the two of us exchanging an awkward nod as I left the room. I didn't bother trying to see Minnie, or Sassie. That would only complicate things, make it more likely for someone to try to stick me in quarantine. Adrian was here, and I trusted him to do right by them.

I hoped I would remain flesh and blood long enough to come back and see that I was right.

9

"CARINA!" I yelled into Sassie's dark, quiet house. The dragon was probably still sleeping. There were no remnants of breakfast in the sink, just my empty coffee mug from an hour or two earlier.

"Cariiiiiiina," I cooed as I made my way to my old bedroom. Scrunching up my nose, I wondered if the smoke smell had been this strong when I'd left. Was I just noticing it now after being out in the fresh air? Had I smelled like a campfire when I'd been talking to Adrian?

"Carina," I said more firmly, my hand twisting the doorknob. I pushed open the door and was met with that muddled darkness of a bedroom whose blinds were shut tight against the daylight. Cracks of sunshine crept through the space, highlighting swirls of smoke dancing through the air. I coughed.

The sound of me hacking up my lungs caused something to stir under the covers of my bed, and it didn't look entirely human. "Carina," I growled as I strode forward and ripped off the covers in one sweeping motion, one arm pressed over my nose and mouth.

I jumped back quickly, chased by a razor-sharp talon that was curled around one of the teddy bears from my childhood I still couldn't believe Sassie hadn't thrown away. The bear died in a puff of white stuffing and ripped stitches, and I bit my cheek in annoyance.

This was new.

Was Carina still asleep? Did she even know she had shifted? Sleepwalking was dangerous enough when you were human—sleep-dragoning would be a whole different story.

Grumbling, I backed out of the room and booked it to the kitchen, where I grabbed the plastic pitcher Sassie used for iced tea and filled it up with cold water from the tap.

Either this would create a sauna in my room or a pissed-off little girl—maybe both. Whatever happened, it would be better than the current situation.

Carina changed back before the water hit her. I had probably woken her with my running around and barging in, but I wasn't going to pause long enough to take any chances.

She stared at me with narrowed eyes and soaked hair plastered to her face, water dripping off the tip of her nose.

My eyes dropped, focusing on her hands—which weren't hands at the moment. The dead teddy bear was still impaled on a long, silvery talon, resting grimly on Carina's knee.

Her eyes followed mine, and she screamed.

"Getoutgetoutgetoutgetoutgetout!" Her scream turned into a jumble of words as she jumped off the bed and rushed at me, pushing me back through the door.

It slammed behind me, and I stood there staring at it for only a few seconds before heaving a sigh and turning around to make myself another cup of coffee.

Thirty minutes later, Carina came shambling out into the kitchen looking fully human, and fully dressed. I suspected her sleep clothes had not made it out of that ordeal in one piece.

I pushed a box of crunchy health cereal at her, the best peace offering I could find in Sassie's kitchen. "So . . ." I said as she poured some in a bowl.

She looked up at me and reached for the milk. "So, what?"

"So, how worried should I be about what just happened?" Gods, I hadn't expected my years of guarding idiotic politicians to grant me the exact level of serenity I needed now to deal with this pre-pubescent dragon, but somehow it had.

"I'm fine," she answered.

"Not what I asked."

She rolled her eyes. "Well, then it depends on what exactly you're worried about."

"Living and driving and possibly working in close proximity to a shifter who can't control the change—for one. How long has this been going on?"

Carina shoved a big bite of cereal in her mouth, crunching hard to mask her growl. "I'm working on it," she said firmly once she'd swallowed. Then, before I could answer: "Wait, what did you mean by 'possibly working'?"

I swirled my coffee around in my mug, weighing my options. If I pressed too hard now, when she was still flustered from waking up all dragony, she would only shut down further. And we did have a lot of other things to be worrying about.

"I may have taken on a job you'd be interested in," I said. "Involving Oya—"

"No!" she yelled. I raised my eyebrows. "I mean, yes!" she quickly corrected. "Oya? For real?"

"Yes, and I was going to ask for your help with it today, but—"

"I'll go get ready." Her spoon splashed down into the milk and clattered against the edge of the bowl as she jumped up and ran back into the bedroom.

I narrowed my eyes. She hadn't even asked what the job was, and I'd prepared so many vague, diplomatic responses . . . I was a little disappointed.

When she came out again, she looked like she'd aged a few years. A bright orange flouncy skirt showed off her slender, tanned legs, and a billowy white tank top was tucked in at her waist, emphasizing an hourglass figure she'd entirely fabricated by stealing one of my smallest bras and stuffing it with something lumpy.

I opened my mouth to disapprove, a knee-jerk reaction to seeing an eight-year-old looking like she was thirteen, but then closed it again when I remembered where we were going. She would fit right in among the child-star hopefuls in LA. Not to mention it was heartening to see her unbothered by the burn scars that were visible on her bare arms and legs.

"Okay," I said instead. "Take whatever that is out of the bra and put some of my socks in—they'll be more even."

Her eyes bugged open wide, making me wonder for a moment if I was the worst aunt on the planet. But no, letting an eight-year-old stuff her bra was nothing compared to what I was about to ask of her.

"There's something else we need to do before we go," I said, trying not to grit my teeth.

"What?" Carina asked as she dug around inside her shirt.

"I need to contact Popo, ask him something important."

She stopped moving with her hand still down her shirt and looked up at me with paralyzing disappointment in her eyes.

I shifted my weight from foot to foot. "So . . . I need you to tell me how to talk to him."

She pressed her lips together and gently puffed out her cheeks as she stared at me, her eyes flickering briefly to the ankle where my mage mark used to be before she'd torn it off me.

"Do I just, like, press a button on one of the rabbits?" I continued. "Or do we need something to sacrifice?" I forced out a little laugh, hoping the humor would get her to forget that I'd just reminded her of her impending doom—of the decision we both knew she would need to make soon.

Carina huffed and looked away from me, finally withdrawing the handful of colorful scrunchies she'd apparently packed into the bra. She dropped them on the counter. "We don't need the rabbits and we don't need a sacrifice," she said. "We just need the dark."

I raised my eyebrows. "A dark room, or—"

"Nightfall," she clarified.

"Okay," I said, nodding slowly. "So we'll go see Oya now, and then tonight you'll help me with the god seance thing?"

"Deal," she said, although her excitement had obviously been dampened. Not even the prospect of meeting her idol was good enough to outweigh the dread of meeting with her god.

She hadn't always been like this . . . She'd been as devout a witch as any not too long ago. I slurped the cereal milk left in my bowl and tried to ignore the tingling flames licking the insides of my ribs as I wondered when she had taken over my place as the family heretic.

Two hours later, I found myself in a room full of hair gel and false eyelashes, trying not to suffocate from the oppressive absence of magic in the air. The bright lights overhead weren't helping, but the real problem was the sheer number of magic users all crowded under one roof.

I closed my eyes, trying to shake the disturbing sensation that I was in a vacuum and would burst open at any second. I'd never felt this bad crammed into the clinic with other mages of the coven as a child—but I hadn't been dealing with an immensely powerful magic bird inside me then, either. It must have been dormant, lying in wait all those years until I was reunited with its other half.

My phone rang. Carina glared at me sharply. She had a big string of numbers pinned to her chest that made her look like she was about to run a race. They would be calling her in to audition any minute now, and I still hadn't told her what we were here to do.

"Can you talk?" Dirk said softly in my ear when I answered the phone.

"Not really," I replied.

"Can you listen?" He was all business, a real rarity for him.

"Yep," I said.

"You have a new mission."

Great, one more thing to add to the to-do list.

"I've just been notified you're in the same building as a high-risk target we've been enlisted to protect. He already has one of ours on him, but we have solid intel that a hit's been ordered on his life."

No kidding. "Who?" I asked, although of course I already knew.

"Oya Vane."

I sighed, glancing down at Carina. "Hang on, ok? I'll call you back."

I hung up on him and cursed. I really should have a separate phone to bring with me if I was going to start taking on assassination jobs. But up until now, I hadn't really minded that the Guardians always knew where I was.

I patted Carina on the shoulder and told her I needed to pee, but she hardly noticed. She was off in her own little world chatting with another girl about how much they both loved Oya's hair.

"It's sooo fluffy—almost like feathers!"

I didn't go to the bathroom, which was usually the worst place in any building to hold sensitive conversations. It was where everyone went to talk when they wanted an illusion of privacy, and that meant it would almost always be bugged in a building like this.

Instead, I walked down the hall until I found the tiny storage closet I'd spotted on my way in.

It was locked.

I frowned as my hand jiggled the knob unsuccessfully. But then the tips of my fingers tingled, all that magic inside me finally pushing for a way out that felt intentional rather than an explosive pressure release.

Out of habit, I held it in. Then, glancing around, I realized maybe I didn't need to. Now that I'd officially accepted the power of my god, was there any reason to keep such a tight rein on the phoenix and what it could do?

Unpredictability. There was that.

But the only reason it was unpredictable was because it was unfamiliar. The smart thing to do would be to familiarize myself with it as much as possible in low-stakes scenarios so it would be less unpredictable when my life was on the line. Right?

A locked door in an empty hallway felt like a pretty low-stakes scenario, so I breathed out with my fingers on the lock and relaxed.

At first, nothing happened. But just as I was about to reach my hand into my jacket to find a lock-picking tool, the doorknob started to glow.

I squinted at it.

It melted, dripping down the door in a slow, hissing flow as low flames burst out from beneath it.

I scrunched my nose at the fumes and stepped back, shaking out my hand. That was not what I'd expected. And not very convenient, either.

The whole point of hiding in a closet would be to escape unwanted attention, and now the door to said closet was a mutilated beacon that screamed "Something weird's going on over here!"

I walked away briskly and found another closet around the corner. This door, I unlocked with one of my knives. Slipping inside the dark room, I pulled out my phone and called back Dirk.

"Do you know why someone wants the target eliminated?" I asked when he answered.

"Yes," he said, then paused. I had a feeling he might tell me it was need-to-know, and I was ready to make a case that the information would help me keep Oya alive, but instead he just went ahead and told me.

My heart sank a little when Dirk's information sounded almost identical to Tula's. Vampires. Trafficking. One of the victim's families had gotten wind of it and tried to talk to local law enforcement, and they'd been quietly massacred in a tragic traffic incident not long after. Mother, father, uncle, and baby sister, all dead and gone just like that in a fiery crash that would never be investigated because that kind of thing happened all too frequently for mundane reasons.

Then the local vampire elder had decided to take out Oya to be on the safe side—better to burn one point of supply than to risk discovery of the whole network. "Don't ask how we know that," Dirk warned before I could question it.

That must have been who'd hired Tula, and why. "And we're not letting them"—*me*—"kill this fucker because . . .?"

"Because we want to discover the whole network. And another victim's family—with more smarts than the first—is paying us to do it."

Birds. Frowning, I switched the phone from one ear to the other as my eyes started to adjust to the dark in the supply closet. It was bigger than I'd anticipated.

"Or money," I said.

"What?"

"The family that died in the car crash, that went to the police —it wasn't necessarily a lack of smarts that did them in. Maybe they couldn't afford our fees."

"Do I really need to remind you about the myriad of options we have for just those situations?"

I groaned. He didn't need to remind me. There were Guardians whose sole job description it was to investigate in cases like this and *find* people who would pay us to take on the cases we wanted to take on. The Guardians weren't mercenaries, although we often looked and felt a lot like it.

I knew this. I was just trying to stall to give my mind a chance to come to terms with the decision I now needed to make.

"Who's currently assigned to protect the target?"

"Now, *that* I can't tell you," Dirk said. "They're deep cover, been dark for months. And they don't know you're there, so be discreet."

Excellent. In a perfect world, my new objective was to milk Oya for enough information to uncover his entire network of movers and buyers, then kill him while evading his unknown Guardian protector.

In reality, that meant I'd likely have to choose what I cared about more: keeping my bargain with Tula or staying in the Guardians' good graces.

"Got it," I said. "Time frame?"

"Unknown. Do what you can to stay near the target as long as possible."

I huffed. "Okay, I'll have Carina put on her very best dragon charm and hope she gets picked."

"Is that what you're doing there? Carina is—"

"Carina?" A sharp squeal broke through Dirk's low voice on the other end of the line, and a calm warmth filled my chest. I would recognize that squeal anywhere. "I wanna talk to Carina!"

Noah's little voice came through louder now, and I pictured his bright curls bouncing as he ran up to Dirk.

"You're with Noah?" I asked. "Can you put him on and go get Etty? I want to say hi."

"Etty's at work," Dirk said.

"Then who's—" I was about to ask who was looking after the kid when I realized what an incredibly stupid question that was. "Oh," I said instead, a confusing mess of emotions suddenly tumbling around inside me.

Dirk had babysat Noah before, but that had only been for short periods of time and before Etty was in the picture. The fact that he was there now, while Etty was working, suggested something more regular—more permanent. I wasn't sure how okay I was with that. And even less sure that I even had a right to feel uncomfortable about it.

I wasn't there to take care of him myself, and Etty had just as much say in his upbringing now as I did—I'd made sure of that when I'd forced her into coparenting as part of my bargain with the fae to set her free.

"Hi Darcy," a sweet, pouty voice said into my ear, interrupting my thoughts. "Are you and Carina going to be back soon?"

"I don't know," I lied. Or maybe I really didn't know . . . but it felt like a lie because at least one of us had no intention of being back soon. "I hope so."

"Well can you tell her she left her snake here and I've been trying to keep it from dying but it's not easy when it keeps trying to eat Etty's shoes?"

"Of course," I said, suddenly at a loss for words. Just hearing his voice made my brain go blank and my skin prickle with cold. It was wrong that I wasn't there with him. He didn't need me, clearly—he sounded fine, and Etty was taking great care of him, even if that meant leaving him with Dirk sometimes. But it just felt . . . wrong.

Was this what it felt like to be homesick? Was this what it felt like to *have* a home?

"I miss you, Darcy. Can you bring me a big fish from the ocean? I heard there were big fishes in California."

Laughter welled up in my chest and tried to make its way to my eyes before I choked it down. "You got it, kid."

"I'm not a k—"

"I miss you too, Noah," I said quickly. "Tell Dirk I gotta go, and give Etty a big hug for me."

"Okay, but I want my big fish to be a football fish," he went on. "They live really far down deep but I bet you could get one. Their teeth are sharp as glass so I think Carina would like it, and they even have glowing hats on their heads to catch food."

"Sure," I said. "I'm blowing a kiss through the phone right now and then I'm gonna g—"

"Okay but there's also the giant sea bass and they're *huge*, probably too big to fit in your car, but you can get me a baby one and that would be alright; they're bright orange with polka dots."

I breathed out through pursed lips before saying, "I'll see what I can do. I'm gonna go now, Noah. Bye b—"

"Okay but—"

"Bye bye, Noah. Big hugs!" I hung up. If I didn't, I might end up sitting here for hours getting sucked into the little boy's cute, ridiculous world of crazy fish.

That wouldn't work, as fun as it sounded. I had a job to do.

Two jobs, now.

Two contradicting jobs.

Kill Oya *and* keep him alive.

Birds.

I groaned as I put my phone away, my eyes sweeping the room that no longer looked like a closet now that my eyes had fully adjusted to the dark. Closets usually didn't have doors leading to other rooms in them—nor did they usually have studio lighting equipment or needles and tubes for blood collection.

This one did. The big light stands were pointed at a cushy black chair decorated with manacles and flanked by IV stands, a table of bloodletting tools just to its side.

Great, a vampire porn dungeon. And possible further evidence of a trafficking outfit behind the scenes of Oya's show.

Footsteps sounded through the thin walls, and a light flicked on behind a small window in one of the doors. I crept toward it and peeked through, counting on the darkness on my side of the glass to keep me hidden.

It was like I'd been teleported back to the clinic and was peering into the lab where we processed patients' blood tests. Stainless steel gleamed at me, industrial refrigeration units lining the walls while test tubes littered the surfaces.

Someone who looked like a lab tech was labeling a handful of new blood samples.

I rapped my fingernails lightly against the door, ducking my head below the window. That room was probably filled with cameras, so I couldn't just go barging in. I'd have to draw out my prey.

Nothing happened, so I rapped my fingernails on the door again. A few moments later, it tentatively cracked open, and I pulled my prey into the darkness.

He hissed at me, exposing fangs that made him look too wild to be wearing that lab coat.

Evidence of vampire operation? Check.

I gripped my knife, ready to lunge for his heart, then stopped. This could be another good opportunity to test the phoenix's magic. Hadn't I, just a few minutes ago, produced enough heat with my fingertip to melt a doorknob? Maybe I could be a sort of human flamethrower. That would make killing vampires so much simpler.

He struck his head out at me, fangs first, and I lifted my palm to his chest. Heat swelled within my scrye and rushed out of my hand, flames dancing through my fingers as the vampire's white coat turned to ash.

He snarled, jerking away from me and crumpling to a panicked blob on the floor. The flames lit him up quickly, engulfing every inch of him until they rose to his neck. Then they began to die out.

Ashes and soot fell to the ground around him, leaving him huddled up, nude, skin dark gray with the remnants of his burned clothing.

I stared at him, curling my fingers around my knife again as my forehead creased. This didn't make any sense.

He looked up at me tentatively—unharmed except for his pride.

"Is this some kind of a sex thing?" he asked. "Because I might be—"

I lunged forward, knife aimed at his heart.

He jumped up and screeched at me, and my knife sliced into the side of his midsection. Blood welled up from the cut and dripped down his exposed genitals, which looked shrunken and soft.

I cringed. You could never really call a vampire unarmed, but even so this didn't feel like a fair fight.

Then he reached down and began stroking himself, and I cringed harder. He brought his bloody hand up to his mouth and licked, showing me a fanged smile. "It's going to be a sex thing now," he said, taking a step towards me. "I'm going to rip your head off and fuck one end while I drain the other."

I smiled. Vampires were just so damn reliable. I could always count on them to give me good reason to kill them.

With a shrug, I backed away from him slowly. "Come and get me then," I said as my thighs bumped into the chair that was set up to drain victims. I sat down and crossed my legs, holding the knife against the arm of the chair. Vampires were strong. If I let this one pounce on me while I was standing, he would take me to the ground.

He ran straight for me, hands outstretched to take off my head just like he'd promised. I swiveled the chair around, and he collided with the back of it. Letting go of my knife, I grasped one of his arms and pressed it into the arm of the chair, clasping together the manacles designed to hold victims in place.

His other hand grabbed a fistful of my hair while I worked, and he snarled. I grimaced as he pulled my head back, the roots of the hair stinging. He might yank out a chunk of my scalp if I didn't end this soon.

But he only had the one hand free, and I had both of mine. I found my knife again and slashed at his wrist, which surprised him just enough to loosen his grip on my hair. I yanked my head away and clenched my teeth at the pain. I'd probably lost some hair, but my scalp was still intact. He reached around the chair as soon as he lost me, trying to free his other arm from the restraint.

I was quicker with my knife than he was with the manacle. I came around behind him and stabbed up through his ribs. The back of the chair against his chest kept him steady for me as my knife pierced his heart, and then he went completely still.

I closed my eyes and let out a breath, standing up slowly and inspecting myself for damage. Nothing that I could see or feel— the only thing he'd gotten hold of was my hair.

But now I had a stunned vampire who'd seen me snooping where I shouldn't be. I couldn't let him live, and the phoenix's fire hadn't burned him.

Why not?

I shook my head. Answering that question was a problem for later.

I pulled out my serrated hunting knife and sawed the naked

vamp's head off, using the chair to brace myself while I worked. It was tough and messy, and my boots were slipping in the blood on the ground before it was done. This vampire, unlike most of the ones I'd beheaded recently, had never been beheaded before.

And he won't ever be again, I thought as I severed the last bit of flesh and wiped my knife on the chair.

Stepping forward, I grabbed the heavy black cloth hanging as a backdrop behind the torture chair and swung it over my head, then pulled it around my shoulders like a hooded cape.

Sufficiently hidden from whatever cameras might be present, I made my way to the room the vampire had been in and stepped into the light. I found a trashcan quickly and dropped the severed head inside, then headed to the sink to wash up.

Looking down at myself in the shadows of the curtain-cape and the dark clothing I wore underneath, I had the fleeting thought that maybe this was why Tula seemed to love wearing white. If she ever got any blood on her, she would be aware of every drop. Me? I was going to be a walking crime scene on my way out of the building, unless I found a new set of clothes. At least it wouldn't be obvious to anyone unless they looked closely.

Once I was as clean as I could manage, I pulled the trash bag out of the can and tied it shut, hefting it over my shoulder with the severed head inside. It would be coming with me everywhere I went until I found a way to destroy it. I had learned my lesson.

My eyes landed on the new tubes of blood the vampire had been handling before I'd lured him out. I took out my phone and got closer, snapping pics for Dirk as I read the labels.

Annabel Merrick, forest sprite, starting bid: $10,000

Nausea laced my insides as I recalled the face of the treeish girl from the diner last night. Had she knowingly participated in a staged hero stunt to gain fame and fortune? Probably, yeah. But she also probably had no idea her blood was sitting here in this lab with a price for her life on it, and no one deserved that.

I frowned. Opening up one of the refrigerator doors, I bit my cheek and snapped more pictures. It was all filled with similar vials, all with names and abilities and starting bids.

They must distribute these as samples to their network of buyers. Like a mail-order catalog of exquisite snacks. Did that mean everyone whose name was written on a label in this fridge was still alive and could be saved?

I hoped so.

Sighing, I closed the refrigerator door and tucked my phone carefully into my pocket. This was pretty damning evidence that the intel from Tula and Dirk was good. I should find Carina and tell her the plan . . . once I figured out what the plan was.

I headed back into the dark murder closet and dropped the curtain on the ground. Clutching the knotted garbage bag closely, I emerged into the hallway and wished I'd brought a bag big enough to stash vampire heads in. I'd always preferred pockets to handbags, but that was going to have to change if I couldn't easily burn up vampires wherever I was.

Miraculously, no one stopped me to ask what was in the plastic bag, and I made it to the parking lot without any fuss. But when I opened up the trunk of my car to toss the vampire head inside, smoke wafted out.

I scrunched my nose and brought my arm up to cover my face. "What the . . .?" Had the volcano bunnies burnt something in here?

Frowning, I shut the trunk and walked around to peer in the window. Carina was curled up on her side in the back seat of the car, crying.

I knocked on the glass. She startled, then spotted me out of the corner of her eye and promptly covered her face.

I opened the door and coughed as more smoke billowed out.

"What is this?" I asked when I could speak. "Trying to asphyxiate me? I thought we were friends."

I expected Carina to ignore me, but I must have touched a nerve. She sat up pin straight and stared at me, her hands clenched into tight fists and her teeth bared.

"I. Can't. Control. It," she yelled. I waited a moment for her to offer more explanation, but it wasn't happening.

"Okay," I said calmly. "Let's start with what you can control. Why are you in the car and not in there?" I pointed at the building I'd just come out of.

Carina grunted, and two streams of dark smoke puffed out of her nostrils. But then she took in a small breath and spoke. "Because they told me to leave. I failed the audition and"—her words caught in her throat, and she swallowed—"and now I'll never meet Oya and I won't be a hero and I'll have to leave the country and be alone like my mom and I'll never be able to do anything with my life except kill people!"

"Don't you help your dad make weapons?" I asked, too quickly. It was the wrong thing to say.

Carina let out a muted angry scream, and I reminded myself it wouldn't help to point out the logic holes in her argument that her life was utterly ruined. I'd been young once. I knew how that felt.

"Ok, I get it; I'm sorry," I said. "But there's something I should have told you earlier."

Carina focused her eyes on me. "What?"

"We were never here so that Oya could make you a hero— Oya doesn't make heroes. He kills them. He's a bad guy. And I brought you here to help stop him."

Carina didn't move. Her expression didn't change except for her eyes getting just slightly narrower. I hadn't been planning on telling her so bluntly, but with her emotions already raw like this, there wasn't going to be any good way to do it.

Before she could run out of the car screaming about how insane I was, I popped out my phone and brought up some of the photos of victims Tula had given me. Carina was a fan of Oya's program, so she should recognize some of the bodies as his hopefuls.

"That's what would have happened to you if he had picked you—and if you weren't here with me."

"But . . ." Carina shook her head. "Why would he do that when he's so perfect and famous and rich already? Isn't it better to be . . . better than *that*?" She glared at the pictures on my phone.

I nodded silently. Carina wasn't calling me a liar, which was what I'd expected. She trusted me more than I'd thought.

"He's a vampire," I answered. "Perfect and famous and rich only goes so far without blood and lots of it."

"But he has so many willing fans!" Carina protested, and I frowned. She was kind of right.

I was so salty about vampires in general after everything that had happened that I hadn't thought to ask these same questions. Why would Oya be doing this when he already had plenty of money, especially since he was trafficking his victims and not draining them himself?

"Could be he's just an evil fucker," I said.

Carina was silent.

"Wait a minute." I cocked my head at her. "Why did he tell you to leave? You're saying he had the chance to recruit an adorable *dragon* and he turned you down?"

The little girl huffed out another puff of smoke, then wiped her tears away and clambered up into the front seat to get away from me. "Donwannatalkaboutit," she mumbled, but I wasn't letting it go.

"I mean, you're basically the high-end barbecue of vampire victims, right?" I said to the back of her head. "All that fire and magic's gotta make you super tasty."

I smacked my lips. I hated myself a little for it, but Carina needed me to not be too serious right now. The little girl who'd been forced to face death and destruction at every turn of her life needed to be allowed to laugh about it, or it would suffocate her.

"I would be *delicious*," she said with a disturbing amount of ferocity, turning her head to glare at me. Then she looked away again and got quiet. After a long moment, she said, "But he didn't believe me."

I scrunched my forehead in confusion. "What do you mean? Believe you about what?"

"That I'm a dragon."

"How could he not believe? It's very obvious when you shift into a winged creature with a long, spiny tail and breathe fire."

"I couldn't do that."

"Why not?"

"Because I CAN'T—I can't shift when I want, ok? I can't control it anymore. I just can't." She hung her head low and hugged her knees, and I pressed my lips together to keep quiet. After a minute or so, she whispered, "Not since they stole me."

I hummed a low note of frustration in my throat, wanting to wrap my arms around her and comfort her. But she would hate that. Instead, I said, "Come on," and I got up out of the car. I walked around to the passenger-side door and opened it, holding my hand out to the huddled-up little girl inside.

She looked up at me, sooty tears running down her cheeks.

"You're still a dragon," I said firmly. "You'll always be a dragon, no matter how good you are at deciding when you want to have wings." I smiled. "And this is actually a perfect opportunity for us to go after Oya. You want to be a hero? Let's go back in there and get you recruited so we can take the evil fucker down."

"What?" she questioned in a wavering voice.

"Come on," I repeated.

She took my hand. I pulled her out of the car and led her beside me as I marched back up to the building, trying to channel the obnoxious dance-mom persona I never knew I needed in my repertoire. If I made a scene—and recorded it with my phone, that was key—Oya would have to show himself to defuse the situation. I hoped. He also might just have a horde of his vampire minions try to make us disappear before we could do too much damage.

Either way, we would make it work.

We walked in the door and marched straight back through the halls to where we'd been waiting for Carina's audition, and then I pulled Carina straight through into the room the hopefuls disappeared into when their names were called. Only at this point did she begin to pull back on my hand, slowing me down.

The room was empty except for Oya, two of his assistants, and a ferret that was doing tricks. Maybe an auditioning shifter.

"How dare you?" I asked in a booming voice, eyes locking with Oya as I held up my recording phone.

And then I was engulfed by flames.

Oya disappeared, the ferret disappeared, the room disappeared, and Carina's tight grip on my hand disappeared.

Everything around me was gone, replaced with nothing but fire and wind.

10

FUCK, fuck, fuck, fuck . . . It was all I could think when my world turned into a rushing inferno around me.

Icy cold mist prickled my cheeks and fingertips relentlessly, and I shivered even as the flames around me seemed to heat me from within. It didn't make sense in my body, and it didn't make sense in my mind.

Where was I?

Flying.

I didn't know how I knew, but I knew. I wasn't flying with my wings, but I was moving far above the ground. Carried by a phoenix that was both corporeal and not, and within its magic I was alone in the clouds.

Alone.

Carina.

There were two possibilities when it came to Carina. Either she'd been burned up along with everyone else in my immediate vicinity, or she was alone in a room with Oya and his vampire minions after I'd dragged her back in there and put a neon sign on her that said: "Eat me! I'm trouble!"

Fuck.

I wasn't worried for my safety right now. Fire and wind were hallmarks of the phoenix's very un-amusing shenanigans. And it couldn't hurt me without hurting itself . . . probably.

But what the fuck was Carina going to do without me?

The flames around me began to take shape, and the phoenix's great wings beat the misty air into a whirlwind. I couldn't see the bird's head, but I could hear it screech in a high-pitched wail that drowned all the thoughts from my mind.

Time stretched and slowed and danced to the erratic beat of my heart. Up was down and down was up and everywhere was nothing except flight.

Then I was assaulted by rocks. Hot, sharp edges and scratchy tufts of grass dug into my skin and rattled my bones. I tried to roll as I hit the ground, but I was too disoriented. Instead, I just lay there and groaned, feeling broken and lost.

A second sack of flesh and bones dropped down beside me with similar protests, and I blinked my eyes until the blurry lump took shape as my brother.

Ray. The phoenix's other half.

I groaned again. We must have really pissed off the bird by separating.

"Darcy?" Ray was quicker to recover from being dropped on the rocks than I was. He was already standing and crouching over me.

I sat up, grimacing, and held out my hand. When Ray grabbed it, his touch did nothing to help me heal the cuts and bruises covering me—which I should have been able to heal even without him close, now that I'd embraced the witch life.

The screeching around us became shriller as I stood, until it seemed to penetrate my skull and expand in a reverberating whistle of words.

"You play, like children, with my fire."

I looked at Ray, and he nodded. He heard it too.

"Sorry?" I called out.

"You do not understand."

"That's true," I muttered bitterly, but Ray was already on his knees, head lowered.

I clenched my fists as the swirling fire gathered before us. I wasn't going to get on my knees and bow to this bird that had possibly just gotten my niece killed by failing to ask before whisking me away to wherever the fuck this was.

"One devout and one rebellious. This is good. This is what we are."

"What?" I snapped.

"We are two. We are both. We are contrary. We are life."

"Okay, I get it," I said. "We're bumbling idiots and don't know what you want us to do. But can you put us back where you found us for now and let's reschedule the lecture?"

"We are not you. We are we. We cannot."

"Motherfucker," I muttered, and Ray yanked down on my hand. I scowled at him. "No," I said. "I'm not doing this. I need to get back to Carina."

"We cannot," the bird said as its swirling flames died down. What was left looked like the wings that sprouted from my back and Ray's when we wanted to fly. Feathers in varying shades of brown, fluffy and shimmering, wavering—incorporeal. It was as tall as a small house, intimidatingly huge even with its wings cooled down and folded on its back. *"We need time to refresh."*

"Refresh . . ." I repeated.

"The magic," Ray said. "It takes an incredible amount of energy for the phoenix to act independently of us—just bringing us here would have been enough to deplete it."

I narrowed my eyes. "How *much* time do you need?"

The bird screeched again and stretched out its wings, giving them a majestically aggressive half-flap before folding them again on its back.

"You are here for a reason. Do not squander it."

"The mountain," Ray said. "You brought us to the mountain."

"It is the only place we can separate."

I looked around, noting the rocky cliffs surrounding us on all sides and the round depression in the ground a few feet away. There was smoke coming out of it.

"Does it always do that?" I asked, not wanting to test whether we'd be immune to the effects of a volcanic eruption just for being the volcano god's not-so-loyal servants.

"It does not. These are dangerous times. We are to warn you."

"Warn us about the volcano erupting by bringing us to its crater?"

"Not erupting. He is building strength. Preparing to fight."

"Preparing to fight what? Or who?"

"The cold that would eclipse his fire."

"Itztlacoliuhqui . . ." Ray said.

I tensed. That was the ice god who had taken over the Sweepers and then seduced Simeon into his little death cult. Okay . . . It probably wasn't little.

"Popo's rival, right?" I asked, and Ray nodded. Well, good. At least my god and I had a common enemy.

"He also builds strength. Much greater strength."

"How do we stop him?" I asked. If the phoenix had brought us here to warn us about this enemy god, then it must have some useful advice to impart on the subject . . . right?

"Protect the witches."

"The witches . . ."

"He steals them."

"The witches . . ." I repeated again under my breath, staring at the little pebbles of volcanic rock covering the ground at my feet. "Which witches?" I asked even though a small part of me already knew.

"All," came the phoenix's answer.

Ice crept up my spine. Not literally, though. Not yet.

Did this mean the ice god was the architect behind so many witches all over the world turning to stone?

"The more he steals, the more powerful he becomes."

"So he's petrifying witches to steal their power? Then why are they all turning into different things? Shouldn't they be turning to ice if the ice god is causing it?"

"Through the witches, he steals power from their gods."

I bit my cheek, letting out a short breath. Of course. It would probably drain his own power to turn so many people into ice. And that was all witches were, right? Little batteries working to generate and store power for their—our—respective gods? We would be destroyed in the wake of their insane war, which I didn't even know what had caused.

"How?" I asked. "How do we protect the witches?"

The phoenix screeched again and stretched out its wings, this time stomping its little bird feet on the rocks as luminescent brown feathers fell at its sides.

"It doesn't know," Ray said quietly, and I looked over to him. I'd almost forgotten he was here. How could that be?

I looked down at my hands, turning my consciousness inward to feel for my scrye. It was there, as always, but it felt small and cold and alone, as it had during my adolescence. As if Ray weren't here and we were still separated.

"We must refresh," the phoenix shrieked. Then it leapt up into the sky. Gusts of wind blew down on us as it flapped its great wings once, twice, three times. Then it tipped its beak forward and dove down.

It fell through the air like a missile, not stopping as it neared the rocky ground of the crater. Piercing the clouds of smoke wafting up from the hole, it fell directly into the opening and beyond, shrieking all the while.

I opened my eyes wide and looked at Ray, who shrugged. Together, we clambered to the opening and leaned over to look inside. It was a long way down, and there was a glowing pit of golden red magma churning gently at the bottom.

"This is the rejuvenating spa treatment for phoenixes?" I asked Ray. "A lovely soak inside an active volcano?"

"This is why it likes our god so much," Ray answered.

The wind changed directions, and smoke blew in my eyes. I coughed and stepped back. Ray followed me.

"You know what witches it was talking about?" he asked.

"Unfortunately," I said, and then I told him everything I could recall about the people being petrified.

He frowned. "More than I would have thought," he murmured.

"What?"

He looked up at me, a hint of shock in his expression. "I never realized there were so many other active gods with witches in the world. They've been so quiet, secretive . . ."

"Haven't you and all of Popo's crew been doing the same?"

"I suppose." He shook his head. "I heard about a few people getting petrified in DC recently—friends of friends—but I never thought they could be witches."

"Same. I didn't realize until Adrian spelled it out for me."

"I never thought we could be next," he added. "We have to find out how he's choosing his victims . . . and how to stop him."

"Agreed. Any idea how we do that?"

"We can ask Popo, to start. He may have an idea."

"Well, we're in the right place for that," I said, but Ray shook his head.

"He sleeps during the day," Ray explained. "Many gods do. Their power is born of darkness and dreams, hope and sorrow —things there isn't as much space for under the glare of the sun."

That was interesting. A small part of me wondered whether that was the real truth behind the mages in the coven using the moon as our focus. Was it all tied to the gods we or our ancestors had escaped, even down to the smallest details?

I looked around again. Nothing but jutting rock surfaces in every direction, smoke and clouds swirling above and fire below. I wasn't sure if we would still be here when night fell, and I wasn't sure if I would even *want* to wait that long when I'd left Carina in such a precarious position.

But we couldn't leave without the bird. If I climbed up these rocks and then hiked down the mountain, I'd have to hitchhike a ride back into the States—without my passport. Even if that worked, it would take days.

"How long do you think the volcano birdbath will take?" I asked Ray.

"It will be done before dark. The phoenix knew what it was doing. It wanted to be here while the god slumbered."

"Why?" I asked.

"Popo can be . . ." Ray twisted his mouth and shrugged one shoulder before he said, "distracting."

"Distracting. From the enormous fiery mystical bird that normally lives inside us?"

"Distracting at best. Yes. Have you ever met a god before—that you remember?"

"No."

"You won't forget it again, once you do."

I took a deep breath as my bare arms prickled in the wind. I hadn't been wearing my jacket when the bird had grabbed me, and it was nippy at this altitude even at this time of year.

Patting the pockets on my pants, I grumbled. They were empty.

No phone. No wallet.

Nothing to help me get out of here faster and back to Carina.

"Where is my daughter?" Ray asked, staring at me levelly.

Oh, nowhere special. Just one of those crazy LA vampire dens masquerading as reality TV. I couldn't say that to her dad. But I also couldn't lie. Wouldn't lie.

"I took her to meet my family in California," I said. "She needed some time to cool off and process what happened before coming back here."

To my surprise, Ray nodded. He stuck his hands in his pockets and looked away from me. "Probably smart," he said.

"We were in a complicated situation when I left, though. I really need to get back to her."

"Complicated situation . . ." he repeated. "Do I want to know?"

I opened my mouth, but he shook his head.

"No. The more you tell me, the more I'll want to go find her and drag her back home." He looked at me with wet eyes, daring me to tell him otherwise. "And if I follow her before she comes back on her own, she'll only run faster and farther."

I shifted my stance. If we'd been having this conversation yesterday, or even a few hours ago, I'd have said that was a great attitude. But I couldn't assure Ray that she was in safe hands with me when I'd put her in such a dangerous position and then been ripped away from her.

If I got back to find she'd been turned into vampire food, I'd never forgive myself. Never be able to look my brother in the eye again.

But Oya wouldn't work that quickly. Even if Carina couldn't control her shifting at the moment, she was still a dragon. They would still be able to taste the magic in her veins at the very first sip. And then, they wouldn't want to waste her by draining her quickly. Her blood would go into sample vials like the ones I'd taken pictures of, and she would be auctioned off to the highest bidder. That would take time.

How much time? More than the phoenix spa day, I had to hope.

"I'll do my best," I said to Ray after far too long, "to keep her safe."

"Fuck safe," he said. "Just keep her sane."

I smiled softly and sat down on the bumpy gravel of shiny black pebbles, my back against the jagged rock face at the perimeter of the crater. Nothing to do now but wait for the bird and marvel at the fact that I actually might like my crazy witch-cult-following brother.

"That's a bigger ask," I said. "But I'll try."

THE FIRST PINK hints of dusk had just begun to creep into the clouds when the phoenix's shriek whistled out of the crater. It echoed in my ears, bouncing off the rock in every direction as Ray sprang to his feet beside me.

His eyes met mine, and he gave me a short nod. He was counting on me to get back to Carina, and I was counting on him to help figure out how we were supposed to keep all the witches in the world from turning to stone and letting their magic fuel the evil ice god who wanted to obliterate all life on earth.

Seemed proportionate.

The whistling shrieks grew louder, and the air wafting from the crater grew hotter.

I tried to step back, but I was already as far as I could go without climbing the cliffs.

Sparks danced out of the crater, searing pathways of light into the cloud of smoke. Something roared below our feet.

I couldn't help but flinch away when the phoenix emerged. Flinging my hands in front of my face, I cursed as the wave of intense heat rolled into me. The bare skin on my arms stung as though they'd been blasted by steam from an oven.

Apparently, I could only comfortably handle fire when my half of the phoenix was comfortably resting inside me.

The heat dissipated as the bird flew straight up into the air, and I uncovered my face. It was a mistake.

I froze, staring up at the bird flapping its molten wings. The whole thing glowed, its edges turning black before cracking and falling off to crash down against the pebbles at my feet. Bright orange lava dripped from the wings as they beat, flinging semi-soft rocks of hot death in every direction.

Still shrieking, it rooted its face in its own molten feathers and then threw its head back as its beak opened and closed around a mouthful of lava, which it slurped down greedily before rooting for more.

I screamed involuntarily as one of the hot death rocks hit my left arm, right above the elbow. It bounced off and landed at my feet, but not before burning enough flesh to take a chunk of me with it.

I sank to my knees, trying to resist the urge to clutch the wound with my right hand while I reminded myself to breathe. I couldn't move, and I couldn't look away from the fiery bird above me.

I'd never seen anything more terrifying in my life.

"We are refreshed," it sang in my head, and it was a miracle I could make out the words over all the screaming. Ray, the bird, and I—we were all three of us screaming.

Another death rock struck me, this time in the shoulder. And then another in my ribs. The thin layer of fabric over my torso burned where the rocks touched it, ashes fusing with my melting skin before falling away in chunks.

I didn't dare look over at Ray. As long as I could hear his screams, it meant he wasn't dead. That was all that mattered.

"We will return?" It was a question.

I wanted to yell "yes" at the bird, but was it asking about returning us to where it had taken us or about returning itself to us, its corporeal hosts? Why did it even need us? It seemed pretty fucking corporeal right now.

"Take us back to where we were," I said.

"First we will return."

It swooped up in the air as the words echoed in my head, wings crusting into black as the glowing parts underneath blurred into a mesmerizing swirl of light.

Then it dove straight towards us.

I tore my eyes away from the sight of oncoming sudden death and finally looked at Ray. He had fewer chunks missing from him than I did, so that was good. If the phoenix didn't kill us in the next moment, he would survive.

I didn't need to look back to know it had almost reached us. The shrieking deafened me, and the heat was so intense it stopped me breathing. I shut my eyes tight against it and braced myself on the rocks behind me.

The pain magnified when the heat dissipated. All the intensity, the magic, the feral force of life that was the molten bird had jumped inside me in the same brutish way that errant souls tended to return to their bodies when I pushed them.

I wasn't hurt, not physically—but for the span of this unmeasurably long moment, I *was* pain.

I crumbled to the ground, only to find there was no ground beneath my feet. There was only mist.

We were flying again, me and the bird inside me, wrapped in a whirlwind of its fiery wings and a cloud of misty wind. The icy fog of water vapor clashing against the heat on my skin only made the pain worse.

How long had it been since before I'd started screaming? How long would it be before I could stop?

I couldn't know. I could only lose myself in the pain and the clouds and hope I was conscious enough to protect Carina when I got back.

11

My HEAD HAD SPLIT in two. There was no other explanation for the wrenching ache inhabiting my skull.

Something was wrong.

Something other than the searing aftereffects of the phoenix's return to my body.

The world was wobbling. I was wobbling.

I blinked my eyes open.

My feet were moving over the blue carpet in Oya's studio, but I wasn't walking. Someone was dragging me.

Two someones, I realized as I felt their hands gripping under my shoulders.

Fuck.

The bird had apparently done exactly as I'd asked, deposited me right where I'd been when it had taken me—and I'd been unconscious, and probably still bleeding. The perfect little vampire treat.

I kept still, not wanting to clue in my captors that I'd woken. Closing my eyes again, I took stock of my body.

Feel beyond the pain. That was the key when it came to healing wounds on myself. Pain was a terrible indicator of damage when magic was involved. I had to see my body from within, feel the tingle of energy that told me things were working as they should, home in on all the places where the flow of energy was disrupted.

It wasn't too many places, but they were big. The lava rocks had taken a lot out of me—flesh and blood and even some muscle. I couldn't fix them all the way with magic, but at least I could stop the bleeding. Clot the fluids, repair the broken vessels, bring together thin layers of skin over the missing pieces.

The phoenix wasn't lying when it had said we were refreshed. Even without Ray by my side, it was easy.

No wonder such an ancient, terrifyingly powerful creature had tied itself to the relatively young volcano god. A hot bath could be a powerful thing.

The tinny, boppy beat of one of Oya's songs filtered through into the hallway and made me want to close my ears.

Now was as good a time as any.

I swung my feet off the ground and pulled them up under me, then pressed the soles down quickly to push myself up. My captors weren't trying to restrain me—just carry me—so the sudden shift in weight and position threw off their grip.

I put distance between us before the surprise could wear off, crouching down a few feet away from them in the middle of the hall. The only knife I knew I still had on me was in my boot.

One knife. One me. Two vampires.

I gripped my knife.

A muffled shriek drifted out from behind a door on the other side of the vampires. One of them turned away from me to look towards the sound, and the other walked over to knock on the door.

My grip on the knife loosened.

What was this? They weren't even paying attention to me.

The one who had knocked on the door opened it quickly after, and both the music and the shrieking got louder.

"You're crazy!" a girl yelled. "What are you doing?"

It was Carina. I gripped the knife again and leapt towards the door.

"No!" she shrieked as I pushed past the vampire who had opened the door. "Absolutely not!"

I ran in with my knife raised, expecting to see Carina bleeding and bound.

Instead, she stood on a raised platform before a paneled mirror, covered in colorful feathers and glittering gemstones. Her hands were at her cheeks, mouth open in an exaggerated O as she shrieked once more.

She was covered in so many stones that my heart dropped for a second while I considered the possibility she was being petrified. But none of it was spreading, and she didn't look even the slightest bit afraid.

She might be screaming, but her eyes were laughing.

"Don't you dare put that—" She stopped, gaze centering on me in the mirror. "Darcy?"

I stood up straight and relaxed my grip on the knife.

Carina spun around, a whirlwind of color and sparkle, and ran towards me. I braced myself and stood firm against her tackling me as she flung her feathered arms around my waist. Her left hand came back around to grab my wrist as she squealed into my ribs, and the knife disappeared from my hand.

Way to disarm me, kid. I awkwardly patted her head with my hand that no longer had a knife in it. *Message received.*

"Darcy, where did you go?" She pulled away from me and beamed. "Never mind, I don't care—look at this!"

I raised my eyebrows. "You look like a bedazzled chicken."

"You're just jealous," she said with a spin, unfazed.

"I take it you made it past the auditions?" I looked away from Carina to stare at Oya. He stood by the mirror, where he was holding a giant feathered headpiece.

"She did," he said with a pointed glare at me. "Thanks to you."

Carina shook her head. "I was so shocked when you flew away like that—I shifted partway without realizing it. And then Oya saw and he was like, 'Oh, I guess you really are a dragon.' And now we're trying to pin down my look because it's actually happening and I'm going to be a hero!"

"Yay," I said without an ounce of enthusiasm. I couldn't tell whether Carina was legitimately excited about this. Had she forgotten what I'd told her about Oya and what he did to his "heroes"?

"Are you her mother?" Oya asked. "She has oh so much to offer; I'm sorry I didn't see it at first."

"I'm her aunt," I said coolly, and Carina groaned.

"Darcy," she whined. "Chill out, he's fine." She turned to Oya and clasped her hands together, looking like a perfect little princess. "Can I please tell her? She might try to kill you if I don't."

Try? So touching, how much faith Carina had in my ability to kill people.

"He made me sign an NDA," she said to me.

"Your aunt will have to sign one too, if you want her to know," Oya said.

Carina squealed and grabbed my hand. "Come on, come on, come on! You won't believe what I found out!"

I scowled as she dragged me to a corner of the dressing room where there was a desk.

"In the drawer," Oya called, and Carina had a paper and pen in my shaking hands before I could blink.

I sat down and tried to calm my pounding heart. Too much adrenaline for this kind of thing. But there was no way I was signing anything here without reading every sentence twice. Carina bounced back to Oya while I read, and she carried right on with what she'd apparently been doing before I interrupted—

screaming at him that the headpiece he wanted her to wear was one step too far.

"But a dragon needs her horns," Oya said emphatically.

"I have real horns," Carina protested, and I tuned out their screeching, giggly chatter.

This was insanity.

But the form she'd handed me was pretty straightforward. Nothing suspicious or even too confusing. There was even a whole stack of them in the drawer she'd pulled it from.

Oya must have people sign it on a regular basis. What kind of secret would even be worth protecting if he was going to let so many people in on it?

I sighed and signed on the dotted line.

"Done," I called out in Carina's direction, but she didn't hear me. She was too busy posing with the headpiece, which Oya had finally wrangled onto her head.

I marched over to them and stuck the paper in front of Oya.

He turned to me, perfectly manicured brows arching up as he took the paper from my hands. Up close, he was wearing so much glittery highlighter that he almost looked fae. But the glittery sheen on Etty's skin didn't rely on light or movement to sparkle.

"Are you ready?" He smiled at me.

"I have no idea," I said.

"Don't laugh . . . or do." He waved his hand and shrugged. "I guess I can't complain if I manage to put a smile on that unhappy face." He lifted his hand again and touched his index finger to the tip of my nose.

My scowl deepened.

Oya fluttered his fingers and moved his arms in a circle to frame his face before settling his hands on his hips. He tilted his chin at his assistant in the corner of the room and said, "Hit it."

His most popular song started playing, and Carina bounced

up and down to the beat.

"Birds of a feather . . ." she sang, spinning until the feathers on her getup danced with her.

Oya started spinning as well, then paused to stick his foot out to the side with a flourish.

It turned into an elongated hooflike thing and sprouted a single thick claw.

"Don't always flock together . . ." Carina sang.

Oya spun again, stretching his right arm out behind his back until it curved into a shape human bones just couldn't make.

It sprouted black and white feathers.

"But when they do . . ." Carina sang.

Oya tilted his head up to the sky as his neck stretched up and up and up. His head shrank into a tiny beaked thing covered in white fuzz. It chirped at me while Carina finished the chorus of the song.

"They shake their tail feathers!"

Carina swirled her butt around in the signature dance move for the song, and Oya did the same—only his butt was more like a feathered hump.

By now, I was scowling so deeply I wasn't sure my face would ever be the same. Oya hooted and growled at me, and Carina said, "Well?"

I looked at her and blinked.

"It's a very . . . statuesque bird." I didn't know what to say. Truly. I'd never seen an ostrich in person before.

Oya pawed at the ground with one of his bird hoofs and then changed back into a human with a poof. "Thank you," he said. "I do think I'm stunning in my feathers, but my managers don't think the world is quite ready for me yet."

"See, Darcy?" Carina said, jutting her head forward with her hands on her hips. "He's not really a vampire. He's an ostrich. So he's not going to eat me."

"Were you nervous about her spending time with a vampire?" Oya asked brightly. "Oh, there's no need to be nervous. I'm harmless!"

I opened my mouth, not sure what to say. Then I heard the distinct buzz of my phone. Only it was in Carina's hands.

Her face fell.

"My ride's here," she said.

"Your ride?" Wasn't I her ride?

"Yeah, well, you were gone—and then your car got towed because it was here for too long. And I needed to call someone to come get me because I can't spend the night here without getting Oya in legal trouble. And you even left your phone, so . . ."

I breathed in and shook my head. My car had been towed? What a nice cherry on top of this bird-shit show.

"Let's get this off you," Oya said, unzipping the feathery getup at Carina's back. She was still wearing her clothes underneath, complete with the stuffing in her bra. "I'll see you here tomorrow at nine o'clock sharp. Are you her legal guardian?" he asked, looking at me.

"Yes," I said. We were lying about her name and age anyway to avoid getting her arrested, so it wouldn't hurt to lie about this too.

"You'll need to come with her. We have more forms for you to sign."

I nodded, and then my eye twitched as Carina ran up to Oya and wrapped her arms around him.

"Thank you thank you thank you for everything! I'll be here for sure!"

After giving him a quick squeeze, she bounced away from him and caught my hand, dragging me out of the room. As she led me down the hallway towards the exit, I caught a glance of the lock I'd picked earlier to find my way into the murder closet.

Had they found the vampire I'd beheaded yet? Had they seen

me chuck his head in the trash on the cameras? Would the head still be there in the trunk of my car when I picked it up from the impound lot?

More importantly—how was I going to convince Carina that Oya being an ostrich shifter didn't mean she wouldn't become vampire food just like so many of his other recruits? Even if he wasn't the one selling them, someone was.

I didn't even want to think about whether I was still going to kill him for Tula, or what I would tell Dirk. I was just relieved Carina was okay. I wanted to make sure she stayed that way.

"Who did you call to come get you?" I asked as Carina pushed open the door to the parking lot and I plucked my knife out of the pocket of her skirt.

"The clinic," she said as I bent over to tuck the knife back in my boot. "But Sassie couldn't come."

"So who . . ." I stood back up and stopped when I saw the DSC van pull up to the curb. Black with red trim and darkened windows, it loomed in front of me.

The passenger-side window rolled down, and Adrian peered down at us from the driver's seat. Had it just been this morning that I'd seen him last? His face was shadowed with stubble, and he was wearing his glasses. It had been a long enough day that he'd had to take out his contacts.

"You told me Darcy wasn't here," he said, eyes on Carina.

"She wasn't," Carina said as she opened the door. "Now she's back. I get shotgun!"

"I thought you said we were good—you and I," I said tentatively over Carina's head as she climbed in beside Adrian.

"We are," he said. "I didn't mean to imply—it's fine. Get in."

I took a deep breath and got in the back, strapping myself in behind Carina. When I looked up, I caught Adrian's eyes on me in the rear-view mirror.

"What happened to you?" he asked as he pulled out of the parking lot.

"What do you mean?"

"That shirt was a different shade of black when I saw you this morning. And it didn't have massive holes in it. Neither did you, for that matter."

Oh, right. My clothes were soaked in vampire blood, and I was still missing chunks of muscle where the lava rocks had hit me.

"Killed a vampire and went sunbathing on a volcano," I said.

Carina whipped her head around and gripped the back of her seat with white knuckles.

"You went to the mountain without me?" She gaped. "That's where you were?"

"Not by choice," I said. "The phoenix took me without asking. Took your dad, too."

Carina's face softened, and her eyes ran over me in earnest for the first time since I'd come back. Was she finally noticing just how terrible I looked?

"Is he ok?" she whispered.

"He'll live," I said. Not that I had much reason to be sure of that . . . I just assumed that, as feral as the bird inside us was, it wouldn't be reckless enough to accidentally kill one of us all the way. Or that at least I'd know if it did. "We should give him a call when we get home. But first we need to talk to Popo."

"You still haven't done that?" Adrian asked.

"Couldn't. Apparently he sleeps during the day." I paused, expecting Carina to say something snarky, but she was quiet. Probably worried about Ray. "The bird had something interesting to say, though."

"What?" Adrian's eyes met mine in the mirror again.

"The witches being petrified . . . it's the work of the same ice god who took over the Sweepers. He's doing it to drain them of their gods' power—gaining strength."

"Gaining strength for what?" Adrian asked with a frown.

"That's a good fucking question," I said, and a brief aftershock of too much adrenaline made my voice break. I swallowed. "I don't know. It just told us we needed to stop him. 'Protect the witches,' it said."

Adrian stopped at a light and twisted his shoulders around to stare at me intently. His look went right through me, prodding at the wall I'd built around all the fear and pain and helplessness the events of the day had conjured inside me.

I fought the urge to wipe my eyes. My hands trembled. Was he even looking at me, or was it the phoenix and its knowledge of the gods he wanted to see?

He opened his mouth but then closed it without saying anything.

"It's green," I said.

He turned back around and asked, "Where am I going?"

I gave him Sassie's address, then sat back while Carina chattered to Adrian up front, telling him all about her day with Oya and how excited she was to go back tomorrow. I tried to close my eyes for a little rest, but they just kept opening again, all the energy inside me certain I should still be on the lookout for something to fight.

When we got back to Sassie's, the house was dark and empty.

"My aunt still in quarantine?" I asked Adrian as we followed Carina inside. She ran straight to my old room, hefting the bag of goodies Oya had given her on her shoulder.

"Yes," he answered. "Is it ok that I'm here?"

"What do you mean?"

"You're going to talk to your god, right? Will it be a problem if I'm here?"

"I doubt it," I said.

"It's okay," Carina chirped as she came back into the living room carrying a different bag. "She won't really be *here* so it doesn't matter where you are."

I raised my eyebrows at her. "Am I calling the god without you?"

"Obviously," she said, directing Adrian to the couch. "If he sees me, it will be all 'Where are you and when are you coming back to add your breath to my fire?' and I am *not* letting him make me leave before my date with Oya tomorrow."

Taking a deep breath, I forced myself to sit down next to Adrian. Carina reached into her backpack and pulled out a thick, white candle. Its wick had never been burnt.

"So, Popo is all about his torch," she said. "When he was human, he died holding it in watch over the tomb of his lover, *La Mujer Dormida*. The sleeping woman. The other mountain next to his. It's what keeps him going still—he'll keep watch over her until she wakes, even if that never happens. And our job is to help keep his fire lit."

"Sounds healthy." I held out my hand. "So I light this candle to call him?"

"Kind of," she said, not handing it over. "You don't really need the candle. I don't need to use it anymore, but my dad makes me carry it around anyway just in case. The important thing is to light the torch inside you."

"Inside me?"

"Like think of something you love so much you would watch over it until you die. Something you want to protect. For me it's my dad."

I raised my eyebrows at her, surprised she would admit such a thing—to me or to herself. I was also surprised by how . . . not sinister it all sounded. In my head, this god was a tyrant who kept his witches on a short leash and controlled the way they lived their lives.

But if it were really so short a leash, would he have allowed us to dilly-dally this long on our way to see him? I let out a breath, pushing those thoughts aside. Now wasn't the time to contemplate the goodness of our god. It was the time to pump him for information.

"You can think about Noah," Carina said as she pulled out her matches. "Or his dead mom you loved so much."

I sighed and took the candle from her, my eyes shifting over to Adrian. He was watching me intently.

"I'll find out as much as I can," I said. "Will you stay with Carina while I'm gone?"

Carina rolled her eyes at that, but Adrian nodded. "At this point, you and your god are my best leads," he said. "I'm not going anywhere."

I held out my hand to Carina, and she struck a match for me. Holding the small flame against the candle's wick, I brought the image of the fire into my mind and closed my eyes.

Who did I want to protect? Who would I watch over until the day I died? Or what?

I wasn't sure. Noah, yes. Obviously. But it didn't feel right. I loved him, but soon he would grow up and—if Etty and I did our job right—be able to protect himself.

It felt silly for me to even hesitate with this, given how strong of a compulsion it always was for me to protect . . . well, everyone. But then that was the thing—it was really everyone. It wasn't just the people I knew and cared about. It was the world I lived in. I wanted it to be a good world.

Until the day I died, I would never be able to hold myself back if I had the opportunity to protect *anyone* in this world. And fuck if that wasn't a terrifying thought.

I shuddered as warm air blew over my arms.

I opened my eyes. Obsidian glittered all around me.

12

IT WAS the same cave I'd found myself in what felt like ages ago, when I'd chased Ray just after Becca's death. Now it made more sense that I'd ended up there . . . I'd been feeling pretty strongly protective right after seeing my friend burn on the pole. Protective of her memory, even though I knew she was already dead. Protective of the possibility that there was something—anything —I could still do for her.

Was that how Popo felt about his sleeping woman?

I looked around, remembering the pain I'd felt when I'd landed here before. Too much magic frying my scrye. I didn't have the same sensation now. Was it because I'd gotten rid of my mage mark and fully returned to my status as a witch of the mountain? I didn't have to convince this place that I belonged here this time; it already knew.

Tinkling, scratching noises echoed around me, getting closer and louder, as a horde of black rabbits scurried towards me along the walls of the cave. They bumped their noses into my legs, a few of them climbing to make their way up to my shoulders, where they gently pushed their faces and ears into my neck and cheeks.

They were warm, as usual. Not the delicate warmth of beating little hearts encased in fur, but rather the aggressive warmth of a hot shower scouring you clean.

A sharp pain caught me at my collarbone, and I looked down to see a rabbit sinking its teeth into me. Blood welled up through the puncture and quickly disappeared into the rabbit's head. Not its mouth—it wasn't drinking my blood. It was pushing its forehead against the wound to absorb it.

The walls shook. Rabbits scurried in a chaotic frenzy as the ceiling cracked and flew upwards, pelting me with small pebbles and dust.

When the dust cleared, I found myself staring up into the night sky, stars twinkling their peaceful dance as if each one weren't a great inferno raging far away.

A wisp of smoke traveled up the space, and I lowered my gaze to see a hole in the ground, glowing with light spilling up out of it along with the smoke.

A booming voice echoed from the hole.

"My little flame," it said. "You have returned."

"I . . ." I coughed, fingers coming instinctively to my throat as I cleared it. This voice resonated in my memories. Which ones, I couldn't pinpoint. I only knew that it was there. It had always been there.

"I have tried to forgive you," it said.

"For what?" I asked, unnerved by the implication.

"For leaving me. I know it was not your choice. But nor was your return." It paused. "Not yet."

I swallowed. There it was, the accusation I'd known was coming because it was true. "I don't know you," I said. "Not yet."

It was the only answer I could give. The only answer that wasn't an automatic "fuck off and fuck you for trying to own me." I was here of my own volition. I needed his help. And I didn't know enough yet to really know whether I would regret it.

"You will," he said.

I breathed in. I would know him? Or I would regret it? Probably both.

"Why have you come?" he asked.

"Itztlacoliuhqui," I said slowly, trying to remember the way Ray had said it. "Your rival god. He's been 'stealing witches' and turning them to stone."

"Rival god?" Popo's voice vibrated through the space. "No, there is no such thing."

I blinked. That wasn't what Ray had said.

"We are all one," Popo continued. "Different shapes blooming from the same divine energy. That he wants something different than I does not make him my rival, for there is no competition. There are only our desires, which change shape with us as old gods become new."

Oh, birds. Getting any concrete information out of this philosophizing volcano was going to be like pulling teeth, wasn't it?

"Tell me, my little flame," Popo asked into the silence. "Why does he concern you?"

"Doesn't the witch-stealing concern *you*?" I asked in return. "Who's to say he won't target your witches, if he hasn't already?"

A low hum emanated through the cave, and the rabbits on the walls click-clacked their discomfort as they shifted.

"It concerns me. He would snuff out our fire if he could. He tries but has yet to succeed."

"I need to know how to stop him," I said bluntly. "That's why I'm here."

A thick plume of smoke rose from the hole and drifted up into the stars. The rabbits click-clacked again.

"To stop him," Popo finally said. "You would take on this task? You, who have been gone for most of your brief life?"

"I haven't been gone," I said without thinking. "Just elsewhere.

And I'd want to stop him regardless of that—he's affecting the whole world." I shifted my weight, bunnies scuffling around my feet. "Is anyone else already working on it?"

"No one else has asked." Popo paused briefly, and I waited. "How did you know to ask?"

"The phoenix," I answered. "It warned me. It also doesn't want to see your fire snuffed out."

"This is true," Popo said. "And so, it will be you."

I nodded. The philosophizing volcano was decisive. I liked that. "Good, so . . . how do I do it?"

"This is a complicated question," Popo said slowly. "In order to understand how to undo a god, you must first understand how he came to be."

I sighed and sat down on the rocky cave floor, welcoming the rabbits that scurried into my lap when I did. Why did I get the sense that trying to hurry a god would be more difficult than trying to undo one?

"I'm listening," I said stiffly.

"You think of the sun and the moon and the planets in the heavens as dependable—you, with your lifespan so short you will never see them stray from their course. But they are gods, all of them, just as this mountain is not only a mountain, and they do not always act as you might expect."

He paused for a moment while I scratched a rabbit between the ears, wishing I had Adrian here to make sense of all this. I understood what Popo was saying, but at the same time it didn't mean anything to me. A philosophy lesson on the nature of gods wasn't going to give me something to *do*.

"This god you seek, Itztlacoliuhqui, was not always himself," Popo continued. "Many ages ago, before I lived and died, he was the god of the dawn. Both the morning and evening star, he guided the sun on its path to light the skies. Until one morning, the sun refused to move."

The sun refusing to move. I couldn't comprehend that. All I could picture was a hungover teenager in bed wearing a sun costume and his mom pounding on his bedroom door yelling at him to get his ass up.

"Why?" I asked.

"No one knows. It was a new sun, brother of the god who was meant to shine in his stead. Some say he did not have the confidence to blaze his own path across the sky."

"A new sun?"

"We have had many suns. All gods who have sacrificed to become such."

"Right . . . and this one didn't want to be the sun, so he just refused to move? Wait—" I narrowed my eyes. "The sun doesn't move. It's the earth that orbits around it."

"Move, burn, pull the other gods on their orbits . . . these are unimportant distinctions. He did not do what the sun must do, and so the god of the dawn shot an arrow at him."

I blinked. Dawn picking a fight with the sun. Yet another concept I couldn't wrap my head around. "Wouldn't the arrow just burn up?" I asked.

Popo laughed. "The sun is only the sun as you know it when you perceive it with human eyes and a human mind. It is also always a god, and gods are never invulnerable."

"So, dawn killed the sun? But we still have a sun . . ."

"Dawn did not kill the sun. The sun defended itself, turning the arrow around and shooting it back at his attacker. It struck the god of the dawn in his eye, and he was carried by the arrow to the underworld to be reborn as Itztlacoliuhqui as you know him, god of frost and death."

"An ice god . . . created by the sun?" If that wasn't the definition of ass-backwards, I didn't know what was.

"You may choose to think of it this way."

"Ok . . ." I gave my head a brief shake. It would be a miracle if I remembered all this nonsense later. "How does that help me stop him?"

"The arrow was the catalyst for his rebirth, and so it may be the catalyst for his undoing."

"The arrow shot at him by the sun."

"Indeed. You must find this arrow."

I raised my eyebrows. "How?"

"That, I do not know. Perhaps start in the underworld, for that is where the arrow took him such a long time ago."

"The underworld . . ." I muttered. "You want me to go to hell?" I shook my head again as the volcano hummed. "Wait," I said as a pit formed in my gut. "That's a real thing? There's an underworld? Is it where people's souls go when they die?"

"Not anymore," Popo answered. "It has been abandoned by its old god, and now nameless terrors reign."

I took a deep breath. "Find the arrow in hell guarded by nameless terrors . . . Great, okay. Is that all?"

"You will also need an archer and a bow, I presume," Popo said.

I narrowed my eyes and bit my cheek, trying not to say something I might regret.

"To shoot the arrow," he elaborated.

"Yeah, I got that," I said. "One more question . . ."

The volcano shuddered around me, and the rabbits began to scurry back the way they'd come.

"You have many questions for one who has not yet come to swear your oath."

I clenched my fists, fighting against the urge to rudely point out that I was a little busy trying to save his ass and all his witches from his rival-not-rival. Now more than ever, I needed this god and his power and his knowledge. I might be able to slap on a new mage mark and save *myself* from becoming a petrified "stolen" witch, but I couldn't save all the other witches that way—

and there were too many of them in danger for me to even consider walking away.

I needed Popo's help, and the price for that was letting him think he owned me. Or letting him actually own me. At least for now.

"I'll come as soon as I'm able," I said politely through half-gritted teeth. "But I want to know, is there anything I can do to protect myself and Carina from being stolen by Itztlacoliuhqui? While I'm looking for the arrow?"

"Perhaps," Popo said, "you can—"

And then my gut wrenched. Darkness blanketed my world.

My head was spinning and my skin freezing.

Was this it? Was I turning to obsidian? Was the ice god stealing me away right under Popo's nose?

Long seconds enveloped me. Blood thumped in my ears.

No. I could still hear. And too much time had passed. Unless I was turning slowly like Minnie, I couldn't be petrified.

Someone grunted near me, and another someone growled.

I tried to open my eyes and only managed a slight crack. The world was sideways.

I was sideways. My cheek was smushed against the tile floor in Sassie's bathroom. No wonder I was cold.

People were fighting in the other room, but I couldn't see them.

Something heavy thumped against the floor, and glass shattered. A man groaned.

I tried to move my arms to push myself up, but a sharp pain bloomed in my side. My fingers slipped on the tile, and when I brought them in front of my face I saw red.

Was I bleeding out on the bathroom floor?

I gritted my teeth and pushed through the pain to sit up.

Blinking the blur out of my eyes, I swallowed down a wave of nausea as the world spun.

A blood-stained towel was wrapped around my mid-section. With a wince, I unpeeled it to reveal a bullet hole in my side.

Fuck.

Even with a fully charged phoenix and all my witchy power, I couldn't heal myself if there was a bullet stuck inside me. Not unless I wanted a killer infection and surprise internal bleeding later.

Bracing myself with one hand on the toilet, I reached around to my back and hoped to find an exit wound.

No such luck.

The only good news was that there wasn't actually that much blood. It was a wide smear on the floor, but not a puddle. The wound wasn't gushing, and the towel wasn't soaked.

Still, a trickling gunshot wound would kill me just as surely as a gushing one—it was only a matter of time.

The grunting and smashing and thumping was still going on in the next room, so I let out a slow breath and pulled myself up to stand.

If I ignored the pain, I could fight.

If it was Adrian and Carina out there, I would have to.

Sassie's first aid kit was right where it always was, behind the mirror above the sink. I let it fall onto the counter and dumped its contents out to find the dressings and gauze, then did a quick patch job that was worlds better than the towel.

I reached down for the knife in my boot, but it wasn't there. Grumbling, I picked up the scissors from the first aid kit and pushed open the bathroom door.

There were two bodies down and two bodies up. The down bodies were strewn across the living room floor while the up ones made a wreck of Sassie's furniture. None of them were small enough to be Carina, so I had to assume that one of the people fighting was Adrian.

Had he taken out the two that were down?

My eyes finally focused on him as he went crashing into a wall. He had his chin tucked, so his back took the brunt of the hit and he seemed to bounce off unscathed.

His left arm swept out to the side, catching his attacker's attention while his right arm went in for a stab to the chest.

He was holding my knife.

I growled as he missed his attacker's heart, my knife slashing a new smear of red into the room as it glanced off the man's ribs. This must be a vampire Adrian was trying to stun, or he wouldn't have aimed for the heart at all—he would have gone in with something non-lethal.

The vampire hissed at him and grabbed Adrian's forearm, holding the knife away while he attempted to clutch at Adrian's throat with his other hand.

Neither of them were paying me any attention, so I crept closer to them and tried to work out whether I could get to a vampire heart with this tiny pair of scissors that was my only available weapon.

Probably not.

As I made my way across the room, Adrian managed to curl his free arm around the vampire's chest and twist his arm into a position that wouldn't hold long without someone breaking a bone.

The vampire couldn't move unless he let go of Adrian's wrist.

He did, but then he sent his elbow flying back into Adrian's face, and more blood painted the scene as Adrian's glasses cracked on his face.

It was a flurry of flying limbs as I dropped to the ground and crawled towards them, scissors in hand.

This had to be the most ridiculous way I'd ever entered a fight.

They tumbled to the ground in front of me when I got past the couch, Adrian's eyes finally connecting with mine as his glasses fell away and the vampire pinned his head against the hardwood floor.

What I saw there wasn't like anything I'd ever seen in him.

Rage.

The sweet, peaceful man I'd thought I'd known was gone or buried deep, and in his place was a hard face shining with sweat and blood, snarling with rage.

The slight hint of relief when he saw me wasn't enough to counteract it, and it shook me.

"No," he grunted at me.

No, what?

"No Darcy, don't hurt yourself more trying to save me"? *"No Darcy, don't kill this asshole—he's mine"?*

Or was it *"No Darcy, don't look at me like this"?*

Careful not to touch his attacker, whose head was still facing away from me, I slipped my little pair of scissors into Adrian's hand. With the position they were in, he should have just enough range of motion to make use of the weapon even though he couldn't reach anything bare-handed.

Then I ducked back behind the couch and sucked in a breath.

What was I doing?

My heart pounded. My fingers twitched.

Adrian grunted and something squelched. The attacker yelled an incoherent curse.

I dug my fingernails into my thighs.

Don't get up. Not yet.

Adrian wanted me to give him this one, for whatever reason— and from the look in his eyes and the two bodies already downed, I didn't doubt that he could do it.

Still, all I could think was what if he couldn't . . .

Simeon's face flashed in my mind, the familiar smile returning to taunt me with the memory of the last time I'd seen Adrian grappling with a vampire.

He hadn't won then. And I'd wanted so fiercely to protect him.

I wanted it even more now.

Not only from the vampire currently trying to kill him, but also from whatever was fueling the rage in his eyes.

Something thudded loudly, and then it was silent but for Adrian's labored breathing.

It had to be him breathing.

I gritted my teeth against the pain and pulled myself up using the couch for support.

Adrian sat with his back against the other side of the couch, his attacker prone beside him. The scissors were wedged into the vampire's right eye, blood smeared liberally over his face. One of the DSC's stun devices rested over the vampire's heart, keeping it from pumping. My knife was slick with blood, once more in Adrian's hand. He must have recovered it and gone for the heart after distracting his attacker with the scissors in the eye.

Good move.

"Are you hurt?" I asked without coming any closer.

"Not badly," he said without looking at me.

I wanted to crouch down in front of him, reach out and touch him and let the magic tell me he was really okay—or help me make him so. Instead, I asked, "Where's Carina?"

Adrian looked at me sharply. "She's not with you?" He closed his eyes and leaned his head back against the couch. "I shut her in the bathroom with you and told her to stay out of sight."

In typical Carina fashion, it seemed she hadn't listened.

"I'll find her," I said just as a man's scream drifted through the walls. It sounded like it was coming from the kitchen.

I ran—*no, fuck, ouch.* I doubled over in pain trying to run, a wave of dizziness incapacitating my brain as I stared at the broken glass and blood at my feet.

With a groan, I stood back up and walked, clutching my side, into the kitchen. By the time I got there, the screams had died because the man making them no longer had a mouth.

Carina, standing on a footstool with one of her hands transformed into a dragon claw, was holding his head down onto the lit burner of Sassie's gas stove. His hair and flesh were gone, the remains of his face charred and crispy as smoke wafted up into the hood vent.

His body was still struggling, limbs flailing, but he had no voice left to scream—and apparently he wasn't strong enough to escape from a dragon's clutches.

Carina looked up at me, her eyes wild and unreadable.

Keep her sane, Ray's words echoed in my memory. I didn't want to admit that it might already be too late for that.

I strode forward, grabbing Sassie's boning knife off the counter, and stabbed it into the man's chest without saying anything to Carina.

He stopped flailing instantly. Another vampire.

"Get him off there," I snapped at the dragon. "He's stunned for now but not dead—and you'll burn down the house before you kill him like that."

"I wasn't trying to kill him," Carina said as her claws transformed back into the hand of a little girl. "Just wanted him to tell me who sent him to kill us."

"Is that why you melted off his mouth? Great way to get a guy to talk." I groaned, cringing at my lack of tact as soon as I saw Carina's face fall.

"I didn't think it through completely," she admitted. "But I knew he wouldn't die. I wasn't trying to kill him," she repeated. Her eyes were still wild, but they were wet with tears now.

"Okay," I said, letting out a shaky breath and trying to soften my voice. "It's fine. You kept him from hurting you, and that's all that matters."

She licked her lips and swallowed as she stared at the mutilated vampire lying stunned on the kitchen floor. I could almost see the nausea fighting to creep up her throat.

"Did he tell you who sent him?" I asked, trying to keep her focused.

"No, but . . ." She looked at me, and I nodded. She didn't have to say it.

"I know," I said. It had to be Oya. He must have had us followed here.

"Why would he . . ." she started, trailing off as she looked back down at the body at her feet.

"He probably put two and two together after finding the vampire I killed in his studio."

"Wait, what?" Carina snapped her head up to me, her mouth twisted in confusion. "Not Oya—he's not even a vampire, remember?" Her hands moved to her hips. "What about your crazy ex-boyfriend, the evil vampire mastermind that tried to kill us last time?"

I grunted. It sounded like she might have a point, when she put it like that.

"Is that another . . ." Adrian's voice trailed off behind me, and I turned around to see the few non-bloodied parts of his face go white as he looked at the vampire Carina had barbecued. How well could he even see it, without his glasses? Too well, it seemed. He took a deep breath and then said, "I'm all out of stunners."

"Can I have my knife back?" I asked. It was still gripped tightly in his right hand.

He looked down at it as if surprised to see it there, then held it out towards me.

"Carina," I said as I walked gingerly towards Adrian, "Go get my knife bag, please."

She scurried past me out of the kitchen, her shoes dragging blood into the hallway.

I stepped closer to Adrian than I probably should have—close enough that I could feel the heat coming off him—before I curled my fingers around his and pressed into them to loosen his grip on my knife.

I let a little magic loose when I touched him, unable to resist, and let out an audible sigh when the tingling clarity passed through us and told me he really was okay. He hadn't been hurt any more badly than he looked.

Heat rushed to my face as I realized just how relieved I was. A small part of me had been worried he was hurt even worse than me, that he'd lost too much blood or sustained too much damage to some vital organ and I would be unable to save him.

There were just too many unknowns, walking into a fight that was already halfway done like this. I hated it. Hated that I hadn't been here with my body when they'd needed me.

The knife slipped from Adrian's fingers into mine, and I looked up to find him staring down at me. His gray eyes stood out, shining bright amidst the blood that covered the rest of his face and clumped in his hair.

Part of me loved him less to see him like this—a warrior, so much like me—and another part of me loved him more. Wait. No, I didn't *love* him. Not like that.

I shook my head and broke away from his stare, taking the knife to the kitchen sink to rinse the blood off.

"Thank you," he said from behind me.

"For what?" I asked.

"The scissors. I needed . . ." He stopped as I placed the knife onto a dry towel and shook the water off my hands.

I turned around to look at him, suddenly desperate to hear what he had to say. To understand the rage I'd seen in him earlier.

"I was—" he started, but Carina's voice boomed out from the hallway in the same instant.

"Got the knives!" she yelled.

I bit the inside of my cheek as Carina bounced into the room and hefted my bag onto the counter. I turned back to Adrian, looking him in the eyes.

"We're going to kill these bloodsuckers," I said. "Will you be helping us, or do you need to leave?" Damn, why had that sounded so bitchy? "I'd like for you to stay," I added, and my voice only wavered slightly. "But I'll understand if you can't."

"Are you sure killing them is the best move?" he asked, eyebrows raised. "I can arrest them and question them, find out why they came in the first place and keep it from happening again."

"There are only two people who might have sent them," I said coolly, "and I'll be going after both of them in a very illegal capacity regardless of which one it was. So, no . . ." I gave him a single, slow nod. "I don't want any official record of this incident."

"Ah." He broke away from my stare to look down at his hands, still slippery with blood. His eyes rested on the vampire at his feet, whose charred face was slowly reforming into something that looked human.

After a moment, he looked back up at me and closed the distance between us in only three long strides. His bloody fingers caught the hem of my tattered shirt and lifted it up to my ribs, my skin tingling where his knuckles grazed against it.

The dressing I'd slapped on my gunshot wound was already bloodied, and it stung as Adrian gently turned me to the side to get a look at my unmarred back.

He knew what it meant that there was only one hole in me, and not two.

His eyes traveled back up to my face, and he held my cheek with one hand to keep me looking at him.

"If you promise to tell me everything," he said slowly, carefully, "I'll stay."

13

IN NORMAL CIRCUMSTANCES, if you were to get shot in the abdomen—or anywhere, really—with no exit wound, the worst thing you could do would be to remove the bullet.

Without a skilled surgeon at the ready, you'd only do more damage fishing around for it, and then removing it would make you bleed out faster.

Things were a little different with magical healers like me. Forget eyes in the back of my head—I had eyes in every cell of my body, the ability to send a current of awareness throughout myself and tinker where things weren't right.

I knew already that the bullet hadn't hit anything that would kill me quickly, although it would kill me slowly if I didn't patch it up and pound some antibiotics. Still, the three not-quite-dead vampires decorating my childhood home felt like a more pressing problem to deal with.

Was I extra paranoid about downed vampires popping back up to ruin my life? Fuck yeah. But who could blame me?

Smoke stung my eyes.

I applied light pressure to my wound as I watched Adrian haul the last headless vampire onto the stone firepit that was far too small to serve as a decent cremation device.

He hadn't let me help, insisting that I at least sit down and rest if I wouldn't let him tend to my wound until the vampires were dead.

A small part of me felt bad, pressuring him yet again to break the rules for me. Whether he was still a cop or DSC now, murdering people wasn't a side gig that would go over well if anyone he worked with found out. And I knew how much he cared about doing things by the book.

But I still had to keep Carina off the law-enforcement radar, which meant either not engaging in any conflict or keeping the conflict under wraps.

And beyond that, I was done. Done fucking with vampires and done letting them fuck with me. Any bloodsucker who tried to kill me or mine would end the day in ashes.

Except for the one whose head was still locked in the trunk of my impounded car.

That one would have to wait a bit longer.

Carina stood near the fire, staring into it with a blank face and her hands in the pockets of her oversized yellow hoodie. She hadn't moved while we'd watched the first two bodies burn.

Adrian held up a shovel in front of her. She blinked and then took it, a little bit of life returning to her expression. He said something to her I couldn't hear from where he'd insisted I sit about ten feet away, and she nodded. He was pointing to the vampire's arm, which was dangling over the side of the firepit. It would need to be pushed into the flames, along with all the other limbs, but only after enough of the torso had burned to make room for it.

Keep her sane, Ray's words echoed in my head again.

This wasn't that.

The urge to jump to my feet and do something about it hit me just as a wave of dizziness made me feel like I was swimming in fire rather than watching it burn. My brain was made of bubblegum threatening to pop, and my feet wouldn't move without sharp pain searing through my midsection.

The bullet inside me had shifted when I'd moved, and that slow death I'd predicted would maybe be coming a little faster now.

This must be why Adrian had turned over the reins to Carina as soon as all the heavy lifting was done.

Well, not quite all.

He stood in front of me now, saying something that smushed into my sticky bubble-gum brain without making it all the way through.

Leaning me against him, he pulled me to my feet and then somehow got an arm under my knees to pluck me off the ground.

The sharp pain melded with the comforting warmth of my cheek against his arm, and the gum in my head started to melt.

He laid me down on the couch, and I felt my mouth moving even though I wasn't telling it to.

"First aid . . . in the bathroom. Alcohol . . . ice . . . and coffee."

"Coffee?" I finally heard his voice.

"I need to stay conscious." I blinked as my brain stopped melting slightly; it helped to tell it what it needed to do. "I need to do this."

"I'm here," he said. "I can do it if you just tell me what to do."

"Coffee," I repeated, breathing in against the pain and pushing his chest away with an open palm. "With sugar. Now."

He disappeared obediently, and the world floated in bursts of pink bubbles as I clawed my way to a seated position before he returned with something that smelled fucking amazing.

I sipped the hot liquid and groaned as it hit the back of my throat. Warmth swelled inside me. When the sugar hit my bloodstream, the bubblegum in my head popped softly, and my thoughts began to snap back to their rightful shapes.

Closing my eyes, I breathed in a deep breath and then gulped down the coffee. When it was half-gone and no longer quite as scorching, I handed it back to Adrian and licked my lips.

"I need to ice it," I said, holding out my hand. "Can you wipe the forceps with alcohol while I do that?"

He dropped an ice bag in my hand, and his other hand moved away from my knee to open up the first aid kit. I hadn't even noticed him touching me until then, but the sudden absence of warmth on my knee was somehow more jarring than the freezing plastic he'd given me.

I licked my lips again and peeled the bloodied dressing off my wound, replacing it with the bag of ice. Wincing, I tried to welcome the harsh sting of cold against my broken skin.

Alcohol fumes tickled the inside of my nose, doing away with the remnants of smoke and coffee and planting me firmly back in the world of medicine I'd spent so much time in—but as a healer, not as a patient.

Today I would need to be both.

I held out my hands to Adrian as he finished wiping down the forceps from Sassie's kit. "My hands now."

He frowned at me. "Are you—"

"It would be better to wash them at the sink, but not worth the risk of getting up again."

He looked at me sternly. "You're planning to operate on yourself."

"Yes."

"That can't be necessary," he said. "Isn't this a community of healers? There should be help literally right next door."

As usual, Adrian was right. There were plenty of mages living in the houses surrounding Sassie's who had the skills to fix me up. Problem was, Sassie herself was still in quarantine and I'd been gone so long that I didn't know who else I could trust.

"Not worth the risk," I said. "I can do this as long as I can stay conscious."

"And if you can't?"

I briefly closed my eyes and pressed my lips together. "Ask for Fred," I finally said, "my uncle." I hoped I wouldn't regret it.

Adrian gave me a barely perceptible nod before taking the alcohol wipe to my hands and carefully rubbing it over my skin. Between the fingers, underneath the nails, palms and knuckles and wrists and forearms.

The cool cloth and firm pressure of his hands helped me begin to separate myself from the pain in my abdomen.

He looked me in the eyes when he was done and asked, "How can I help?"

Something crumpled in my chest as he held my stare, eyes soft and sincere despite the blood and bruises all over the rest of his face. So different than he'd looked earlier in the night when he'd been fighting.

"Sit with me," I replied, nodding my head at the space next to me on the couch. "Help me stay in position while I work." *Help keep me grounded through the pain.*

He sighed and slid in beside me, leaning back against the armrest to my right and slipping his left leg around to extend it beside mine. Without saying a word, he gripped underneath my shoulders and pulled me into him, my back lying flush against his chest, my cheek just inches from his throat and my temple brushing against his chin.

"Like this?" he asked. "Or more reclined?"

I fought the urge to nestle my face in the crook of his neck and close my eyes. "Like this is good."

"Do you need a mirror?"

"No," I said. "I'll have a better view from within."

"What about something to bite down on?"

"No, I . . . actually, yes. That's probably a good idea."

His hands crept beneath the small of my back to undo his belt buckle. My heart rate increased.

Maybe this wasn't such a good idea. I needed to be calm and focused, and apparently there was a fine line between relaxed and aroused when it came to this man's effect on me.

I let out a breath, then opened my mouth to accept the folded leather belt Adrian held in front of my face. I bit down when he placed it between my teeth.

No more talking. No more waiting.

Time to go in.

I closed my eyes.

Magic filled my scrye as my other senses came to life, but even so the first thing I noticed was the foreign heartbeat behind me and the warmth that came with it. Adrian's chest rose and fell in long breaths, which I gratefully matched with my own lungs. His arms curved around me loosely, hands resting on the tops of my thighs, giving me a sturdy framework to rest my own arms on while I worked.

I moved into position, forceps in hand, hovering just above my wound as I narrowed my focus to my abdomen.

The low current of magic traveled deep, through healthy tissue to the ruptured small intestines and torn muscles and pooling blood, and then all the way to the small chunk of steel-plated lead that didn't belong there.

I could see it more clearly than if I had eyes on it. I could feel it with every surrounding cell.

I moved my hand towards it.

Muscles in my jaw and my sides and my limbs tensed involuntarily as the metal tips of the forceps met the broken tissue of the wound.

I paused. I had trained for this. Not this, specifically—but I had trained to work through extreme pain.

Where were those breaths? I needed to breathe.

There, with the extra heartbeat and warmth, making it just a little bit easier to hold my own steady rhythm.

I breathed in and out, in and out until the pain became background noise—and then I pressed deeper. The noise got louder.

My jaw clenched, teeth pressing into bitter leather. I paused again.

In and out. In and out. In and out until I could ease the tension and keep moving.

Pink swirls drifted at the edges of my focus, the bubble gum threatening to return and forcing me to narrow even further. I dug deeper, faster now—I couldn't keep this going long.

A strangled whine resonated in my throat as I tore through more muscle to get to the chunk of metal. I didn't need to be careful here. I just needed to keep my head.

The arms at my sides—not mine—held me tighter. Was I moving?

I squeezed my fingers together, praying my hold on the metal wouldn't slip, and yanked unceremoniously.

My inner awareness collapsed in an inferno of searing pain.

Was it out? I couldn't see.

My eyes squeezed shut against the tears as my jaw clenched around a cry in my throat I couldn't get out or hold in.

The hands on my thighs pressed down, a low voice vibrating against my spine reminding me to breathe. I did.

When I opened my eyes, the damn bullet was looking back at me from the grip of the forceps. My fingers holding it were covered in blood, but if they weren't then the knuckles would probably be white.

I let go.

"Fuck," I gasped as I let the leather fall from my mouth. The bubble gum was coming back, this time with an enticing heaviness that wanted me to sleep. The hands on my thighs moved, one to my arm and the other to my hair, gentle and soothing—"No," I grunted.

"No, what?" The voice vibrated against my spine again softly, like a purr.

"Sit me up," I said, gripping the other hands with my own. They were warm and rough. "I need to be awake to fix the damage I just did." He didn't understand. I hadn't explained it to him fully.

But he did as I asked, curling an arm around my chest as he pushed me up.

His frown beckoned to me out of the corner of my eye.

My head swayed forward.

Gods, I just wanted to sleep.

I leaned to the side, falling into him and catching the corner of his mouth with my lips.

"Wake me up," I pleaded against his prickly cheek.

He turned his head, lips connecting with mine tentatively— too tentatively. He needed to be louder to pop through the gum.

I lifted my hands to his neck, fingernails clawing at the back of his head to press him harder against me. There was a groan, and it wasn't mine.

The stinging ache in my gut screamed as I moved; I'd stopped even attempting to baby the wound. But the electric current of arousal was louder still as I relished in the hot liquid motion of his tongue on my lips, the vibration from his throat now more a growl than a purr.

This.

I was alive now. No chance of drifting to sleep in the midst of this powerful *wanting*.

The abundant energy was enough for me to connect with my scrye again without even trying, reluctantly sending some aware-

ness back to my torn-up insides to accomplish the far more practiced task of repairing them so I would stop bleeding.

I worked from the inside out, letting Adrian take the reins of
the other thing, the better thing, while I divided cells and
smoothed over damaged intestinal walls and stitched together
tiny fibers of torn muscles. By the time I was ready to close the
flesh wound, sticky fluid was dripping out of it. A mixture of
blood and bile. I hoped enough of it had gotten out that it
wouldn't give me problems later.

Enough of that.

Back to the more pressing issue of the heart beating against
mine, the soft lips moving roughly against my own, the whimper
coming up from my chest that had nothing to do with pain.

He was the first to break away, fingers grasping the hair at the
back of my head to keep me from hungrily following, eyes travelling down between us.

"Are you . . ." His free hand moved to my hip, where his
fingertips brushed upwards over my blood-stained but smooth
abdomen.

"Fixed it," I said after I'd caught my breath. "Thank you."

His chest heaved with the release of a sharp breath, and then
he ran his eyes over the rest of us. We were both still, neither of
us moving closer together or further apart.

"It's done," I clarified, not sure if it was necessary. "If you were
doing this just to help, I don't need—"

His mouth was back on mine so fast I nearly choked on my
next breath. Blinking away the heat that rushed to my face, I felt
my head fill with a different kind of haze. Not gum, this stuff—
this was more like hot chocolate, full of sweetness and steam and
with the velvety bitter edge of knowing something dreamlike was
real.

Adrian's fingers loosened their grip on my hair, caressing my
scalp briefly before trailing down my neck, down my collarbone,

over my breast . . . lingering on my breast. His thumb brushed against the nipple through my thin t-shirt and bra, and I bit his lip while humming with pleasure.

The vibrations in his throat came back with a vengeance. He liked that. His hand trailed further down, leaving my chest feeling cold and alone. I wanted to tear off my shirt but that would mean moving away from him, and I couldn't do that—so instead I pressed closer.

There was another reason why I shouldn't tear off my shirt, I knew somewhere in the back of my mind, but gods help me I had no idea what it could be.

His fingers stroked down over my abdomen, over the newly mended flesh, and I jerked at the sharp twinge of pain it sent through my nerves.

He hesitated, pulling his hand back just a bit. The flesh where I'd been shot might be healed now, but it would take a while for my nervous system to get the memo.

He didn't know that.

I didn't care.

I moved my hand down over his and pressed it back against my belly, breathing out through my nose to welcome the pain it caused. It only added more depth to the sensations I was swimming in. My nerves were alive and attuned to his touch.

He reached lower, sliding his fingers over the button of my jeans and in between my legs and why—fuck, *why* had I worn the thick denim today?

It still sent my mind whirling, the heat blooming beneath my skin everywhere we touched. My lips released his as I drew in a small gasp, and he squeezed at the nape of my neck while dipping his head in to taste the tender spot below my ear.

It was everything and not enough. The bittersweet haze engulfing me demanded more. Could I magic our clothes off somehow? Then I wouldn't need to stop touching him.

I was digging my hands beneath his shirt, palms running over hard muscle, when ice crashed through the haze and shocked my whole system.

For the second time that night, I wondered if this was it—the ice god pulling the life from my body, stealing away my fire and freezing me in time. If so, he'd picked a fucking terrible time.

But no—once again, I could still hear.

Someone was yelling in my ear.

"That's what you get!" a little girl shrieked with laughter.

I blinked the icy water away from my eyelashes. Adrian rolled away from me and onto the floor, leaving me even colder and taking away the myriad of sensations that had been masking the harshness of the pain in my gut.

"Aaaah . . ." I groaned and cracked my eyes open, staring up into Carina's mad Cheshire grin.

"Serves you right," she yelled gleefully, "for getting me all wet this morning!"

I groaned again, finally putting together what was happening as I picked up an actual ice cube that had settled between my breasts. I held it up in front of me. "I didn't use *ice*," I said.

"Same difference." Carina crossed her arms in front of her. "When you take into account my higher body temperature. Besides," she added, eyeing us both with clear contempt, "you were getting blood everywhere. The cold will keep the stains from setting."

Excuses and bitter retorts popped through my head one at a time. *There was already blood everywhere* and *You don't need to clean up to suck up to my aunt.*

But they were eclipsed by the fact that I was *her* aunt. I was the adult here. And I'd just been getting sexy in full view of an eight-year-old after saddling her with finishing up our dead-body disposal.

I was the worst aunt ever. Even worse than Sassie.

"Sorry," I said, "and don't worry about the blood." I swallowed as she looked at me, her face blank. Had she expected a fight? "You did good today," I added. "You should get some sleep—it's probably late."

"Are we still going to see Oya in the morning?"

Good question, kid. "I'm not sure yet," I said honestly. "Let's discuss it over breakfast? We both need rest before we can make any big decisions."

Carina's eyes flitted briefly to Adrian, who was standing a few feet from me now in the middle of the room.

Yeah girl, I see that side eye.

She at least seemed convinced that I wasn't bullshitting her about not being able to make good decisions right now.

"Okay," she said, "but we'll do breakfast at seven so I have time to get ready—Oya said to be there at nine."

"Deal," I said. "I'll throw ice at you if you're not up by six forty-five."

Carina rolled her eyes at me and stretched her shoulder out, flexing her fingers, before turning around and walking away.

Was that a flash of claw I saw? I shook my head.

"Goodnight," Adrian called after her, but she didn't acknowledge it.

I turned around to look at him with wide eyes. He looked terrible and amazing all at once, with crusted blood flaking off his face and my fresh blood smeared over the front of his shirt. His long sleeves were rolled up to his elbows, muscles in his forearms shifting as he attempted to adjust his hair.

What now? So many things I needed to say to him—so many things I wanted to do to him. Where could I even start?

When I opened my mouth and nothing came out, he stepped up to me and put his hands on my shoulders, fingers squeezing tightly as if he were afraid to move them anywhere else. He leaned down so his head was closer to mine and said into my hair, "We need to talk . . ." He paused while I tried not to huff at such a gross understatement. "And you need to shower," he added.

I snorted into his shoulder. "You need to shower too," I said, "badly." *We could shower together*, I wanted to add, my nerves already relighting at his closeness.

But it wouldn't be right. Not with Carina in the other room, not after what she'd been through today . . . and not with the mountain of impossible, time-sensitive tasks on my plate.

"I need to go to hell and find an arrow the sun shot at the dawn," I blurted out into his chest, cringing at how insane it sounded. I couldn't count on my ability to stay awake or coherent for much longer, and I had promised to tell him everything. Before he could reply, I pulled away from him just enough to look up into his face. "How did I get shot, anyway?"

"Through the window," he said slowly, "before we even knew we were being attacked. Seemed like they were under orders to take you out first—I don't think they realized you weren't conscious."

I nodded, grateful the vampires hadn't been great snipers. As an unmoving target, I was lucky they hadn't landed a head shot. More likely, they'd been ordered to take me alive for questioning.

"An arrow shot by the sun?" Adrian cocked his head at me, the familiar spark of curiosity lighting up his eyes. Now sex would *really* be off the table, until I explained myself.

I took a deep breath and let it out, searching my mind and failing to come up with a way to make it make sense. I hadn't forgotten what Popo had told me—the information was there—but I was already too far gone tonight to relay it.

I weighed my options.

Drag Adrian into the shower with me and fuck him senseless until my brain wakes up enough to tell him what he needs to know.

Something deep inside me was trying hard to get me to

believe this would work. It wouldn't. If I hadn't been woken up enough by the wanting and the ice bath, a hot shower and satisfied bits weren't going to help the situation.

Be a responsible adult and go the fuck to sleep.

"Tell you later," I murmured as I rested my head against his chest, all the gum and adrenaline bouncing around in me now melting into him with everything else. I could no longer tell where he stopped and I started. Were my eyes closed, or were they even eyes anymore?

My body was making my decision for me.

Later, I thought. I was going to have words with this traitorous meat sack of mine later.

14

THE WARM BODY pressing against mine morphed into something cold.

The gum in my brain that had melted away was rubbery now, its remnants making it hard to remember who I even was. The whole of my awareness was a mixture of anger and confusion.

"Darcy," the cold body beneath mine pleaded.

Simeon.

I must be dreaming.

He was calm, staring at me unwaveringly as I pressed my hands harder into his soft neck. He wasn't smiling, but it was there in the twitch of his cheeks and the glint in his eyes.

"You don't want to do this," he said firmly. He wasn't trying to convince me. Just vocalizing something he knew was the truth.

He was right. I didn't want to press any harder. Didn't want to push the magic into him. Didn't want to feel him explode into those ribbons of vampire gore. But why?

"You want to be with me again," he continued, his hands coming up to rest gently underneath my elbows.

No. He wasn't right about that. I didn't want to be anywhere near him. Wished I could get out of this dream and never come back.

"*I* want you to be with me again," he amended, his cheeks softening as his dark eyes turned down and blinked.

There. Something snapped inside me, the short burst of a sob coming out of my throat before I could stop it. That was the truth that had been nagging at me since our last encounter.

He'd wanted me, still. It was the only reason I'd been able to stun him so easily, without a fight.

Despite having become a fanatic of this homicidal god, despite losing sight of all his noble aspirations, he hadn't lost sight of his feelings for me.

And if that could still be salvaged, maybe the rest of him could be salvaged as well.

If I hadn't let his head escape me—if I'd burned him when I'd had the chance—I would never be able to find out.

But what would finding out cost me now? Too much. Time and energy I wasn't willing to give. He didn't deserve it. If only that would stop the possibility from gnawing at my conscience, tormenting me in my dreams.

"Too bad," I said and pushed the sharp wind into him. It sliced at my awareness as the air dropped out of my lungs, the blackness taking me before I could feel the cool spatter of his blood on my face.

A SOFT DRAFT tickled my nose. I scrunched it. I wanted to rub it with my hand, but I didn't know where my hands were.

My eyes were sealed shut, weighted by drowsiness, and the rest of my body felt like it was suspended in a bath of thick, warm pudding. I couldn't move easily, but why would I want to?

I sighed, turning my head a little to the side, and my tickling nose rubbed against something rough.

"Darcy," someone said into my ear.

I grunted in response, pressing my eyelids down even further. I hoped I wasn't still dreaming.

Something warm brushed across my forehead and then down my cheek, then below my jaw and down the side of my neck, just light enough to wake up my nerves and make my skin tingle.

I blinked without thinking about it, bleary eyes landing on Adrian's bloodied shirt, the top few buttons undone to grant me a glimpse of his chest—which I was currently using as a pillow.

His hand rested beneath my ear as he repeated, "Darcy." A little more firmly this time.

I grunted again, wanting to get up even less now.

His fingers ran through my hair against my scalp. He grasped a handful of curls and tugged gently.

"Fuck me . . ." I mumbled. If anyone else had laid a hand on me while I was sleeping, they would be begging for their life right now. It was like my body knew not to pump me full of adrenaline just because I could smell him. It knew I was safe.

Which was terrifying. Because I was never safe.

"We need to talk first," he said without releasing his hold on my hair.

Ha ha, I thought, shifting my body in an attempt to find all my limbs. But he wasn't laughing. And if I was going to be honest, neither was I.

"It's six AM," he said, his voice low.

I blinked again, stretching my fingers and toes after finding my limbs entwined with his. Was he saying there was enough time for me to have my way with him before waking up Carina?

"We need to talk and clean up before breakfast," he said, dashing my hopes to the ground. But maybe, if we were quick . . .

I ripped off the bandaid, sitting up forcefully even though one of my legs was still pinned underneath his.

"Ahhh," I winced, face contorting in a grimace as I clutched my side.

Adrian was sitting up next to me by the time I breathed out and looked over at him. "Are you still hurt?" he asked.

"Not really," I said in a strained voice. "Still need antibiotics— but even if I'm fine, the pain won't go away for a while. That's how it works with magic."

Narrowing my eyes, I reached out and touched his face. There were still some flecks of dried blood scattered about, but enough of it had rubbed off that I could see his skin underneath.

"I must have healed you at some point," I said softly, a little unnerved that I couldn't remember doing so. Using magic for any reason wasn't something I ever wanted to do without thinking about it enough to remember it.

"Definitely still stings," he said, but he made no move to pull away from me.

Our eyes met. I licked my lips.

"About what happened—" I started, but he shook his head quickly. I raised my eyebrows.

"As much as I'd love to discuss what happened—what's been happening—between us, there are more important things we need to talk about." He lifted his hand and placed it over mine, pulling it down from his cheek. It might have felt like a rejection except for his thumb rubbing my palm as he set it down between us.

"That's not what I was going to say." I tilted my head, remembering further back in the night than either of us probably wanted to. "I was going to ask about the . . ." I glanced around, nodding my head at the congealed pools and smears of blood on the floor. Then I held my hand up and pretended to stab him in the face while making a high-pitched sound in my throat. "With the scissors, you know."

He caught my wrist, gripping a little tighter than I expected, and I stopped the fake stabbing. His eyes hardened.

"That's . . ." He shifted his jaw and gave a subtle shake of his head. "Still. More important things than that."

I nodded, frowning at the memory of seeing him so full of fury. I twisted my arm out of his grasp, and he pulled his hand away as quick as though I'd burned him. I resisted the urge to rub my wrist as I looked at him—the attentive gray eyes focused on me, the strong arms that had held me steady last night . . .

It was like he'd been another person entirely for one brief moment, fighting that vampire. And right now, understanding who that person was felt like the most important thing in the world.

I mean, maybe only because fucking him was off the table. But still.

"Fine," I said. "But we're going to talk about it later. Tit for tat. If I tell you everything, you do the same."

He nodded slowly. "You still haven't told me anything," he reminded me. "Except that you're going to hell? For an arrow?"

"Right," I said as I stretched my arms out, feeling itchy and crusty and gross.

"An arrow shot by the sun?" he prompted.

"Exactly." I smiled. "See? I told you the important part." At his frown, I shook my head and put my hand on his knee. "Just kidding." I closed my eyes, willing myself to remember what Popo and the phoenix had told me. "Remember the ice god that's causing all the petrification?"

"Itztlacoliuhqui," he stated without missing a beat. It took effort not to call him a teacher's pet.

"What the phoenix told me, that he's 'stealing' witches from other gods—or stealing their power. Gathering strength for something. That's still the only thing I know for sure."

Adrian nodded and pulled out his phone. He started tapping at it, probably writing down everything I was saying.

"When I asked how to stop him, Popo just told me the guy's origin story." I relayed it as best I could, the god of the dawn trying to keep the sun in line and his attack backfiring, landing him in hell to be reborn as this new god of icy death. "Popo doesn't know how to stop him," I emphasized. "But he thought finding the arrow would be our best bet."

"The dawn and the sun . . ." Adrian muttered, still tapping at his phone. He looked up at me, intense focus in his eyes. "Anything about the moon?"

"No." I shook my head slowly. "Why?"

"It's what Minnie said to you, right? It was in the report." He looked down at his phone again, tapped again, and read, "'The moon brought this death.' She said that after touching the petrified corpse in the garden."

"She did," I confirmed. "No idea what that was about."

"Okay," he said. "What else?"

I shrugged. "I think that's it."

Adrian lowered his phone, looked up at me and laughed.

Warmth fluttered in my belly. It had been a long time since I'd seen him laugh. It wasn't even a full laugh, just a half smile and slightly crinkled eyes, one cheek lifting and a promise in his stare that we would laugh together again sooner or later.

"Darcy," he said, reaching his hand out to pull up my ruined shirt. He stopped when he got to the bottom of my bra, running his thumb over the spot near my ribs where a lava rock had taken a chunk out of me. His other hand grasped me at my elbow, running up my arm where another rock had hit. "What about these?" he said. "And the fact that your clothes were soaked in blood before we even got here last night? And what are you doing taking Carina to Oya's auditions in the first place? You said you'd tell me everything. I meant everything."

The warmth fluttering in my belly turned into a hollow pit.

The phoenix and its lava rocks of death—I could tell Adrian about that, easy.

But why was I messing around taking Carina to auditions? Well, that was because I needed to assassinate Oya—because I'd traded tasks with Minnie's murderous wife—because she knew how to find Simeon—because I needed to get Simeon dead and out of my nightmares for good.

I swallowed and nodded, looking off to the side. "It's a whole complicated mess," I said, then added quickly, "and I'll lay it all out for you, I promise." I took in a breath and looked Adrian in the eyes. "But we should maybe do that over drinks—lots of drinks—once we get done saving all the witches in the world from becoming statues, yeah?"

Adrian held my stare for a moment, not saying anything.

"And you can tell me about the scissors?" I added.

His lips parted, and he breathed out. "Yeah," he finally said. "Lots of drinks."

"Great." I shifted and planted my feet on the ground. "Gotta go shower. There's another bathroom in there." I pointed to Sassie's room and then leaned over, my body instinctively moving to kiss him goodbye. *Fucking awkward.* I stopped myself inches from his face, narrowing my eyes. My hand extended and gave him a single pat on the head. "Okay," I said, and then I retreated into the bathroom as quickly as I could.

TWENTY MINUTES LATER, I emerged wrapped in a towel to find the wood floors spotless. The living room rug was rolled up and leaning against the couch, which was the only thing still stained with blood. No one was around, but I could hear the water running from Sassie's shower.

Adrian had cleaned up the mess before taking care of himself. But he'd been the one that caused most of it, and somehow I didn't think this attempted scrubbing of the scene was a selfless act. He didn't want the reminder of what had happened.

Adjusting my towel to make sure it was tight enough to hold on its own, I went to the kitchen and made myself a cup of coffee. Then I filled another cup with ice. Not enough to be a real nuisance—just enough for teasing Carina. All my clean clothes were in the room she was sleeping in, so I'd have to wake her up before getting dressed.

I looked at the time on my phone. Six forty-one. Close enough.

I'd only taken two steps into the hall when the doorbell rang.

Shit.

I tiptoed my way to the door, not quite remembering where the creaky floorboard was around here. When I peeked through the peephole, I held my breath and gripped the towel tighter.

The man outside was wearing a faded brown cowboy hat, the same one I'd pretended was a boat for my stuffed animals when I was a child.

"Fred," I said under my breath. My uncle. Sassie's husband. Ex-husband? Whatever. I should have known. He was the only mage in this damn place who was a morning person.

Had he seen the smoke coming from our firepit last night? Had he seen the blood-soaked patio out back this morning? Either way, if I didn't answer the door, he was going to stir up more trouble.

I ducked into the coat closet and pulled out Sassie's long rain jacket.

Wrapping it around me, I let the towel fall. Then I twisted the doorknob and swung the door open.

He looked up at me and opened his mouth, but nothing came out. How many years had it been since he'd seen me? I swallowed.

"Do I look that different?" I asked, the ice in my hands somehow travelling up into my throat.

He cocked his head, still peering at me silently. His brow furrowed. "You naked under there, little D?"

"Yes," I said, quietly fuming at how easy it was for me to take slow, even breaths right now. Here was another man who only had to let me hear his voice to convince my body he was no threat—and yet, it wasn't up to the little girl inside me to decide those things anymore.

"No slip-ups then," he said with a shake of his head as he stepped in and crushed me against his chest, his arms wrapping tightly around me. "Don't want to see something I shouldn't."

I took a deep breath, which was shaky because of how tightly Fred was squeezing me, and cleared my throat.

He released me and stepped back, nodding slowly. "Were you going to tell me you were back?" he asked.

"I'm not back," I said. "Just passing through." I shook my head. *Were you ever going to talk to me again if I hadn't come? Would you have been happy to forget I ever existed?* "He wanted more children," Sassie's words floated in my head.

"Even more reason to come say hi," he said, "if you don't know when you'll get the chance to do it again."

"I was going to," I said. Was it a lie? I didn't know. "It's been hectic."

His face darkened. "You know anything about what's happening at the clinic?"

"Yes," I said again. He waited, staring at me, but I didn't elaborate.

Footsteps creaking on the floorboards behind me saved me from having to think of what to say next. I turned my head to see

Adrian walking up, fully dressed in fresh clothes with a DSC emblem on his shirt. He must keep extras in his car. Finally free of all the blood, his face looked perfect—no trace of the injuries he'd sustained in the fight.

"Who's this?" Fred asked while Adrian stayed quiet.

I didn't answer. Instead, I turned to Adrian and held out the cup of ice. "Go wake Carina for me?"

He nodded, took the ice, and turned on his heel. I turned away from him reluctantly, looking back at Fred.

What did I have to say to this man?

If I weren't dealing with what seemed like a looming witch genocide, maybe I'd ask him about his life. Find out what he was doing off in that other house away from Sassie. Why he hadn't tried to contact me even though he knew she was the reason I'd left. Why he'd decided so late in life that he wanted a family. Whether he had really considered me such.

But I *was* dealing with a looming witch genocide. And I'd gone and made myself back into a witch. I'd left not only Fred and Sassie but also the protection they'd offered me, and just being here—spending time with them—wouldn't buy it back.

"Would you happen to know anything about how to get to hell?" I asked.

He stared at me for a long moment. I half expected him to start laughing, but instead he took off his hat and hung it on a hook by the door, rubbing his messy gray hair underneath.

He came close to me and put his hands on my shoulders. I fleetingly wondered whether taller women constantly had men touching their shoulders like this. He was looking at me like he'd looked at me before telling me our cat had died when I was nine. I didn't move.

"You're in the shit, huh?" was all he said.

Heat rushed to my face. My eyes stung. What the actual fuck.

I blinked, praying no tears would escape, and turned my head away from him to look back down the hallway.

Adrian was coming back. Moving too fast.

Something was wrong.

"She's gone," he said, and I tore myself free from Fred's grasp.

I ran past both of them without saying a word. The door to my old room was already slightly open, so I kicked it until it swung open all the way and crashed against the wall.

Carina wasn't here, just like Adrian had said. But that wasn't the worst part.

The worst part was that the bed was still perfectly made, just the way I'd made her make it yesterday morning before we'd headed off to the audition.

Carina wasn't just gone—she'd been gone all night.

15

"Just take me to my car," I said as I hefted my bag of weapons into the back seat of Adrian's van.

"It will be faster if we go straight there," he protested.

"*We're* not going there," I said. "I am."

Fred cleared his throat, making us both glance at him. He was already sitting in the passenger seat. It would be a fun ride to the impound lot for him, I supposed.

I gripped Adrian's arm, my fingers barely making it halfway around it, and turned him away from Fred. I lowered my voice. "Remember those drinks we need to have?" He stared down at me, eyebrows raised. "Until we have them, you'll be more a hindrance to me than a help where Carina is concerned."

Adrian tilted his head at me, leaning into my hand. "I can kick this guy out of my car right now and you can say whatever you need to say while we drive." I took in a breath and opened my mouth to speak, but he leaned even closer and said, "Darcy. You don't need to be drunk to—"

"I know," I said quickly. "I know. But we can't afford to both get tied up in this. Carina is my responsibility—I have to go after her. And none of it will matter if she and I turn to stone. I need you to do what you do best."

"And what's that?" he asked.

"Research." There was that half smile of his again. He didn't bother arguing with me because we both knew I was right. "See if you can find anything about the arrow we're looking for, possible entrances to the underworld, maybe anything Popo didn't tell me about Itztlaco—"

"Itztlacoliuhqui," he said, correcting my heinous pronunciation.

"Right. Him." I swallowed as a heavy feeling shifted inside me. "And call Ray. He should already be looking into Itztla . . .coliuhqui, but he might not know about the arrow—and there might be something he knows that we don't."

"Should I—"

"Don't mention Carina," I said. "He doesn't want to know. Not until I find her."

Adrian nodded. I moved to turn away from him, back to the car, but he snuck his hand around my back and yanked me towards him. I nearly punched him before I realized what he was doing, my forehead bumping up against his as he bent to get his face level with mine.

Fucking awkward, I thought once again. But it didn't stop the rush of heat that flared through my spine when he dug his fingers into the small of my back, staring into my eyes.

"Call me as soon as you're done," he said. "I need you with me."

You what? I thought, frozen in his grasp.

"So I'm not constantly distracted wondering whether you've turned into a Darcy statue and how much I'm going to have to pay to get it shipped back home in one piece."

I let out a short chuckle. "I'm not even going to picture that—"

He pressed his mouth against mine, stopping me mid-speech

178 | ERIN EMBLY

with a hard kiss that was over before I could tell myself I didn't have time to enjoy it.

Then he was gone, walking around the van to get into the driver's seat, leaving me standing awkwardly in front of the open door while Fred did his best to avoid eye contact.

"Birds," I muttered, though I didn't quite know why. A tumultuous mess of emotions was roiling in my stomach, and I didn't know when I would have the time or energy to spare for untangling them.

I got into the car, shut the door behind me, and quietly set to work hiding knives in every nook and cranny of my outfit.

Fred's eyes were on me when I finished and looked up. He had his head turned just enough to peer at me where I was sitting on the other side of the van, behind Adrian. The look on his face wasn't one I could recall ever seeing on him before.

"This . . ." He gestured to the less-full bag of weapons at my feet. "This is what you do now?" I could see a more loaded question hovering behind his sad eyes. *This is what you left us for?*

"Weren't you the one always telling me I should do something I love?" I shot back.

"Violence is what you love?"

"Yes," I said, surprising myself a little in how much I really meant it. I could easily have said no, argued that violence was a means to an end—and it was. "It's what lets me keep the people I care about safe." That was true. But I also loved the fight—the sharp, cold steel between my fingers, the adrenaline in my veins, the movement and the challenge and the blood.

"Violence is never the answer," Fred said. "If I had known . . ."

"What?" I snapped, digging my knuckles into the leather seat. "If you'd known what I'd end up doing, would you have backed Sassie and tried to force me into medicine?"

"Of course not," he said evenly. "Don't you realize you're doing exactly what she wanted?"

I narrowed my eyes. What was he getting at?

He chuckled to himself, shaking his head. "You are. And you're both too bullheaded to realize it."

I bit my tongue, wanting in equal parts to run away from this conversation and to jump in headfirst. Now was not the time for either.

Ignoring Fred, I looked down at my phone and tried to call Carina for the umpteenth time. No joy. I crushed my fingers into the sides of the phone and let out a breath.

After a glance up at Adrian, his eyes on the road, I texted Dirk:

What exactly do you need before I can let O go?

The three dots danced a fleeting dance in response. He was probably pissed I'd texted about Guardian business. But I'd made it vague enough. Hadn't spelled out Oya's name or exactly how much I wanted to kill the bastard. I was the picture of discretion.

Adrian stopped the car, and I looked up. We were at the lot.

Both men were twisted slightly in their seats, looking back at me expectantly.

"Yeah," I said. "Thanks for the ride."

I took a deep breath and reached up front with my left hand to give Adrian's arm a quick squeeze. *Not mad at you*, I tried to convey silently despite how bitchy I knew I must look right now.

Then I grabbed my bag and slid out of the van, not giving either of them a chance to distract me any further.

POPO'S BUNNIES swarmed me once I was back in my car, climbing onto my lap and into my hair and scurrying around at my feet. It was all I could do not to step on any of them while I sped my way to Oya's studio.

Their warm little bodies pressed into mine, ever so slightly vibrating with energy. Were they lending me their fire, or were they basking in mine? They hadn't acted this way before the phoenix's bird bath.

I glanced at my phone as I pulled into the parking lot. Still nothing from Dirk.

Gripping the steering wheel tightly, I let out a growl.

I wanted to run in there and kill every vampire or ostrich in my path to Carina. Then I wanted to throw her in a dragon sack and haul her back to Sassie's—no, back even further than that, safe with her father somewhere before she'd been made into a killer.

You think that like it's such a bad thing, a small voice in my mind taunted. Hadn't I just admitted I enjoyed being a killer, myself? It was different, though. Carina was too young to process the nuance. And she had been forced to kill innocents.

I couldn't save her from what had already happened. Not by brute force, at least. But I could try to save her from whatever she was about to do.

It couldn't be anything good. The possibilities tumbled through my mind. Either Carina had snuck out last night on her own, or she had been taken. Either way, she'd have ended up with Oya—because even if Simeon had been the one who'd sent the assassins, he'd have had no reason to go after Carina specifically. And if she was with Oya, it was only a matter of time before shit hit the fan.

But I couldn't barge in and kill Oya or blow up his trafficking outfit until I got the go-ahead from Dirk. My Guardian mission was still to protect him long enough to get them the information they needed on his buyers.

Tapping my fingernails rapidly on the dash, I glanced at my phone again and then stuffed it in my pocket. I got out of the car and walked around to the trunk, which I opened just enough to verify that the vampire head I'd tossed in there yesterday was still there.

Good.

I stuck my hands in my pockets instead and forced myself to walk calmly inside the building.

No one stopped me until I got to the hallway just outside his dressing room where we'd been last night. One of the vampires who had dragged my unconscious phoenix-fried ass to Oya was here now, standing outside his door.

Just my luck, it was the big, muscly one.

"Hi." I forced a smile. Should I have said good morning? I never remembered to say good morning.

"Hi," he grunted. I supposed vampires also were not fond of this time of day.

"I'm looking for my niece," I said. "The girl I was here with last night? She may have come early to our appointment."

My heart pounded in my chest as the big vampire eyed me. I couldn't stop it. It was such a slim chance that Carina was actually here and nothing was amiss. She'd been gone all night, after all. And it was fifty-fifty that Oya was the one who'd tried to have us killed.

"Haven't seen her," the big vampire eventually said.

"Ah." I swallowed. "What about your boss?"

"What about him?"

"Is he here? Can I talk to him?"

"No." The big vampire shifted in his stance, and the hair pricked up on the back of my neck. He was preparing to fight me.

"Which one?" I asked. "He's not here or I can't talk to him yet? I do have an appointment."

"No," he said again. "All appointments canceled today."

"Hmm," I said. That was interesting. I stretched out my fingers and licked my lips, ready to reach for a knife. If I did, I might have to kill every vampire in this building right now. If I didn't, how would I know whether Carina was even here? She could have gone to find Oya somewhere else last night, like I had the night I'd watched him pick up the tree girl.

I should have checked his social media in the car.

"Well, have you seen my phone? I had it with me last night and haven't seen it since you and your friend were dragging me around."

"No," he grumbled, relaxing his stance just a bit.

I did my best to look distressed. "Can you check in there for it? I really need it—I need to call my niece."

"No." He tightened his fists. "You need to leave."

"I didn't want to have to do this . . ." I sighed and tilted my head at him. He tensed. "You're Oya's security, right? It's your job to make sure no one hurts him, stalks him, annoys him . . . bugs his dressing room by hiding their phone in it?"

He grunted.

"What will make him madder, do you think?" I asked, inching my way closer. "You going in there to find my phone—or you knowingly leaving my recording device in his personal space?"

The big vein on his temple pulsed. His jaw shifted. A flash of fangs wanting to come out to play. I didn't blame him. I'd been in his position before, and I was being really fucking annoying.

I gave him a moment, staring at him with big eyes, until he grunted again and turned to push the door open.

I smiled and craned my neck to look inside.

No Oya.

No Carina.

But at least this big fucker was now out of sight of the cameras in the hall.

He turned back towards me, the open door resting against his side. "Where is it?" he asked. When I stepped forward, he held out a hand to stop me and shook his head. "Where?"

"I *think* it's over there, on the desk with the form I had to sign . . ." I squinted.

He turned his back to me.

Knife in hand, I pounced.

He sidestepped just as I got within stabbing range, and my knife slashed across his arm instead of sinking into his back.

His head jutted towards me, mouth open wide, fangs gleaming as he hissed. Those teeth seemed longer than usual, even for a vampire.

I narrowed my eyes at him, noting the faint edges of red lining his eyes and the gums above his teeth. The telltale sign of a new vampire. If he had just been turned recently, he might be easier to kill—new vampires didn't heal as fast as the old ones.

His fingers gripped the wound on his arm, blood welling up between them and dripping onto the floor.

I shifted on my feet and pounced toward him again, knife slashing intentionally this time. He swatted me away, but not fast enough.

By the time I crashed to the ground and looked up, he was gurgling and trying to clasp his fingers over the gash I'd made in his neck.

I got to my feet. I'd need to be relentless if I was going to try to bleed him down.

But I paused, standing back and blinking, when his skin started to turn gray. That wasn't something I'd seen happen to any vampire before.

And was he getting even bigger?

My mouth twisted into a deep frown as I pulled out a second knife.

Okay, getting bigger was an understatement. He was getting fucking huge.

So huge that he might be able to kill me just by flicking a wrist because there wasn't enough space in this room for me to dodge him.

Except he didn't have wrists anymore.

He had . . . fins?

I darted forward, sinking my knife into his side and then pulling it out quickly to step back. I couldn't back away far enough quick enough, though, and he smacked me to the side with one of his fins.

I flew across the room and slammed into the wall.

My limbs froze at the impact, spine vibrating in agony, and it was all I could do to tell my feet to carry my weight when I slid down to the ground.

I looked down at my knife. It was six inches long, and there was no blood on it. But I'd gotten it in him down to the hilt.

What gives? He waddled towards me awkwardly, and I spotted the hole I'd made in him. A spongy whitish substance was just poking through beneath the torn leathery gray skin.

My legs finally listened to me, and I dashed to the door. The vampire was already at least ten feet wide and still growing, those fangs now each longer than my head.

He finally seemed to solidify as I backed out of the doorway and he slammed into it, his girth punctuated in the middle of the opening by a whiskered face with dopey-looking round eyes.

And those fangs? They were tusks.

This guy had just turned into a walrus.

And he was too fat to fit through the doorway.

Lucky me.

What was it with this place and ridiculous animal shifters masquerading as vampires?

I put my knives away when my back hit the wall of the hallway and the walrus roared at me, unable to move forward any further.

I eyed one of the security cameras down the hall. My knives couldn't penetrate the blubber, but I could maybe rip out one of those tusks and stick it through his eye. If I tried it, I'd just be giving the rest of Oya's people in this building more time to come get me.

The walrus roared again, its jowls flapping as its fishy, bloody breath blew in my face.

I couldn't help but think it was a little bit cute when the roar ended in a rumbling whimper that was distinctly doglike.

What is wrong with me? I shook my head and took off, knowing it was only a matter of time before the vampire-walrus turned back into a vampire-person who could walk through doors.

Vampire-walrus. Oh my god.

I ran out of the building all the way to my car and shoved away the black bunnies that had piled up in the driver's seat in my absence.

My phone rang just as I had finished backing out of my parking spot and put the car in Drive.

I let it ring and stepped on the gas.

It was still ringing once I'd gotten out of the parking lot and started breathing again, so I picked it up.

Dirk.

I answered the call and held the phone to my ear, not bothering to mess with the car's speakers.

"They have a walrus," I said, still a little out of breath.

"It's done," he said in response.

"What? What's done?" Had he not heard me about the walrus?

"We have the evidence we need. Our plant was able to retrieve it this morning. Your protection services are no longer required." He paused, and his voice got a little lower as he shed the formalities. "You make out any assassination attempts?"

"No," I said as an odd feeling ran through me. They'd gotten the evidence. But who exactly was "they"? And why had they just managed to retrieve the evidence this morning if they'd been undercover here for months?

"But you saw a walrus," Dirk said flatly.

"Yes," I said, still thinking. Could it have something to do with Carina? Had the events of last night created a break in Oya's usual routine that had given Dirk's plant an opening to get what they needed?

"Did you kill it?" Dirk asked.

"What?" I shifted my shoulders. "No. Do you have any idea how hard walruses are to kill?"

"So you tried to kill it."

"I—"

"Darcy, why are you moonlighting as an assassin?"

Birds.

"Do I not pay you enough? No, don't answer that," he said quickly before I could remind him he wasn't paying me dick in liquid cash. All my Guardian funds were tied up in obscure investments to ensure discretion. "The real question is what will you give me to keep me from telling Etty?"

"You wouldn't."

"You bet your pretty little ass I would. You left her high and dry to take care of your club and your kid, and she let you because she thought you were taking some family time. Turns out you're just working somewhere else—and chasing out more danger. She's gonna be pissed."

"They're hers, too," I said. "The club and the kid." I shook my head. I was getting defensive. "You can't tell her without outing yourself. Otherwise how would you know?" I groaned as soon as I asked that dumb question. Dirk could easily make up some shit about finding out through police channels. "Fine," I said before he could point it out himself. "Just don't tell her, *please*. I'm going to tell her all about it when I get back home and I don't want her worrying about misleading out-of-context speculation before then."

Dirk was silent on the other end. Where were his near-constant taunting chuckles? I pulled the phone away from my ear and looked at it to make sure the call was still connected.

"Well," he said finally, and I put the phone back to my ear. "That just might be the most mature thing I've ever heard you say, little lady."

I scowled and gripped the steering wheel tighter. There was no part of me that didn't want to punch Dirk for that patronizing comment, but it was kind of true.

This whole *having friends and keeping them* thing was new to me, but I was learning.

"I gotta go, dickwad," I said.

"With the moonlighting," he said, "which I just accidentally gave you the green light on."

"Sure," I said.

"Burn him to a crisp," Dirk said and then hung up.

I licked my lips, pulling over into a packed supermarket parking lot. If anyone was following me, I'd be less of a sitting duck in here.

Pulling up Oya's social media feeds, I took a deep breath and glanced over at the empty passenger seat. The candy wrappers had all been herded to the floor, and a single obsidian bunny sat staring at me from Carina's usual spot.

"What would the little dragon do?" I whispered softly as I flicked through the videos he had posted last night. My heart beat faster as the clear answer drowned out all the useful thoughts in my head.

Burn him to a crisp.

16

OYA STOOD above the twinkling city lights of Los Angeles at night. Even on the small screen of my phone, it was beautiful. The lights blended together and pulsed, giving the impression of a neon heartbeat with veins running throughout a massive metropolitan beast. Far in the distance, the tall halo of Celestial glowed.

He had some new recruit under his wing, cozying up to the teen boy so they would both fit in the frame while he mooned about whatever the latest fake hero action had been. Probably saving someone from a drug overdose or black-market vampire blood, given the location of Griffith Observatory. Southern California's gateway to the cosmos, supposedly. Except when Oya's camera tilted up, I couldn't spot a single star in the sky. The light from the city below was far too bright.

I frowned as the video ended—the last one he'd posted last night. The time stamp indicated it had been posted while Carina was still burning vampires in Sassie's backyard. Would she have seen it and come to look for him at the observatory?

If she had, there was no chance they would still be there. Even if Oya really wasn't a vampire, I couldn't see him staying outdoors to watch the sunrise and then lingering for a slow breakfast.

I sighed and brought up the directions to Oya's house on my phone. One good thing about this city was that it was never hard to figure out where any celebrities lived. But it also meant that Oya's house would be the hardest place for me to get to him—it was sure to be smothered in guards.

Hopefully he only had one vampire-walrus.

My phone rang after I'd been driving a few minutes, and Etty's voice came through loud and clear when I answered the call.

"Darcy."

It sent an uncomfortable twang through my chest, both comforting and unsettling at the same time. I missed her, and this was the first time I'd heard her voice since I'd left her a few days ago in DC.

Had I really left her "high and dry" like Dirk had said? Did she see it that way?

"What's up?" I asked. "Are you doing okay?"

"Me?" she hummed. "Yes, okay. But Noah hurt his foot."

"His foot? How? Is it bad?" I wanted to ask a million more questions. My mind was busy racing around the inconvenient fact that between me and Etty, I was hands down the best one to be there in the event of any sort of injury or medical emergency.

"It's . . . weird," she said. "Hard to say how bad it is. Don't know how it happened, either. He just woke up this morning and it looked all raisiny."

"Raisiny?" I questioned.

"Shriveled up," she clarified. "Wrinkly and dry. He can't move it."

That . . . really didn't sound good. I scrunched up my brow as I glared at the road in front of me.

"Anyway, I know you're busy," she continued over my silence.

"The really weird thing is that it seems similar to what Baz has been freaking out about lately. I'm on my way to the prison now to see for myself, and I'm taking Noah to a specialist later today. I just wanted to keep you in the loop because, you know . . ."

I breathed out, frustrated. Yes, I was busy. But I was never too busy to care about something like this. As for what I could do about it . . . that was another question. "It sounds like you have it covered for now," I said reluctantly. "Can I talk to him?"

"He's at school," Etty reminded me.

"Right, of course." I frowned, something in my stomach fluttering.

"He's handling it well, though," Etty went on, clearly trying to reassure me. "Was all excited about the cane I made him so he could walk around without falling on his face."

"I'll bet he was," I said.

"I'll let you know as soon as I know more," she replied, not waiting for me to say anything else.

"Thank you, Etty," I choked out, not knowing what else to say. I owe you. I miss you. What would I do without you? "I'll be back as soon as I can."

"Sounds good," she said. "But don't you dare come back without some kinda fish for the little one. He won't shut up about how excited he is for the damn fish."

I couldn't help but smile. "You got it," I said just before she hung up. And on to the ever-growing to-do list in my head, right next to "fish for Noah," I added: "sell my soul to get Etty an *epic* thank-you gift for taking such good care of him."

WHEN I PULLED up to the spot my GPS told me was Oya's address, it was so heavily surrounded by foliage that I couldn't see any part of the house itself. I took in as much as I could as quickly as I could and kept driving past it without slowing down.

After parking on a busier street a few blocks away, I licked my lips and did my best to shove Noah and Etty out of my mind so I could properly battle with indecision about what weapons to take with me. If I were just going to be fighting vampires, it would be knives, knives, and more knives. It took precision to get to their hearts, and I wasn't the greatest aim with a firearm. But Oya himself had shown me he was a shifter, and now I knew at least one of his guards to be one as well. What other deadly animals might I encounter in his arsenal?

Probably more than I was prepared to fight with mine. I had one short sword in my bag, and it wasn't silver. I slung the scabbard over my shoulder anyway. I didn't have any rifles with me, so the handgun would have to do. I tucked it into the denim jacket I'd slipped on despite the heat.

I stepped lightly through the outskirts of Oya's forested estate, keeping my eyes only partially open and my scrye on high alert. By focusing on the ambient magic around me, I could identify potential adversaries from further away. Even regular humans with no sense for channeling magic disrupted the flow in the ambience. I'd only done this once or twice because, for most of my life, it was the kind of thing that wore me out quickly. It was just another way the magic could fail me if I let myself rely on it. Now, though . . . it was different. Since aligning with Popo, and even more so since the phoenix took its bird bath, I knew somehow that the magic wouldn't fail me. So I might as well make the most of it.

If there were cameras, I had no way of identifying them— except the years of experience that told me where I would put them if I were in charge of Oya's security. But if I were in charge of his security, I would have had these trees burned down long ago. They were great for privacy, but poor visibility went both ways.

He was clearly more afraid of paparazzi than assassins. Maybe he wasn't the one who had sent the assassins after me, then—you know what they say about people in glass houses throwing stones.

Or maybe he was just an idiot.

I was about ten feet away when a tingling flush of energy touched the edges of my scrye. Magic radiated off of two beings on the other side of the tall, vine-covered wall in front of me. And another two beings lurked on opposite sides of a large area behind them.

None of them were regular humans. Beyond that, I couldn't tell anything.

I stepped forward, adjusted my scabbard, and started to climb.

I moved painfully slowly, careful not to use momentum to sling my weight around, careful not to commit to a handhold or foothold until I knew it was secure, careful even not to breathe too hard. If they heard me before I got to the top, I'd be dead.

Magic washed over my scrye in waves as I climbed, indicating that the beings on the other side of the wall weren't just existing there—they were doing something magical.

And then one of them was gone.

I paused. Breathed.

Not gone. Sped away, down to the left. At an insane speed.

Were they driving cars in there?

I kept climbing.

Not a minute later, the being sped back around from the right and stopped short. Did Oya have a racetrack circling his home? Either that or it was a vampire-dolphin swimming in a moat.

My fingertips crept over the top of the wall, curling around thick patches of vines as I slowly pulled myself up. I only went high enough to poke my head up and get a visual on the scene below.

It was a racetrack, but not for cars.

Narrow lanes were marked out on a paved pathway that ran around the house in either direction as far as I could see. A wide awning jutted out from the house above it, keeping it shaded while the midday sun bore down on the narrow space of manicured garden between the racetrack and the wall I was clinging to.

A clever design for a vampire mansion. Oya could be outside on his track—or lounging beside it—enjoying the fresh air and the beauty of the garden without ever being exposed to direct sunlight.

And right now, he was doing just that. Standing on the track in pearlescent blue leggings and a sheer white tank, stretching his bare arms in the air as he smiled at Carina.

"Just like that," he said.

Carina stared up at him, her face unreadable. She was dressed in normal clothes today, her usual stretchy jeans and baggy yellow sweatshirt even though she couldn't need it in this weather. Was it a good sign or a bad one that she was back to hiding her scars?

"Wow," she said, and I instantly knew it was a bad sign. Oya might not recognize the sarcasm in her voice, but I did.

"Want to see it again?" he asked, still preening.

"Oh, yes." Carina nodded her head up and down with a little too much gusto.

I bit my lip to keep from muttering a curse. She was really going to kill him, wasn't she?

Oya lifted his head up and let out a deep yell as he stomped one foot against the ground. He started to run, and the transformation was almost instant. He was an ostrich before his second step was finished. He sped along the track, disappearing around the side of the house to the right.

Time seemed to stretch longer this time as I watched Carina stand there alone, hands in the front pocket of her sweatshirt, a tiny wisp of smoke coming from her nose as she stared waiting for Oya to return.

When he did, he lingered in bird form this time, his long neck bending his head down to meet Carina's shoulder. He prodded her with the top of his fluffy little face and stomped the ground again.

Carina huffed out a larger puff of smoke.

Oya changed back again quickly, clapping Carina on the arm with his hand. "That's it! The smoke is a start," he said. "What does it mean to you to be a dragon? Is it the fire in your breath? I can get you some hot sauce—it might help."

"No," Carina said, "it's not that."

"What, then?"

She shrugged and tilted her head down. "I don't know."

Oya crossed his arms.

Carina turned away from him and peered at something inside the house. I couldn't see what. Maybe she was just looking at her reflection in the glass.

"I just keep thinking *why*," she eventually said.

"Why what?"

"Why be a dragon?" she said. "I can fly, but the last time I tried to fight a monster from the air I just got blown off a building." Was she talking about Salma? "I can burn and slash and kill, but that just means it's easy for me to hurt people by accident. And on top of that, I'm supposed to be alone—stay away from all my family and never make any friends. How can I do anything *good* with this kind of beast?"

Oya nodded, and I swallowed. The sarcasm was all gone. She was being real with him now. Maybe she wasn't planning to kill him, after all. Why did that feel worse?

Maybe because he was having the conversation with her that I should have had with her days ago.

"Look at me," Oya said, briefly turning into an ostrich again and then back. How did he do that so quickly? "You think I haven't wondered the exact same thing? People take one look at me and burst out laughing. I'm an ostrich—a joke of a bird." He paused to peel his lips away from his teeth, running his tongue over one of his fangs. "But it's not all I am. My beast is only a joke if I let other people define it."

Carina's eyes widened. "You really are a vampire too . . ." she whispered.

Oya shrugged. "I was lying about it at first, but then I found an elder willing to take a chance on me when no one else would."

"I didn't think shifters could be vampires," Carina said, echoing my thoughts.

"Only because the elders have so many restrictions on who they allow us to turn."

His face changed into the ostrich's face so briefly I would have missed it if I'd blinked, and he hissed through the beak. I frowned. I'd never been around a shifter who could shift so fluidly. If he were anything but an ostrich, it would be a terrifying capability.

I need coffee, I told myself silently as the previous thought sank like lead in my gut. Of course it was terrifying—he was an ostrich *and* a vampire. And unlike the walrus, he wasn't a brand-new weak baby vampire, either. Fluid shifting was probably only one of his many terrifying capabilities I'd never seen.

"I'm changing that, too," Oya continued. "The world needs more heroes. There are too many humans with odd magic they don't know what to do with—so I give them the opportunity to be useful. And there are too many rare shifters who get caught up in what the world thinks of their beasts. Just like you. Our beasts are all different, but the blood could tie us together. Give us a true community. Acceptance. More feet to stand on so we can better help others."

"Are you saying I could be a vampire too?" Carina asked.

"You'll have to figure out how to be a dragon first." He shook his head as Carina opened her mouth to say something. "I can't tell you why," he said. "You need to answer that question yourself."

Carina shut her mouth, staring at him quietly.

"But when you do," he continued, "it's going to be amazing."

With another brief pat to her shoulder, he looked down the track again and stomped his foot.

I sucked in a breath.

He was going to run again.

I moved just as he did, pulling myself up and over the top of the wall in just a few short motions. One leg over and then the other. I couldn't stop myself from letting out a grunt. If they were going to hear me, they were going to hear me—but this was my best chance.

I hung from my arms just long enough to look down and ensure I had flat ground to land on before I let go.

No wings, please, I begged the phoenix silently, then bent my knees as my feet hit the ground to land in a deep squat.

Shockwaves flowed up my bones, and I grunted again softly. I could do lateral jumps all day, but a straight-down drop was fucking painful. At least I'd gotten down without rustling the foliage or spending too much time in plain view.

Crouched behind a shrub, I held still and turned my awareness back to my scrye to see if the two unknown figures I'd identified before had moved.

They had.

But so had Carina.

She was walking towards me.

Fuck.

She stopped when Oya ran back around from the other side of the house.

I held my breath.

The two beings I hadn't seen were converging in the house on the other side of Carina and Oya.

One of them walked outside.

"Boss," she said with a curt nod. "We canceled all your appointments for the day, but Rose didn't take it well. She's here demanding to see you."

I let out my breath. They hadn't mobilized to come get me. Rose . . . that was the name of one of the blood buyers on the list Tula had given me.

Oya growled with a roll of his head before saying, "I'll be right with her. Is that all?"

"We've made the calls you requested about the breach."

"*Potential* breach," Oya corrected. "We don't know for sure what happened to it."

"What happened to what?" Carina piped up.

Oya shook his head at her, but she puffed out her chest.

"No, I want to know," she said. "I want to help. It's why I ran away from my aunt last night—she said she wanted to hurt you."

Oya twisted his neck to regard her slowly. His minion took a tiny step forward, but he held out his hand to stop the woman.

"It was you that tried to kill her, wasn't it?" Carina continued. "What did she do to you?"

"You think I tried to kill your aunt, and you came here to help me?" Oya asked.

"Yeah," Carina said, crossing her arms. "Have you met her? She's kind of a bitch."

Oya crinkled his forehead. Was he buying this?

"Seriously," Carina said. "People try to kill her all the time—they must have a reason. And I'm fucking sick of it." She breathed out another puff of smoke. "So what did she do to you?"

Nodding slowly, he looked straight down at her and said, "She murdered one of my employees in my studio yesterday."

I swallowed. There it was. Confirmation that Oya was the one who'd tried to have us killed last night.

Dread settled in my stomach like molten steel.

This meant I had no reason to check up on Tula about Simeon before finishing my job. And it meant that Oya now had more than one reason to hurt Carina. Would she make it through to his blood auctions, or was she too much of a liability now that she knew he'd attacked her family?

Carina huffed and crossed her arms. "I knew she'd do anything to sabotage my chance with you."

"You . . ." Oya paused and narrowed his eyes at her. "You might be more useful than I expected."

"What can I do?" Carina asked.

"Come," he said with a nod as he beckoned her towards the house. "Want to see how we really make heroes here?"

Carina nodded vigorously.

"You won't be disappointed."

17

ROSE TURNED out to be one of the rare vampires that looked as old as she was. Well, I didn't know exactly how old she was. But her hair was completely gray, and underneath it she looked like a shriveled mummy in a sparkly dress. Her skin had the same luminescent sheen as Soma's, but without his youthful appearance it conjured thoughts of slimy reptilian things rather than ethereal beauty.

She licked her fangs as Oya's people dragged tree girl—Annabel—into the spacious living room.

From the upper landing where I was hiding, it seemed like the girl was sedated. Unconscious but not beaten or bloodied.

Carina stood beside Oya, arms crossed, one of her fingers scratching her elbow relentlessly through her sweater.

A sign of stress? *Good*, I thought. She'd better be stressed—what with this nice little death trap she'd walked right into.

"You say she is fae infused?" Rose asked, and my breath caught briefly at the sound of it. Her voice was softer than Soma's, but it still screamed *threat* to my nervous system with every syllable.

"Forest sprite in the ancestry," Oya said, holding out his phone in front of her.

Rose peered down her nose at it and then fluttered her papery eyelids towards the unconscious girl. "The sample was impressive. I'll take her."

"Lovely. Would you like to step outside to settle payment then?"

"Outside?"

"You'll find I have a secure shaded area just out the—"

Rose turned a withering stare on Oya, and he snapped his mouth shut with a nod. "All right—payment in here. Today it will be . . ." He beckoned to a short balding man who was standing between his guards. "Dave."

"Dave." Rose sighed, holding her right hand out to the assistant standing behind her. Seconds later, those shriveled fingers closed around a gleaming little blade. "And just what kind of a creature is this Dave?"

Dave stepped forward on shaky legs. "Thank you for asking, ma'am," he said, words coming too fast. "I'm a—"

"Just show her," Oya snapped.

"I . . ." Dave scratched his head, mouth open. "Okay." And then he started shrinking. He got hairier as he got smaller, until eventually he was about three feet tall with goofy little round ears sticking out from the sides of his head.

Rose scoffed at Oya. "You want me to grant eternity to an ape?"

"Only if you want the tree sprite," Oya replied as Dave the chimpanzee climbed up to his shoulder.

Rose moved inhumanly quickly, her hand darting out and grabbing Dave by the neck. She pulled him to her face and grasped him with both of her spiny hands as she tore out his throat with her teeth. Blood spilled down the front of her face and chest, splashes of it falling all the way to the pale blue rug beneath her feet.

Oya cringed.

Rose clamped her mouth over Dave's open throat and sucked, hands wringing his limp body as if he were a wet washcloth she wanted to squeeze every single drop of liquid out of.

When she was done, she dropped him at her feet and bent over him. With the blade in her hand, she opened a vein in her wrist. Dark, syrupy blood trickled out of it and onto Dave's mangled corpse.

For a long moment, I wondered if anything would happen. The blood dripped and slid and seeped through his black fur. Rose massaged her forearm to squeeze more of it out, but her wound was closing.

She was moving her blade to reopen the wound when Dave sprang into motion with a high-pitched shriek. His whole body leapt up to Rose's wrist, embracing her bony arm with a ferocity I'd have thought would be reserved for crack bananas.

She let him drink for less than a minute before peeling him off and tossing him back to the ground. Dave hissed at her and writhed on the rug, scrambling to get his bearings. But before he could launch himself back at Rose, one of Oya's guards restrained him and dragged him away. He left a trail of dark, sticky blood on Oya's rug and then the hardwood that led into the hallway. His chimp screeches turned into deeper yells through the walls of the house, and then they stopped completely.

I clutched at the knives hidden in my sleeves, wondering if all vampire births were so quick and dirty—and whether Dave would even survive. I glanced at Carina and was surprised to see her keeping so quiet. Whatever she thought of what had just happened, she wasn't showing it.

Oya's remaining guard lifted Annabel from beneath her shoulders and dragged her towards Rose, avoiding the bloody parts of the rug at her feet.

"Cut me a finger," Rose said as she wiped Dave's blood off her face with a wet towel her assistant had handed her. She handed the bloodied towel back, exchanging it for something small and black.

Oya's guard hesitated only briefly before taking Rose's offered blade and using it to cut off Annabel's left-hand pinky finger.

Rose snatched it up as soon as it was severed and popped the end in her mouth like a cigarette, pursing her lips around it and closing her eyes as she sucked. In her other hand, she cradled the small black thing against her chest.

For a brief moment, her skin rippled like water and sparkled like Etty's. When I blinked, the shriveled gray mummy in a dress became smooth, supple and dark. Black, bony protrusions grew from her back, stretching out into giant leathery wings.

I blinked again, and she was ancient again—and wingless.

She held tree girl's severed finger out and dropped it in her assistant's hand.

"Pack her up," she said with a slight smack of her lips. "This one should last quite a while."

Then her eyes snapped to Carina, whose face was still impressively blank.

"You, little girl," she said. Carina lifted her chin. "Would you like to be next?"

Carina uncrossed her arms and opened her mouth. "Depends—"

"No," Oya interrupted. "She isn't ready. I only had one for you here, and we shouldn't be doing this at all today anyway."

"Your little security breach?" Rose tilted her head back and let out a low cackle. "I have no reason to care about that. Not anymore."

"What does that mean?" Oya asked, forehead crinkling.

Rose jutted one shoulder forward in something that might have been a shrug if she weren't so skeletal. "Time to go," she said to her assistant, handing him back the small black thing she'd been cradling. Was it moving?

The assistant produced a tiny birdcage, no bigger than the size of his hand, and stuffed the black thing inside. It was definitely moving.

"No," Oya said, and his voice rose a little in pitch as it got louder. "What did you mean? Are you threatening me? It sounded like you were threatening me."

"Ha," Rose scoffed. "Why would I bother to threaten you? I have nothing to gain from your demise. I wanted to save you, even. Asked you to join us in our cleanse. You declined."

"Save me from *what?*" Oya's eyes were darting around the room now. I moved my head back behind the pillar I was using for cover, losing my visual on the scene. If I could see them, they could see me—and that was only fine as long as they weren't looking.

"You'll find out soon enough," Rose said. Now that I couldn't see her, the effect of her voice travelling straight through to my bones was even more pronounced. I shivered.

"Don't let them leave," Oya muttered.

Someone roared.

I poked my head out again.

Oya had changed back into his ostrich, and now that he was indoors it struck me just how tall he was. Nearly ten feet tall, I'd guess—more than twice Carina's height.

He extended his wings, puffing them forward and out like billowing black clouds. To his left, Carina disappeared behind the feathery fluff. On his other side, a tiger crouched low to the ground. That must be what had roared.

Rose held her arms in front of her, bony fingers clawing at the air. Her lips curled away from her teeth as she snarled at Oya.

Oya's hoof-like foot stomped the ground.

I bit my cheek. I never would have thought I'd be saying it, but my money here was on the ostrich.

I got off my ass just as Oya started to run and crept quickly down the stairs towards Carina. I could kill Oya later—if Rose didn't do it for me. This was the best chance I'd get to pluck Carina out of there unnoticed.

Maybe unnoticed wasn't the right word.

Rose, I was sure, had noticed me long ago. A vampire that old would be able to hear my heartbeat from miles away. But she didn't know I wasn't supposed to be there.

Oya was certainly noticing me now, as I breezed past his outstretched wings . . . but he was on a collision course that couldn't be stopped, and I wasn't the one he'd fluffed his feathers at with so much menace.

I grabbed Carina's arm and locked eyes with her, daring her to challenge me.

For once, she didn't.

She ran with me towards the glass door to the backyard, both of us bounding over a sofa and coffee table to get there. I was about to slide open the door when I heard a scream that sounded far too human for my liking.

I stopped, hand on the door.

"What are you doing?" Carina whisper-yelled at me.

I turned around to look back at the clash of freakshow vampires.

Oya had run straight into Rose's spindly claws and trampled her like a cat pouncing on a spider. She was still moving, but obviously on the losing end of this fight.

The tiger at his side had Rose's assistant wrapped in a fierce cuddle on the ground, claws digging into the man's heart to stun him. Enormous jaws closed around the man's head, which looked comically small sandwiched between such massive sets of sharp teeth.

The tiger closed its jaws.

Beside me, Carina flinched at the wet crunching sound that cut through the rest of the chaos. Blood and bone and pulpy gore spilled out from between the tiger's teeth as he shook his head, and the assistant's body was flung across the room with a shredded stump for a neck.

I nodded appreciatively. Death by tiger seemed like a great way to ensure no heads remained to get reattached to vampire bodies.

I stilled as my eyes swept over to the source of the scream.

Annabel sat on the ground beside Rose, who now resembled something like a bucket of grapes being smashed by foot to make wine.

The tree girl had stopped screaming and was weeping now as she clutched the wrist attached to her bleeding hand, staring at the tiny stump where her pinky finger should be. Blood flowed down her arm like melting ice cream on a hot day, dripping onto her pale green dress in a sticky mess of bittersweet regret.

At least she was still alive.

I groaned, glancing down at Carina. I couldn't leave this room without doing something to make sure Annabel stayed alive. If I did, I'd have to admit I was lying to myself about being here—at least in part—to save the victims of Oya's weird little trafficking outfit.

And I wasn't lying to myself. Not fully.

"Get outside," I growled at Carina. "I'll be right there."

Then I drew my sword.

It felt hefty in my grip, only because I'd been favoring my smaller blades since reentering the civilian world, where I usually wanted to be discreet.

Here, the added length and thicker hilt on my blade felt like a burst of promise, extending out in front of me as I rushed towards the tree girl.

Still weeping, she looked up at me charging her and only weeped harder.

Oya turned my way and emitted a booming sound from his

slender throat. His long pink legs were stained red up to the knees, which bent the wrong way.

I needed to get off the ground or my blood would be staining his feathers next. With only a gentle prod at the phoenix in my scrye, the spectral brown wings sprouted from my back and tried to lift me up. I fought to keep them folded just a moment longer.

Annabel squeezed her eyes shut when I halted in front of her.

I let the wings spread open as I dipped my front end down to loop my left arm around her chest while my right arm brandished the sword in Oya's direction.

"Grab on!" I yelled at the girl, and miraculously she did.

It took Oya less than two strides to reach us. His powerful clawed hoof shot out, catching me in the ribs as my blade slashed into nothing but feathers.

I gasped, the breath knocked out of me as the edges of my vision blurred. Oya's legs were far longer than my weapon; I would need a spear to do any damage to him in a straight-on match.

Birds. Shifters were the absolute worst. Why hadn't my Guardian instructors taken me to a zoo as part of my training? If I survived this, I would be making the suggestion to Dirk.

Retreat, I commanded the wings, but I couldn't fly very high with Annabel weighing me down.

I managed to get halfway to where Carina was before dropping the tree girl behind the sofa. Except Carina wasn't there anymore.

I didn't have the luxury of looking around to find her because, while Oya had returned to stomping on the puddle of mush that used to be Rose, his tiger friend was prowling my way.

Tiger—yay. At least this was something I shouldn't need a spear or an atomic bomb to kill.

I folded my wings back down and made myself small.

The big cat growled.

I waited.

When it pounced, I sprang forward and dove underneath it, the tip of my sword slashing upwards through its belly. I rolled away from its claws as soon as I hit the ground.

This time, its roar faltered.

But when I turned to face it, the big cat was already gearing up to pounce at me again.

It was bleeding. The wound wouldn't heal quickly, but it also wouldn't be fatal. I had to remember this tiger was also a vampire, albeit a young one. *Through its heart or off with its head.* Those were the only ways to incapacitate it.

I swung my sword in a half-circle, altering my grip.

The tiger leapt at me.

I let out my breath, aimed the point of my blade, and narrowed my eyes.

The tiger never made it to me.

Mid-pounce, it was swept up in a blaze of billowing flames and reduced to a pile of black dust.

The tip of my sword turned red.

Was my face melting? My sword was melting, and it felt like my face might be melting too.

I turned my head to the left, where the fire was coming from.

A small black dragon crouched on the landing where I'd been hiding earlier, spitting flames mercilessly from behind toothy jaws.

I stood up and stepped back as the flames swept along the rug that was once bloodstained and, before that, pale blue.

Carina lifted her claws and then dug them deeper into the floorboards underneath her. The firelight glinted off her deep black scales as the muscles in her neck slowly shifted to push out more flames.

She was beautiful. Deadliest thing I'd seen after the phoenix— and she might even give that hellish bird a run for its money.

And then she withered and sputtered out sparks, deflating like a giant dragon balloon as her scales lightened and softened into flesh.

The roar of her flames transformed into a piercing scream, mouth still open and fingernails still gripping the floorboards in fury.

The fire had reached the edge of the rug and then died down, consuming an entire sofa and chaise lounge in its wake. I made a mental note to ask Oya what kind of magical elixir he sealed his wood floors with that it could withstand dragon fire.

When I looked his way, he was a person again, leaving the pile of Rose mush behind as he advanced towards Carina.

On second thought, maybe I'd just ask one of his minions about the floors after I killed him.

"That was incredible," he called up to Carina, hands pressed together in front of his chest. "I knew you could do it."

Carina glared down at him, crouched naked and snarling on the upper landing.

Why was it only the vampire shifters who managed to keep their clothes on throughout the change?

"You would do so many great things with us . . ." Oya continued, ignoring the snarling. "And I have so much more to show you. I know you didn't mean to hurt Tag." He gestured to the place where the tiger's ashes had fused with the remains of the rug. "You didn't expect for *her* to be here—I get it. It's hard to let our family go, even when we know they're wrong."

Um, hello? I'm right here. I bit my tongue and kept from saying it out loud. My whole body tensed, every part of me itching to charge Oya with my sword. But I wanted to let Carina make a decision before I took away her opportunity to do so.

"You're not helping anyone!" Carina yelled, finally looking out at Oya with a red face stained with tears and soot. "I believed your hero bullshit, even after you sent *assassins* after me, because

I wanted to believe I could be a hero too . . . But that's the problem, isn't it?"

"It's not bullshit," Oya said, stepping closer to her.

"You just want people to think you're a hero. You just want to think of yourself that way. But you can't even protect the people closest to you. You're just like me. And we're both just killers."

"You haven't seen the whole operation," Oya said calmly. "You don't know the context. We aren't vigilantes—we're insurgents."

My ears perked up. That wasn't something I'd expected.

"You have no idea what the vampire elders are planning," Oya went on. "How dangerous they really are. We can only stop them if we can play on their level. But they keep such a tight rein on anyone able to administer the change . . . we have no choice but to resort to extraordinary means to obtain it."

"What are the vampire elders planning?" I asked, and Oya whipped his head around to me. "It didn't sound like you knew much about it, either, when Rose was goading you into a fight."

Oya twitched his shoulders, probably debating whether to entertain my question or switch back into kill mode. But he didn't get a chance to do either.

"Boss," called a nervous voice from the entrance hall. "I couldn't reach anyone else because—"

"Not now," Oya snapped at what appeared to be one of his assistants lucky enough to have missed the fight.

The assistant stopped short, her eyes sweeping over the carnage that used to be Oya's living room.

Oya rubbed a hand over his face and let out a gruff sigh. "Fine," he said coolly. "Why couldn't you reach anyone else?"

"They're all at Celestial," the assistant said as she did her best to look at Oya and not all the chaos around him.

"Celestial?" Oya narrowed his eyes, twitching with indecision yet again. "Are you sure?"

"That's what their humans all said. But they didn't know why."

"Celestial doesn't allow vampires on the premises," Oya stated, but his assistant just shook her head helplessly.

"I take it 'they' are a bunch of vampires then?" I asked. "The other buyers you were notifying of your breach?" At Oya's glare, I added, "That wasn't me, by the way." But I would love to know who Dirk's other plant was, if they were still alive.

"Yes," Oya seethed, legs twitching underneath him as he fought off his ostrich. He didn't believe me one bit, but that didn't matter right now.

A wet, gurgling cackle sounded from across the room.

I looked over to see that the mangled blob of Rose's remains had regrown its face and some semblance of four disjointed limbs. She pushed herself up off the floor, her sticky dead flesh stretching like gory taffy.

The cackling stopped just long enough for her to say, "Finally. Our time has finally come." She twisted her headless face in a circular motion until her eyes landed on the crushed head of her dead assistant, and she began to crawl over to him.

I cringed, swallowing against the urge to vomit.

Then I realized the Rose puddle wasn't really crawling towards her dead assistant.

She was crawling towards the black creature he'd put in the tiny cage.

I moved, more on instinct than anything else, diving in front of her and scooping it up before she could. Her melted blob of a face snarled at me, but she could only move so far before her pulpy body threatened to tear itself in half—most of it was still stuck to the floor.

I stepped away from her and looked down at the cage in my hands. Inside it was a small bat.

Beady black eyes stared at me amidst dark fur and two disproportionately enormous ears. I realized now that, despite my constant cursing of them as a historically unfair symbol of vampirism, I'd never seen a real bat before.

It was pretty cute.

And there was something . . .

Something called to my scrye.

"No," Rose gurgle-screamed, but I stuck my finger in the cage and gave the bat a little scratch on the head. It was soft. Before I knew it, I was opening the cage and letting the thing climb out into my hand.

My fingers curled around it, but it didn't struggle to get free of my grip. Instead, it looked me in the eyes—no, not in the eyes. It looked straight through to my scrye.

Then it bit me.

Fangs sank into the fleshy space between my fingers and thumb, but instead of pain it was a refreshing current of cool energy that ran through my veins.

Something happened to my scrye as my stomach turned over inside me. My scrye felt heavier somehow. But not full. Coated? Plated. Like it had been covered in a layer of protective steel.

The bat pulled its tiny fangs away and shifted slightly in my hand, nestling its soft little head in the crook of my palm.

Rose wailed, a wet guttural noise, and stretched out her hand in a desperate attempt to reach me.

But her fingers turned to ice before she could.

Her wail cut off abruptly as her lips frosted over and then solidified completely, the gory stretched skin of her smushed-up torso becoming icicles. Clear and pristine and sharp. Not so much as a drop of blood left on her, although there was plenty surrounding her on the floor.

A quick glance to the side told me her assistant had suffered the same fate.

I looked down at the bat in my hands.

It looked up at me.

If what I thought had just happened had really just happened, I was never letting go of this little guy.

I stood up and tucked him down the front of my shirt. I was wearing a sports bra today, so there was a nice little shelf to support him between my girls.

When I turned back in Carina's direction, neither she nor Oya were even looking my way.

Carina was claws deep in the stair landing again, wings braced at her sides, jaws parted and mouth gaping . . . but no fire was coming out.

Oya was just walking calmly towards her, calling her name.

"You don't really want to hurt me, Carina. It won't work like that, remember? *Why* do you want to be a dragon and breathe fire? It's not to hurt people like me."

Carina went fully human again, the process slower this time. Not that her shifting was ever as fast as Oya's, but lately it had still been sort of frantic, some parts of her shifting abruptly while other parts lagged.

Now, for the first time in a long time, it seemed like her whole body was shifting back to human at the same steady pace.

When she was done, she looked at Oya and just sobbed.

"What if it is, though?" she finally said.

He frowned. "Then I would kill you first."

That was enough for me.

I lifted my sword.

Oya turned around to glance at me and huffed. "Again? Didn't you see what I did to—" He stopped, finally taking in Rose's icy remains.

"I saw you fail to kill an old-ass mummy of a vampire, and then I finished the job," I bluffed. "But you didn't see that, did you? You were too busy trying to impress a traumatized eight-year-old."

The eight-year-old in question yelled, "Kill him, Darcy," just as Oya stomped his foot on the ground.

The ostrich stood in front of me again, pink knobby knees almost level with my eyes. Luscious black feathers billowed at its sides as Oya pushed his wings forward to intimidate me.

The wings were the least intimidating thing about him.

His neck stretched up all the way to where Carina was perched, more than double my height, while his heart lay in the middle of a giant ball of feathery fluff. I couldn't reach either, unless . . .

Unless my wings could be the most intimidating thing about *me*.

I hadn't even finished the thought when the spectral feathers fluttered at my sides, pulling warm air past my face. Didn't it used to hurt when these things popped out?

Bird against bird, I thought as the wings lifted me over Oya's head.

It was our second face-off; but this time, tree girl was safely over by the door instead of in my arms weighing me down.

Oya's ostrich face looked even sillier up close, an itty-bitty knob at the end of a giant murderous feather duster. When he opened his beak to hiss up at me, it just looked like a baby bird begging its mother for food.

I swung my sword down in an arc and connected right at the top of his neck.

The small beaked knob of a head fell to the side, and I didn't even hear it when it hit the ground.

A fountain of blood burst from the top of Oya's long neck, spraying the room in red circles as the neck spun out of control.

Oya's legs were running rampant as well, and it wasn't long until he'd crushed the ice sculpture of Rose just like he'd crushed her when she was made of skin and bones and blood.

Apparently all birds were the same in the end. Headless ostrich, headless chicken, whatever.

Would the phoenix follow suit, if anything ever managed to cut off its terrifying head? I didn't want to find out.

I stepped back and wiped my sword on a soft gold curtain, painting Oya's crimson blood on yet one more surface.

When the ostrich's body finally fell, it lay still for only a few seconds before shrinking into Oya's headless human-shaped corpse.

Not quite a corpse, though. Not yet.

With stiff shoulders and a silent scowl, Carina descended the stairs. I slipped off my denim jacket and handed it to her, and she grabbed it without looking at my face.

She yanked the jacket over her shoulders as she walked right past me to where Oya's tiny bird head had fallen; it still hadn't turned back into anything that looked human.

Bending over, she picked it up by the beak and clutched it in her hands.

A grip that wouldn't relent until she found the fire in her breath to turn it to ashes.

What I should have done with Simeon's head when I'd had it in my clutches.

I wouldn't stop her. I'd bring the ashes to Tula as proof of death if need be.

I looked over to the ice sculpture of Rose's mutilated form.

Ice.

When Itztla stole a witch, he was really stealing power from their god, and so it turned them into the preferred material of that corresponding god.

But Itztla's preferred material was ice.

Did that mean Rose was one of Itztla's witches? Had he stolen her from *himself*?

I looked down at the tiny bat nestled between my breasts. It had seemed like she and her assistant were using it for protection, somehow. And I could feel it in my scrye, that it was protecting me from something now.

So maybe whatever Itztla was doing to steal witches couldn't discriminate between his own witches and all the others. And maybe this bat was one of many carried by his own to keep them safe from their ruinous god.

Why a bat, though?

I raised an eyebrow at it. That was a question for Adrian and Ray.

Me, on the other hand . . . I needed to go back to Celestial.

Oya's assistant, who had fled the room upon getting ostrich blood sprayed in her face, had told him a bunch of his vampire buyers were at Celestial. And that information had meant something to Rose.

Rose who looked a hell of a lot like a stolen ice witch right now.

Did that mean I would find more of Itztla's witches at Celestial?

Would Simeon be one of them?

I frowned.

That thought felt just a little too convenient, after I'd set one of Celestial's assassins after him just a couple days ago.

Absently, I scooped the little bat out of my tits and held it out towards Carina. "Touch it," I said when she looked at me like I was a loon.

She did as I asked, resting Oya's bird head on her hip to maintain two points of contact with it.

"Do you feel it in your magic?"

She nodded. "What is it?"

"I don't know," I said. "But I think we just got very, very lucky."

18

I STOOD outside the clinic of my childhood nightmares, watching a bloody little girl wearing my jacket stalk in with a severed head clutched in her hands.

It had turned back from bird to human on the drive here.

Well, not quite human. Vampire human. I supposed that wasn't implied anymore now that I'd seen vampire walruses and monkeys and ostriches. Oh my.

The ringtone on my phone just kept humming in my ear. Again and again and again. Insulting me with every tone until I finally worked up the fury to smash End Call with my thumb.

Tula wasn't picking up.

That didn't necessarily mean things had gone sideways.

If she was with Simeon, it'd be a bit awkward chatting on the phone with his nemesis human ex-girlfriend.

But she could at least text.

I put the phone away.

I needed to go to Celestial, but I didn't want to show up blind and unprepared. If I couldn't get any intel from Tula—and if things really had gone sideways with her—then maybe I could get something from her wife.

Carina wasn't in the front room when I entered, but the trail of Oya's dripping blood on the ground told me she'd headed towards Adrian's temporary office.

I headed in the other direction. It wasn't long before I found Sassie shuffling through charts at the desk nearby Minnie's room.

She looked up at me with alert eyes and frayed nerves when my footsteps gave me away. On seeing me, she let out an aggressive breath and shook her head, dropping the charts in her hands.

"I can't make sense of it," she said.

Did I need to ask what?

"It's random and it's not . . ." She frowned, looking down at the charts again. "It seems like it's coming in waves, whatever it is that's doing this—turning people into statues."

"What do you mean both random and not?"

"I've been keeping track of the timing, when petrified patients are brought in here and at the nearby hospitals—based on what I'm hearing from my contacts—and the materials are consistent with each wave. Only one at a time."

"One material at a time?"

"Exactly. We'll get a wave of citrine and then a wave of iron, then clay and then slate. It changes every hour, on the dot. But some repeat, some don't, and it's always a different number of patients. No pattern at all except the timing of the waves."

"You're calling them patients."

"As opposed to . . .?"

I raised my eyebrows.

"Ah," Sassie said. "You mean why aren't they at the morgue?"

I nodded.

"We don't know yet that they're corpses. Not while we have at least one patient who was only partially petrified and still very much alive. As long as there's hope for her, we have to presume there could be hope for the others."

"Minnie, I take it?" I asked. "How's she doing?"

Sassie cocked her head to the side and gave me a very small shrug. "That depends on how you look at it." At my questioning glare, she came around the desk and beckoned me to follow her.

I couldn't see through the glass to Minnie's room because of all the mages in brown tunics standing just on the other side. I opened my eyes wide. There was "not in quarantine anymore" and then there was this. Yikes.

Sassie pushed through the door, and I followed.

The air was warm in Minnie's room, probably from all the extra body heat of these mages who were just standing there staring at her.

Yes, they were also taking notes and monitoring her energy levels, but it still seemed creepy and unnecessary. Leading them, Kia stood just at the foot of Minnie's bed, her eyes closed, hands on Minnie's bare feet. Still searching for magical curses?

I craned my head to look around her, eager to see how much of Minnie was left. But the hand that had been crystallized was covered with a blanket that went all the way up her arm and was folded just underneath her chin.

My fingers twitched. I wanted to do something to help her.

"Is this a glass half-empty, half-full situation?" I questioned, wondering why Sassie had said what she had.

"No." She scoffed. "That's not what I meant. Just that we've made some interesting discoveries."

I frowned as I looked over Minnie, whose sleeping face seemed just as I'd left it a couple days ago. Usually when patients were bedridden, unconscious or not, you could see it in their skin after a while, in the shadows under their eyes and the chap on their lips and the extra frizz in their hair. Minnie still looked bright and fresh, like she'd just gotten a restful night's sleep and hopped out of the shower.

That was a strange sign, but it didn't seem like a bad one.

"What discoveries?" I asked.

"She's pregnant, for one," Sassie said.

My head snapped up. "Excuse me?"

"Still early on, by the looks of it. She might not even know. We ran all the blood tests we could think of, and that was the only unexpected anomaly."

My head whirled with new thoughts. I wanted to ask Minnie if this pregnancy was planned. She seemed to genuinely love her batshit crazy ancient wife, but it wasn't exactly easy or cheap to get pregnant without infidelity in a same-sex monogamous relationship.

And if it *was* planned . . . this news could be great leverage to arm myself with heading into a possible confrontation with Tula.

"Did you look through her things?" I asked. "Find any prenatal vitamins?"

"Of course we didn't snoop through her things," Sassie said. "That's no way to treat a guest."

Just your teenage niece then? I bit my tongue to keep from saying it aloud, but I couldn't keep the wave of bitterness from rushing through me upon remembering the day I'd come home from school to find my room torn apart after Sassie had seen the half-completed Guardian application on my desk.

She'd been certain I was out of my mind, coerced somehow by some bad influence I must be hiding in my bedsheets. If only. Maybe if I'd had a bad influence to hide in my bedsheets at that age I wouldn't have graduated to hiding in Simeon's as an adult.

"We were thinking the pregnancy could be why she's responding differently than the other patients to whatever is causing the petrification," Sassie continued, shaking me from my memories.

I narrowed my eyes. That was a thought. Don't want to turn

into a statue? Go get knocked up and you'll be fine. Or, if not fine, whatever this was.

"We haven't seen any other pregnant victims," she went on. "But that doesn't mean there aren't any. The DSC man who's holding us all hostage said he'd check his files on the victims worldwide and get back to us."

I snorted at the bite in Sassie's voice. Adrian holding them hostage? I doubted that. But of course she wouldn't like an outsider barging in and commandeering the ship she'd been captain of for over thirty years.

He would love it if he knew I was thinking pirate jokes about him.

I loved it that he was pissing off my aunt.

Sassie must have seen the smile I was trying to hide. "Is this funny to you?"

"Not at all," I said. "Just happy about the baby." That was sort of true. "What other discoveries?" I asked. She had said discoveries, plural.

She nodded, eyes going distant—what she did whenever she had to discuss something complicated. "This one is . . ." She paused and looked at me. "It might be easier to show you. Step up and touch her."

I scrunched up my forehead. "You want me to touch—"

"Her skin," Sassie clarified.

I licked my lips, hesitating. I'd touched Minnie before, and it hadn't been my idea of a good time. "I'm aware of her abilities, if that's what this is about."

"And you didn't warn us?" Sassie asked.

"I did tell you not to touch her," I said. "I told you not to let anyone in the same room as her. You didn't listen."

"That's . . ." Sassie shook her head. "It would have been nice to know why."

"Sorry," I said, blinking. "I don't know much about her abilities besides they fuck things up when she touches anything or anyone. Her wife told me she's dangerous when she wakes—that's all I had to go on."

"In any case," Sassie said with a wave of her hand, "that's not quite what we discovered."

I raised my eyebrows.

"It's not her abilities, but the fact that they aren't working the way they should. Instead of perceiving, she's projecting."

"So . . ." I started.

"You should touch her and see." As Sassie gestured, Kia opened her eyes and let go of Minnie, stepping back to where the other mages were standing.

Grumbling internally, I stepped forward and laid my hand on Minnie's exposed foot where Kia had been touching.

My skin stuck to hers like a magnet, pulling me into a world that zoomed and blurred around me until it dropped me in a sunny little bakeshop filled with people chatting and sipping tea. The scents of chocolate and cinnamon and coffee swirled together in my head, delivering an instant rush of calm pleasure at odds with my restless nerves.

A light giggle sounded beside me. I turned my head to see a girl, younger than Carina and probably younger than Noah, holding an iced teacake up to her mouth. Her wispy red-blonde hair was breaking free of its braid in every direction, and the smile on her face was directed at the tall woman who stood before her.

I almost didn't recognize the woman because of what she was wearing—not a stitch of white in sight. Instead, she had on loose brown pants and a flowy pink blouse underneath a colorful patchwork apron. Her light blonde hair was tied up in a messy bun, but the features on her face were Tula's—apart from the cheery smile. The Tula I knew smiled often, but never in a way that didn't strike me as sinister.

This Tula dipped her finger in the icing on the little girl's teacake, then transferred a smudge of it to the girl's nose. This elicited many more giggles, calmed only by a few pats of Tula's hand on the girl's red hair. She patted my head next, and it filled me with a calm so still I thought it might be death itself. But death was cold, and this woman's touch was oh so warm.

I pulled my hand away from Minnie's foot. I might get lost in her memories if I didn't. Eyes hot and gut twisting, I stepped away.

Minnie had known Tula since she was a young child? I had really tried to give their weird relationship the benefit of the doubt, but while "I'm married to a psychotic assassin" hadn't quite swayed me, this blatant case of child grooming seemed up to the task.

"What did you see?" Sassie asked, and my disgust deepened.

"None of your business," I said. "And no one should be touching her, if this is what happens. It's a violation of her privacy."

Sassie's brow furrowed.

"An *unnecessary* violation of her privacy," I amended. I knew there were plenty of necessary ones, in times like these. I wasn't sure where rifling through Minnie's things for prenatal vitamins would fall, but leave it to me and my aunt to disagree about literally everything.

"We only touched her enough to figure out what was happening. To learn the way her ability normally functions and assess the difference."

"And?"

"Like I said, she's projecting instead of perceiving."

I tried to remember what Minnie had said about how it

worked. "Her memories, then. Instead of seeing all the memories around her, she's projecting her own."

"Exactly." Sassie's face darkened as her eyes settled back on me.

Oh no.

"I saw you . . ." she said, then shook her head.

Oh fuck no.

"You could have—"

"No," I said to cut her off. "We're not doing this. Talk about a violation of privacy . . ." I wanted to heave as the memories Minnie had recently returned to me came up to the forefront of my thoughts. Sassie would have seen it from Minnie's perspective, which was even worse—a front-row seat to me losing my shit after watching Simeon die. All I could remember was the way it felt, the way he looked, the complete terror and loss of control that had followed when I hadn't been able to handle the fact that I'd fucked up so badly.

How would that have looked to someone watching? I didn't know, but now Sassie did. She may as well have been there in the room with me on the most vulnerable day of my existence.

For a second time.

I squeezed my eyes shut, waiting for the barrage of excuses and platitudes to come.

"I'm sorry," was all she said.

When I opened my eyes, Kia and the watching mages were all gone. Good thing, because there were tears threatening to trickle down my cheeks.

A strong urge was bubbling up inside me to go slit Minnie's throat right now—that way she couldn't reveal my secrets to anyone else.

No, not my secrets. It wasn't a secret, what had happened. It was more than that. It was my pain. My naivete. My failure. My shame.

I stretched out my fingers, fighting the urge to draw one of my blades.

This is how monsters are born, isn't it?

It would be nothing short of villainous for me to hurt Minnie to protect my feelings. To protect my cowardice at those feelings being exposed.

Which made me wonder. What cowardice was Oya trying to protect by killing all those "fae-infused" victims? He'd claimed he and his army of vampire-shifters were insurgents, fighting against an oppressive leadership of vampire elders plotting gods knew what. But Oya hadn't been doing any fighting, from what I'd seen. Just bulking up, killing innocents to amass his own power, driven by fear.

And what about Simeon? Was he driven by some fear as well? I might never know.

I swallowed, then sighed. "There's a lot more to the story than what Minnie saw," I said. It wasn't a defense, just the truth. "Simeon is still alive, and he's tried to destroy me since then. Me and so many others."

"I'm proud of you," Sassie said with a nod of her head.

"For what?" I asked.

"For not letting him do it."

"That remains to be seen," I said. Until Simeon was dead and burned, everything he did was something I was allowing him to do. That was what it had felt like ever since I'd had the opportunity to kill him and fucked it up. Maybe that was another reason I'd gone to Tula for help; I knew if I actually found him myself, I'd have to see what terrible new things he was up to and feel guilty for letting them happen.

As I let my eyes focus on Minnie's unconscious face, I let my mind focus on a truth I hadn't wanted to confront consciously. Simeon had done this to her. Had done it to all the witches who were now statues. And as much as I knew I shouldn't, I'd been carrying around the guilt of it all ever since I'd been birded to the volcano.

The phoenix had told us it was Itztla behind the witch-stealing. Itztla, who would always mean more to me as the one pulling Simeon's strings than as any rival-not-rival of my own god.

If there were vampires at Celestial now, I knew it in my bones that one of them had to be Simeon. Him and Tula and his god, and whatever it was they were doing to suck the life out of witches all over the world.

And whatever they were using to protect their own witches from the aforementioned life-sucking.

I looked down at the bat in my tits.

"Mind if I try something?"

Sassie gave me a pointed look, as if to say I should know better than to ask that sort of question without any elaboration.

"I'm going to try something," I said instead, but Sassie put a hand out to stop me before I could scoop the bat out of the front of my shirt.

"There's more we discovered," she said.

"More?" I asked, trying not to sound as exhausted as I felt.

Sassie licked her lips and nodded, then carefully pulled the blanket away from Minnie's afflicted arm.

I blinked, then fell to my knees beside the bed as a strangled moan resonated deep in my chest.

There were no more crystals on Minnie's hand. No crystals anywhere on her.

Instead, her entire arm had turned into a shriveled, withered thing, fingers curled up in an unmoving claw covered in dry, wrinkly leather that extended all the way up to her neck.

It looked just like what Etty'd said had happened to Noah's foot.

And just like that, my mild background worry about what was happening to him exploded into the forefront of all my thoughts.

He wasn't a witch, but neither was Minnie—and this "raisin" effect on her was obviously connected to the crystals she'd picked up from touching one of Itztla's petrified victims.

Which meant that Noah's raisin foot was probably connected somehow as well.

19

"Do you know why it changed?" I asked, cold desperation seeping into my words.

"No," Sassie said. "That's what Kia's been trying to discover. That's why we're making use of the projections."

I was much less inclined to argue about violating Minnie's privacy now than I'd been a few minutes ago.

"I'm going to try something," I repeated, and this time Sassie didn't object when I knelt by Minnie's side and brought the bat out of my bra.

I had no idea how this worked.

For me, I'd just picked the thing up and let it bite me before I'd felt it shielding my scrye. Carina had only touched it. But it'd seemed like Rose and her assistant were using the one bat to protect them both, and my taking it had negated their protection. Until I knew why that was, I had to assume giving it to anyone else could negate my own protection.

"Have you had any waves of obsidian statues?" I asked Sassie.

"Not since yesterday," she said, and I breathed a little easier. Carina and I had escaped yesterday's wave by sheer luck, then. If there hadn't been another wave since I'd picked up the bat, there was no bogeyman lying in wait to turn me into a statue as soon as I lost it—like I assumed had happened with Rose.

So this was worth a shot.

The bat chirped at me, and I rubbed my finger over its fluffy little head. It stuck out its thin, pink tongue and reached it up to touch the spot where my finger had been.

My heart melted.

What kind of crazy sorcery was this? Did it need to be this cute to make the magic work? Ugh.

I held out the little wily thing and dropped it gently on Minnie's chest. It slowly spread out paper-thin wings punctuated by spindly claws. So delicate and yet still the stuff of nightmares. It shuffled its way up to her face, using its bony elbows to help pull itself along with its tiny feet. Then it curled up again and sank into the hollow at the base of her neck.

I felt a slight tug on my scrye as the thick shielding cracked against it, only to then stretch and thin before solidifying again.

I blinked.

That answered that, then. Somewhat. I could share the protection by sharing the bat, but it wasn't a limitless resource.

Nothing appeared to happen to Minnie. Which I should have been prepared for. I knew full well that preventatives and cures rarely worked the same way.

"I had to try," I said to Sassie, then sighed and stood up. "I don't know how or why, but I think this thing's been protecting me from getting petrified."

Sassie narrowed her eyes, leaning in to get a closer look at the bat.

"I can run some tests," she said slowly. "If someone's worked protective magic on the animal, we might be able to reverse engineer the effect it's meant to protect against—maybe even figure out our own way to stop it."

I scooped up the bat quickly, and Sassie stood upright to look at me. "Let's wait a bit on that," I said. As much as I wanted to bottle up the bat's magic so I could work it on Noah right now, I had to be careful and efficient about it.

"Darcy—"

"I know," I said to stop her. "I know it makes sense to run tests. It's a good idea. But we might not need to. Just let me check in with the DSC people first to see if they have any theories."

Sassie blinked once and said, "If you must."

And with that, I nodded and left the room, popping the bat back in my bra. I sent a quick text to Etty suggesting she find Noah a pet bat and then headed back through the front room, this time following the blood trail Carina had left when she'd come in.

I grimaced and ducked into a supply closet to pull out a mop, almost without even thinking about it. There were very few places in the world where I would clean up a blood trail without being asked to do so, and I was a little surprised to realize this was still one of them.

It felt good, pushing the wet strands of fabric along the floor and watching them absorb the blood. Eggshell tiles gleamed beneath remnants of water that was still slightly pink. I went back to the entryway and did another pass with fresh water, and by the time I got to the old room Adrian was using as an office, the tightness in my chest had loosened a good deal.

"You know I'm the least-qualified person in the building for this," I heard Adrian say through the cracked door.

I paused, something stopping me from going in.

"It's not like it's hard," I heard Carina say, and I took a step back to peer through the crack. "Just clean it and put on the goopy stuff."

She was sitting on the cot that had been pushed into a corner, wearing a rolled-up pair of his sweatpants and my jacket pulled over her chest instead of her back. He was standing behind her, looking a bit ill as he stared down at her back.

"You sure you don't need stitches?" he asked.

"I heal fast," she said. "It's not bleeding, is it? Dragon claws are hot when they slash—should have cauterized the flesh."

"It's not bleeding," Adrian said, but he didn't look happy about her explanation. "How did you manage this anyway?"

She was quiet for a moment, and my legs itched to walk me in there—either that or back away to avoid eavesdropping.

"I was trying to hold on to the dragon, and it was trying to leave me," she eventually said, then shook her head. "I don't know how to get it to do what I want anymore."

Adrian dabbed at Carina's back, and she winced. "I don't have any personal experience shifting," he said, "but I doubt slashing yourself up is the answer."

"That's not what I was trying to do—obviously," she said. "I was just frustrated. When I'm only partway shifted, it's hard to tell where everything is going because the proportions and nerve pathways are all wrong."

Had Carina really clawed herself in the back without me noticing? I'd been pretty distracted by Rose and Oya, and I had handed her my jacket without really looking at her after the fight.

"Nerve pathways?" I could hear the smile in Adrian's voice. "Wouldn't've thought someone your age would know what that was."

"That's because most kids my age aren't dragons or witches or murderers," Carina said sharply.

Adrian stopped. He put down the cloth in his hand and stood still behind her. I wished I could see him better through the crack, but the light was too dim and there was too much junk in the way.

Just go in, I told myself. But my feet still didn't move.

"Are you done?" Carina eventually said, twisting to look at him. "Did you get the goopy stuff?"

Adrian's shoulders jerked slightly, and he reached down to pick something up. "Gooping now," he said. Then, in a quieter voice: "Is that what you really think you are?"

"What?" Carina asked.

"A murderer."

Without missing a beat, Carina answered, "I've killed people. Innocent and unprovoked."

"The ones from the Metro?" Adrian asked.

Carina nodded. "And don't bother telling me that I wasn't myself or it wasn't my fault. Control and intent are already messy when you're a shifter—I've never really been one person, always two, and the second has bad impulse control. It's still always my responsibility, whatever that second part does. It's still me that's doing things even when they're things I'd rather not be doing."

"But this wasn't the second you—it wasn't you at all. Your soul wasn't there in your body."

"What even *is* a soul?" Carina said with a snort. "It's just another part of me. Not the whole thing. What don't you get? Whatever *any* part of me does—it's mine. Something I did."

Carina winced as Adrian's hands moved over her back. He finished what he was doing in silence and put the goop down as she stared blankly ahead.

"I've only ever been one person," Adrian eventually said. "But I know what it feels like to be a murderer too."

"You only kill bad guys," Carina said, twisting around to look at him. "That makes you a hero, not a murderer."

"I've only ever killed *three* bad guys," Adrian replied, "and it didn't feel very heroic."

"The three vampires from last night?"

He nodded, and she twisted back around to hop off the cot.

"They were trying to kill us," she said.

"I know," he agreed. "But I've killed my share of people who didn't deserve it too. A long time ago."

I sucked in a breath. This was it. My feet really needed to move. In or out.

I could eavesdrop on Carina without too much guilt because she was a kid and my responsibility while we were away from her dad. He'd asked me to keep her sane, and she only seemed to want to talk to everyone other than me.

Adrian, on the other hand . . . I shouldn't know anything he didn't want to tell me to my face.

I stepped backwards, adrenaline rushing through me as I heard Carina ask him for clarification. I needed to get out of here fast.

Except I'd just mopped a blood trail off the floor, and the tiles were still wet.

In an impressive feat of ridiculous normalcy, I slipped and fell on my ass.

"Birds," I cursed, and the bat in my tits stared up at me with wide eyes. "Sorry, little thing."

I looked up with a frown as Carina opened the door and stuck her head out. At least I'd made it far enough before falling that it shouldn't be obvious I'd been listening to them.

"Hey," I said to her sternly. "The next time you want to carry a freshly severed head into a civilized space, you need to ask where the mop is."

She looked at me like I'd grown another head to be severed.

"I did it for you this time, but it won't happen again." Before she could argue with me, I asked, "Is Adrian in there?"

He appeared behind her in the doorway and swiftly walked out past her when he saw me. His hand stretched out to me as his eyes met mine.

"Thanks," I said as I put my own hand in his.

He didn't pull, just gave me a firm grip to pull myself up with.

When I did, he stood still instead of stepping back, and I ended up with my face just a couple inches from his chest. I breathed in, my heart slowing as I felt the warmth coming off him and his familiar scent cut through the medicinal smell of the clinic.

Who did he kill—and how, and why? The questions flashed through my mind, but I shooed them away. He would tell me eventually, if it mattered. And right now, it didn't.

He was smiling calmly when I looked up at his face. "You got her," he said.

"I did." I nodded, wishing things were simple enough that I had time to celebrate the small victories.

Carina scoffed loudly behind him. "You wasted your time is what you did," she called out. "I was fine. Oya wasn't going to hurt me."

"He needed to die anyway," I called back to her. No sense in arguing with the girl. "And now we have another lead," I said in a lower voice, looking back up at Adrian.

He led me back into his makeshift office, and I told him what Oya's assistant had said about the vampires at Celestial, then about what had happened with Rose and her assistant and the bat.

"Where is it?" he asked when I was done. I leaned over and pulled the top of my shirt away from my chest. His eyebrows came together as he stared into my cleavage. "You did that on purpose, didn't you?"

"No," I said, "but are you complaining?"

He shook his head only slightly. I went ahead and scooped the bat out of my boobs so Carina wouldn't have to watch this turn into something inappropriate.

Adrian made no move to touch the small creature, just turned his head and bent closer to look at it. He brought out his phone and took a picture. "Not sure what species it is, but I can find out."

"Alright, I'm out," Carina said from across the room. She'd been listening intently to me recounting our story, but apparently discussing bat species was where she drew her line. "Your aunt owes me a dead body to study."

She hopped off the cot, still wearing my jacket across her front, and walked to the door. A pinkish-brown gash of scar tissue ran diagonally across her lower back. She did heal fast, apparently, if that wound had been goop-able not too long ago.

I moved my feet, wanting to follow her, but she'd be safe for now in Sassie's hands. I'd sit her down for a nice, long chat as soon as I ended the vampire witches who were trying to turn her and everyone she knew into obsidian statues.

Which reminded me. "Have you heard from Ray since yesterday?" I asked Adrian once Carina had left the room. Yesterday was when Sassie had said the last obsidian wave had been.

"I just tried calling him," Adrian said. "Figured it was a good time while I had his daughter here to say hi, but he didn't pick up."

"So that's a no," I said as something sank deep in my chest. I pulled out my phone and found Ray's number. "I'm going to try him. We need to show him the bat." *And I need to know he's still alive.*

Ray didn't answer on the first ring, or the second, but after the third he responded, "Bueno," and then his face showed up on my screen.

"Oh, thank our batshit crazy god," I said after letting out a breath. Ray looked like hell, but at least he wasn't a statue.

"For what?" he asked. "I hear you went back to the mountain with your torch."

I nodded slowly. It felt like so long ago already that I'd spoken with Popo. So long ago that he'd given me the impossible task of finding an arrow in the underworld, which I was no closer to even knowing where to begin on.

"I'm just happy you're alive," I said. "No witch is safe right now, that I know of—except for me and Carina."

"¿Cómo?"

I took out the bat and held it up in front of the phone. "See it?"

"Yes, but why?" he replied.

"Can you . . . I don't know, touch the picture on the phone and pretend you're touching the bat?"

Ray looked at me just like Carina had when I'd lectured her on cleaning up her own blood trails. Like daughter like father.

"Just try it, please?" I needed to entertain the very unlikely possibility that I could protect Noah via video call before moving on to more complicated options.

"I did it," Ray said.

"And do you feel anything?"

He lifted his shoulders in a shrug. "Like what?"

I sighed, wondering why I bothered ever expecting anything to be simple. "Ok, so it only works in person."

"What does?" Ray started walking somewhere. "I don't have time for these games—just tell me what is going on."

"I think the bat is protecting us—me and Carina, and now probably Minnie—from Itztla. I wanted to see if I could get it to work for you too. My aunt says the victims are coming in waves of different materials, which means he's targeting only one god's witches at a time in small increments, changing every hour. We haven't seen any obsidian since yesterday, but more of Popo's witches could be next."

"And how did you get the guard-bat?" Ray asked as he quirked up an eyebrow.

"I stole it from one of Itztla's witches. A vampire."

Ray dipped his head as if to concede my story made perfect sense. "How does it work?"

"No idea. I was hoping to ask if you knew."

Ray squinted at the screen and grunted. "If you took it from one of Itztla's witches, then it will be closely linked to what he is doing. But we still have not been able to come up with any plausible theories on *how* he is doing it."

Behind me, Adrian was typing away at his laptop. "There's a death god associated with bats in Maya mythology," he offered. "Camazotz."

Ray shook his head, then tilted it to the side. "Wait one second."

I met Adrian's eyes and gave him a small shrug.

"Have you heard of Itzpapalotl?" Ray asked after a moment, his eyes cast down.

"No," I said at the same time as Adrian said, "Yes."

"She is a goddess," Ray said, "often known as the Obsidian Butterfly."

More obsidian—just what we need. "And?" I asked aloud.

"Bats are sometimes called black butterflies in old stories, and some say they have seen Itzpapalotl with the clawed, leather-like wings of a bat."

I breathed in deep, poking around at my memories of what had happened earlier in the day. "Rose grew wings like that," I said slowly, "when she tasted the tree-girl's blood. She said it was fae infused. And she was holding this bat when she did it."

"Fae infused," Adrian muttered, eyes cast down as he typed furiously. When he looked up, he was frowning. "Still seems like a stretch," he said. "All we really have that points to this goddess are a magic guard-bat and bat wings growing on a vampire."

"Except," Ray said, "Itzpapalotl is also famously one of the cihuateteo."

At my blank look, Adrian supplied, "Divine Women. The Aztecs believed that childbirth was violent work, just like battle, and so the spirits of women who died in childbirth were honored like warriors who had died in battle."

"So this goddess with bat wings was originally the spirit of a woman who died giving birth?" I asked. "Why does that matter?"

"The cihuateteo . . ." Ray repeated, "because they died while giving life, some of the spirits are motivated to steal that life back. And they can—and do."

"What do you mean?" I asked, but something cold was creeping through my gut at his words.

"Some of them are known to haunt crossroads at night and steal children who wander by," Ray explained. "But they don't steal the whole child—only its life force, leaving it a shriveled husk even its mother couldn't recognize."

The cold in my gut crept up into my heart, and I let out my breath with a groan. "Shriveled husk?" That sounded a lot like what I'd just seen where Minnie's arm used to be. She wasn't a child . . . but Noah with his raisin foot certainly was.

I swept away from Ray's face on my phone and brought up the picture Etty had sent me, then forwarded it to Ray.

"Would it look something like that?" I asked as Adrian peered over my shoulder to see. "It's Noah," I added when their affirmative noises confirmed what I'd already guessed. "But the same thing is happening to Minnie's arm; the crystals are gone."

Adrian's hand found its way to my back, fingers pressing in around my spine and sending a tingling warmth all the way through me. I breathed out slowly.

"Why did you say some of them?" Adrian asked, looking at Ray's face that was back up on my screen. "Some of them are known to haunt crossroads and steal children—not all?"

Ray shrugged. "Most of these spirits reside safely in the underworld, where they help the fallen warriors to guide the sun through the darkness from dusk until dawn."

"That . . ." I started, my brain working to find some connection to Itztla's story involving the sun and the underworld.

"That is not the point," Ray said quickly. "The ability to steal a life force—this is something one can obtain from the corpse of any of these women that has not been properly guarded."

My heart dropped. How many women died in childbirth in the world every day? I didn't know the number—didn't want to know—but I was sure it was too many.

"And what happens when you try to steal the life force of a god?" Adrian asked in a quiet voice, his eyes unfocused.

"If that god has no witches in their following? I don't know," Ray answered. "But if they do? A small portion of their life force would be residing in every one of their witches. I expect the result looks something like what we are seeing right now."

"So he isn't 'stealing witches' exactly," I said slowly. "He isn't trying to weaken other gods. He's trying to kill them. And not only gods with witches—those are just the ones we're noticing."

"That could be why we're seeing something different with Minnie and Noah," Adrian suggested. "They aren't witches, and not gods either, but it's possible they each command their own divine energy—maybe they're being affected the same way a god with no witches would be."

"Etty did say something strange was happening to Baz in prison too. And he's a djinn, like Noah."

"Maybe," Ray said. "I don't know why Itztla would be trying to kill other gods."

"Do you see another alternative?" I asked.

"Maybe he doesn't care what happens to the other gods. Maybe he's motivated by what he can do with all the life force he steals."

"What can he do with it?" I asked.

Ray and Adrian were both silent. Adrian lost in his thoughts and Ray looking like the world was about to end.

"That's impossible to say," Ray eventually said. "I don't know if there is anything he *couldn't* do . . . with the life force of every other god in existence."

I bit the inside of my cheek.

That didn't sound good at all.

"What can we do?" I asked, thinking aloud. "Any luck finding a way into the underworld?"

"Not yet," Adrian said. "There are various entrances mentioned in many, many different myths and old stories—from many different cultures all over the world. None are known to be in working order."

"Not surprising," I said. "If they were, someone would have capitalized on it by now. 'Spend a weekend in hell to visit your ancestors and maybe torture them . . .' Sounds fun."

"Heh." Adrian gave me another half-smile, but it didn't have the same spark as usual. "I have people on it, checking out the closest ones in person. So far, no luck."

"It may be better to focus on the bats," Ray said.

"How so?" I asked.

"You want to get to the underworld to find the arrow we need to take down Itztlacoliuhqui himself. But if he is using one or more of the cihuateteo to do what he is doing, then we can stop him by stopping them."

I nodded. "Okay, let me get this straight. He could be using one or more of these spirits of divine women to help him drain the life forces of all these gods . . . or he could be using the corpses they left behind when they died giving birth. But could he be working with the black-butterfly goddess herself?" If so, that wouldn't make my task any easier. Instead of finding the hell arrow to kill one god, I'd have to do something potentially equally impossible to kill a goddess.

"No." Ray actually chuckled. "He can't be working with Itzpapalotl herself because she's dead."

My spine straightened a little. A goddess had died? Had someone killed her? If so, whatever it had taken to do so must not have been impossible. "How did she die?"

"Crushed by a cactus," Ray said with a smile, "while trying to eat another god's heart."

I opened my mouth, then closed it again and blinked. "A . . . cactus," I eventually said. Ray ignored me.

"But even dead," he continued, "no god or goddess truly ceases to exist while people still remember them. The cihuateteo will always recognize her as one of their own, even if it is only her memory. This is why bats can be used to appease them."

"You've got to be fucking with me," I said, and he gave me a confused look. "A *cactus?*"

"That's what I—"

"How does a cactus even *crush* someone? It's not like it can go walking around looking for wrestling partners—it's a plant!"

Ray stared at me for a moment before answering, "It fell from the sky."

"No," I said, shaking my head. This was too much. "No. That's—"

Adrians's hand made its way to my upper back, fingers working their magic on the tense muscles that might just be the only thing holding me together at this point.

I took a deep breath, then let it out. "You're telling me I can't kill the god we need to kill without finding a way to the underworld and then looking for a very specific arrow in a stack of demonic torture devices so we can shoot him with it—but here's this other goddess that was so easy to kill someone just needed to drop a fucking cactus on her head?"

"No," Ray said. "I'm not telling you that. Who told you there was only one way to kill Itztlacoliuhqui or even that the arrow would certainly work?"

I clenched my teeth together, thinking back to what Popo had said. He didn't know how to kill Itztla. There was likely no one answer. This hell arrow was just his best guess. And that was what really pissed me off about the idea of going to the underworld to find it. Not that it might be impossible—because how many other impossible things had I already managed to pull off? —but that even if I could do it, it might all be for nothing.

"So we focus on the bats," I said as I dug my fingernails into my palms. That was what Ray had said. Focus on the tool the evil fucker was using rather than the god himself.

"If he is using any cihuateteo spirits, the bats will appease them. If he is using their corpses, you can destroy them."

"Dad?" Carina's voice carried from behind me, and I turned to see her standing at the door. My jacket was gone, as were Adrian's pants; someone had put her in a brown tunic. Because of-fucking-course I had to distance her from one weird magic cult just to get her sucked into another.

Ray's face froze, a deer in daughter headlights. When I turned my phone so he could see her, it melted in an absurd combination of fear and relief.

"Mija," he said in a strained but cheerful voice, "I've missed you."

"Miss you too, Dad," Carina said easily.

He just looked at her, eyes wandering over her drab outfit and the blood and soot in her hair, biting back all the questions I was sure he was desperate to ask. None of them could be answered while we were facing something so huge and outside of ourselves.

Carina had her eyes on the bat.

"Sassie sent me to bring that in for tests," she said. "And to tell you that it's stopped spreading."

"Absolutely not on the tests," I said as I gave the bat a little nudge and dropped it back in my boobs. "What's stopped spreading?"

"The gross mummy arm on your redheaded friend," she replied. "Still there but Sassie's been tracking the rate of growth and noticed that it's stopped."

"That's amazing," I said. "It's really working then." When I noticed Adrian and Ray looking at me, I added, "I tried putting the bat on Minnie and felt its protection stretch when I did. I don't think it could stretch much further, though."

"So one bat only goes so far," Adrian mused. "How many do you think we'll need to get the cihuateteo to stop?"

And how are we going to acquire a bunch of bats? I wondered.

"None," Ray said.

"What?" I asked. Wasn't that the opposite of what he'd just been telling us?

"You shouldn't need actual bats," he went on. "Typical offerings are pieces of bread shaped like bats."

I turned to Carina. "Minnie's still unconscious?" The girl nodded. "Then I don't know where we're going to get all this bat bread. Actual bats may be easier."

"'Bread' can be interpreted loosely," Ray said with a glint in his eye, and I wondered what absurd idea he was going to hit me with next.

20

An hour later, I sat in my car parked on Magnolia Blvd waiting for Carina to come out of the gaudy shop in front of me.

My eyes were glued to my phone.

Deal is off. Can't help myself. Tell Minnie I tried.

That was the message Tula had sent me at some point during the drive from the clinic. And I had no idea what it meant.

The first part, sure—she had no intention of making good on her end of the deal despite the fact that I'd already held up mine. Fine. Whatever. I'd kill Simeon on my own. At least now I probably knew where he was.

But *why* would she call it off? And what about the rest of it? Can't help herself? Was she some kind of an addict? What had she tried to do that Minnie would care about, and why couldn't she tell her wife herself?

There were way too many possible answers to those questions, and I could think of none that were good.

Something banged on the passenger-side window, and I looked up to see Carina holding up a huge plastic bag with orange and black lettering on it. She was also snuggled up in a fluffy feather boa made up of black and white ostrich feathers.

"Too soon?" she asked when I unlocked the door and she slid inside.

I opened my mouth to answer, but she flung a handful of black confetti in my face before I could.

I squeezed my eyes shut and clenched my fingers around my phone so I wouldn't be tempted to hit her. When I felt the little plastic bits settle in my hair and on my cheeks, I opened my eyes and picked one of the pieces up from my lap. It was in the shape of a small bat.

"Bat confetti?" I asked. "We drove all the way to an all-year Halloween shop to get bat confetti? This isn't even loosely in the same category as bread."

"I think it'll work," she said. "They're both for celebrations. But you should at least pretend to like it—intent matters when you make offerings to appease gods and monsters."

"Is that all you got?" I asked as my eye twitched.

"Found some stamps, too." Carina stuck her whole arm in the bag and rustled around until she found something at the bottom. She brought it out to show me, a plastic figurine of a bat with outstretched wings and a little round ink pad attached to its feet.

I sighed as I watched her bat-stamp the back of her hand to show me. These were not the kinds of weapons I was used to taking into battle. But then, life clearly had no fucks to give when it came to keeping me in my comfort zone.

I started the car. We had one more stop to make, which would hopefully make me feel a little better.

"How are you doing?" I asked the little dragon draped in ostrich feathers as I pulled into traffic.

She pulled her boa tighter around her and plucked a feather out of it. Then another.

"Are you upset that I killed Oya?" I prodded. She'd asked me to kill him, in the moment. Yet here she was, wrapping herself in ostrich, looking like she missed the fucker.

Three more feathers were plucked and thrown to the bunnies before she said, "I'm upset that I didn't."

"Couldn't," I corrected.

Carina looked up at me, a sour expression on her face.

"You would have killed him if you could," I said. "But you're still learning how to use the tools you have at your disposal. Know how many years it took me to get good enough with weapons to know I could hold my own? How many assholes I wish I could have killed before I did?"

Carina gave me a twisted shrug. "Probably a lot?"

"Right, but I don't feel guilty about not killing any of them because as much as they deserved it, it would have been irresponsible for me to even try. Know what I *do* feel guilty about?"

"Probably a lot," Carina said with a giggle and sat straighter in her seat.

I shook my head. "I feel guilty about not killing Simeon when I had the chance—because I *did* have the chance. I had his head in my hands with none of his allies nearby. I could have found some matches to burn it or a discreet bag to stuff it in and carry it with me, but instead I set it down somewhere I had no reason to believe was secure and then cried about it when it found its way back to him."

"Yeah, that was a dumb move," Carina said, and I tried not to regret having filled her in on what had happened with the vampire mastermind behind the chaneques who had stolen her soul. "But he was the senator you were boning, right?"

That I hadn't told her. "How did—" I stopped myself and grunted. "Yes, sure," I conceded. "But that's exactly my point. I *chose* not to destroy his head then and there because there was still a part of me that didn't want to." Something I hadn't admitted while conscious until right now. "And I chose not to keep it with me because I didn't want to carry around a reminder of that."

"Definitely dumb," Carina said.

"Yes," I agreed. "But *you* tried. You chose to kill Oya, and you would have if your dragon had cooperated. It didn't, so you did the next best thing and asked me for help. He ended up dead in the end."

"Not yet," Carina whispered. When I looked over, she'd gone a bit pale.

"Didn't you burn his head at the clinic?" I asked.

"Not yet," she repeated, head turned down. More feathers fell to the bunnies. "I wanted to do it with my breath, but the dragon still wouldn't come."

I bit the inside of my cheek in frustration. I was the absolute worst aunt. Maybe even worse than Sassie. Had I really just told that whole story to make the point that Carina was just as dumb as me?

"You left it somewhere secure though," I tried.

"With Adrian," she said.

"Don't worry." I jerked the steering wheel over to make a sharp turn into the studio parking lot I'd almost missed. "He'll keep it safe for you."

I pulled up to the guard house, rolled down my window, glanced at the name tag (Kevin) on the guard who asked for my name, and said, "Darcy. I'm here to make some s'mores."

"Perfect," Kevin said smoothly, turning away from me without making eye contact. "I have your marshmallows right here, if you'll just pop your trunk."

I bent down to pull the lever while Kevin walked around to the back of the car. He lifted open the hatch and hefted a long canvas bag inside. After giving it a pat, he closed the trunk and walked back around, instructing me on where to drive before exiting so it wouldn't look like I'd come here just to see him. Which, of course, I had.

"Thanks, Dirk," I mumbled after I'd rolled my window back

up, glad he'd set up this little hand-off when I'd updated him. Louder, I said, "With marshmallows back there, we won't need to cart around any more vampire heads if we don't want to—dragon or no dragon."

Carina looked away from me and rested her head against the window, and I gripped the wheel tighter.

We would make this work.

We had to.

ADRIAN WAS STANDING on a street corner just a couple blocks away by the time we made it to Celestial. In plain clothes, hands in the pockets of a loose gray coat—perfect for a cool spring LA night of killing. Had he taken a page out of my book and hidden weapons under there?

I rolled to a stop in front of him, and he picked up a black bag at his feet before getting in the back.

"I didn't think you were coming," I said, avoiding the urge to stare at him in the rearview mirror.

"DSC won't go near Celestial, but that doesn't mean I can't take a night off."

"Are you here as an East Coast police officer then, or . . .?"

"Just me," he said, catching my eye in the mirror.

It sent a current of excitement through me, and I looked away. "Just you and whatever's under that coat."

"Gross," Carina said.

I reached over to give her a flick on the shoulder.

"I couldn't bring the DSC van," Adrian said, "so I raided it instead." He opened up his coat and brought something out, then handed it up to us.

Carina took it, and I looked to the side while I pulled into a parking space on the street. It was one of the stunners he'd been using to keep vampires' hearts from healing. Worked better than just leaving the knife in there after stabbing them because their bodies would eventually expel any blade or bullet—the point of these was that they stayed put.

"I have sixty of them," Adrian said. "Think that'll be enough?"

I raised my eyebrows. "I love that you think we have enough weapons and stamina and luck to take on sixty vampires and get them all through the heart."

"I think you have enough of all that to take on seventy," he said, "but sixty was all I had."

I couldn't not smile. "You know you don't have to say that to get in my—" I stopped myself with a glance at Carina, then swallowed. "You know I'm going to have to kill some of them, if not most."

"I know," he said. "But with more options for incapacitating them, you're more likely to come out of it alive."

I turned off the engine and unclipped my seatbelt, twisting in my seat to face him. I wanted to ask what had changed in him, and why, that all his qualms about killing vampires had seemingly vanished. Instead, I held out my hand to take the small object he was handing me. It looked like a button, with a little clip in the back.

"Camera," he said. "If we're your backup, we're going to do it properly. This too." He handed me an earpiece, which I popped in my left ear after clipping the button-camera to my jacket. He looked at me expectantly as he tapped on the microphone of a headset, and I nodded when the sound came through in my ear.

"Stay together in the car if you can," I said. I'd parked close enough that they could see the building without sitting conspicuously right in front of it. "If I see an opening to get you in, I'll do it. If I can smoke any of them out, I'll do that too. Best thing you can do for me, if none of that works, is make sure I don't miss it when I find the spirits I'm supposed to appease."

"Or their corpses to destroy," Carina reminded me as she handed me the bag full of confetti and stamps.

I paused as I took it from her, wondering why she wasn't fighting to go with me rather than stay in the car as backup. I hadn't wanted her here at all, but she'd insisted, and I'd assumed she would keep pressing. But Celestial's reputation was no joke. Carina may be more mature than the average eight-year-old, but even she must know she had no chance of walking in where I was about to go. I held her stare for a moment and then nodded, glad that Adrian had shown up.

Before I could say anything, she turned away from me and leaned around her seat to look at Adrian. "Did you get my text?"

"I did." He picked up the bag he'd set beside him and passed it up to Carina.

She glanced inside quickly before passing it straight to me.

"What is th—" I stopped when I poked the top open and saw Oya's bulging dead eyes staring back at me.

"Burn it for me," Carina said, "since I can't."

I tried not to grimace, but that's easier said than done when a surprise severed head lands in your lap. "You don't want me to just find you some fire?"

She shook her head. "You were right. I didn't do it because I couldn't. I won't fix that by taking shortcuts. I need to work on my dragon before I try to kill anything else—if I even want to."

"You—"

"I'm going to stay with Sassie for . . . I don't know how long. I just need to learn how to do something *else*. Separate myself from the killing so I have the space to . . ." She tightened her mouth in a frown as her forehead scrunched, and I wasn't sure if she didn't know what she wanted to say or just didn't want to say it.

"To separate the fighting from the murder?" Adrian's voice was clear, commanding even though he was asking a question, and Carina's shoulders relaxed upon hearing it.

"My dad will hate me for it," she said, her eyes cast down.

"He won't," I said. "He would have left Popo a long time ago if it weren't for you. That's the whole reason he brought you to DC to find me—so he would be useful enough to stay with Popo, because he thought that was what you wanted."

"It *was* what I wanted," Carina said, fingering her phone in her lap. "But did he really think I wouldn't have gone with him?"

"Maybe he thought you would hate him for it," I offered. Like daughter, like father. Carina was silent, but the bunnies had begun chittering at my feet. "Oh, shut up," I said to them. "You wanna go tell the mountain what bad witches we are? So disloyal we're about to save our god's life. Go tell him that." I held my hand down towards the churning mass of shiny black rodents. "Or you can come help me instead."

There was more chittering, more churning, and even the occasional flash of a glowing red eye. But after a few long moments, one of the bunnies hopped onto my hand. Warm and heavy, it climbed up my arm onto my shoulder and perched under my hair at the back of my neck.

I closed my eyes and breathed in. It felt like getting a hot-stone massage, which wasn't exactly relaxing so soon after the phoenix had pummeled me with stones so hot they were molten.

When I opened my eyes, something unmoving glinted beside the mass of bunnies at my feet. I reached down and picked up Tula's necklace, which I had completely forgotten about by now. Had it been keeping the rabbits company this whole time? I was certain it hadn't been there just a second ago when I'd looked at the same spot.

It'd probably popped up because it knew where I was headed. Back into Celestial. I slipped the necklace into my pocket. A sentient piece of jewelry eager to return to its master? Nothing creepy about that at all. But I was eager to be rid of it.

Popping the trunk, I got out of the car. I had to reach all the way in the back of the trunk to get the head I'd taken off the vampire in Oya's studio lab. When I pulled the black plastic open to look at it, it was in exactly the same condition as Oya's. Dead, but still fresh. Not decaying. Which meant it still wasn't *really* dead.

I plopped it down on the sidewalk and then dropped Oya's head right next to it. Then I opened the bag I'd picked up from Kevin and peered inside.

Just like Dirk had promised. I smiled. Good thing he had developed an obsession with flamethrowers. And good thing no one in LA ever batted an eye at crazy shit going down on the street, I thought as I took it out of its bag.

The weapon was lighter and smaller than any of its kind I'd ever seen, and I felt a zing as it immediately connected with my scrye. I licked my lips. I'd never used a weapon designed to work with magic, but now seemed like a good time to start.

I aimed it at the two heads. One squeeze of the trigger and they were burning. Another squeeze, and they were unrecognizable lumps of coal. Without the magic boost, it would have taken a lot more sustained heat to burn something so wet and squishy.

Good. Maybe I had a chance in hell of not dying in there after all.

"Done," I said to Carina through the open door as I packed the flamethrower back in its case and slung it over my shoulder.

Carina climbed over the middle console and leaned out over the edge of the driver's seat to inspect my work.

Her fingers tightened over the seat cushion, and for a second there was a flash of claw digging into the stuffing. Then she looked up at me and asked, "You really think my dad will want to leave Popo if I do?" Her voice was small, softer than I'd ever heard it. She almost sounded like Noah, the innocent little kid asking me for a big ocean fish.

"I think your dad would do anything for you," I answered

truthfully. And wasn't she lucky for that? It was something I wasn't sure I'd ever had, not from Sassie or Fred and not from either of the birth parents I'd never known.

Carina shifted to sit back in her seat, sucking her cheeks in briefly before saying, "Thanks, Darcy."

I nodded, and my eyes drifted over to Adrian, who'd been watching us quietly. I pulled an empty paper bag from the trunk and handed it to him. "For the stunners?"

He emptied his pockets into the bag, and I slipped it over my wrist next to the gaudy Halloween one filled with confetti. Hopefully I looked more like someone who'd just been shopping than someone ready to rain death on a bunch of vampire witches. It probably helped that I'd put on a stretchier bra and a lower-cut shirt so that the bat would be more comfortable.

Adrian's eyes were on my face, though, when I looked back in the car with my hand on the open door, ready to close it. It was a rare sight, him not standing tall over me. His shoulders were hunched over just a bit, that powerful frame packed up all neat and tidy, as if the new glasses and the coat and the soft smile could hide what was in his nature. I'd seen him in action. I couldn't unsee it.

I *wanted* him to come with me. Could taste how delicious it would feel to really fight alongside him. But this time, I was going alone out of necessity.

He brought the mic on his headset close to his mouth while holding my stare. "Good hunting," he said in a low voice. I could barely hear him across the few feet between us, but his voice resonated deep in my ear. It was something I'd never heard him say before—and it meant he *was* coming with me, in the way that mattered most.

With yet another small smile I couldn't hold back, I closed the door and was on my way.

Celestial loomed ahead of me, its mirrored windows

reflecting the sun from the other side of the street. With every step I took, it was more difficult to see all the way to the top, more difficult to ignore the gnawing uncertainty in my gut.

The last time I'd walked in there, I'd come dangerously close to being scorpion food—would have, if Tula hadn't rescued me. I couldn't count on her doing that again.

But things were different now. Different enough?

Only one way to find out.

21

I SLIPPED my sunglasses on and walked into Celestial with my eyes closed.

The phoenix raged within me.

How long had it been doing that?

Since I was a child, there'd always been a small part of me that thought this tumultuous, explosive beast inside me was a part of my own being, something to rein in and push down and control, control, control. Maybe even something like Carina's capricious dragon.

When I'd seen the molten bird fly out of the volcano, flapping and shrieking and burning, I hadn't wanted to admit that it felt so familiar.

But it did. It was like looking in a mirror, seeing yourself for the first time and realizing that was never you at all.

After so long, though, maybe now it *was* me too.

This was the thought I clung to with every step, head held high, boots clomping on the polished floors of this fake little civilization that was a classroom for immortal beings.

They were pretending to be something they weren't.

I was done pretending.

Fake shopkeepers made polite noises at me, but the phoenix didn't care, so neither did I. I kept my eyes shut firmly as I walked right by.

Nothing to see here but pathetic freakshows floundering in their old age, desperate to be born anew.

We could help them with that, the phoenix and I.

We could be just what they needed.

Warm air shifted behind me as my wings stretched up and out. They felt different, this time. No pain, and no feathers. They licked the back of my neck and my shoulders like flames as cool wind rushed under them, ready to lift me into the heavens at the slightest command.

My boots no longer clomped on tiles; rather, they floated on ashes. Everything I touched may as well be ashes.

An elevator dinged ahead.

A smooth voice in my ear told me to stop.

I rustled up the courage to open my eyes.

The man part of the scorpion man stood before me—suit pristine, neck intact, no creepy-crawly exoskeleton in sight.

I said nothing. Stayed with the phoenix. Raging and burning and floating in place.

He reached up and removed his hat, then held it against his chest and lowered his head.

"Welcome to Celestial," he said in the same melodic voice he'd used the other day, right before he'd tried to kill me. Only a tiny hint of click-clacking in the back of his throat. The elevator doors opened, and he gestured toward the open space with his free hand. "If you'll please proceed to level B4, we'll get your membership processed right away."

I stepped in the elevator and paused while the doors closed, finger hovering over the buttons. After a moment, I pressed B4.

Then I waited, standing still and stoking the inferno raging in my scrye.

If I were just Darcy right now, I might be in a hurry to root out the vampires and break up their little games.

But the phoenix was never in a hurry. The notion did not compute.

When the elevator doors opened again, I stepped out into a dark little slice of wild illusions. Straight ahead, a man sat behind a desk. He looked almost identical to the scorpion man who had met me at the elevator. Brothers? How many in their brood of bloodthirsty bugs?

As my eyes shifted across the space, so too did the colors and shapes around me. Thick gray tree trunks covered in vines turned to sparkling ocean, then to dripping stone, then dark clouds sparking with flashes of light, only to circle back again and again before finally landing on the steaming rocks in the crater of a rumbling volcano.

"Apologies," the man said in a voice just as melodic as his brother's. "We've never had one of your kind before. I hope the scenery is to your liking." It wasn't a question.

I stepped forward, slightly distracted by the sudden urge to take off my shoes and relish in the sting of the hot pebbles under my feet.

Fake pebbles, I was reminded. Ashes. All of this was ashes.

The man reached out over the desk, presenting me with a long, thick piece of paper covered in tiny words.

The human part of me wanted to read it.

The human part of me would get us all killed if she wanted anything too loudly in here.

There was something resting on top of the paper. I picked it up. A tiny knife to go with the tiny words.

I pricked my thumb with the blade and then slipped it in my

pocket. Human or bird or blazing inferno, one could never have enough knives.

Two drops of blood fell on the page before the man whisked it away.

"Congratulations on your membership," he said slowly, delicately.

These words were made to last. The phoenix took note.

I shivered.

"Your welcome pack." He handed over a shiny gold bag, which I slipped over my wrist right next to the others. "And your key."

I tilted the smooth metal object between my fingers, holding back the fire so I wouldn't melt it.

Was it safe to hold back the fire now that I'd signed their forms with my blood? No takey-backsies, even if I were to start looking more human than scary old bird?

Maybe wait a bit longer. At least until the creepy-crawly scorpion bros were out of sight.

I dropped the key into the bag and let the fire keep raging. It took me back to the elevator, floating on ashes as my awareness fought to stay in the background without disappearing entirely.

The bird wanted to go to our new digs, whatever room that key would open. When the elevator doors closed, I pushed forward and pressed the button for Tula's floor instead.

Nausea twisted my insides as my body resisted the command. It wasn't the bird fighting me; it wasn't really anything *fighting* me. It was just the profound weirdness of one vehicle trying to respond to two drivers at the same time. It wasn't built that way. No one was.

We were.

Another twist of nausea hit me as the thought that wasn't mine echoed through my head. The phoenix had spoken to me when I'd seen it at the mountain, but this was the first time it had done so from inside me.

Always two, never one, it continued.

I breathed in and closed my eyes. The elevator kept dinging as we rose. "Why?" I asked. "Why are you a . . . two-person bird?"

The fire in our heart is the kiss of death, the wind under our wings the breath of life.

I opened my eyes and tilted my head as I tried to make that make sense. The elevator dinged another floor.

Together, we are too much for one vessel.

I grunted my confusion and then asked, "If the fire is death and the wind is life, why can't I burn vampires to death but I can blow them into confetti?"

You play games without understanding the rules. Sometimes you'll win; sometimes you'll lose.

I twisted my face to match the nausea in my gut. Not many more dings left to go, but the bird wasn't done.

Our fire can only bring death where our wind can also bring life. What is undead cannot be reborn.

I nodded slowly. The last ding sounded as the elevator settled at Tula's floor. "So if I tried to bring someone dead back to life with the wind, I couldn't do it without also burning them. But I can use both for other things?"

The elevator doors opened as the phoenix filled my head with echoes of, *You should not.*

I wanted to ask why, but my jaw hung open instead, refusing to obey my command. Waiting in the hallway just outside the elevator was a giant purple caterpillar that looked like it could swallow me whole. Its dark mouth was surrounded with striking markings of black and bright yellow, fake eyes that stared at me unseeing above a cavernous pit full of shiny pincers and teeth.

Closing my mouth, I swallowed and let the phoenix tell my feet where to move. Caterpillars were afraid of birds, right?

Probably not this one.

It lumbered forward after I'd vacated the elevator, round feet thumping and pushing as the squishy body folded over itself to fit in the small space.

"Have a nice day," I said once the doors started to close. Human manners were the thing here, right? Was that another member? And if so, how old was it? Had it just been slowly eating and growing for thousands of years? Would it turn into some kind of monstrous butterfly soon?

I really didn't want to find out.

I tried not to grumble as I made my way to Tula's room, taking a bit more control from the phoenix with every step.

Tula's door was closed when I stopped in front of it. I licked my lips, lifted a fist, and knocked.

Adrenaline coursed through me as I mentally shook the bird out of my muscles, imagining the movements I'd need to make to draw a weapon quickly.

No one answered.

I breathed out. What had I been expecting? A vampire butler to open up and welcome me into a big vampire party?

Honestly, maybe.

Reaching forward, I pulled some birdfire into my finger and melted the doorknob. Definitely much better than picking locks when I didn't care about anyone knowing I'd been here.

You should not, the phoenix repeated.

"Why?" I asked as sparks fluttered down around the molten sizzle of dripping metal. Then I pushed the door open and walked in. This place had terrible internal security, but maybe that was all part of the learning experience it offered.

Games. The word echoed ominously around my skull as my footsteps filled Tula's empty apartment.

It was a simple answer, and my stomach sank as the full meaning of it finally clicked in my head.

The Darcy I'd been just a few months ago was poking her nose back into my consciousness, scolding me for needing to be reminded of something so basic. That Darcy never would have used magic for anything bigger than enhancing a drink or fixing her hair. The Darcy raised by mages understood that the magic wasn't hers—that it would only do what she wanted until it didn't. That becoming reliant on it was a recipe for disaster.

The Darcy from a few months ago had never encountered anything she really couldn't kill without it, though. Hadn't lain dying in a puddle of blood and rainwater with a vampire sucking the last remnants of her strength away. Hadn't watched helplessly from the ground as two innocent children flew above on dragon wings into certain death and destruction.

It had been proven to me so many times of late that I *was* reliant on magic, whether I liked it or not. That I could either risk using it or die without it. It was a risk, yes—but I no longer had the luxury of keeping risks to a happy minimum when so much was at stake.

I'd come to a point where it felt safer to be well practiced with the risky magic than to only bust it out in emergencies.

The thought was terrifying, and also freeing.

"Some games, you'll lose anyway if you don't play," I said in a low voice.

The phoenix was silent. So was Tula's apartment.

It wasn't just empty as in no one was home. It looked like it hadn't been lived in recently at all. The furniture was all there, just as it had been a few days ago, but there were no shoes, clothes, bags strewn about. Not even any throw blankets folded or coasters waiting to be placed under drinks.

I moved from room to room, opening up closet doors expecting to find them empty or sparse. But they were all full, packed neatly full of clean, color-coordinated belongings as if this were a museum and not a home.

I stopped when I came to the kitchen.

A lone piece of paper was hanging on the refrigerator door. Ice blue with black lettering and shimmering accents of blood red. When I plucked it off and held it up, it read like a wedding invitation from hell.

"A little lower, please," Adrian said in my ear. I almost jumped. God, he'd been so quiet I'd forgotten he was in there.

I lowered the invitation closer to the camera on my chest and read through it more carefully.

"We, the Excised and Edged, request your presence at Celestial's Crown for our first and only Crystal Gala. Arrangements have been made for admission of non-member invitees." I muttered a curse, then flipped it to the back to see if there was anything else. "Black tie required," was all I could find.

I muttered another curse before dropping the invitation and heading to Tula's closets.

Adrian was quiet while I stripped off my clothes (sans the camera, which I clipped to my bra) and flipped through Tula's dresses to find something appropriate. Carina, on the other hand, was chattering away in the background, alternating between excited and disgusted noises at my every move. I ignored her.

An assassin's wardrobe was a good place to be, because there wasn't anything here I couldn't move in. But Tula was so much thinner and taller than me that there was quite a bit I probably couldn't fit in. Not to mention that almost everything was varying shades of white or cream. Much harder to hide weapons and blood with those colors. Surprisingly impractical—but then, how often did Tula actually need to use weapons?

My fingers stopped when I touched something with a magic zing hidden in the back. It was the same kind of zing I'd gotten when I'd touched the new flamethrower, except this was a feathery soft garment. I pulled it out from between two white jumpsuits and sighed. Finally. Something black.

It was black feathers and leather from head to toe, with a few silvery metal accents around the middle that made it look something like glammed-up armor. Absolutely perfect. And the feathers might help me keep up the birdy appearance I needed to not get eaten by the scorpion sentinels of this crazed club.

"I don't like it," Carina yelled faintly in my ear, making me grateful Adrian was keeping the mic away from her. "It's overdone."

It just reminds you of the feathery getup Oya put you in, I thought as I continued to ignore her. *Birds, birds, everywhere.*

I peered at the garment uncertainly as I stepped into it. It was definitely going to be too tight, too long. But something made me pull it up anyway.

There was a slight resistance when I worked it over my hips, but the fabric quickly gave way with a tingle that ran all the way through to my scrye. A dress charmed to fit anyone with magic who put it on?

It seemed too good to be true. Had Tula expected me to come here? Had she left it specifically for me?

No. If she had, it would have been out in the open with my name on it. Or at least not hidden behind all her other clothes.

I decided not to look the gift dress in its seams when I pulled it over my boobs and transferred the bat inside. I didn't even need a bra—this dress made a perfect little pocket for the creature, lined with soft feathers.

After moving the camera to the dress and ditching the bra, I spun around once in front of Tula's mirror. Catching a glimpse of skin on my back, I twisted around to do a double take. Holy bats, there were even elegant slits in the fabric for my wings to poke through. That was unnecessary, since my wings were never quite fully corporeal and so didn't rip holes in clothes, but it would certainly look nicer to wear something designed around them.

Looking down, I kicked a leg out to test the flexibility of the skirt. The material gave way like a dream, as if it were floating around me rather than hanging off me.

"You look lovely," a voice whispered in my ear as I smoothed down the feathers of the skirt.

It took me just a moment too long to realize it was the wrong ear.

22

A PERSON with ice running through their veins will always have an unfair advantage when it comes to sneaking up on little old warm-blooded human-bird-thing me.

His voice was in my ear, but there was no warm breath, no looming presence behind me to signal that I wasn't alone until it was too late. I might have seen him in the mirror had I not been looking down at the dreamy skirt on this damn dreamy dress.

By the time I spun towards him, one of his hands was already wrapped around my neck. The other shoved into my waist, pushing me against the mirror so hard and fast that it cracked.

I held still, gasping, limbs frozen when normally they would be going for whatever weapons I could reach. I had none on me. They were all in a pile on the other side of the room with the clothes I'd been wearing when I came in.

"It's ok." Adrian's voice sounded distant in my ear, but I could still hear the calm breaths he was encouraging me to match, if only in my memory. "You can—"

Simeon hit me. The hand that was on my neck lifted for just long enough to swing into my cheek, making my world spin as the opposite side of my head crashed into the mirror.

Pain burst across my face in ripples, which turned into waves as they found their way to my jostled brain.

Something felt wrong. Empty.

"And who is this?" Simeon asked in his raspy voice, fingers pinching something small in front of me.

I blinked. Once. Twice. Three times before the blur cleared enough for me to see he was holding the insert that had just been in my ear. He must have hit me to knock it out after hearing Adrian. Not every vampire would have been able to hear that, but Simeon was old enough and strong enough that there was no hiding anything from him.

I blinked again as he crushed Adrian's voice between his fingers and moved his hand back to my neck. His smile hovered in front of me, fangs out and ready, every detail of his face the same as when I'd last seen him. But the exuberance was gone.

The thing I'd always loved most about him—his determination to enjoy even the most mundane things in life, which had always been written in his smile and in his eyes in a way that anyone could read without trying. It had still been there, the last time I'd seen him, when he'd tried to convince me to join him.

When there was still something left of the man I'd loved.

Now, though, he was not enjoying anything. Holding me. Hurting me.

The stiff grin stopped halfway up his cheeks, leaving his dark eyes glowering at me with a sinister menace.

In my dreams, the only one filled with anger was usually me. In my dreams, it was me with my hands around his throat. In my dreams, I still hadn't been able to truly accept that this man had changed so completely.

The stilted smile here, the casual violence—it was real. It was pain. It was everything I hadn't given him the chance to prove to me at our last encounter.

"She told me you might show up here," he said when I didn't reply. "I didn't believe her."

I couldn't answer him with the pressure he was putting on my windpipe. With my left hand, I pointed to my neck as I crinkled my brow.

He loosened his grip enough to let me suck in some air. Instead of exhaling it, I lashed out at him with a piece of the cracked mirror I'd broken off with my right hand.

It sliced into his side through his white dress shirt, which quickly bloomed with blood. He growled and jerked, his muscles jumping with shock and indecision just long enough for me to slip out of his grasp.

I wanted to run across the room to all my weapons. Knives. Stunners. Flamethrower. Fuck.

But I would never make it without him catching me first.

If I threw myself at him, he would overpower me. So instead I threw the mirror fragment, aiming for his face. While he blocked that, I grabbed the tall lamp beside us and yanked until the cord popped away from the wall.

I swung it at his head. See if we could test just how fragile that new neck of his was.

He backed away just in time, feet stumbling as his upper body swerved out.

"Darcy," he said as he got his bearings, rolling up the sleeves of a shirt that was already ruined. "Why are you here?"

To kill you, I wanted to say. I wanted that to be true, but it wasn't. Not anymore. Killing him would just be a happy bonus.

"Have you reconsidered my offer?" he asked, taking a tentative step towards me. I gripped the lamp more firmly. "Come to join me at the gala? See the magnitude of what we could achieve with a god at our side?"

I tried and failed to hold in my scoff. "I didn't need to come *here* to see what you and your god have been up to. A witch genocide, Simeon? Really?"

"The witches were never the point," he said, but his voice had gotten quieter. "Collateral damage."

"I thought you wanted a world with *less* violence in it," I snapped, my voice getting louder as his retreated. "All your talk of stabilizing relations between humans and vampires. How is petrifying millions of people going to achieve that?"

He stared at me for a moment, silent, eyes boring into mine. I wanted him to answer me—wanted it to be a good answer. How far did he need to go to get me to stop trying to give him the benefit of the doubt?

"Tell me," I pressed. "What *is* the point? Are you just chasing power? If all you wanted was an almighty god to hold your hand and kiss your boo-boos, there are plenty others that aren't completely evil fuckers."

The corner of his mouth quirked up, but his eyes were now avoiding mine. "The point," he said slowly, softly, "was always to have a fresh start. I wanted you to have it with me, but clearly that was a mistake."

He darted forward while I was trying to work out what kind of fresh start he could be hoping for.

I swung at him with the lamp, but I didn't have time to aim it properly. Instead of having to dodge it, he reached out and grabbed it, then tore it away from me. It flew across the room and crashed into a wall, which gave in and crumbled around it.

I made a dash for my weapons, but he was on me before I'd taken two steps. He knocked me to the ground, pinning me underneath him, fingers digging into my arms as his eyes frosted over with ice. Cold penetrated where his skin met mine.

He was going to use his witchy powers on me? Fine. Two could play at that game.

Games, the phoenix echoed in my head. I ignored it.

Simeon's fangs came closer to my neck. Would he try to drain me? The one thing he'd promised over and over he would never do?

I breathed in, drawing the air through my lungs and into my scrye, where it transformed into energy and gained force and speed as I channeled it towards the cold. All the little worries that'd been holding me back from blowing this man into confetti disappeared. If I had to burn this whole building to the ground afterward to make sure I turned every last bit of him to ashes, I would do it.

I let the energy flow into him, the same way it had in my dreams except without the overwhelming regret that usually came with it. All the breath in me rushed through my skin, and I waited with empty lungs to see what it would do. The ribbons of vampire gore I'd seen so many times in my dreams floated in my subconscious, but they failed to appear in front of me.

Simeon grunted and then snarled, still whole, fangs gleaming over my face as he pressed up and away from me. But I was still pinned by his ice. Sturdy, rounded bricks of it encased my upper arms where he'd been holding me and over my hips where he'd been kneeling.

Where had the magic wind gone?

The ice was getting heavier.

Games, the phoenix repeated.

I gasped, lungs tired of waiting, and my icy prison burst. Sparkling shards of cold death filled the space between us, all white and misty until they turned pink.

Was it my blood or his? Or both?

Pain lanced the skin on my arms, my neck, my face. I sat up and looked down.

There were my ribbons of gore. All up and down my arms, like I'd been sliced with hundreds of tiny knives. The cuts weren't deep, and there were none at all where the ice had been touching.

The phoenix's wind had directed the pressure away from me. If it hadn't, I wouldn't have arms attached to me anymore.

I groaned as my awareness drifted to the pain, reflexively working to heal the wounds. Healed wounds were all well and good, but when there were so many of them and probably someone still trying to kill me, it would be better to wait.

Pulling my spinning mind away, I tried to focus on what was in front of me. Simeon. Bloody and angry.

Tiny shards of ice were melting in his wounds, rivulets of diluted blood flowing over every bit of exposed skin. The bloody shirt was sliced to shreds.

But he was already healing. Unlike me, he didn't need focus to do so.

He charged me as I pulled myself to my feet, mind scrambling to come up with something that would hurt him more than me.

The magic wind hadn't worked. It had just been absorbed by his magic ice, which he'd used like armor.

He stopped short, just a foot away from me. Strategizing—hesitating—just like me.

When I'd blown away the other vampire, he'd been feeding on me. I'd sent the wind through my blood.

Simeon wiped the wetness from his face, leaving a red smear to frame his piercing glare. He'd always hated leaving blood on his face. Hated being surrounded by it even more. That was why he'd requested me as his Guardian, back in the day. Send the healer to the vampire so she can keep the blood contained. Keep the hunger at bay.

I lifted my chin. Turned it to the side. Leaned forward. Let my heart race.

Would he take the bait? How could he not? Unless his fake death and witchy transformation had somehow dulled his bloodlust.

He growled and sprang for me.

I braced myself.

He collided with something, but it wasn't me.

It took him clear across the room, until he crumpled next to the ruined lamp with a short spear lodged in his chest. The blood that pumped out around its shaft was not diluted.

I looked in the opposite direction.

Tula stood in the doorway, hand on hip, wearing a formal white jumpsuit with an unblemished sheen that mocked the sorry state of me and Simeon.

Where had she been keeping the spear?

"Nobody kills anybody in my home without me," she said as she stepped into the room. She stopped in front of me. "*Why* are you wearing my armor?"

Armor? I cleared my throat and calmed my breathing before answering, "I didn't want to show up to the party in jeans."

"I'll have to cut it off you." She pressed her lips together in a crooked grin as she eyed me. "Or should I cut you up with it?"

"We had a deal," I said, voice cracking as I rubbed my sore neck. "How much money did I just make you, taking out your target? And you're threatening me instead of thanking me?"

"I just saved your life," she countered with a nod at Simeon, who was still crumpled around her spear. It must have gone through his heart. "We are even, yes? Except . . ." She looked around the room, which was destroyed.

I got up and went over to my pile of belongings. Finally. But instead of a weapon, I grabbed the little gold bag the scorpion man had given me.

"Here." I tossed it over to her. "Don't want this apartment anymore? You can have mine."

"Hm?" Tula tilted her head at me. "You wooed Girt into letting you in? Impressive."

"Yes," I said as I picked up the flamethrower. "I killed your mark, became a member of your weird little club, and now I'm going to finish the job that you decided to fuck me over on."

When I slipped the cover off the weapon and hoisted it in Simeon's direction, Tula was on me in a flash. She put her hand over mine, lowering it as she stared me down. "No."

"No?" I echoed. "Are you kidding? You just threw a spear at him, but you won't let me kill him?"

"We still need him for the ceremony."

Dare I ask? I sighed bitterly. "What ceremony?"

"The usual." Tula rolled her eyes. "Lots of death . . . to get more power . . . to bring more death . . . very boring."

"Doesn't sound like your scene."

"Thank you," she said. "I appreciate that. I worked hard to get away from—" She breathed in sharply. "Not hard enough." Quick as lightning, she snatched the flamethrower out of my grasp and twirled a finger in the air, then nodded over to the living room. "Shall we have a drink? We have some time before it starts."

I breathed out through my nose, a low growl forming in my throat as my fingers opened and closed around air. Yes, I'd managed to get myself in here by channeling the phoenix, but I'd probably still lose in a fight with any one of Celestial's other members, including this psychotic blonde in front of me.

"One second," I said, then grabbed one of Adrian's stunners and held it up to show her. She didn't stop me as I walked briskly over to Simeon, pulled out the spear, and lodged the stunner firmly in its place.

"That was not necessary," Tula said with a shrug. "My spears are inescapable." But she gave me a nod when I handed it back to her. "Come."

23

I FOLLOWED Tula into the living room, healing my cuts and bruises along the way. Pain prickled up my arms and face, and I realized abruptly that the black feathered dress was completely unharmed—as was all my flesh underneath. Armor, indeed.

"I don't have much here," Tula said as she poured from a dusty bottle of clear liquor she'd dug out from the back of a cupboard. "I was in the process of moving out—no point being here now that he's found me."

"Now that who's found you?" I asked, taking the glass from her. I sniffed it and immediately regretted it. Nostrils burning, I took a very small sip.

Tula downed her drink in one swallow and poured another. "This new god, the 'lord of frost.' I believe you know the one." She shook her head. "That's the problem with gods . . . You kill one and think you've got away, and then another finds you and it starts all over again. They are all made of the same stuff." She put her drink down and mimed squishing something big in her hands. "Killing a god is only like crushing one arm of an octopus with millions of tentacles. It will not be the same, but it will still regrow."

"You've killed a god?" I asked, sitting up straighter. "How?"

"You didn't hear me?" she asked. "With gods, it is not really killing."

"It's like octopus whack-a-mole, yeah, I heard." I took another sip of the burning liquid. "Give me the hammer and I'll whack away."

Tula laughed, full on, eyes crinkled, then took a breath and threw back another shot. "I would love to give you the hammer, but I can't as long as he has me."

"I don't understand . . ." I started.

"You can't understand," she agreed. "You are human—*mostly* human. No one wants anything from you. You could be born, wiggle around, and die, like a worm, and no one would pluck you out of your little worm hole to turn you into a bird. You would just get eaten by the bird, and no one would care."

"I don't know where you're going with this, but I'm not sure the bird analogy is working, considering—"

"I am the last of my kind," Tula said, eyes boring into mine. "But even when there were more, we were never many. We were created with a purpose. A responsibility that could never be shrugged off so long as there was a god in need of it. If I try to resist, I stop existing."

"What responsibility?" I asked.

"To guide the souls of the slain to the afterlife."

I stared at her. Was I drinking with a *reaper*? Would her pretty face turn into a rotting skull if I looked hard enough?

I looked down at the black, feathered dress. Her armor. Raven black. No. She wasn't just any reaper. "Valkyrie?" I didn't need Adrian in my ear to get that one. Even I knew the stories of valkyries.

"A long time ago." She filled up her glass again. "Now everyone who knew me by that name is dead."

"What happened to the others?"

"I killed them." Tula brought her glass to her mouth again, but this time she only took a small sip before putting it down, lips pursed.

"You killed—"

"All my sisters, yes," she said quickly. "And the gods who created me and passed me around like their personal death slave."

"You killed all the . . . Norse gods?" I didn't know whether to be impressed or horrified. No, I did—it was both. Definitely both.

"Not quite all," she said with a small, twisted smile. "Only the ones who had use for me. Which was *most* . . . it is rare to find a god who is not violent."

"So you . . ." Something clicked in my head, and I put my glass down. "Gods use you to take away the souls of the people they kill? Where do you bring them?"

"*That* is the point," she said. "My job is not simply to take them away. Most will go away on their own—but the eternal realm is a big place." She leaned forward and spread her hands. "*Boundless.* And if a god wants someone dead, they don't always want that someone free to roam the halls of Valhalla."

"The eternal realm," I repeated. "Is that the same thing as the underworld?"

"The underworld is part of the eternal realm," she answered, then looked at me with narrowed eyes. "Why do you ask about the underworld? Are you planning to go there on vacation? The weather is horrible, but you can always find a fire."

"Can you take me there?" I was leaning closer to her now, on the edge of my seat.

She sat back and gave me an appraising look. "Yes," she eventually answered. "But why should I?"

"You owe me," I replied, nodding over to Simeon's paralyzed body.

"I really don't," she said with a gesture over to the spear I'd pulled out of him. "Why won't you tell me why you want to go?"

I picked up the glass in front of me and tapped my fingernail against it. "Because I think you would rather not know." If what she'd just told me was true, that Itztla *had* her and she would stop existing if she resisted him, then helping me find the arrow I needed to kill him might count as resisting. But if she was just giving a friend a ride from Point A to Point B . . . not that I was exactly a friend.

"I see," she said.

I couldn't tell whether she'd picked up on my meaning. It didn't matter, though, because at that point we were interrupted by an overwhelming musical hum coming from all around us. The leather sofa vibrated under me, and the walls shook.

The hum picked up in volume without changing pitch, getting louder and louder until abruptly, it stopped. I blinked. Everything was still.

"Mm," Tula said, standing up. "That means it's time for the party. Come with me." She made a show of craning her neck off to the side. "Just don't show me what all you have in your bags."

"What about him?" I asked, gesturing towards Simeon.

Tula picked up the spear again, making sure to hold it away from her body, and tossed it at him. Then another spear materialized in her hand, and she tossed that one too.

They caught him in his shoulders, somehow, and pulled him up into the air as if they were strong men instead of lengths of metal and wood.

Head slumped over and feet dragging on the ground, Simeon followed us silently as we made our way out of Tula's apartment and through the hallway.

My fingers twitched. What would she do if I just turned around and ignited him right now?

Eyes on the prize, Darcy. I wished I still had Adrian in my ear.

Even if Tula didn't kill me outright for lighting up Simeon, she'd at least disinvite me from this gala. And I was willing to bet that was where I'd find the things I really needed to kill.

The hum sounded again as we entered the elevator and rose upward, with a slightly more metallic tone this time. Vibrations rose through my feet and prickled the hair on my arms.

I breathed out, unable to take my eyes off Simeon's limp frame. My fingers twitched again. "What is that hum?" I asked Tula.

"Celestial is not just a place to start a new life," she explained. "It is also where great beings come to die."

I raised my eyebrows, not sure I liked where this was going.

"Even gods," she whispered playfully. "Remember the octopus?" She waited for me to nod before continuing, "When a god comes here to die, they give their energy to the building. It is trapped here, and so they can be sure it will not morph into something else later on. Same for all the lesser creatures and their magic. They may have been destined for any number of unsavory places in the eternal realm—but if they die here, they can stay here forever."

"How is that—"

"And today, for the ceremony, the reason I brought this new god to Celestial with all of his followers . . ." She peeled her lips away from her teeth, hunching forward in a shrug as if to say she was sorry for being so amazing. "We are using the ashes of a goddess to help him in his endeavor." Tula ran her hand along the wall of the elevator as the building hummed again. "This is her, letting us know she is looking forward to it."

Oh, this bitch was definitely not sorry. I grunted, then looked down as I realized the small bat was vibrating softly against my chest. Responding to the hum. "What goddess?" I asked, but I already knew the answer.

It had to be the one Ray had told me about. The Obsidian

Butterfly. Patron goddess of the cihuateteo, divine women who had died in childbirth and become expert little life-force vacuums in death. Ray had said she'd been crushed by a cactus, so how had she ended up here?

"She is an interesting one to chat with. Maybe you'll see, if you stay here as a member." Tula looked up at the dinging lights above the elevator doors. They were nearing the end of the line. "There was not much left of her when she arrived. She had been hurt badly and had two choices: die, in a way of her choosing, or commit to years of regeneration during which she would be vulnerable to the worst her enemies could conjure."

"She must have had a lot of enemies," I offered. Plenty worse ways to go than death by cactus.

Tula's eyes sparkled as the elevator made its final ding and shuffled to a stop. I wondered whether she also had a lot of enemies. Probably not. She probably killed anyone she encountered who might become one. Should I be flattered or insulted that she'd left me alive this long?

The doors opened with another hum, this one stronger than all the others. It had been coming from the top of the tower, and now we were at the source. It sounded in my ears and swirled around my head with the piercing tone of a mournful violin, which was matched by the fluttering vibrations of the bat against my chest.

I stepped out after Tula, gently stoking the phoenix's fire in my scrye. I didn't want to lose myself here, but I also didn't want to get eaten alive for appearing too weak.

We emerged in a small, mirrored lobby, which seemed a bit overkill for a building with only one elevator. Tula ignored me while I stashed my bags behind a potted plant, quickly tucking some bat confetti, vamp stunners, and a small knife into the pockets of the valkyrie armor dress. Because of course the valkyrie armor dress had pockets.

Catching a glimpse of myself in the mirror as I straightened the dress, I saw a flash of black underneath my hair at the base of my neck. The bunny's hard, warm body pressed against my shoulder as I adjusted my hair to cover it.

Where were you when the vampire was crushing my windpipe? I asked the bunny silently.

Where were you when you swore a blood oath to this building? it responded in kind.

I almost jumped. The bunny's red eyes glowed at me from beneath my curls. No. It wasn't the rabbit speaking in my head. It was Popo.

I shifted my eyes around. What was it about this place? First the phoenix communicating with me, and now the god I'd had to transport myself to a mountain to speak to earlier.

Blood oath, I wondered, mind reaching back to the hazy fire of when I'd given the phoenix control. Two drops of blood on parchment. Was that what that was?

And you still have yet to swear your oath to me. The thought vibrated through my head as the bunny's eyes glowed.

Jealous much? I thought with a scoff. I'd done far more for Popo already than I'd done for any other god—or building—and he was still complaining.

"Are you finished staring at yourself?" Tula asked before he could respond. "The armor doesn't suit you. You should have gone with one of my champagne gowns. You look too pale in black."

"So I'll fit right in next to a bunch of vamps," I said.

Tula started laughing again, so hard she had to fight to catch her breath again once she was done. With a slow shake of her head, she walked up close to me. "One thing," she said as she held up the necklace she had given me days ago.

I furrowed my brow. I hadn't given it back to her. Had she

gone through my things in her apartment when I hadn't been looking?

"This will help." She hooked the necklace to the black feathers underneath my chest, her fingers gently brushing the camera I'd already pinned on.

I was left thoroughly creeped out and wondering why she hadn't put it around my neck as she turned from me to the elegant double doors to the right.

They opened on their own, revealing a ballroom encased in glass.

It wasn't just windows all around from floor to ceiling, the way it looked from outside—from this perspective, the ceiling was glass, too. As if the whole top level were a huge cake platter resting underneath a glass dome, which could only be lifted by a god in the heavens.

Except the gods weren't in the heavens. They were in here.

Pale, slender bodies filled the expansive ballroom, some chatting around the edges of the room, others twirling on the dance floor to an old, orchestrated piece of music I couldn't place. All were dressed impeccably, which was collectively the most inhuman thing about them.

At every black-tie event I'd ever been to (and there'd been many in my days as the bodyguard of a senator), there were always several men whose jackets hung too far off their shoulders or pinched too tightly across their guts, always several women wearing undergarments that created awkward lines and lumps under their dresses. I was an expert in noticing these things because it had been my job to determine whether an ill-fitting garment was a matter of human error or an assassin hiding weapons. More often than not, it was the former.

Here, there were neither. No human error, because there were no humans. No hidden weapons, because the two weapons in each vampire's mouth were all they needed. The only odd details were the unhidden scars wrapped around most of the vampires' necks and the bat cages dangling from so many of their wrists.

In a way, the scars were comforting. A small reassurance that this death god had only sucked in the dregs of the vampire society, the outcasts—that this wasn't part of a huge conspiracy of all vampires, like Oya had suggested, to eliminate everyone else and take over the world.

But of course it wasn't. For normal vampires, the world was their playground. For these weak-necked rejects, it was a prized possession they'd loved and lost—and if they couldn't have it, why should anyone else?

None of them batted an eyelash when Tula walked through the doors, Simeon floating gruesomely at her side. Apparently dripping blood on the ground wasn't a vampire party foul unless it was human blood.

When I followed them through, the collective air whooshed out of a room full of lungs that didn't actually need to breathe. All eyes turned to me.

I let a low groan build in my throat as I resisted the urge to check myself for cuts. I wasn't bleeding, but it didn't matter. I was the only thing in this room with a heartbeat, so I might as well have introduced myself as Darcy the Blood Buffet.

"Can you tone down the 'delicious snack' thing at all?" Tula muttered at me without losing her demure smile.

I started to say no, but maybe I *could* tone it down. Be less human and more bird. I blinked my eyes and bit my lip, pulling at the fire inside me until I felt it brimming at the back of my mind —or was it the front?

The room became instantly less beautiful. Instead of sculpted immortal bodies wearing shimmering fabrics and sparkling jewels, there was stiff flesh and sunken eyes, too much silence, and the pervasive scent of decay beneath the floral perfume in the air.

A flare of rage grew within me, rippling out from my scrye to the blood in my veins and bringing a flush of heat to my skin. Birds. Wouldn't this make me look *more* delicious to the room full of vampires? I couldn't help it, though. The phoenix really, *really* didn't like undead things.

Bones creaked as soft necks turned away from me again, followed by whispers of chatter and the sloshing of stale blood in glass bottles. Maybe undead things didn't like the phoenix, either.

One of the bodies came forward, skin and hair chalk white, eyes black. This one was not a vampire. Was he even part of this world? My eyes ran over him too quickly, unable to properly focus. It was like a character in a video game stood before me: details perfectly designed from a distance, but nothing was moving the way it should. This man should not exist in three dimensions. Should it be two, or should it be six? No way to tell. He was just *wrong*.

He opened his mouth, and words came out despite his lips not moving. "You broke him." The voice was lighter than I expected, almost airy, yet still I wanted to cover my ears to dull the way it bounced around in my head. I resisted the urge.

"He was already broken," Tula replied, her eyes on Simeon. "He was going to betray you."

The chalky man cocked his head, grotesquely far, and stared at Simeon with unblinking eyes.

Tula gestured at me. "See? I found him with his human lover." She leaned over toward the chalky man, who was a good deal shorter than her. "She is the witch of another god."

Oh birds. This was him.

The evil god. Itztlacoliuhqui. And Tula was serving me to him on a silver platter.

Maybe she thought this half-truth was better than telling him

I was the reason his favorite toy was "broken." At least this way, Simeon would go down with me.

My skin prickled with cold as the god turned his unblinking stare on me. "She is not all human," he said, mouth agape like a bizarre speaker. I half expected flies to come crawling out.

The phoenix bristled. What did the creature of fire and life think of this monstrosity that called itself a god? Nothing good. Behind the fire, all I could think was that this must be why Popo hadn't appeared to me as anything resembling a human. Even though he had been human once, if *this* was what he was like now, as a god . . . I could understand why he would prefer to remain a mountain.

"Does it matter?" Tula asked the god. "She is a witch, and not yours. I thought you would like to have her here for the ceremony, a demonstration for your own eyes of what will be happening to every other witch outside these walls."

The fire burned hotter in my scrye with every second. The phoenix was eager to take flight. Me, though? I just stared at Tula with a calm grin on my face. She was helping me. Reminding the god that his plans would take care of me and there was no reason for him to dispose of me sooner. Of course, she didn't know about the bat in my tits, so she probably thought she was just sparing me a worse death or delaying the inevitable.

But still, she was helping. As much as she could without working against her god's interests. *Why?*

Itztla was still for too long. Or was he? Time had begun to feel funny. Vampires all around me moved some limbs in slow motion, some in fast. Eventually, the god's mouth gaped open again and emitted, "She'll stay with me." He disappeared from in front of us then as cold bloomed behind me.

He grasped my upper arms in the same places Simeon's ice had frozen me not long ago. Fleetingly, I wondered whether I should try to blow up the god with the magic wind. The phoenix flapped and shook with laughter inside me. Then it shrieked and folded over on itself in pain.

The fire in my scrye shrank down as cold penetrated every cell in my body. The massive inferno that had once burned freely now pushed itself into such a dense ball of energy that it felt like another lead bullet threatening to punch a hole in me.

"Sit," the god's voice commanded, and I obeyed. There was no chair, so I sat cross-legged on the floor at his feet. The haze of the phoenix fire was gone, but a sheen of ice coated my nerves in its place. The realization that I hadn't *meant* to obey his command sent a spike of yet more ice straight into my gut.

Why was Itztla even here? Weren't gods supposed to lurk in their dark little god lairs and send their witches out to do their dirty work? If I'd known this terrifying *thing* would be here in the flesh, would I still have come?

Probably, but I might have called bullshit on Ray's plan of focusing on the god's tools rather than the god himself.

"Shall I lead the ceremony, or would you still have the traitor?" I heard Tula ask above me. The god must have given her some form of a nod, because she followed it with, "Splendid," and Simeon dropped to the ground in front of me. Tula had removed the floating spears that were holding him up, leaving two gaping wounds in his shoulders. They wouldn't heal while the stunner remained in his heart.

Blood crept out of his wounds as Tula made her way across the dance floor, and I pulled as much of the feathered skirt as I could away from the growing pool of red.

Tula stopped before the spherical ice sculpture at center of the dance floor, which was also the very center of the room. She stared directly up at the highest point of the glass dome and let her hands splay out at her sides. The music cut out and the building hummed as the floor rose beneath her, tiles shifting and grinding to form a platform that lifted her high enough to give everyone in the room a good view. A narrow pillar rose even higher directly in front of her, and I watched as the top of it transformed into some kind of stone pot.

Finally, the shifting stopped, and the piercing hum faded to a buzz in the background.

"Friends of Itztlacoliuhqui," Tula said, her voice carrying throughout the space. "Welcome to Celestial." She reached behind her and produced a caged bat just like the ones clutched by most of the vampires around me. "Do you wonder why we are here? What we are to celebrate *now* when the first stage of our venture was not supposed to be finished for another month yet?"

Murmurs fluttered around the room, and I stared on as icicles of dread continued to creep along my insides.

Tula grinned, then lifted the lid off the stone pot in front of her and thrust her hand inside. When she pulled it out again, her fist was dusky gray and full of ashes. "The spirits who have been doing your bidding all bow to a dead goddess—you know this. It is how you are able to protect yourself from them by carrying her symbol." She held up the caged bat for emphasis. "Here, though . . ." She raised her fist of ashes, some of it already filtering through her fingers and floating into the air around her. "Here is the goddess herself."

The murmurs grew louder, more chaotic. The words "another month yet" bounced around in my head as a horrifying backdrop to all the other words coming out of the mouth of the assassin— no, valkyrie—I'd sent straight into the hands of the enemy.

"With her blessing," Tula went on, "the first stage of our venture can be finished *today*. Millions of souls siphoned of divine energy all at once instead of just a few every hour."

I squeezed my eyes shut for a brief moment, sick to my stomach. Tula certainly seemed to be going above and beyond when it came to "not resisting" the call of her new god. How could she want to *amplify* his antics after hearing about the effect they were having on Minnie? Maybe she wasn't as reluctant as she'd let on. Or maybe she just wanted it all to be over already.

Noah's face floated in the back of my mind, all perfect squishy cheeks and fiery blue eyes. So much life and growth and promise that I never wanted to see sucked dry. All I could do was hope Etty had found him a bat in time as I dug my hands into my pockets, closing fists around as much confetti as I could gather. It stuck to my sweaty palms, mocking me with how flimsy and ordinary it was. How could *this* help me here?

"Begin." The god's voice sounded behind me, rattling around like ice cubes through my bones.

Tula gave him a curt nod and then closed her eyes, muttering something under her breath as she sifted some of the ashes from her fist onto the bat in its cage. Then she opened her eyes and set the bat down at her feet, leaving her arms free to welcome the misty spirit that swirled down to meet her from above. Its long, wispy hair flowed freely through the air, as did its skirts, while above the waist its ghostly round breasts were exposed, ready even in death to nurse the child they would never meet.

The spirit wailed as Tula held out an ashy hand in its direction. It grasped her hand tightly, clinging on as if for dear life. Tula moved her other hand to the spherical ice sculpture and closed her eyes again, continuing to mutter.

This was happening too quickly. I had to move *now*.

Huffing out a short breath, I lunged up to my feet and charged at the spirit. The tendrils of cold behind me stretched as I ran, their hooks never leaving me.

It only took me a few strides to get close enough, and I didn't hesitate to fling all the bat confetti I had straight into the cihuateteo's misty form. This was the spirit of a woman who had died in childbirth, not her dead body, which meant I couldn't destroy it; it needed to be appeased instead.

The bits of glossy black plastic puffed through the air in front

286 | ERIN EMBLY

of me, some sticking in odd places to the spirit while others traveled through it and fell to the ground. As I watched them, I kept my mind on the bat that was still vibrating softly against my chest, working to infuse the confetti with my intent.

Tula looked genuinely shocked. More than surprise, it felt like disappointment and maybe a little bit of embarrassment that she was emanating with her stare. It didn't suit her.

The cihuateteo spirit did nothing to acknowledge what I'd just done. The bits of confetti remained, merely decorating it in Halloween festivity as it began to amass an aura of bright energy.

Birds.

I could have told myself that wasn't going to fucking work. I needed to stop letting optimistic people convince me that stupid shit like confetti might actually work.

Tula shook her head at me, eyes crinkling with laughter.

You're killing your pregnant wife, I wanted to say. The words formed a lump in my throat.

She wouldn't care. Telling her about Minnie's baby would be as useless as the confetti. I could see that now. What good were a wife and child if you didn't exist anymore to enjoy them?

There would be no reasoning with Tula. Not when Itztla held her very existence in his clutches.

The cihuateteo spirit glowed brighter. On instinct, I reached out and touched it. My fingers slid against its skirts, buzzing at the contact with the energy it was amassing. Such a familiar feeling.

How many times had I grasped the souls of the dying and ushered them back into their bodies? Too many to count. And despite this woman already being dead, despite her having turned into a monster capable of killing millions of people, her spirit felt just the same in my grasp. I didn't know where her body was, or if it was anything more than ashes or worms by now, but maybe I could still usher her back to it.

As soon as I had the thought, the god's icy hooks pulled back on my scrye. Pain tore through me.

I let out a guttural noise, planting my feet on the ground and thrusting my hands further into the spirit's skirts. But Itztla wasn't trying to move me away; he'd come up to meet me instead.

His chalky face hovered over me, staring intently, head tilted too far to the side again as if I were a curiosity in a zoo. I squeezed my eyes shut, trying to ignore him as I felt for the spirit and connected to it with my scrye.

It was getting too hot. The spirit was there, but with every moment that passed it was buried further and further beneath the insane amount of energy it was channeling. Energy from the millions of witches it was petrifying. My scrye faltered, distracted, the part of me designed to channel magic gravitating toward this massive font of endless possibility.

Itztla's hooks pulled harder. When I opened my eyes, his teeth were bared. And there were the crawling flies. Twitchy little black things on a surreal backdrop of pasty white.

I froze. Ice coursed through my veins, searing pain surrounding it.

"You dare steal from me?" he emitted, the unmoving mouth gaping directly above me.

I could only stare. In the corner of my eye, my arm was beginning to change color and shape, frosting over at the edges with white. This wasn't the cihuateteo drawing power through me from my god. I wasn't being stolen, petrified like the others. Itztla himself was turning me to ice.

A small bit of warmth touched the back of my neck. The rabbit. Great—maybe it could melt me into a Darcy puddle after this god finished icing me over.

Or was Popo just jealous enough to keep Itztla's paws off me, despite my still unsworn oath?

The warmth grew to a pleasant burn as the ground rumbled

beneath my feet. The sound of clattering pebbles cascaded towards me from behind, followed closely by a whole horde of scurrying obsidian rabbits. They swarmed me, climbing in rows up the feathered skirt of Tula's dress. Their little stone claws dug into my chest and arms and neck as they perched on me, covering me from head to toe in obsidian armor.

Was this the volcano god version of "fuck off, she's mine"? If so, I wasn't going to complain. And that thought didn't even scare me, although it probably should.

I couldn't feel Itztla's hooks in me any longer, but I also couldn't feel the cihuateteo spirit. The energy it had amassed was draining away quickly, through Tula and into the spherical ice sculpture, which now glowed like the moon. Minnie's words from the garden came back to me. *"The moon brought this death,"* she'd said. Was this what she'd meant?

I shook my fingers vigorously, dislodging some of the bunnies from my hands so I could regain contact with the spirit. I sighed when my scrye reconnected. There it was again. The familiar feel of a soul too far from its body. Without another second of hesitation, I sent it home. It was happy to go. Tired. Limp. Ready for an eternity of rest.

My skin crawled, but I couldn't pinpoint exactly why.

Itztla had turned away from me, leaving me and my army of bunnies without a foe to defend against. He was looking at the glowing sphere like a child would look at his favorite candy. I hadn't thought that inhuman face could smile, but apparently I was wrong.

The final bit of glowing energy transferred from Tula to the sphere, and she let go of it just as the god pounced. He transformed in the air, his human form giving way to an enormous shadow that engulfed the glowing sphere in darkness.

For a moment, the entire room went dark. The vampires around me, the stars above—everything disappeared, not only the sights but the sounds and smells and chills as well. Then, just as quick, it was back. Except the god and his new toy were gone.

"Not even a thank-you," Tula complained into the awkward silence as dozens of vampires stared at her expectantly. She brushed her hands together, signaling the completion of a good job.

I didn't have it in me to answer her. I didn't have it in me to process what had just happened. That I had completely failed to stop her. How many witches had just breathed their last breaths? Would Noah be with them?

I didn't have the luxury to think too hard about it. Not with the vampires inching closer as their uncertain whispers around the room gained force. I would *not* be their dessert course.

"Flamethrower," I muttered out of the corner of my mouth to the bunny by my ear, and a small chunk of the obsidian horde broke off to fetch my weapon.

"I have work to do," Tula said with a small lift of her shoulder. Sure she did. All those people she had just killed needed to be put in their proper place in hell. She turned to me just in time to see the bunnies scurry up with my weapon, and she swung a finger back and forth at me. "Don't be naughty."

I pointed the flamethrower at Simeon. The only vampire in here I could be reasonably certain *wasn't* about to try to eat me. Very smart, Darcy.

"You don't need to do that," Tula said, stepping in front of the weapon. She snapped her fingers in the air three times. "I'll hold up my end of the deal, now that my god has no use for him." She shot me a mischievous grin and then walked up to Simeon.

I narrowed my eyes. A scorpion man appeared beside her, its arachnoid legs tapping eagerly on the wood floor. "You called?" he said.

"Thank you, Girt," she replied without looking at him. "I'd like to rescind the invitations I extended to the blood-drinkers."

Shifting her eyes around the room, she called out in a flat voice, "Party's over."

Faster than I could blink, the room filled with monstrous scorpions, pincers tearing off the heads and limbs of vampires while scuttling legs dragged the carnage straight through the ballroom to the elevator. The previously golden wood floors glistened with red as rivers of blood flowed to the edges of the room.

I stopped breathing, the sheer speed and scale of the violence happening around me freezing me in a rare moment of shock. After a few beats of my heart that felt like an eternity, I moved my feet to step away from the flowing blood and calmed my nerves with the observation that the scorpions were paying me no mind.

Tula's laughter drew my eyes back to her.

"If you want to keep your membership," she said to me, "you're going to have to start thinking bigger." Then she bent over Simeon, the only vamp she'd shooed the scorpions away from, and lifted him with her arms underneath his shoulders. His blood streamed down the front of her white outfit, painting it crimson.

She shook herself, and the white garment fell away to reveal her black feathered armor underneath. It looked similar to what I was wearing, except it wasn't a dress.

Black wings unfolded behind her, and she lifted herself straight up into the air. Simeon's limp body hung from her arms as she spun upward, and suddenly I felt the wind on my cheeks.

The glass dome was gone.

I ran, following underneath Tula as she flew overhead until I got to the edge of the room. I tried to follow her into the air, but my wings failed to appear. Frantic, I scraped at the bottom of my scrye in search of the phoenix, but all I found was the cold, hard ball of lead.

All I could do was watch as Tula let go of Simeon and they

parted ways. She soared off into the distance. He hurtled downward.

And just like that, they were both gone.

The glass reappeared.

I turned around, alone in a room full of scorpions and blood.

My heart pounded. I'd never felt so impotent in my life.

What had I accomplished by being here?

What would have happened differently had I not come?

Simeon was the only thing I could think of.

I'd come armed with bat confetti, focused on sabotaging the tool of a genocidal god. That never would have been enough, and millions of people had just died because of it.

Tula was right. I should have been thinking bigger.

I should never have stopped looking for a way to kill the god himself.

It wasn't a mistake I would make again.

24

BODY COUNT.

That was all I could think of as I dodged scorpions and slid through vampire blood and escaped yet more weird giant caterpillars on my way out of Celestial.

It wasn't the dead bodies I was worried about counting. I already knew those would be uncountable. Tula had said millions. All at once. I had no reason to doubt her.

It was the live ones I needed to see. Everyone I cared about. Were they still breathing?

I found Adrian and Carina two blocks from where I'd left them, huddled in the middle of the street with Adrian's van blocking a lane of traffic.

I stopped walking and breathed out, relieved that Carina hadn't turned into a hunk of obsidian and Adrian hadn't been eaten by some rogue vampire who'd escaped the scorpions. Before they saw me, I pulled out my phone and dialed Etty.

The tone rang in my ear as I walked up closer to Adrian and Carina, dodging the cars that were speeding by. Light reflected off the pavement by their feet as if the street was wet, but it hadn't rained. When I stepped up behind them, I saw why.

The thing they were huddled over was Simeon's . . . I turned my head and squinted. You couldn't really call that a body.

Remains. Remains was more appropriate. Vampire goo was even better.

My face scrunched up in an involuntary grimace.

"Darcy," Etty said over the phone. Her voice sounded heavy, but not tired.

My heart raced. "How's Noah?"

Adrian twisted around when he heard my voice, standing to meet me, mouth open and then quickly shut when he saw me on the phone. Carina was still crouched over the vampire goo, entranced.

"Noah?" Etty asked against my ear. *Yes!* I wanted to scream. Who else would I be calling in a panic about? "He's fine," she added, but there was something hollow in the way she said it that made my gut twist.

"His leg?" I prompted. Maybe he was alive but the withered parts had spread?

"Fine," she said. "I mean—he still has a little raisin foot, but it's stopped spreading."

More relief. Heat rushed to my face as I dared to let out a small smile. "Ol' raisin foot," I said affectionately. "Sounds like a new nickname."

Adrian matched my grin, but Etty remained silent.

"Etty?" I asked, but there were only footsteps and muttering on her end. "Etty, what's wrong?"

"Hang on, I'm sending you a picture."

Worry gnawed at me as I took the phone away from my ear and put her on speaker. The picture came through.

I opened it up and stared, trying to make sense of what I was seeing.

An obsidian statue in the entryway of our apartment. A man.

Adrian peered over my shoulder. "Is that . . .?"

"Your brother showed up here with some bat bread for Noah," Etty explained as the cold, heavy feeling in my scrye came to the forefront of my awareness. "We already had a real bat, but I guess he didn't know that, and . . . I don't know, it happened so quickly that he didn't get the chance to . . . make sure he had something for himself?"

"Ray . . ." I whispered, zooming in on the picture to see the facets of obsidian that had formed on his face. He was mid-stride, determination written in his frozen expression. He'd been more worried about saving Noah than protecting himself, and that had gotten him killed.

Just having a bat in the vicinity wasn't enough—I knew that from what had happened to Rose after I'd taken hers. And who knew if Ray's bat bread would have been any more effective than my confetti?

"Are you talking to my dad?" Carina asked, finally looking up from the Simeon goo. "I want to tell him I'm coming home—the mountain can eat a butt."

"Fuck," I said too quickly, tears now coming to my eyes. If we were in any other situation, I'd be laughing and grilling Carina on where she'd even heard that expression. She must know something was really wrong when I did none of that.

Adrian's hand moved on my back. How did it get there? I wanted to fold into him, crush the phone between us so Carina would never have to look at what was on it. But the little dragon was already pulling it out of my hands.

She knew what she was looking at as soon as she saw it. Didn't even need to zoom. I could see it on her face. In the white blooms on her fingertips as they pressed too hard into the back of the phone.

I wanted to look away, give her this moment to herself. Let her process her shock until it had a chance to turn to grief.

But we were still in the middle of the street, and her tail was growing. Long and spiky, it slid against the gravelly pavement from side to side as she stared into the phone, getting dangerously close to the Simeon goo she'd been crouched over a moment ago.

I pulled out the flamethrower, pointed it at the goo, felt the magic zing, and finally let the fire fly loose. It raged, flames lapping up every speck of spattered vampire like a cat lapping up spilled milk. What was left of his face melted, blurring and stretching and popping before ultimately turning to dust. I hated every moment of it.

Carina was even more the dragon by the time it was done. Not just a tail now but also wings and legs. Her little girl head tilted up to the sky, eyes blazing, and she let out a roar that no sane person would believe was coming from so small a mouth.

Claws scraped against the pavement as she sprang upward, taking my phone with her into the night sky.

I couldn't follow her. The phoenix's wings still wouldn't come, no matter how hard I searched for them.

Now, at least, I had a good idea of why that might be.

WE TRACKED my phone to the clinic, which was bursting at the seams with people. No, not people.

Patients? Not quite that either.

I doubted there was any point in trying to treat the petrification victims that were decorating most of the otherwise empty rooms. Not now that I'd felt the stolen energy for myself, the life force of their gods, and seen it in Itztla's grimy grasp.

I didn't know what he was doing with it, but I was willing to bet he wouldn't be changing his mind and letting it go anytime soon. And I couldn't pry it away from him until I found a way to kill him.

Adrian cleared his throat behind me in the entryway as his

phone rang. When I looked back, he was frowning at the small device and declining the call.

I sent him a questioning glance.

"I'm probably fired," he said slowly, and then, "It's what I expected."

"You expected to fail?" I asked.

"Not exactly. I expected to lose the job regardless of whether we succeeded or failed."

"Is that why you still haven't quit your old job?"

He nodded. "DSC only hired me provisionally to research the petrification. I think they regretted it as soon as it became obvious there wasn't some family defect in Miriam's line just petrifying their replicants," he continued, now in full-on nervous rambling mode. "They never cared about saving any of these witches. It's not the way they work. They might care about catching whoever did it, if it weren't an actual *god* and he hadn't been camped out at Celestial. I can't see why they'd want to keep me on now, after all this."

"I'm sorry," I said, my chest tight. It was never my job to help him, not technically. But it was always my job to keep homicidal lunatics from doing what Itztla had just done. I was sorry for my part in our fuck-up, and I was sorry for what it now meant for Adrian's career.

"Why?" he asked softly, although he had to know.

"I know you've always wanted to work for the DSC," I answered.

He shrugged. "I have, now. It wasn't what I'd imagined."

I took a step towards him, not caring about anyone who might be watching as I slipped my arms around his waist.

I wanted to ask him again about why the DSC would never hire him before, whether it had something to do with the killing he'd been talking about with Carina. But my curiosity wasn't his problem, and now was a bad time if there ever was one. I loved him despite whatever bad things he might have done in the past.

I pressed my cheek to his chest as he rested one hand in my hair and the other on my shoulder. My eyes grew hot. I closed them.

We'd fucked up so bad.

The both of us had, in so many ways.

If the phoenix were still anything more than a cold lump at the bottom of my scrye, it would be knocking its *Games* taunt through my head again. We'd played with magic we didn't understand, trusting the path of least resistance to work because sometimes it did and because the only other paths were too overgrown and dark to even contemplate exploring.

And millions of people had been petrified because of it. I'd lost my brother. Undone whatever progress my niece had made towards coming to terms with her trauma. Adrian would lose his job. It meant more to him than he was willing to tell me.

I pressed my face against him harder, letting the tears soak through his shirt. The Darcy from a few months ago would be hating herself right now, consumed with guilt, obsessed with finding a way to make things right. But I wasn't crying now because of any guilt. I was crying because I finally understood there was no way to keep myself from fucking up again. The only way to be sure I wouldn't lose the evil god's games would be to not play at all—and that would surely be a far greater loss.

All I could do was keep trying and hope for a win.

I would do it. But I was tired.

Adrian's fingers worked their way through my hair, massaging my scalp as he turned my face upward and planted his warm lips on my temple. I unwrapped one of my arms from around him to wipe the wetness from my face.

"Time to face the music," he said, and I nodded.

We parted awkwardly, mechanically, like two robots who'd

gotten tangled together by accident. He walked off towards his provisional office with his phone to his ear, and I finished drying my face as I made my way to Sassie's desk.

"Where's Carina?" I asked my aunt when she looked up at me. Dark circles shadowed the flesh beneath her eyes, and her lips were parted in permanent readiness to bark a command or breathe out in a frustrated huff. Yeah. It had been a long night for her too.

She tilted her head at me. "I'm not sure Carina is ready to—"

Clicking, scraping footsteps raced behind me. I turned to see my niece running towards Minnie's room, a cloud of smoke drifting along behind her as her hands and feet shifted haphazardly from skin to scales and back again. Without even a glance at me, she pressed her face up against the window and snarled as her claws etched cracks into the glass. Then she peeled herself away from it and tumbled through the door.

"Birds," I said out loud as I followed her, heart racing.

There were no mages in the room, but Minnie wasn't alone.

She was awake and smiling, despite her bad arm still looking shriveled and dead. Her other arm was resting on her belly.

But that wasn't why Carina had run in here.

No—that probably had to do with Tula, who was sitting at Minnie's side with her cheek pressed to her wife's belly.

The fucking gall of this woman.

Carina stopped short just at the end of Minnie's bed, and I stopped even shorter just behind her.

"What are you doing here?" Carina asked. Her voice was gravelly, and the temperature of the room soared as she let the words out of her mouth.

I frowned as beads of sweat formed on my forehead, but so far all three of them were ignoring my presence.

"Visiting my wife," Tula said cheerfully, sitting up. "And our baby."

"Carina," I said, stepping forward to put my hand on her scaly shoulder. "Let's get out of here. I know you want to kill her—so do I—but now is not the time." I didn't know when the time would be to kill the terrifying valkyrie, or if it would ever come, but that didn't seem like a very comforting thing to say to the grieving dragon.

"No," Carina said, yanking her shoulder away from me. "I want to understand."

"Understand what?" Tula asked innocently.

"You're married to her?" Carina pointed at Minnie.

"Yes."

"You're *married*?" Carina pressed.

"Yes," Tula repeated. "Why is it so hard to comprehend?"

"I didn't think someone like you could have a family."

Tula bristled, sitting up straighter in her chair. "I've had many families." She flicked her eyes to Minnie, whose smile didn't falter, before asking, "What do you mean someone like me?"

"A killer," Carina answered quickly, more fire in her voice.

I coughed as smoke filled my nostrils. Minnie had finally begun to look a little worried; her fingers pressed harder against her belly.

"The last of your kind," Carina added after Tula kept looking at her expectantly.

"You heard all that?" Tula finally asked, a small smile pulling at her cheeks. "Little spy, aren't you?"

Carina stared at her. Silent, confident. She'd been listening during my conversation with Tula at Celestial. And she'd seen everything that had happened afterward through the camera on my dress.

She knew what this woman was. What she'd done. Whom specifically she'd killed.

"It's because I'm a killer that I should also create life," Tula said, giving Minnie's belly a circular rub.

Carina snorted, and it was more than smoke that came out of her when she did. Actual flames licked the air above Minnie's legs, and the pregnant woman scooted to the other end of her bed with a small yelp.

"You don't get to do that," Carina said as her claws opened and closed. She was getting taller. Darker. Shinier. "You don't get to take my dad and have your family too."

Tula watched with calm, curious eyes as Carina grew larger and reached a clawed arm behind her.

Oh birds. Could she really be about to—

Her claws shot forward at Minnie.

I didn't think. I just moved.

Somehow, the necklace Tula had clipped on me made its way from my dress to my hands. Somehow, I touched it to Carina's side before she could reach Minnie, who had stood up on the bed by now to press herself flat against the wall.

The dragon disappeared as soon as the hard, black feathers touched her hard, black scales.

Only the girl remained, naked and snarling, clawing her way across the bed with human-shaped hands and feet.

I threw a blanket over her and then my arms around her, holding her tight.

She writhed in my grasp, animal noises eventually turning to sobs before she stopped fighting and curled herself into a tight ball.

Minnie's eyes were wide as she sat back down on the bed, staring at the little-girl lump under the blanket at her feet.

Tula had barely moved the whole time. Had she known I would act to save Minnie and her baby?

That wasn't why I'd done it. I'd done it to save Carina.

Keep her sane, Ray's voice haunted my memories.

That train may have already left the station. But I wanted to believe it could still come back. If I let Carina murder Minnie's unborn child, the train and the station both would be blown to smithereens.

I looked at the necklace in my hand as the Carina lump heaved with sobs under the blanket. How had I known that would work? I hadn't. Not consciously.

I glanced at Minnie's earrings. Felt the flash of deathlike calm I'd felt in her memories. Was it something she knew that'd gotten mixed in my head throughout all the times our minds had collided?

"Each of my feathers is a link to the void," Tula supplied, accurately guessing what I'd been wondering. "They have magic nullification properties. Quite useful in a pinch. And now . . ." She plucked the necklace out of my grasp. "I'll have it back, since our work together is completed."

My fingers itched where the necklace had touched as I opened and closed my empty palm. A link to the void? Magic nullification properties? That was some powerful nullification, considering how quickly it had just banished Carina's unruly beast.

Had Tula considered that when she'd made sure I had access to it before bringing me up to the murder-fest at the top of Celestial? If I had touched the necklace to the cihuateteo instead of throwing the damn confetti, would Ray still be alive?

It didn't matter now. Whatever small ways Tula may have tried to help me, it hadn't been nearly enough. And it didn't make up for the fervor with which she'd helped Itztla.

Carina stilled beneath the blanket as I wondered how in hell I was going to get her out of this room in one piece. Would she walk out with me without making another suicidal attempt on Minnie's life? Or would I have to knock her out to get her away?

I opened my mouth, hoping to ask Tula and Minnie to get out instead, but Carina sat back up before I could. Her body was covered in soot again, face streaked with gray tears. But her expression was hard.

"You *should* be alone," Carina said boldly, forcefully, as she glared at Tula. "Even if I can't make you."

"It's because I'm the last of my kind that I make an effort to not be alone," Tula answered.

Carina shifted her jaw, still glaring at Tula, but her eyes were slightly softer now.

My urge to grab her and run out of the room got stronger. I pushed it down. "You could have just . . . I don't know . . . *not* killed all your sisters," I interjected warily, edging my way between Tula and Carina. "Seems like that would have been less of an effort."

Carina snapped her head at me with something that was halfway between a growl and a shush, but it was Minnie who responded. "I knew one of her sisters when I was a child. She lived a full life, and she died for a good cause."

Oh god, they were both lunatics. My mind flashed again to Minnie's memory, the one I'd seen when Sassie had encouraged me to touch her. That might have been Tula's sister and not Tula herself interacting with the little girls. I wasn't sure that made it all any less gross.

Carina breathed out through her nose, but there was no smoke this time. "I'm not the last of my kind," she said quietly. "But there aren't many others. And we're supposed to stay away from each other. Dragons are supposed to be alone."

"Nobody is supposed to be alone," Tula replied, and something broke inside Carina at the words.

The little girl's face contorted again, tears threatening to return for a long moment before she composed herself. "I *am* alone now," she eventually said softly. "My dad is gone."

I'm right here, I wanted to say. But something held me back. I didn't need to say it. Carina was looking right at me. She knew.

And she still thought she was alone. That was another failure on my part.

"And I'm a killer too," she said even more quietly, looking away from me again.

Something panicky scrambled in my chest.

How had Carina gone so quickly from seeking revenge to finding common ground with the person who'd just killed her father?

It *hadn't* happened quickly, though, I realized as I watched Tula's smile grow.

It had been eating away at Carina this whole time—that she was a killer, and not the excusable kind. Had one of her victims been someone else's father? Maybe.

And now she fully understood just what that meant.

Tula held out her free hand to Carina. "Would you like to spend some time with us? We're going out for dinner as soon as Minnie gets discharged."

The little dragon took the valkyrie's hand.

"Do you like steak?" Minnie asked. I felt sick.

Carina nodded vigorously as I ducked out of the room. Letting the door slam behind me, I bolted straight for Sassie's desk and the small trash can that sat behind it. Sharp pain stabbed at my insides as I curled myself over it and heaved.

This newest failure had snuck up on me, and now it was hitting me so much harder than all the others.

I hadn't seen it coming because I hadn't understood it. I was a different kind of killer than the ones in the room I'd just fled. I'd never grappled with the kind of guilt that had been forced on Carina when the chaneques had stolen her soul. It was foolish of me to think I could help her by treating her like a younger version of myself.

I groaned into the trash can as the last remnants of my stomach contents vacated me. When I finally looked up, Sassie was there with a wet washcloth and a cup of water. Just seeing her made my stomach clench again, but there was nothing left for it to expel.

"Not so easy, is it?" I expected her to say. But she was silent.

Had I made the same mistakes with my niece that Sassie had made with me?

I'd tried to fit her into my shoes and then offered her measly bandages and socks when it was clear they were the wrong size.

But in Carina's case, the outcome was so much worse.

I took the cloth and cup from Sassie, wiped and rinsed my mouth. Just like old times.

I'd been sick in this clinic more times than I could count, the natural consequence of a job well done stuffing souls back into bodies they didn't want to be in. Was Carina just like one of those souls? Was it futile and torturous, all my effort to stuff her back into a sane little girl?

It couldn't be. I wouldn't let it.

"Thank you," I said to Sassie before standing up again.

"I was wrong," she said in response, before I could walk away. I looked at her blankly, and she continued, "I thought you would get worse when you left. I thought you wouldn't be able to handle the pressure, if you couldn't handle this . . ."

I breathed in as I watched her gesture at our surroundings.

"I was just trying to protect you. I'm sorry," she said with a subtle shake of her head. "I should have trusted you instead."

"I'm sorry too," I said, and the corners of her eyes crinkled just a little. I almost leaned forward to hug her, but there was no time for that.

I hugged myself instead as I turned away from my aunt and walked back to Minnie's room.

It was empty.

My phone buzzed. It was sitting on top of Minnie's crumpled bedsheets where Carina had left it for me.

Don't come after me, she had texted already. **I got this.**

"I got this?" I mumbled under my breath, my heart pounding in my chest. What did that mean? Was the wild little dragon trying to play some long game, hanging out with Tula to uncover her secrets like she'd done with Oya?

Was she asking me to trust her?

I scoffed. Fat chance of that, regardless of how much I agreed with what Sassie had just admitted. Carina was eight, not eighteen. There was only so much slack I could give her before it turned into straight-up neglect.

But maybe I could give her a little.

Just a little.

No matter what, I wasn't letting the valkyrie assassin sink her claws into my niece.

And I wasn't letting Tula get out of helping me take down her god, once and for all. The psychotic woman was still my best shot at a ticket into the underworld—as long as I could keep her in the dark about what I would be doing down there.

That was a problem for another day, though. I didn't like it, but I'd let Carina eat her steak. Something told me she'd need a bit of time to cool off, anyway, before anything I could think to say would get through to her.

Maybe I needed the time, too, to think of what to say.

There was one thing I was sure of, at least: I was going to need a whole lot of sleep before I'd be ready to go traipsing through hell.

25

I DON'T KNOW how long I slept, but there was a warm body lying next to mine when I woke.

Carina?

I breathed in, hoping for the scent of smoke from her little dragon snores. Eyes still closed, my hands reached out and found hard muscle.

Not Carina.

It was easy to push the disappointment away as I rolled over to press myself against Adrian, fitting my head into the crook of his neck.

"What day is it?" I mumbled.

"Tomorrow," he said, and I understood. It was the day after everything had gone down, which meant I hadn't slept for very long at all. "I'm leaving tonight," he added.

"Back to DC?" I asked.

He grunted affirmatively and then said, "I'm not fired."

"Oh?" I opened my eyes and propped myself up just enough to see Adrian's face. He had shaved, and his slightly damp hair was light and soft around his eyes. "Is that a good thing?" I asked.

"I don't know yet," he said. "But it means I'm going to have to tell Dirk."

I flopped back down on his chest with a chuckle, surprised I had any laughter left in me after yesterday. "He's not going to take it well."

"He'll be happy for me," Adrian said, but there was no mirth in his tone. "He doesn't know why the DSC never hired me before this."

I didn't know that, either. "Is that . . . a reason to not be happy about this?" I tried, not sure what he was getting at.

"Maybe," he said. "It's the reason I can't say no to them. Even if I wanted to."

"Are you ever going to let me in on this big secret you've been keeping, after all the lectures you've given me on how I'm a terrible person if I don't tell you *everything*?"

"I never said you were a terrible—"

"Shh." I put my finger over his lips. I'd only been teasing him. But I didn't want to delve into any of that now.

He looked at me expectantly, and I took a deep breath. Was this real? After everything that had gone horribly, horribly wrong over the past couple days—over the past few months, really—Adrian was in my bed, and neither of us was in any immediate danger.

There were still so many problems to fix. So many. But none of them could be fixed by me getting out of bed *right now*.

Was this finally something good happening to me? Did I even deserve it?

That was a stupid question.

If I hadn't learned by now to seize every tiny win by its horns and appreciate the fuck out of it, I never would.

"There's just so much I need to say," I finally whispered, taking my finger away from his lips.

His throat vibrated with a low chuckle. "Like what?"

"That I like what you're wearing, mostly," I said, running my hands down the sides of his arms.

He grunted as I brushed my lips against his neck and let my fingers wander further down to linger on the elastic of his boxer briefs, the only article of clothing he had on.

I stopped, pulling my head up again to say, "That I'm coming back to DC with you tonight." I moved my fingers underneath the elastic. "That I'm going to find my way to the underworld after that." My palm lay flat against the silky, hard length of his cock. He drew in a sharp breath. "And that you can wait as long as you want to tell me your secrets." I curled my hand around my prize and drew my face up close to his ear. "But if you don't fuck me right now, I'm done telling you any of mine."

He burst into motion, lax muscles tensing as they closed around my arms and pulled me closer. The leafy scent of his aftershave filled my head as he pressed his mouth against mine, and I ran my fingers over the smooth, hard line of his jaw.

His hands found their way under my thin sleep shirt and trailed up along my back, pushing the fabric up until it barely covered my breasts.

"Is there still a bat in there?" he asked softly, breath hot on the side of my neck.

"Worried you'll catch rabies?" I teased, then nipped my teeth on his chin as I arched my back to press my boobs further out from under the shirt.

He looked down, humming appreciatively at the view—all tit, no small, furry animals. The bat was on the other side of my old room, snuggling with my childhood stuffed animals. "I just didn't want to squish it," Adrian said, and I couldn't hold back my smile.

Of course that was what he was worried about.

I still didn't know much about this man, when all was said and done—but some things are important, and some aren't. He might be a fuck-up just as much as I was, but at the end of the day he would walk through hell to avoid hurting anything that didn't deserve it. Or he would hold my hand while I did the walking.

Don't you dare cry, Darcy, I told myself as the blood rushed to my face and heat filled my eyes. I'd been doing too much of that lately, and it was the last thing I wanted to be doing right now.

I let out a groan as Adrian closed a palm around my breast, thumb gently teasing the nipple as his other hand reached down between my legs. Ripples of pleasure coursed through me when he found the slick bundle of nerves beneath my panties, and the threat of tears left me as the blood in my face rushed elsewhere.

I shifted my hips, eager to shimmy out of the small bit of impeding fabric, but he gripped it at the side seam and tore it easily apart. That was better, yes.

My lips parted, a moan escaping as he slid two fingers around the edges of my clit. "Fuck," I gasped against his jaw before moving my mouth back to his. His erection rubbed against my inner thigh, just slightly hesitant.

I needed him inside me, but at the same time I was afraid I might implode if he stopped touching me. The vampire ostrich and the ice god and the scorpion man hadn't gotten me, but this just might be the thing to do me in.

"Condom," I managed to say after gasping in another breath, and he reached over to pluck up the small packet that was sitting right next to his keys and phone. Mr. Goody-Goody had come prepared. It sent a buzzing warmth through my chest, knowing that I wasn't asking him for anything he hadn't already decided to give me.

I flipped myself over beneath him, lifting my hips into him and guiding his hand back around to where I wanted it. He planted his other arm over my shoulder, holding himself above me so his solid chest just grazed my spine.

I lifted my hips again, insistent. "Don't make me beg."

He didn't.

He slid inside me, his weight pressing into me from above as his fingers flicked against me from below. I stopped breathing.

The fullness was overwhelming, not just inside me but around me in every direction. He had me pinned as he moved through me, slowly stoking a fire in me that had nothing to do with magic—nothing to do with games.

I could hardly move an inch, yet there was no doubt in my mind that I was in control. No doubt that I was safe here beneath him, that he trusted me and would stand by me no matter how many more fuck-ups either of us stumbled our way into. No doubt that he would help me find the energy to keep pressing on.

I whimpered and finally breathed again, fingernails digging into the bicep that was planted by my face.

Adrian lowered his head, pushing the loose curls away from mine with his nose before whispering in my ear, "Now." It was as close to a command as I'd ever heard him give.

I was happy to obey. And it didn't scare me at all to realize there wasn't much I wouldn't do for any chance to be closer to this man—to see him, to understand him, to help him, to enjoy him.

But now. . . now I moved with him, waves of pleasure rocking through me as the fire exploded into an inferno. Faster and harder and wilder until our bodies exhausted each other, heavy as stone, and it was only our panting lungs still fighting for control.

When he finally peeled himself away from me, it felt like all the sleep I'd gotten had been undone. But I didn't want to sleep any more.

Too many people had died. So many I couldn't even wrap my head around it. Yet here I was, alive and doing something just for the joy of it. Something I hadn't done in far too long.

It was the perfect way to mourn, really. A big fuck you to the god who didn't want anyone to live. It left me eager to send him an even bigger one.

"When we get back," Adrian said, chin resting against the top of my head, "are you going to keep working at the club?"

"I hope so," I answered. "If I can get through the whole hell thing alive and kill the ice god so he doesn't do away with all my customers." I tugged at the hair at the base of his neck, lifting his head enough so I could peek at his face. "Why?"

"It's just, with my new DSC salary," he started, giving me one of his little half smiles, "I'd like to come see you dance. I did tell you I was going to make it rain for you."

"You did," I laughed. It felt like so long ago that he'd said that, and I hadn't taken him seriously at the time.

"I keep my promises," he said, and it was so genuine I didn't have the heart to remind him I was a terrible dancer. Fuck, I'd get up there and shake my ass on a slow night just to see his smile.

WE DIDN'T RIDE off into the sunset.

We rode away from it. Apparently happy endings are only reserved for people driving west.

Bright light streamed through the windshield from directly behind us, painting the asphalt ahead with our shadows and blinding me every time I glanced at a mirror.

The last time I'd been blinded by bright lights while driving, it had been the fiery phoenix throwing a fit in front of me on the road.

As much as I knew that wouldn't happen again, there was a hollow, aching part of me that kept looking. Wondering if the bright sunlight would turn into a blaze of feathers the next time I blinked.

It wouldn't.

I grit my teeth and kept my eyes on the road.

We were only driving as far as the airport, but still it felt as though I were retracing my steps—and that felt wrong without Carina feeding candy to the bunnies from the passenger seat.

"You'll tell me the second you have something on her, right?" I asked without looking over at Adrian, who was sitting in her place.

"Of course," he said. "It won't even go through me. I'll have the alerts sent straight to you."

"They're going to regret not firing you," I said with a grin. "I'm a bad influence." But in the grand scheme of things, I didn't think anyone would care about him using DSC resources to look out for my still-a-fugitive niece before she could get herself thrown in prison or into yet more trouble hanging out with the happy assassin family I'd left her with.

To say I was worried about her would be the understatement of the century.

Keep her sane. Ray's words fell on me yet again, so much heavier now that he was gone. But I'd failed him already before the first time he'd said them.

Help her find her way back. That was the best I could do now. And I was going to do it, no matter how long it took.

"Stop the car," Adrian said, twisting around to look behind us. "Pull over."

I put my foot on the brake, only avoiding looking in the mirror until I realized there were no more harsh shadows out in front of us, no more glare behind. The sun must have dipped below the horizon.

"What is it?" I asked as I slowed to a stop, but he was already unclipping his seatbelt and hopping out onto the side of the road.

"What is *that*?" he muttered in a low voice, his hand over his eyes as he squinted into the distance.

I got out of the car and looked where he was looking. "The

moon?" I offered. It was a misty crescent, surrounded by uncharacteristically dark shadows in a dusky sky.

"That's not the moon," he said, something shaking in his voice.

I tilted my head, scrunching my face at the thing in the sky that looked very, very much like the moon. It was getting smaller as I watched, the crescent turning into a tiny sliver. Ok, that wasn't normal. I'd give him that. "Then what—"

"It's the sun." He stood completely still as he stared at it, jaw tensing as I glanced from him to the thing in the sky and back again.

It was getting darker.

By the time the shadows surrounding the misty crescent engulfed it, they had also spread across the rest of the vast sky, black splotches taking over where wispy bits of pink and orange had been just moments before.

The automatic headlights on my car turned on.

I clenched my fists, digging my fingernails into my palms before opening my hands again.

A glowing orb engulfed in shadow. Wasn't that what we'd just seen happen in the sky? Should I really be surprised after I'd watched Itztla turn himself into a giant shadow to consume the glowing sphere containing the life force of all the gods and witches he'd drained?

This must be what he'd planned to do with it. The second phase of his "endeavor."

"If my goal were to turn the world into a haven of ice and death," I said, my voice flat. "Taking out the sun would be at the top of my to-do list."

Adrian looked over to me, eyes wide and lips pressed tightly shut. Then he got back in the car. I followed his lead.

"We have a lot of work to do," he said as I strapped myself in.

I nodded and pressed on the gas. A single obsidian bunny

clawed its way to the top of the steering wheel, red eyes boring into mine as it beckoned for my attention.

"Birds," I cursed.

It is time, Popo's voice vibrated through the steering wheel, through my hands and up my arms until it filled my head with fire.

"Time for what?" I asked in a strained voice. But there could only be one answer.

I braced myself and flung one hand out in a futile attempt to steady Adrian as I spun the steering wheel all the way around.

My right foot pressed harder on the gas while my left one tapped nervously against the inside of the door. My left ankle itched where the tattoo of the moon used to be.

How was it that in all the time I'd just spent back in California around Sassie and Fred, I hadn't actually asked either of them how to get it back?

More importantly—what would my oath to the volcano even be worth, now that my brother was gone and the phoenix with it?

I wasn't sure.

But if I had any chance at all of going up against the god who had just taken the sun out of the sky . . .

I knew I had to swear it.

AFTERWORD

Thank you for reading Obsidian Oath!

This has been the most challenging book in the series to write, but also the most rewarding. And there are still two more books in Darcy's story to come . . .

To stay up to date and be the first to know about upcoming releases, join my mailing list or connect with me on social media. You can find me here:

https://www.erinembly.com

(Psst . . . If you sign up for my newsletter, you'll get a free novella about Minnie and Tula to read right away!)

Want to make an author's day? Please consider leaving a review! Even if it's just a rating or a few words, it will be a great help.

I'm a new author, and every review counts.

Till next time, happy reading!
Erin

Made in the USA
Middletown, DE
29 April 2022